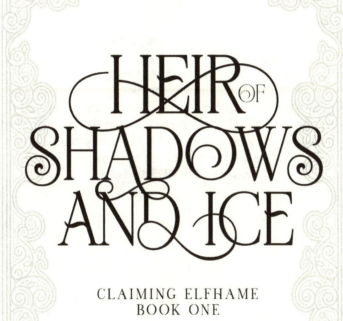

HEIR OF SHADOWS AND ICE

CLAIMING ELFHAME
BOOK ONE

J.M. WALLACE

HEIR OF SHADOWS AND ICE

CLAIMING ELFHAME
BOOK ONE

J.M. WALLACE

To the writer who feels like their dreams are just out of reach. Don't give up. Someone out there needs your story.

Contents

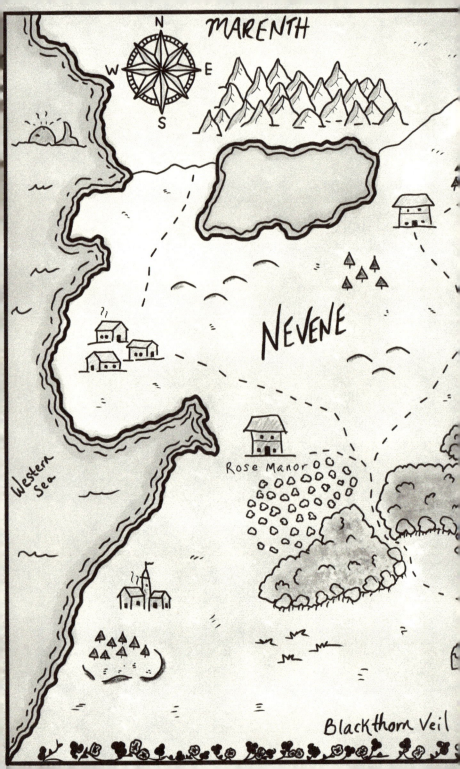

AMARAN

Eastern Sea

Royal Palace

Mortal Realm

Blackth
AUTUMN COURT
Western Sea
unseelie Palace
WINTER COURT
Elfhame

Prologue

Twelve years earlier

Kelera knelt to the ground, trying to catch sight of the ghastly beast again. As she searched, she rubbed at her rosy cheeks, leaving streaks of dirt behind. Calling out to the small Fae creature, she said, "Come out, come out, wherever you are." Hide and seek was one of her favorite games, but she felt annoyance rising in her as her stomach grumbled. Nanny had promised her a piece of cake tonight for doing so well at her reading lessons. But surely Papa would not allow her to have it now that she had missed dinner.

She looked around the clearing, nervous that he would appear by the sheer will of her thoughts. He was going to be livid with her. She was breaking the rules, after all. And that was definitely *not* what little girls were supposed to do when training to be ladies of the Nevene court one day. Not only had she ventured too far south of the palace grounds, but it was dark now. She knew better than to go out alone after the sun had set. Everyone knew things liked to go bump in the night near the Elfhame border. But who could blame her, really? After all, it wasn't her fault that the goblin-like creature had snatched away the new hair bow her father had bought for her.

Something rustled in the tree line up ahead. Kelera jumped to her feet. "Gotchya!" She ran toward the overgrown brush looming up ahead. When she reached it, she skidded to a stop, careful not to run into the brush. The tangled branches, covered in razor sharp thorns, were only inches away from her face. Subconsciously, she reached for the locket hanging around her neck. She rubbed her nail bitten thumb along the intricate details that matched the blackthorn trees standing before her.

"No fair! Papa says I'm not allowed to go in there." She pouted and stomped her foot on the ground.

She crouched down and glimpsed the bogie between the trees. He peeked between the tree trunks with his abnormally tall, hairy ears, and squashed snout. He snickered through his protruding teeth and dangled her hair bow, just out of reach.

For a split second, she thought about grabbing it. But Papa's warning rang in her mind. She was never, under any circumstances, to go near the blackthorn brush—the veil that separated their mortal world from the dwelling of the Fae. But perhaps *she* did not need to go to the bogie when she could make him come to her...

She shut her eyes tight and clenched her tiny hands into fists. She pictured the roots in the ground beneath the bogie's feet and willed them to emerge. Concentrating, she felt the magic of Elfhame answer her call. A strange heat warmed her arms and legs. And it was as if a hundred butterflies were dancing around inside her stomach.

She knew using magic was against the rules. People in Nevene feared it and anyone who wielded it. Papa insisted it was safer for her if no one knew she had inherited her mother's abilities. But Papa wasn't here. Nobody but her and the bogie were around. And who was he going to tell? She giggled playfully as her magic connected to the earth beneath her feet.

The bogie yelped as a root came out and took hold of its foot. Kelera tugged the root back with her magic, forcing the bogie to stumble forward. The hair bow fell from his hand and onto the ground. Just within her reach. Triumphant, she scooped it up and tied it in her long wavy hair, pulling it back so it revealed the slight points on the tips of her ears.

Satisfied with having won the game, she released the magic and turned on her heel to skip away. Part of her felt empty now, with the magic no longer coursing through her veins. How wonderful would it be if she were free to use it all the time? Maybe the other children in the palace would finally want to play with her if they knew she had such a fun gift. Then again, she would not want Papa to worry. She shrugged off the emptiness and started back up to the palace.

Before she made it a few steps, something blocked her path. It towered over her, cloaked with a hood over its face. Kelera took a step back in alarm. She could feel the power illuminating from the dreadfully pale, old creature standing in her way. Its magic was cold and foreign to her. Not at all like the magic she had just wielded herself.

The creature spoke with the soft voice of a woman. "My dear, how far you are from home." The hood slid away from her face and her eyes flicked down to the locket. Kelera's stomach did a somersault as the woman smiled, revealing rotting teeth.

Instinct told Kelera to run, but she couldn't ignore the fascination she was feeling. She had never seen anyone like the woman before. Kelera stuttered, "I'm-I'm not *that* far. My father is just up the hill." She pointed toward the magnificent white-stone palace that stood in the distance.

"Oh, silly child. Not that home. Your *true* home." She tilted her head back toward the blackthorn brush. As she did, the hood on her cloak fell from her head completely, giving Kelera a full view of her wrinkled face. The woman looked much older than she sounded.

The hairs on Kelera's arms rose. Papa wouldn't like her talking to this stranger. Her voice was a mere whisper as she said, "I want to go home. To my Papa."

"What about your mother? Sweet child. Come with me and I can take you to her." The woman smiled and extended her hand. Kelera could not take her eyes from it. She had a nagging instinct that told her to trust the woman.

Kelera had never met her mother. She had dreamed of her often, but the dreams were fading the older she got... she extended her hand and took a step toward the woman. The woman's voice was gentle and encouraging as she said, "All you have to do is prick your finger on the blackthorn..." Her smile grew sinister as Kelera moved to take hold of her hand.

But before their hands could touch, Papa's voice called down to her from the hill. "Kelera, no!"

Kelera snatched her hand away from the woman and looked up the hill to see Papa and two of his squires. An arrow shot at lightning speed, striking the woman in the shoulder. She hissed and reached for Kelera. But Kelera was too fast for her. She ducked out of the woman's reach just as she grabbed hold of the hair bow. The ribbon fell from Kelera's hair as she ran toward Papa.

The woman screeched at him, "She does not belong here! She is a child of Elfhame."

Enraged, Papa shouted back, "She is *my* child! She belongs with me!"

"You cannot protect her from her fate." The woman cackled, and Kelera's adrenaline coursed at the viciousness in that laughter. Magic pooled at the woman's fingertips as she proclaimed, "The world will succumb to frost and be reborn in fire."

With magic still enveloping her hands, she moved to grab Kelera. Afraid of never seeing Papa again, Kelera's magic blazed to life. It lashed out at the woman in a blast of bright light. She staggered away from Kelera with a painful scream.

Terrified, Kelera ran as fast as her little legs could carry her to the hill. Before Papa and his squires had a chance to loose another arrow on the woman, she pulled the cloak around her and disappeared into the night. With her, went the cold magic that had accompanied her presence.

When Kelera reached Papa, she leapt into his arms. Her hair matted to the tears streaming down her face as she clung to him. She gripped his armor, feeling sorrier than she ever had before. The last thing she had wanted was for him to be disappointed in her.

His voice was a mixture of terror and relief as he said, "Never, ever, go near the blackthorns. You know that."

"I only wanted to get my new ribbon back from the bogie." The fear in Papa's eyes was enough to flood her with guilt and embarrassment.

Papa drew her away from his embrace and set her on the ground. He held her shoulders with a firm grip. "The bogie? Kelera, you cannot continue on this way. Chasing down troublesome creatures for your own amusement. How many times do I have to tell you?"

"But Papa, it was easy! I simply thought of the roots, and they did as I told them!" As sorry as Kelera was for causing trouble, she was proud of her accomplishment. Surely her father would be impressed as well.

One of the squires swore under his breath. "Magic? Can she really do that?"

Papa glared at the young man. "You are not to utter a word of this night to anyone, Dodger. Is that understood? Neither of you." He gave the other squire a pointed look. "If anyone finds out, she will become a pariah... or worse. Look at her. She's just a girl." Papa's eyes were welling with tears. "I'm begging you, help me keep her safe."

Dodger looked down at Kelera. He had always been kind to her. He'd even stuck up for her one time when the other children were teasing her about her pointed ears. Would he be frightened of her now that he knew she had magic? She felt ashamed suddenly. She didn't want anyone to be afraid of her.

Dodger watched her carefully as he agreed, "We understand, commander."

The other squire hesitated before nodding.

Papa turned his attention back to her. "Never again, Kelera. Promise me."

"But father—"

"Each time you use magic, you put yourself at risk. It draws these creatures to you. You draw them to Nevene. And that puts us all in danger. If the king finds out you can wield it, then we will lose our place here... our home. I need you to promise me."

She bobbed her head, sending her dark, wavy hair into her face. Determined to keep Papa and herself safe, she tugged at her hair so it covered her ears. "I promise, Papa. I promise."

Chapter One

Twelve years later

T here were two things in this life that Kelera knew
for sure. First, she was never under any circumstances allowed to touch the blackthorn trees, and second, she needed to do everything within her power to
fit in with the mortals.

The first was easily avoided, as she hadn't ventured
south of the palace walls in over a decade. The last time
she dared to go near the tree line that acted as the
magical barrier between the mortal world and the one
ruled by the Fae, her father had been furious with her.
Any time Kelera felt that tug in her heart to go to the
thorny, flowering trees, she would think of the promise
she'd made to him when she was a child.

It was the only time he had ever frightened her. Perhaps it was the fear in his eyes, more than the words he'd spoken, that had stuck with her the most.

Kelera had gotten into trouble plenty of times before that, but it had always been harmless fun. She had learned that night, however, that by pricking her finger on the blackthorn trees, she would gain entry into Elfhame. Her father had been so frightened of losing her that he'd drummed the rules into her from that day forward.

The latter, however, was a constant battle raging within herself. Though everyone at court knew she was half Fae, they still walked on eggshells around her. When her father had found her on his doorstep with a note from her mother, begging for him to protect their baby, the late king had agreed to aid them. With the king's blessing, the people hadn't objected to her presence in the palace... as long as she was careful not to draw attention to herself. That meant shutting away a big part of who she was—the part of her deep down that allowed her to access magic. But even now, as she walked along the dirt road leading to her dearest friend, Cierine's manor, she found herself drawn by the magic buzzing in the air. The familiar presence told her there were pixies nearby. Though mortals could see magical creatures, Kelera could *feel* their presence. It was like the power these beings possessed was calling to her. Beckoning to her like a familiar friend.

This was a sensation Kelera had to constantly fight. She had no desire to single herself out amongst the mortals by getting involved in whatever trouble the creatures were sure to make. The pixie magic grew stronger as she continued down the dirt path. The pesky little things must have slipped through the veil between Elfhame and Nevene early that morning. It was easiest for them and others to pass through during the hours of dawn and dusk.

The sun was just beginning to rise over the hill and Kelera struggled to ignore the urge to seek out the tiny, winged Fae, but it was like a thread tugging on her. There was no doubt in her mind they were there to cause mischief and the part of herself that she'd locked away long ago begged for release. She closed her eyes tight and took a deep breath, trying to ignore the voice in her head that said a little adventure wouldn't do any harm.

Small giggles sounded from behind her, and she spun around to see a cluster of pixies fluttering above the ground. They whispered to one another and continued to laugh behind their tiny hands. Their wings were delicate and almost translucent, with intricate detail that made Kelera want to get a closer look. They were beautiful and harmless looking, but she knew firsthand of the trouble they could cause. Though they were not dangerous, they were quite mischievous, and she wanted no part of that today.

She tried to shoo them away. "Have your fun someplace else. I am far too busy for your games."

One of the pixie's eyes flashed in anger and it beelined for her. It was a mistake to slight them like that. Pixies were notorious for their spiteful attitudes. Before she could react, the fairy took hold of her dark, wavy hair. Its strength surprised her as it pulled at her hair, undoing all the work she had done this morning to tie it up neatly.

Kelera swatted at the little beast while the other pixies laughed from the sidelines. The pixie assaulting her head untied the blue silk ribbon that held her hair in place and flew off with it. The other pixies followed her, disappearing behind a small copse of trees, and leaving Kelera standing in a disheveled mess. Her long hair tumbled down her back, and she tried her best to smooth it down.

Horrid little beasts, Kelera thought, *and now I'm late*. She turned back toward Rose Manor and picked up her pace. She didn't want to keep her friend waiting. It was an important day for Princess Cierine.

As she continued on foot down the dirt path, she heard a carriage coming up behind her. She moved to the side of the path, careful to stay out of its way. The last thing she needed was to show up to the festivities with dust on her new blue gown.

The carriage slowed as it came upon her. Quickly, she rearranged her hair until it covered the slightly pointed tips of her ears. Another thing she had inherited from her Fae mother. Covering them was something she'd taken to doing to blend in better with society. Her eyes, however, were another story with their strange rings of greens and blues in the irises. There was no hiding that.

She turned to greet the family inside. The coachman tipped his hat to her as he brought the horses to a halt. Someone pushed aside the curtain inside of the carriage and a handsome, dark-skinned man peeked his head out of the window. He seemed surprised to see her as he furrowed his brow and said, "Good day, Lady Kelera."

She recognized the man as one of the barons. He owned a prosperous piece of land to the north and only came to court on special occasions. Though he was well liked by the nobles, he had never been very pleasant to her. He and his wife often treated her like a leper. As if they might catch the "bad blood" that ran in her veins.

She plastered a practiced smile on her face, and greeted him pleasantly, "Lord Relon, it is a pleasure to see you again." She gave him a small curtsey.

He looked around as if searching for something and she waited patiently, wishing he would go on his way so she could start walking again.

He squinted at her. "Are you out here alone?" His wife peeked her pinched face out of the window now, too, looking appalled at the idea.

Kelera smiled politely. "My father is going to meet me there. I wanted to lend the Princess a hand as she prepares for the ceremony, and it is such a fine morning for a walk." She did not bother to try to explain to them that she loved being outside in nature with fresh air on her face.

He pursed his lips in displeasure. "Dangerous business, walking alone on the roads. You never know where the *wee ones* may be lurking."

His wife nodded in agreement and curled her upper lip in disdain. The unpleasant woman added, "It is no secret that the beasts are getting bolder. We've heard the horrid rumors of kidnappings on the southern border. To think, poor innocent girls, being subjected to unmentionable torment by those foul monsters. King Tristan really ought to—"

Lord Relon cleared his throat in warning. His wife was clearly loose-lipped. Something she would do well to be more careful of while they were visiting the court. His wife stopped talking but scrunched her nose at Kelera as if it were she who was stealing mortal girls away in the dark of the night. The tiny voice inside of Kelera's head told her she could wipe the look off that woman's face with a little hair pulling of her own.

Instead, she folded her hands in front of her, fighting the urge to curl them into fists. She, too, had heard rumors of the kidnappings, though nothing was substantiated yet. Furthermore, to blame all Fae was unfair. If something nefarious was indeed happening, it surely was not the work of the wee ones, like the pixies she had just encountered.

Still, it was not this couple's fault that they thought of the Fae Folk as they did. Centuries of distrust and fear were difficult to ignore. So Kelera did her best now to appease them. "I am keeping a careful eye out and will do my upmost to make haste."

In response, Lord Relon gave her a curt nod and bid her farewell. "Very well then. We will see you at the ceremony." He hit his hand against the side of the carriage, signaling to the coachman that it was time to go. The reins snapped, and the horses lurched forward, pulling the Baron and his snobby wife down the road and out of sight.

It did not go unnoticed by Kelera how they expressed their disapproval of her being on the road alone, yet still did not offer to give her a ride in their carriage to the manor in which they were both headed to. It had always been like this. The mortals at court tolerated her and treated her pleasantly, but still they kept her at arm's distance. She ignored the pang in her heart and sighed.

Perhaps she should have taken her father's carriage. The walk was taking longer than she would have liked and she desperately wanted to reach Princess Cierine's house before the other ladies, to have a moment alone with her best friend.

Looking down the long road, she decided it would be best to cut through the poppy field in order to reach the manor in time. She knew it was safer to stay on the path, but she didn't want to be any later than she already was. The guests would be arriving soon. She hiked her dress up to keep it from getting ruined.

The early morning air was cool, but Kelera could already tell that it was going to be a warm day. She could often sense these things well before anyone else, though she preferred to keep the thoughts to herself.

She veered away from the path, heading toward the enormous field that stood between her and the manor. As she stepped off the dirt road that she had been following, the brush of magic danced along her skin once again. This time, it was stronger and there was something more sinister about it. Like a chilly breath on the back of her neck.

Panicked, Kelera tried to focus on her breathing, willing the buzz of the magic to go away. Her efforts were fruitless. If anything, the sensation became stronger. *No, no, no. This can't be happening. Not today.* It had been a long time since she'd felt magic like this. The last thing she wanted was a run in with one of the more dangerous Fae. Kelera's thoughts became desperate as she broke into a run, trampling the vibrant reddish-orange flowers.

She made it a few yards, but before she could get any further, someone rose from the flowers. The woman standing before her now was old and haggard. She was wearing a dress patched together with an array of colors like someone had sewed it together with scraps of fabric. Her eyes were ringed with three shades of blue and there was a spider web of wrinkles around them. It was clear that the woman was ancient. Which, according to the history books Kelera had read on Elfhame, also meant that her magic was incredibly strong.

Kelera froze where she stood, unsure of what to do next. She looked back at the road she'd abandoned, hoping to find someone to help her. There was no one. For a moment, she wondered if she should scream. Surely Lord Relon and his wife would still be close enough to hear? But if they did, would they even bother to come to her aid?

It seemed she was on her own, like usual. She turned back to the woman who regarded Kelera's expensive blue gown with fascination as if she had never seen anything so beautiful.

The magic Kelera sensed from the woman was strong and highly volatile. It was like needles on her arms and made her take an alarming step back. It reminded her of the Fae witch that had tried to lure her away from her life in Nevene when she was just a girl.

Witches like this were said to always travel alone. Cast out of Elfhame because of their destructive magic.

The fact that these women were not even permitted to live in the dangerous land of the Unseelie Court told Kelera that they were not to be trifled with. Careful not to offend the witch, or show her fear, she spoke with more confidence than she was feeling. "I don't want any trouble. I am only passing through."

The witch smiled sweetly. "Why, of course, my dear. I am only gathering poppies." She gestured to a basket by her feet, filled with the beautiful flowers from the field. "These are quite potent."

Kelera waited for the witch to go about her business, but she did not move. Instead, the woman stared intently at Kelera as if searching for something within her. She needed to get out of here before the witch decided to take more than flowers from the field. She stepped to the side, but the woman blocked her path.

There was amusement in her voice as she said, "Oh dear, I did not realize..." She studied Kelera and her gaze lingered on the locket that hung down at her chest. The locket her mother had left her with as a baby when she'd abandoned her on her father's doorstep.

Kelera put a defensive hand on it and her heart fluttered. She did not want trouble from this woman. "I'm not sure what you mean." She hadn't meant to sound so defensive, and she chided herself for her carelessness. Lord Relon was right. She should not have ventured out alone this morning.

The witch looked at her with pity as her brow furrowed. "It is dangerous to ignore one's true nature. I should know. I tried to ignore mine, and it only led to the death of those I held most dear."

"Surely you are mistaken in my case. I am nothing more than the daughter of—"

The witch interrupted her, "The daughter of Elfhame. I see you, though you do a fine job of hiding away in that fancy gown. The eyes do not lie." She stared intently into Kelera's eyes which and three shades of green-blue surrounding her pupils in rings. It was a trait only those with Fae blood possessed. As Kelera searched for the right words, the witch's eyes went to her hair, and she pointed.

Self-consciously, Kelera put her hands up to her ears. Her fingers brushed against the small points hidden beneath her hair.

The witch barked out a laugh as she picked up her basket. "Hide from the silly humans all you want, but heed my words. No matter how hard you try, you will never be able to hide from yourself." She continued to pick poppies, but Kelera could feel the witch's magic reaching for her—-testing how close it could get.

Kelera stepped back out of its reach. She maneuvered her way around the witch, intent on putting as much distance between them as she could. The witch hummed a sad tune, catching her attention. Visions of a woman with long, blonde hair cascading like a waterfall over her shoulder flashed in Kelera's mind. A woman that she hadn't dreamt of since she was a child... Her mother. It stirred a longing in her.

Kelera stopped in her tracks. "How do you know that song?"

The witch looked up from her basket and raised an eyebrow. Ignoring the question, she said, "They're true, you know. The rumors of kidnappings beyond the palace grounds."

The shock of the witch's confession overshadowed confusion by the sudden change of conversation. Kelera's heart pounded in her chest. If the Fae were kidnapping humans, then the treaty which stood for thousands of years between their two realms was null and void. King Tristan would have to retaliate.

Warily she asked, "Why are they happening?"

The witch gave her a sly smile. "The dark ones are growing restless. bored with centuries of good behavior. If I were you, I would leave those mortals of yours behind before they turn on you. They will be looking for someone to blame."

Kelera felt like there were rocks in her stomach. Without another word, the witch turned on her heel and wobbled off into the field. Collecting herself, Kelera made her own way through the flowers, leaving behind the old hag and the truth of what she had said. No matter how hard she worked at blending in at court, she knew people whispered about her.

The rules that had been ingrained in her by her father were a constant reminder of how different she was. It was not that he was ashamed to have a daughter with Fae blood running through her veins—he had loved and doted on her since the moment he had first held her in his arms.

Rather than casting her off to the elements as many mortals in his situation would have, he had raised her with the young ladies at court. He had only ever wanted to keep her safe. To help her live a happy, normal life amongst the humans.

Still, there had always been gossip about her. Girls would snicker behind her back at how she was the product of a scandalous night at an autumn revel. Boys would avoid her, worried that they would one day be matched to marry her. And even the adults would tread carefully around her as if she might combust into some horrifying creature with horns and fangs at any moment. Kelera did not hold it against them. There had never been a half-Fae, half-human living amongst them before. And it seemed no one quite knew what to expect.

By the time Kelera reached the edge of the poppy fields, her dress was covered in pollen. She dusted herself off as best she could, irritated at how the day's events had gone so far. From here, she could see Cierine's manor. The beautiful stone home towered high, with rose vines entwining themselves along the walls. The anxiety Kelera had been suffering after the encounter with the witch melted away at the sight of that house. She had spent endless days here as a child, hiding away from court. It was a safe haven away from gossip and the more vindictive girls who had taken to giving her a hard time.

She followed the path up to the steps and smoothed out her hair, careful to cover the tips of her ears. She might not be able to hide her strange eyes, but she would do everything in her power to hide the rest.

Chapter Two

Rose Manor towered before Kelera with its beautiful, clean-cut stone walls and rose vines that wound their way up to the roof. Cierine's family home was one of the most exquisite estates in Nevene. It was the envy of all who visited it. When she reached the steps, the familiar iron horseshoe hanging above the door caught her eye. It was a common adornment amongst the mortals of Nevene. A way for them to feel safe, as if they could ward off any evil Fae who wandered into their territory. Would it keep away the witch in the field if she chose to pay them a visit? Before she could give it much thought, the tall wooden door startled her as it swung open to reveal Cierine still in her white cotton nightgown.

Kelera laughed, "You're not even dressed yet? I thought I was late!"

Cierine blew a strand of copper hair out of her freck-
led face. "You *are* late..." She gestured for Kelera to
join her inside. Once in the large foyer, Cierine added,
"Which is surprising considering you're usually irritatingly early."

Kelera, who was already disappointed in herself for
her tardiness, tried to explain, "I'm sorry. I didn't mean
for it to happen. I even left early, but..." She didn't
want to lie to her best friend, but she also wasn't sure
how to tell her about the encounters she'd had on the
road and in the poppy fields. Cierine had never cared
that Kelera's mother was from Elfhame, but Kelera still
didn't want anyone to know that her draw to magic still
lingered as strongly as it did. It seemed no matter how
hard she tried, she could not escape the ever-present tie
to the Fae.

She tried to think of an excuse to give Cierine, but she
struggled to come up with anything. The conversation
with the witch gave her an unsettling feeling. It had
been years since Kelera had encountered anything as
powerful as the Fae witch. When she was a child, she
had followed any draw of magic, no matter how strong
or dangerous. She had loved playing tricks on courtiers
with the pixies or stealing pies from the kitchen to leave
out for the gnomes in the gardens. But as she grew, and
noticed how differently the courtiers treated her, she
had shut that part of her world out.

It was alarming to her now that lately the draw to
these creatures of Elfhame was getting harder for her to
ignore. The pixies were not even the start of it. Lately,
she had been seeing things around the palace grounds.
A faint shimmer of magic here, and a shadow moving
behind the shrubs there. No matter how much time she
spent making her life as perfectly human as possible,
she still could not escape that other part of her.

Instead of lying, she changed the subject. "It doesn't
matter. What does matter is that you look like you just

rolled out of bed." The girls laughed as Cierine led Kelera up the main stairs and down the hall to her room.

The bedroom was three times the size of Kelera's own back at the palace. Enormous, with a sitting area and a beautiful four-poster bed. The room's walls were adorned with hand-painted flowers. She had always loved this room. Growing up, the girls had spent many nights here, telling stories well after bedtime, or staring out into the gardens to see if they could spot anything lurking in the shadows.

Kelera helped herself to the dress that was hanging on the wooden bureau and removed it from the fabric bag that it was half wrapped in. Her breath hitched in her throat. The pristine white gown was beautifully crafted, long, and flowing with intricate lace detail.

"Oh, it's breathtaking."

Cierine flopped onto the bed and rolled herself dramatically in the heavy quilts. "You're sure it's not too much?"

"Not at all."

Cierine scrunched her nose as she argued, "It just seems so... Perfect."

Kelera grabbed the dress and put a hand on her hip. "And that's a bad thing?"

"Don't you ever just want something to be, I don't know... messy?"

"No." Kelera thought of the pixie who had pulled her hair away from its perfect placement on her head. Cierine would never understand how much effort it took Kelera to be like her. To excel in things like art, writing, and dancing. Each and every day was a battle for her—trying to ignore the draw to magic, or to fight the urge to exact vengeance on the people who slighted her. She had to suppress her very nature just to get through a day at court. She could no longer remember a time where she had wanted life to be anything less than perfect.

Cierine made a funny face at her and sighed. "Fine. I'll put the gown on. But I'm not making any promises that I'll make it to the aisle."

Kelera laughed. She knew her friend was happy about her match to Duke Francis, but Cierine had always had a wild spirit. It was what had first brought the two girls together. Cierine had never minded the rumors about Kelera's connection to the Fae and had loved causing mischief with her when they were children. But whereas Kelera had traded her sense of adventure for duty, Cierine still struggled with the idea of becoming the obedient wife and taking on more responsibility at court.

Kelera helped Cierine into the gown and tied the silk ribbons in the back. She looked incredible, with her sleek, thin frame and delicate features. To Kelera, she looked like the perfect bride.

"Is your father excited about the tournament?" Cierine attempted to tame her unruly hair in the mirror as she asked.

Kelera went to work helping her. "He is. Dodger is convinced he's going to take home the grand prize."

Cierine scoffed. "Too bad you can't enter. You would win for sure."

"Ladies do not compete." Kelera gave Cierine a stern look.

"But you're so talented..."

Kelera spun Cierine to face her and began pinning stray hairs away from her face. "Spending time with my father and Dodger on the training field is an escape from courtly life. That is all. I have no intention of drawing attention to myself by raging about with a sword in front of the entire court."

Cierine teased, "You mean in front of Alexander?"

Kelera laughed, releasing Cierine from her primping. "I would hate to do anything to jeopardize the match..." Cierine scowled, but Kelera didn't let it stop her. "Don't look at me like that. Lord Alexander is the only suitor who has stepped forward. Marriage to him will secure my position in society."

"Others will not accept you until you learn to accept yourself." Cierine was sincere as she repeated the words she had said to Kelera so many times before.

They will never accept the real me, Kelera thought to herself, *I have no choice but to give them a version of myself that they do not fear.* Out loud, she simply said, "Enough about me. This is *your* day."

The girls were interrupted as the door opened to reveal a gaggle of fawning ladies from the court. Kelera moved silently to the side, giving them a wide berth as they scurried into the room. She watched them fuss over Cierine's wild red hair, undoing all of Kelera's work and trying to tame it into submission beneath a glittering tiara.

Cierine looked at Kelera with wide eyes as she mouthed the words, "Help me."

Kelera shrugged her shoulders, leaving her friend to be poked and prodded. When they finished, Cierine was almost unrecognizable. Kelera admired the way Cierine could clean up. Not a hair out of place on her head, and perfect rosy cheeks. Most of all, no pointed ears and eyes that held only one shade of bright blue. So unlike Kelera's own.

The ladies sat on the velvet couches in the sitting area and a lady's maid appeared in the doorway with a tray of tea. She set it out on the short tea table before taking her leave. The ladies didn't bother to offer a word of thanks to the girl as they began to pour the tea into the delicate little cups. Chatter filled the air and Kelera took up a seat to the side of them.

She laid her hands carefully on her lap and listened politely to their gossip. She wondered if any of them would even care if they knew that commoners really were being kidnapped. Or would they go about their day, unbothered? Kelera squeezed her hands together, trying to ignore the pit in her stomach. Perhaps she should tell her father about what the witch had said...

One of the women took a sip of her tea and eyed Kelera over the cup. When she set it down, she spoke, causing the other ladies to fall silent. "Lady Kelera, you look quite lovely today."

Kelera tipped her head to her in thanks. "As do you, Lady Alma." It was a lie. The woman looked dreadful with too much rouge on her cheeks and her dull brown hair pulled too tightly back.

The women were as quite as mice—waiting silently to see if anything exciting was about to unfold. Lady Alma's family was infamous for hunting faeries, no matter how small and harmless. Kelera was all too aware of what the dreadful woman thought of her, and she was not going to give her ammunition to act on those thoughts.

Lady Alma smiled innocently. "It is a wonder you are able to hide those unsightly features of yours so well. I do applaud you for it. I am sure every lady here envies that ability." She laughed haughtily. "I know I would love to be able to hide this horrible blemish that appeared in the dead of the night." She lifted a gloved hand to her chin. "My lady's maid unfortunately does not possess your skills, Lady Kelera." She laughed and the rest of the ladies followed suit.

Kelera's blood boiled at the blatant insult. She thought of how satisfying it would be to remove one of the many hairpins in the woman's hair and stick it in her eye. She bit the inside of her cheek, clouding her vengeful thoughts with the physical pain.

Cierine was not so good at holding back. She looked down at Lady Alma where she was standing as she said, "I agree, it is a shame... the blemish looks quite grotesque. Perhaps if you applied powder, it would not be so distracting."

Lady Alma put a hand over her chin quickly. The ladies stopped laughing and shifted in their seats uncomfortably. Cierine walked over to Kelera and squeezed her shoulder gently in a common show of solidarity between the two of them. Kelera looked up at her gratefully. As the niece of the king, Cierine could dish out all the slights she wished with no social reprimand.

A knock at the door broke the silence. Cierine called out, "Come in."

The young, lady's maid entered and beamed at Cierine in her gown. "They're ready for you, milady."

Cierine looked at Kelera nervously. "Well, what are we waiting for?"

Kelera gave her a reassuring smile. "It's going to be great."

Cierine blushed and took a deep breath before walking to the door. The ladies joined her, bustling out of the room, and holding tight to Cierine's hand as if she might flee at the first chance she had. Kelera, finding herself left behind, sighed as she looked out the window. She could see people already gathering around the altar that had been built in the gardens. She searched the crowd until she found a tall, proud man standing amongst the other lords of court—her father, Sir Aldric. He was dressed in a dazzling green jacket that accented his golden sun kissed skin.

As if he could sense her watching him, he looked up at the window. He smiled ear to ear when he saw her, the soft lines of age crinkling around his eyes as he did. She gave him a small wave before turning away. The ceremony would be starting soon, and it was time for her to face the crowd. Visitors had come from all over the kingdom. Even emissaries and royalty from the kingdoms to the north would be attending the wedding of the year. Surely, they, too, would whisper about her.

She could feel the pressure beginning to weigh on her. With so many strangers visiting, and Lord Alexander attending the wedding, she would need to be at her very best. It was crucial not to do anything to make Lord Alexander question the solidity of their betrothal.

If he changed his mind, then she would have no other marriage prospects. Her place at court would continue to be reliant solely on her ability to show them that she had inherited more from her human father than her Fae mother.

Feeling more anxious than usual, Kelera took a moment to study herself in the mirror on Cierine's vanity. Her dress was wrinkled from her trek through the fields, and she adjusted it carefully over her curves, wishing she, too, had the slim frame that her friend had. The dress was still not back to her standards of flawlessness, but it would have to do for now.

Next, she went to work on her hair. It was less disheveled than it had been when the pixies left her, but she took a moment to smooth it over her slightly pointed ears. She would need to be careful not to let it slip away from them. *Tonight has to be perfect*, she thought to herself, *I have to be perfect.*

Chapter Three

Rose Manor's gardens had been transformed into a wonderland. White lanterns hung from strings, casting a twinkling glow on the people gathered beneath them. King Tristan had spared no expense when it came to throwing his niece the wedding of the year, and the members of his court were taking full advantage of the extravagant event. They were each dressed in their finest clothing and the ladies glittered with jewels. Kelera admired the way they all looked immaculate and poised.

The wedding ceremony had gone off without a hitch. Cierine was the perfect blushing bride and Duke Francis was ever the dotting groom. They had said their vows on the altar, which had been littered with flower petals. And the guests had cheered with joy.

Kelera's father had enjoyed the ceremony as well. When it ended, he leaned in and whispered to her,

"It will be you up there soon enough." Kelera had said nothing in response, but still, she blushed. She was both hopeful and anxious to see her fiancé tonight and knew that it was only a matter of time before they bumped into one another.

Now the reception had begun and Kelera found herself strolling beside the tables lined along the pebble pathways winding through the gardens. Each was piled high with delicate finger foods; cakes, tarts, and slim glasses of champagne littered the tabletops. She ran a hand along the lace tablecloth as she wandered aimlessly past the crowds of people. She had lost sight of the blushing bride hours ago and imagined she was likely off with her new husband, engulfed in marital bliss.

A footman was making his way through the crowd, handing drinks to the guests. Kelera smiled as he walked toward her. When he spotted her waiting eagerly for a refreshment, he brushed past her to hand drinks to a group of ladies standing nearby. It wasn't the first time she had been snubbed, and it wouldn't be the last. But that didn't make the offense hurt any less. Kelera met his eye, and he looked down at her with disdain before heading toward another group of courtiers.

Heat rushed to her cheeks in embarrassment by the blatant slight. She would just have to pour her own drink. She wandered over to the champagne fountain and smiled politely at a small group of noblemen visiting from the north. They eyed her with caution before whispering and moving down the table away from her. She clenched her jaw as she grabbed a tall glass and began to fill it. The men's response didn't shock her. They were not regulars at court and had likely heard rumors about the half-Fae girl masquerading as a mortal in the palace. She sipped on the champagne, enjoying the way the bubbles fizzed on her tongue.

She was lost in thought when a familiar husky voice rang in her ears. "It was a beautiful ceremony." She turned in surprise to find Alexander smiling brightly at her. He was stunningly handsome in his high-cut waistcoat and silver vest. His sandy blonde hair was neatly trimmed, and his dark brown eyes twinkled in the lantern and candlelight. He took her gloved hand in his and kissed it lightly as he bowed to her in greeting.

Kelera nearly forgot her manners. She still was not used to the idea that this was her soon-to-be husband. She had just turned nineteen, and it was unheard of for a woman of her age to not be married and settled into her own estate. Alexander, who was two years her senior, had been her savior for stepping up as a suitor. According to him, he had been far too busy building his political career to marry.

Now he was left with her. Lucky for him, Kelera had spent her life preparing herself to be the dutiful wife. She knew it was what society was expecting of her and she found herself excited to be settled down with a well respected man of high social stature. Perhaps with him by her side, others would no longer turn away from her. She would finally have the security she'd been working so hard to achieve.

Standing before him now, she tried to carry herself with the grace he surely expected from her. She thought of the dolls that her father had commissioned for her when she was a child. Beautiful, obedient, and poised. No longer was she the little girl who had run around in fairy circles, hiding from Papa to explore the gardens. He'd had trouble keeping her in line then. But as she grew up, she had begun to notice the others staring at her. Like she was as strange as the creatures who dwelled south of the palace grounds.

Alexander smiled at her expectantly, and she panicked. How long had she been lost in her own thoughts? Would he think her simple? She set her glass down and cleared her throat before she said, "The reception is quite exquisite as well." Not the most tantalizing conversationalist, but it was better than staring at him, dumb-founded.

He continued the conversation without a second thought. "It is. I was glad we could stay for it. My father and I leave again after the King's Tournament. We have business in the north with Marenth, but it won't be a long trip this time."

Kelera nodded in understanding. Alexander's father, Earl Demetri, was a well respected lord of the court. He oversaw the land to the east of the palace but also had business dealings in trade. Because of that, he and Alexander were often on the road. It also meant that Kelera hadn't spent a lot of time with her betrothed. Not that she minded. She preferred to have her space and thought it might be nice to have a husband who was not always hovering. It would certainly give her a chance to relax and enjoy an ounce of freedom for once. Even though Alexander was aware of her background, she still prayed that he wouldn't notice just how different she was from the other women at court.

As Kelera searched for something else to say to him, her father approached with drinks in hand. He interrupted, handing them each a cup filled with potent wine. "Ah, my future son-in-law has made an appearance. I'm glad to see the two of you found each other in all of this madness." He gestured to the party goers who were having their fill of wine and becoming increasingly boisterous. "How are you, my boy?"

"I'm doing quite well, Sir Aldric." Alexander shook her father's hand firmly. "Does the invitation to join you tomorrow still stand?"

"Absolutely. I'm sure you could teach the squires a thing or two." Her father turned and winked at her, clueless of the blush that was forming across Kelera's face.

She held back a groan. As the Knight Commander, he was in charge of the King's Tournament and would be spending the day practicing in the yard with the other knights. Something she had planned on doing as well, though she was rethinking that choice, knowing now that her fiancé would join them.

Kelera was extensively trained in the arts of battle. She could wield a sword, shoot an arrow, and hold her own in hand-to-hand combat. It was uncommon amongst the women of court, but Kelera found it helped to release the feelings she bottled up throughout her days. Her father had approved, standing firm in his belief that a lady should be prepared for anything. She was not so sure Alexander would share the sentiment.

Someone shouted for her father, and he excused himself, bidding Kelera and Alexander good night. Once he was gone, she shifted awkwardly. Alexander, ever the gentleman, broke the silence as he asked, "Would you like to walk with me?"

Kelera desperately hoped he couldn't see the blush on her face. "A walk sounds lovely."

He offered his arm, and she took it graciously. He led her along the pebbled path, past partygoers who stared and whispered in their presence. Alexander either did not notice or was gallant enough to pretend that he did not.

They walked in silence and Kelera wracked her brain to think of something charming or witty to say. But the further they walked, the more she could feel the buzz of magic. It was becoming so overwhelming that she could think of nothing else except that she wanted to go to it like a moth to a flame. Fighting the urge, she stopped abruptly, nearly jerking Alexander by the arm in the process.

He looked startled. "Is everything okay?"

Kelera bit her cheek. She knew her behavior seemed strange, but whatever was at the end of the path was not of the mortal realm. Likely more pixies who wanted to get a closer look at the human festivities. She rubbed her arms, pretending that the chill of the night was getting to her. "Sorry, it's just a lot colder over here, away from the fire and lanterns..."

"Oh, of course. We can go back." He turned to lead her toward the party.

She relaxed a bit, thinking about how genuinely kind he seemed. He was quite the catch and could have had his pick of any woman in the kingdom. Why tie himself to her and the baggage that came with her?

Before they could get more than a couple of steps, she stopped him. "Alexander, are you happy about this arrangement?" He raised an eyebrow at the bold question and Kelera quickly added, "I just mean, we don't know each other very well. We haven't seen each other since we were so young. I was just wondering if you were disappointed."

He became serious as he spoke. "I could never be disappointed with you. The match was my idea."

Kelera was shocked. "It was?" The engagement had happened so suddenly, she had never even thought to ask. She had assumed their fathers had arranged it. She and Alexander were not getting any younger and their fathers had been friendly for years. It had made sense, but she had been sick with worry that Alexander had felt pressured into agreeing.

He took her hands and squeezed them gently. "You are beautiful, bright, and you excel at practically everything you do. I have no doubt you will make an amazing wife." He raised her hands to his mouth and kissed them gently. Something fluttered in her stomach, and she found herself wondering what his lips would feel like on hers. She had never kissed anyone before—careful to protect her reputation.

As very young children, they had spent summers together at his father's house. But they had always been surrounded by other children visiting; cousins, friends from the village... They had never been alone like this before. It suddenly hit her that they were a good distance away from the party. There were no chaperones nearby, though she figured considering their age, perhaps that was not as big of a deal. Still, she couldn't risk scandalous rumors.

She carefully removed her hands from his and took a step back, putting distance between them. She smiled at him to let him know she wasn't offended by his display of affection as she said, "Perhaps we should return to the party. I would like to bid Cierine farewell before they retire for the night."

Alexander held his arm out for her to take. "Of course. I noticed my father was dipping into the king's wine, too. We might want to steer him away before he starts to gamble. The last time we were at one of these, he lost his pants to Duke Cunningham." They laughed as they made their way back down the path.

They didn't make it more than a few steps before a woman's scream rang through their ears. It came from the opposite direction of the party... In the direction of the magic Kelera had felt. *No. Please don't let this be happening.* Kelera's mind went to the worst. She couldn't help it. Nothing good came from the magic of Elfhame, and there was no mistaking the terror in that scream.

Alexander's brow furrowed with concern. "Someone is in trouble." He turned back to Kelera. "Stay here."

The woman screamed again and Kelera sensed magic swelling in the air. Something stirred inside of her in its presence. Like something begging for release. It was a feeling Kelera hadn't experienced since she called on the roots in the ground as a child. Terrified of the magic she had suppressed for so long, she shut her eyes tight and willed it away.

Meanwhile, Alexander took off at a run, heading straight for the danger. She knew she should do as he had bid, but it felt as if the magic was calling to her. Unable to resist it any longer, she broke out into a run, trying to catch up to him. She stumbled over her gown and paused only for a moment to hike it up. As she ran into the darkness, she could hear Alexander's urgent footsteps ahead of her. There was nothing but the moon to light her path as she hurried away from the gardens.

The screaming continued as Kelera followed it and the growing feeling of the magic. It seemed less like the pixies' magic and more like the Fae witch she had encountered earlier that day. But instead of needles this time, it felt like someone was beating a drum on her body. She rounded the corner, dodging the shrubs that walled off the gardens, and led to the meadow.

Which of the party guests had been stupid enough to wander this far away from the gardens alone? The screaming stopped and Kelera spun around, looking for any sign of trouble.

Alexander jogged back to her and stood by her side. He was panting from the run and brushed his now disheveled hair from his forehead. "I told you to stay by the gardens. It's not safe here." There was a bite to his voice, and Kelera worried she had angered him.

"I know—I just thought I could help."

He relaxed slightly and his voice was softer as he said, "It's okay, just stay close." He squinted his eyes in the darkness. "Do you see anything?"

Kelera's Fae eyes gave her the ability to see more clearly than mortals, even in the dark. Not wanting to share that with Alexander, she pretended she was also having trouble seeing in the dark and squinted too. Though she could see clearly, there was nothing to be found. The field was empty save for a family of rabbits hopping around nearby.

Kelera ventured a few steps further into the darkness and a wave of magic hit her hard. She stumbled back into Alexander's chest. He held tight to her arms as she steadied herself, looking up at him gratefully. Drawing a deep breath, she took a step forward again but was hit with the same force as before.

"What in the world is that?" Alexander looked alarmed, and Kelera felt pity for him. He had grown up far enough north that he had likely never come across creatures from south of the blackthorn border. Even before the rumors of kidnappings had begun, it was not uncommon for mortals living in southern Nevene to have the rare run in at least one time in their life.

Before she could answer him, a shadow caught her eye. The height of it was alarming. Most creatures who were brave enough to sneak into the mortal realm were small and spritely. Whatever was lurking in the dark now was the size of a tall man. Wanting to get a better look, Kelera took a step in its direction, but Alexander held out a hand to stop her.

He sounded nervous as he asked, "Do you see it too?"

"I do."

His voice was firm as he said, "Stay here." Then added gently, "Please."

She relented, though it took every ounce of self-control to hold back. Alexander crept into the shadows as Kelera waited. A woman screamed again, and he took off running in the direction of it. Kelera, unsure of what to do, moved to follow him. Before she could get far, torchlight caught her eye as men from the wedding party came into the clearing. They were armed for a fight and looked her over to make sure she was alright. A few of them eyed her suspiciously, as if it might be a mean trick she was playing on them.

"The scream didn't come from me. It came from there. Lord Alexander went after it." She pointed in the direction that he and the shadow had disappeared to. They nodded to her and proceeded into the night. Kelera was itching to go with them, but knew she shouldn't. A lady was expected to wait for the men to do the fighting. The fact that she had already disobeyed Alexander's order to stay near the gardens was bad enough. There was no need for her to do it a second time.

The magic was still drumming against her as she rubbed at her temples. She was alone in the clearing now, but it felt as if someone was watching her. She looked around nervously. It was too quiet. The rabbits had gone, and she could no longer hear the familiar sound of crickets chiming in the tall grass. Her heart began to thud so hard that it was the only sound in her ears.

Out of the corner of her eye, she saw it again. The shadow of a man was creeping toward her. There was no sign of the mortals who had gone after Alexander and the woman's screams. That meant she was on her own now. She steadied herself and stayed unmoving as it crept closer. Just as it came within reach, she spun around and swung out a fist. It connected with air, and she stumbled forward. Straightening quickly to defend herself from an assault, she was met with laughter. It was arrogant as it laughed at her fruitless efforts to hit it.

"You think this is funny?" Her blood boiled from the slight.

The shadow wavered like it was having trouble holding its form. From what she could make out of it under the moonlight, it was tall and well built. It taunted her with a voice as smooth as honey, "I do not doubt that you are a worthy opponent, but I see the fear in your eyes."

She lied, "I'm not afraid of you. Do not think that I will be so easy to take as the girl you just dragged away." She thought of the girl's screams and how she had not heard them for quite some time now. It was likely that she had already been taken by the time Alexander and the others arrived. Trapped in Elfhame for eternity. If the legends held any truth, once a mortal crossed that threshold, the chances of return dangerously decreased.

"Should we test that theory of yours?" The shadow moved closer to her, but she held her ground. It wanted her to be frightened. That much was clear. But she would not give it the satisfaction. She raised her head high, ready to face the worst.

It reached out a shadowy hand and caressed her face. It felt like ice running along her skin. In response to its touch, a prickling heat flooded her body, and the shadow hissed. Withdrawing its hand like it had been burned, it said, "Interesting. Halfling magic is usually weak. But I sense something more... significant in you." His voice was filled with hunger, as if the thought of power appealed to it.

Little did it know, Kelera had no control over her power. Not anymore. She had suppressed it for so long, she wasn't sure she could call on it by will if she tried. But it was none of the shadow's business. She opened her mouth to deny that she held any magic, but torchlight blazed into the clearing. The men were returning from their hunt. Alexander was leading them and spotted her immediately. He shouted for the others to follow him as he picked up his pace to cross the field to her.

The shadow chuckled, "Another time then." There was a promise in those words that made Kelera shiver. The shadow blinked out of view, and she found herself alone in the clearing by the time Alexander and the other men reached her.

Alexander searched her for any sign of injury. "Did that thing hurt you? What did it say to you?"

She allowed him to take her hands in his and welcomed the solid touch. She assured the concerned group, "I'm fine. He..." She noted the few men who watched her warily. Did they honestly think she could have had anything to do with this? And how would they react if they knew the shadow had shown interest in her magic? She decided to keep the conversation with the shadow to herself. "... it didn't have a chance to say anything."

Alexander let out a gentle sigh. It was comforting to know he cared so much about her safety. The men, on the other hand, still regarded her with uncomfortable gazes. She ignored them, focusing on Alexander's calming presence.

The men searched the clearing once more to see if the shadow was still lingering but came up empty handed. Alexander remained by her side; his brown eyes were filled with concern as he pulled her into a hug. She ignored the bystanders as they returned from their search and thought, *Gossip be damned*. It felt good to be held after the encounter with the shadow and his rough, drumming magic.

After a moment, the men departed, leading the way back to the reception. As Alexander escorted her back to the safety of the gardens, he told her they had found nothing. There was no sign of the girl. They still did not know who she was, and the men had decided they would need to take a headcount back at the party. It would be the only way to know who had been taken.

Kelera simply nodded as he explained that they should be grateful they had not found a body. It meant that the girl was still alive. But Kelera knew from the stories that there were fates worse than death. There had been tales of kidnappings by the Fae through the ages. No one knew for certain what the Fae did with the humans they stole, but there were rumors. The stories ranged from humans being forced to serve the Queen of the Seelie court to them being tortured by the King of the Unseelie court. The fate they met did not matter to Kelera. No matter what it was, it could be nothing other than a nightmare. A nightmare she was determined never to face.

Chapter Four

S leep hadn't come easily after the wedding reception. Not for anyone in the palace. The party had ended shortly after she and the men returned. Alexander had gone straight to King Tristan to tell him of the kidnapping and the shadow they'd seen. King Tristan had been beside himself, barking out orders for guards to move to the blackthorn veil. The reception's atmosphere was heavy with apprehension after that and they had been forced to call it a night.

Even now, as she walked down the velvet carpeted hallway, she could feel the tension rolling off of the courtiers and palace staff in waves. The morning rush was slowing as people dispersed to attend to their business for the day. Kelera tried to greet them as she passed through the halls, but whenever she met their eyes, they would turn their gaze away from her.

Shaking off the unsettling feeling that people were avoiding her more than usual, she continued around the corner. Alexander, who was surrounded by a group of lords, called to her, "Kelera, wait up!" He bid the men farewell, shrugging on his jacket with haste, and jogged to catch up with her.

Kelera slowed to a stop and laughed. "Lord Alexander, your jacket appears to be inside out." She pointed to it, and he blushed.

He chuckled as he removed it. "It has been a rather chaotic morning."

She nodded in understanding but was at a loss for words. She could see his strong build more clearly without the coat and found herself admiring his broad shoulders and muscular arms. He caught her staring and gave her a crooked grin.

As he corrected his jacket, he asked her, "Are you headed to breakfast with the others?"

"No," she hesitated, unsure of how he would respond to where she was actually going. "I was thinking I would pay my father a visit in the training yards." She hoped he was not about to ask if he could accompany her. She didn't want to feel the pressure of his eyes on her while she practiced the sword and bow.

"Would you like some company?" He gave her a hopeful smile.

Worried she would offend him if she was truthful, she nodded. "That would be lovely, thank you."

They strolled through the palace and out past the gardens in a comfortable silence. She liked that he didn't act as if he expected her to carry the brunt of the conversation. He seemed as content as she was just walking together. When they passed the king's gardens, she could see several raised tents up ahead. Each had wooden benches or tables for the knights and squires to rest and replenish themselves. The summer heat was in full force today, and she could imagine that they were miserable underneath all their armor. Lucky for her, a lady did not have to don the sweltering steel suits.

"Have you heard King Tristan is sending soldiers to the border today? Nothing is to pass in or out of Nevene." Alexander fiddled with the buttons on his jacket nervously.

"Does he think it will make a difference? It has been so long since Nevene has required such a thing." She hoped it would. But it had been years since anything other than the odd trick had been enacted on the mortals by the Fae.

Alexander shrugged. "Our proximity to the blackthorns means that we are the only line of defense between Elfhame and the rest of the human realm to the north. King Tristan believes with conviction that it is our duty to put a stop to the kidnappings, regardless of the manpower and resources that it takes."

Kelera had to admit it made her feel better about the situation. Nevene was famous for its military strength and the brave knights who stood ready to fight valiantly for the king. Surely, they would be able to keep things from getting any more out of hand.

They made their way down the path that led to the training fields. The sun felt good on Kelera's face. If she could spend every day outside in the fresh air, then she would. She was wondering about the gardens at Alexander's manor when her father greeted them. Sir Aldric removed his helmet and wiped the sweat from his brow. His dark brown hair was matted, but he was clearly in his element with a smile spread wide across his face. Kelera had always loved visiting him in the training yard. Some of her fondest memories were watching him teach his squires swordplay—an observation that had made the skill easy for her to pick up as well.

Though the other ladies of court disapproved of her extracurriculars, Kelera was determined to be the best in everything. That included sword fighting, archery, and even hand-to-hand combat. Her father had welcomed the idea, knowing that it made his daughter happy. When she was in the field with her father, she felt closer to him than ever.

He greeted her first with a hug and then turned to shake Alexander's hand. "Happy you could join us, Lord Alexander."

Alexander had never taken the title of knighthood, but he'd trained under her father years ago and had earned the respect of the other knights when he was quite young. She imagined it was his own father's expectations of him to continue the family business that had prevented him from pursuing knighthood. Still, Kelera was impressed by the stories she had heard about his abilities and was eager to see him on the field.

Her father turned his attention to her. "Are you here to observe today or were you going to have a go?"

Heat rose to her cheeks. "I thought I would watch for a bit."

Alexander had a look on his face that was somewhere between confusion and intrigue. He gave her a chivalrous bow before following her father to the armory. Kelera lingered, allowing them to get a head start before joining the knights on the sidelines.

It would have been nice to have had the chance to pick up her own sword. After her encounter with the shadow, she desperately needed to work off some of the nervous energy she was feeling, but she was afraid of what Alexander would think if he saw his elegant fiancé with a sword in her hand.

So instead, she followed the sounds of cheering and laughter, slipping through the crowd to get a look at the small makeshift arena her father had set up for the men. It was similar to the one that would hold the King's Tournament but smaller in scale. Alexander had already jumped in to challenge one of the squires. She peered around the other knights to get a better view of the match. The one towering over her, Dodger, shoved the knight standing beside him. He put an arm around Kelera and pulled her up to the front so she could see better.

"There you go Pipsqueak." He bellowed with laughter as he used the nickname he had given her as a child. She rolled her eyes at him but appreciated the help all the same. He was harmless. The knights directly under her father's command had always treated her like a little sister and she was used to their rough-mannered ways. She even welcomed it at times like this. It was easy for her to be around them. She didn't have to worry about what she said or how she acted. These men never whispered about her or stared when her pointed ears peeked through her hair like the other mortals in Nevene often did.

It was one of the things that drew her to the training yards. No matter how much Kelera perfected the arts of things like sewing or dancing, the ladies at court still tiptoed around her. The knights, on the other hand, did not mind that she was half Fae. They only cared how well she held her own when she was around them. The endless hours she had spent on the field with them had earned their respect. It made this her safe space. A sanctuary of sorts.

Dodger, in particular, had always made her feel safe here. It had been over a decade since he had accompanied her father to the blackthorns on the night that the Fae witch had tried to steal Kelera away. He had learned her secret that night, finding out that she indeed possessed magic. Since then, he had kept her secret.

But it wasn't until a few years later that Kelera had begun to consider him a friend. She'd been twelve and had just gotten into an altercation with a particularly cruel girl named Drisella. The nasty girl had pulled Kelera's hair away from her ears to show them off to the other girls in their class.

Kelera had been so consumed with humiliation and anger that she'd pinched Drisella hard on the arm. The girl's pained yelp had filled Kelera with so much satisfaction that it had frightened her. She had felt the warmth of magic rise to the surface of her hands. Afraid that she would do worse if she remained in the girl's presence for another moment, she ran from the palace as fast as her feet could carry her.

When she had shown up looking for her father with tears streaming down her rosy cheeks, she had found Dodger instead. He had sat and listened to her as she told him about how Drisella and the other girls had called her names and told her it was tragic that even her dirty Fae mother hadn't wanted her. He had listened intently before finally telling her that there was only one thing that made him feel better after a run in with miserable, mean people. A good fight.

He had given her a wooden sword and shield, and that was it. Kelera had begun wandering into the yard after her lady's lessons each day and soon she had mastered both sword and bow. Her father never said a word, though he knew what she was doing. She suspected he had preferred her spending her time in the training field where he could keep an eye on her instead of near the blackthorn trees as she had when she was very young.

"Thanks, Dodger." Kelera could see Alexander clearly now. He danced around his opponent with a grace that most of her father's men lacked. His footwork entranced her as she watched him take down one challenger and then the next.

Dodger grunted, "Impressive." When Kelera looked at him with a raised eyebrow, and he added quickly, "For a dandy."

It was on rare occasions that Dodger was impressed with anyone other than himself, and Kelera laughed as she retorted, "Those are not the moves of a dandy."

When he scoffed, she challenged him, "Maybe you should get in there, then."

Dodger took the bait. Without another word, he pushed his way through the crowd that was gathered nearest to the field. He roared out a challenge and Kelera was pleasantly surprised to see Alexander welcome it. As Dodger stepped onto the field, Alexander smiled broadly and spread his arms out wide. Her fiancé may not be a knight, but that certainly did not make him a coward.

Dodger spun his broadsword in a great flourish. He was a showman and loved to keep the crowd on their toes. Kelera wondered how Alexander would fare against someone like him. She squeezed through the crowd until she came to her father's side at the edge of the field.

He raised an eyebrow in suspicion. "Did you have something to do with this?"

She gave him a mischievous smile. "Maybe." It was easy with her father. She didn't have to be the perfect little lady and could let her guard down a bit. As long as she did not lose control, it felt good to stir up some harmless trouble. And she knew the practice field held no real danger. The men were careful not to get carried away. If they did, they risked not only the wrath of her father, but the king as well. Every able-bodied knight was to compete in the tournament, and Dodger knew better than to exert himself too much. He also knew better than to cause any actual harm to a nobleman.

Kelera's father called the match, giving the win to Dodger. She clapped for her fiancé. Though he had lost, it impressed her that he had lasted as long as he did against one of her father's champions.

He picked up his sword and shook hands with Dodger, then came to the side of the arena where Kelera stood with her father. He bowed to her and smiled brightly. She curtseyed in response. His face was covered in sweat and dirt, yet he was still stunningly handsome. She could get used to seeing that face more often.

Kelera was so lost in her thoughts that she almost yelped out in alarm when Dodger shouted at her, "Your turn, milady." He grinned ear to ear and pointed his massive broadsword at her.

Oh no, she thought to herself. *Not with Alexander watching...*

When she paused, a few knights in the crowd began to chant her name. "Kelera! Kelera! Kelera!"

Alexander gaped at her in surprise. She hesitated and felt herself blush. Coming up with the only excuse she could voice out loud, she said, "This is a new dress..."

Dodger gripped his chest in feigned heartbreak. Her father chuckled to himself. "You heard the lady, back to work, lads."

A newcomer slipped through the crowd and spoke with disgust, "That is probably for the best. We wouldn't want King Tristan's men mixing with the likes of her."

Kelera turned to see a young man walking her way. He was a familiar face. A regular at court because of his father's position on the king's council. Though he'd never been particularly friendly toward her, he had never spoken this way to her face. She clenched her fists. "The likes of me?"

His lip curled as he replied, "*Fae* folk. Your kind always resorts to trickery. No doubt you would cheat in a match and hurt someone."

Alexander came to her defense. "Lord Viktor, you are speaking to a lady of King Tristan's court, and you will behave accordingly."

Kelera shook her head slightly. "By all means, let him speak his mind."

Lord Viktor's lip curled. "I only speak the truth. The Fae are nothing without their tricks."

All of her uncertainty and embarrassment were replaced with a seething anger. How dare he come here to her father's domain and insult her? Blinded by anger, she shrugged her shoulders. "Shall we test your theory?" When the words slipped from her mouth, she thought of the shadow and how he had used those very words as a veiled threat against her. Perhaps Lord Viktor was not far off, and she was more like the Fae than she wanted to admit. The thought gave her an unsettling feeling in the pit of her stomach.

The knights who had been standing silent as they watched the exchange hooted with laughter. Lord Viktor's face looked flushed as he sputtered, "You want *me* to match with *you*?"

Still filled with irritation, she said, "Why not? My father has practice swords in the tent."

Dodger didn't give Lord Viktor a chance to respond. He bolted for the supply tent and came back with two dull blades. He tossed one to Lord Viktor, who fumbled as he tried to take hold of it. Dodger winked at her as he handed her the other sword. The weight of it felt comfortable and familiar in her hand as she held it at her side.

She strode confidently past Alexander and onto the field that was acting as their arena. Lord Viktor followed behind, bouncing around on his feet. Kelera had to suppress a snicker at the ridiculous sight.

She caught sight of Dodger in the crowd. He rolled his eyes. Lord Viktor was no warrior. He was a pampered Viscount's son, accustomed to being fawned over by the ladies of the court solely because of his stature. She, on the other hand, had been training with Dodger since she first started coming to the training fields.

Standing in the arena now, she was very much in her element. Lord Viktor wasted no time advancing on her. She blocked strike after strike with ease. They went a few rounds, parrying and swinging at one another until Lord Viktor lunged for her and she pivoted to the side. He had the good sense to look nervous as he stumbled a few steps. This time, she didn't give him the chance to attack first. With expert precision, she kicked out at his legs, sweeping him onto the ground. He rolled to get up, but she put a boot on his sword arm, holding it in place without stepping hard enough to hurt him. She held the tip of her sword to his chest and said, "Concede."

He shook his head as he glared up at her.

She was about to say something rude, but her vision darkened at the edges. Fear crept up her back as she felt the touch of magic. Magic that was not her own. It sparked along her skin and her breath hitched in her throat. She was no longer standing in the training field. Instead, she was in a snow-covered field. Dark clouds blotted out the sun, and she could hear the cries of people in pain. She shook her head. *This can't be real.*

A voice whispered from beside her, but she couldn't see who it belonged to. *You do not belong here.* Belong where? In Nevene? Or in the snow-covered land she was seeing? She wanted to respond, but her voice wouldn't come. The wind carried the whisper away and the snow surrounding her began to melt.

Once again, she was standing in the training field. Lord Viktor was shaking as he repeated, "I concede. I concede!"

She realized she had pressed her foot to his arm harder than she had intended. She removed it quickly and looked for her father. He and Alexander were watching her with wide eyes. *Oh, stars. What just happened to me?*

She offered a hand to help him up. Shying away from her, he scrambled to his feet. Part of her felt like she should apologize, but there was a small piece deep down that was satisfied with the idea that she had frightened him a little.

Lord Viktor stormed off the field and sulked back to the palace. Kelera hoped he would not tell anyone about her episode. Hopefully, he would be too embarrassed about losing the match to her to say a word to anyone about it.

Dodger met her at the edge of the field. He gave her a heavy pat on the back. "Nicely done, Pipsqueak." Her body shook from the impact, and she rolled her shoulders back as he walked away to join his friends. She could hear them making fun of Lord Viktor. And Dodger's voice boomed proudly above the crowd insisting that he had taught her everything she knows.

Kelera dusted herself off and joined her father and Alexander at the side of the field. Her father squeezed her shoulder as he complimented her, "Nicely done, daughter. Now that the fun and games are over, I'd better get these lazy arses back to work. I will see you at dinner." He made no mention of her episode and she wondered if she had imagined it all. He kissed her cheek before taking his leave to bark orders at the squires who were lounging in the shade nearby.

Kelera studied Alexander's face, curious to see what his reaction would be to her in the arena. Would he think she was brutish? She bit her lip, hoping it had not changed his view of her. To her surprise, he shook his head in disbelief. "I heard that you were good at just about everything, but I had no idea it included this." He sounded impressed and something warm bloomed in her chest.

"Not everything." She laughed nervously. "This is just something I do to burn off steam. Being at court can be so..."

"Suffocating." He finished for her.

It amazed her that he understood. "Yes. A bit. I mean, it's not that I don't enjoy it." That was a fib. She had never really enjoyed it. She preferred to be outside in nature. Away from the whispers, judgmental looks, and the pressure of appearing perfectly human.

"You're not what I expected." He was staring at her intently.

She wasn't sure if he meant that as a good thing or a bad thing, so she asked, "Does it bother you that I'm... That my mother is Fae?"

Alexander did not miss a beat as he replied, "Not at all. You can't listen to people like Viktor. They let fear control their words and actions. *You* are a remarkable person, Kelera. I've seen it with my own eyes. Even last night, you ran headfirst into danger to help someone. I think perhaps, if anything, you deserve more than this life at court."

Is that what he was offering her? An escape? She had not thought of it like that before. Though he was a lord, welcome to reside at the palace, he spent most of his time at his family manor or traveling with his father. Perhaps he, too, was trying to escape the pressures of a life at court. Being with him could mean freedom from the burdens of having judgmental eyes on her constantly.

On the other hand, the idea of leaving the palace made her nervous. She had never been away from her father. Come to think of it, she had never been so far from the blackthorns... Did that matter since she wasn't allowed to go near them? Still, it comforted her to know that maybe her mother was still out there somewhere, just beyond that tree line...

"Your kind words are touching." She smiled up at him as he rubbed the back of her hand with his thumb. His hand was strong and calloused. It was unusual for a lord, and it made her think of how different he was from the other men at court. She did not love him like the girls in fairy tales loved their prince charming, but for the first time, she thought maybe one day, she could.

Chapter Five

T he main hall was buzzing with excitement when Kelera came down the grand staircase in the morning. It was the day of the King's Tournament and visitors were coming in from all over Nevene. She had eaten breakfast in her room, hoping to avoid the stares and whispers from strangers in the main dining hall. She thought it would be best to enjoy the solitude she was given in her own room while she had the chance. She would be expected to exchange pleasantries throughout the next few days.

The tournament was always an affair to remember. Kelera's father prided himself in allowing his men to put their skills on display for the whole of the kingdom. Even villagers would travel days across the countryside just to watch from the sidelines.

Kelera could smell the cook's famous fresh baked blackberry pies wafting from the kitchens. All around her, she could hear the chatter that was filling the halls and the sitting rooms nearby. She stood in the middle of the main hall, taking it all in. A few strangers passed by her and leaned in to whisper to one another. One man grimaced when her eyes met his and he herded his friends out the door as if running from someone who was contagious.

Kelera started to worry about how the other people traveling into town for the tournament would react to her, but before she could give it too much thought, Cierine bounded into the hall. Her husband, Duke Francis, was absent from her side. He was likely enjoying an early morning drink and cigars with the other men. Noblemen of Nevene did not partake in the tournament unless they had taken the title of knighthood. Instead, they drank until they were lost in a drunken stupor and placed bets on which knight would emerge the champion.

Cierine was glowing with happiness. "I've been waiting for you!"

The girls embraced in a tight hug. "Look at you! Marriage suits you."

Cierine blushed. "And it will suit you soon enough, too."

"I'm starting to think it will." Kelera walked beside Cierine as they made their way out of the large double doors and down to the tournament fields. She could see the large wooden grandstands that were set up so that the lords and ladies could get a clear view of the field. It also acted as a buffer for the common folk who would watch from down below.

"Are you trying to tell me you are bewitched by the young, dashing Lord Alexander?" Cierine nudged Kelera in the side playfully.

They passed through the already growing crowd of villagers who had arrived early to get the best view of the arena. Kelera smiled at them as she passed, glad to see everyone in such good cheer.

"He is... not what I expected. I knew he was handsome and well mannered, but I didn't think he would be so charming. Did you know that the match was his idea?"

Cierine looked surprised by the revelation. "I did not. Though one could not blame him." She paused for a moment, then, as if she could not contain herself any longer, she said, "Now, I believe I've waited long enough." She lowered her voice to a whisper. "Tell me about the shadow."

Kelera laughed uncomfortably. "Where did you hear about that?"

Cierine waved a hand in the air. "You know how word spreads through these halls. Some are saying that it towered ten feet in the air. Others say that it was not a shadow at all, but a bogie with bloody dripping fangs." Her eyes were bright with excitement. Of course, Cierine would be dying to know every detail.

If Kelera was being honest with herself, she had been eager to talk to her friend about it as well. "No fangs. But it was the strangest thing, like nothing I've ever come across. The magic that he bears must be dangerous."

"What was it like?" Cierine asked in fascination.

"Like a steel drum. It was more power than I've ever felt. It made me uncomfortable, but at the same time..."

"Invigorated." Cierine finished for her.

Kelera looked around cautiously, making sure there was no one near enough to overhear the scandalous conversation. Then she agreed, "Yes. Even so, I am glad to be done with the whole thing. What we must do now is pray to the stars that King Tristan succeeds in strengthening the blackthorn border."

Cierine gave her a small look of disapproval. "Of course."

Kelera changed the subject, ready to forget the whole ugly business. As they continued to walk, she asked

Cierine to fill her in on the details of her new life as a duke's wife. The girls walked with their arms linked together as Cierine talked. "Dear Francis' palace, as beautiful as it is, will surely be quite boring. It is such a long trek to the north, nearly to the Marenth border." She stopped and turned to Kelera. "You must promise to come and visit me."

"Of course." It would be nice to get away for a while.

Ascending the stairs leading to the grandstand, Kelera could see her father and his men across the field. The tents were colorful, each distinguished with banners waving proudly with each knight's unique coat of arms. She loved studying the golden lions barring their teeth and fire-breathing dragons standing proudly on clawed feet.

The girls took their seats to the right of King Tristan's throne. It wasn't typical for a lady of Kelera's stature to receive such an honor, but being there with Princess Cierine afforded her the courtesy. Cierine leaned in to whisper to her, "See that knight there? The one in the red and yellow. That is our man. He grew up in Francis' household and was the youngest man to be dubbed in over twenty years. Sir Jacome." She smiled proudly when she finished.

Kelera took a moment to admire the man. He was not what she would consider handsome. His features were too soft for that. He had high cheekbones and hair that looked as smooth as silk. Her father's knights were going to eat him alive. But she kept that thought to herself. It was clear that Cierine was looking forward to having her very own band of knights fighting for her house and honor; she was perched on the edge of her seat and already ringing her hands in excitement.

Drisella and her flock of friends joined them shortly after. They walked up the stairs as poised as ever and Kelera envied their ability to look as if they were floating on air. They took a moment to bow to King Tristan and Princess Cierine before taking their seats, ignoring Kelera entirely.

She focused her eyes on the tourney field and the knights who were now gathering on it for the first event. She could hear Drisella and the others laughing and whispering behind her. When she turned around to see what had them in such a fit, Drisella put her fan in front of her face and glared at her over it. Kelera clenched her jaw and turned back toward the field.

Cierine gave her a reassuring squeeze on her shoulder. "Ignore them."

Kelera smoothed out the skirts of her dress, making sure there was not a speck of lint on them. Satisfied, she looked up and smiled. She was determined to do as her friend recommended. In any case, the first event of the tournament was beginning. It was her least favorite part of the tourney, in which the knights would be expected to parade around the arena in a grand show of pageantry.

Dressed in their finest armor, with the most magnificent horses, and brand-new weapons—they would impress the locals in what was called *The First Day Procession*. Though she preferred the combat events, she had to admit, she appreciated the effort that went into putting on such a display. The knights rode around the arena, waving to the children and tossing flowers to young women sitting in the crowd. She sat straight backed in her seat, eager to see the action.

She perked up a bit when Dodger rode in on his golden palomino. The light golden-brown horse towered over the other horses in the arena—the only horse that could hold Dodger's massive frame. He ran his hand over his closely shaved head and set his horse off at a gallop when he spotted Kelera. When he reached the edge of the grandstand, he drew a red rose from his saddle pack. Cierine giggled and pushed Kelera. "Go! Go!"

Trying to ignore the embarrassment she was feeling, Kelera walked to the edge of the stand and looked down at him. "Yes, oh *valiant* knight?" She laughed as she teased him.

"For you, milady. Though we both know it should be you down here tossing up the roses." He winked as he tossed her the rose and rode away.

Kelera tried not to grip the thorny rose too tightly as she turned back to face the courtiers, red-faced. Maybe they had not heard him. Or perhaps they had not caught onto his meaning. Of course, with her unfortunate luck...

Drisella's voice was filled with malicious laughter as she said loud enough for all in the stands to hear, "Ha! I should very much like to see that. Lady Kelera riding around down there like a *man*. It would all be very beastly of you."

Kelera remained calm as she said coolly, "Are you calling our most decorated warriors in all the kingdom *beasts*, Lady Drisella? Surely even you would not be that brash."

Drisella stuttered, "I-I did not mean..."

Kelera left her to fumble for her words. She took her seat beside Cierine, who nudged her with approval. After that, the two of them lost themselves in the events of the day, betting on who they thought would prevail in each challenge. They cheered wildly for Kelera's father and his men each time they went round with knights from noble households. They were doing splendidly, and Kelera was feeling a great sense of pride.

The air was sweltering by the time the morning events came to a close. King Tristan and the other courtiers retired for lunch until the afternoon challenges began. Kelera, needing a moment of reprieve, parted ways with Cierine.

She decided to go eat lunch with her father in the tents. It was a tradition of theirs at the Tournaments. She slipped through the crowd, doing her best not to draw too much attention to herself. Her best course of action was to avoid eye contact with the people visiting from the villages or other courts. Walking through the knights' quarters was like walking through a sea of fabric. Tents were huddled close together, and it was difficult for her to navigate her way to her father's quarters.

She caught a glimpse of the king's banner, adorned with a stag beneath a great bow, and hurried around the corner in its direction. She was passing a purple and yellow striped tent when she heard Alexander. Her heart skipped a beat, and she looked around, hoping to see him. She had been disappointed when he had not shown up to the grandstands. Each moment they spent together was another opportunity for her to learn more about him.

His voice grew louder as she neared the tent, but something in his tone gave her pause. The gentle nature in his voice was gone, replaced with something bitter. "It *is* our concern. Anything that happens here at the heart of the country directly affects our estate and the land we are charged with."

Another man interjected. He spoke dismissively, as if Alexander were behaving like a child. "We have bigger things to worry about. Since *you* lost us that deal with Amaran, the coffers are dwindling. You will stay out of the mess King Tristan faces here. That is an order."

Kelera crept closer, looking around to be sure that no one was watching her as she pressed her ear to the fabric of the tent. She knew she shouldn't be listening in on Alexander's private conversation, but curiosity was getting the better of her.

Alexander scoffed, "I do not take orders from you anymore, Father. I am not a child. I will make my own decisions."

"You have made that perfectly clear."

Alexander's tone shifted. There was a hint of warning in his voice as he said, "This isn't about her."

"How is it not? You have hitched yourself to a wagon with a loose wheel. The girl is a liability."

"She comes from a good family of high social standing." Alexander's voice rumbled with frustration, as if this were not the first time they had gone round with this topic. The topic of her. Her cheeks burned with embarrassment.

His father let out a huff before he spoke again. "She is a fine young lady, but you cannot ignore what she is. And now with the kidnappings, all eyes will be on her... And in turn, on *you*."

"I can handle it."

"But can you handle her? As a child, she was always wreaking havoc around the palace grounds. She may not appear to have magic abilities, but the power of Elfhame is still in her veins and it calls to the monstrosities who share it."

"I can and I will." Alexander's words were final.

The men went quiet and Kelera heard footsteps headed toward the flap in the tent. She felt ill and wished she was anywhere but here. The canvas rustled, and she took a few steps back, pretending she had just now happened upon them. Alexander stepped from the tent and halted in his tracks at the sight of her.

She pushed a stray strand of hair from her face and smiled brightly at him, ignoring the empty pit in her stomach. His father did not approve of the match. That much was clear. She supposed she shouldn't be entirely surprised by the revelation. All it meant was that she would need to work that much harder to prove herself to him.

She curtseyed to Alexander and feigned surprise. "Lord Alexander, what a pleasure running into you."

He was once again the gallant gentleman as he took her hand in his and kissed the back of it softly. "You are looking as lovely as ever."

"Thank you, though I do not feel it. The heat is almost unbearable today. Now that I am away from the shade of the stands, I am finding myself succumbing to the elements."

"Well, rest assured, no one would tell it by looking at you." He looked around nervously, as if expecting his father to appear at any moment. "Are you on your way to see your father?"

"I am. It is a little tradition of ours to have lunch together during the tourney."

"That sounds like a charming tradition. I hope it will not offend you if I do not offer to escort you. I still have to pay my respects to King Tristan..."

"No, no. I wouldn't dream of holding you up."

"I will be watching from the grandstands for the rest of the day. I do hope to see you there."

"You will. I will return as soon as lunch is over."

He smiled, and Kelera noted the way his eyes crinkled at the corners. The sight made all the ugliness of his father's words melt away. Alexander had defended his decision to wed her. True, it was an uncomfortable situation, but with time, she hoped they could bring his father around.

They bid one another farewell, and Kelera found her way to her father's tent. Before she could enter, she heard something crash to the ground. Pushing aside the flap, she stepped inside and was confused when she saw no one in there. The tent was cool, giving her a reprieve from the bright sunshine. She walked over to a silver plate that was lying upside down in the dirt and picked it up.

Well, that's odd, she thought to herself as she placed it back on the small table. She had no idea where her father could be and wondered if perhaps she had taken too long to get there. *Maybe he assumed I was not coming...*

She noticed that the coat hanging on the chair was turned inside out and the change of shoes her father kept was set upon the pillows on the small bed in the corner. She looked around at the disorder. A chair laid on its side where the trunk usually was, and the trunk was set in the middle of the room like a centerpiece. Her father always camped in his tent throughout the three-day event and liked to keep it tidy. It was odd that his room would be rearranged in such a haphazard way.

Something was off. Kelera focused on the small area. No human would have gone through the trouble to play a trick like this. But a wee one, on the other hand... She stayed still, waiting for any hint of the strange Fae magic to present itself. Finally, like a chill in the air, she felt it. The magic was a faint pulse all around her, but there was no mistaking it for what it was. She said gently, "The game is up. I know you're here. You may as well show yourself."

Something rattled under the bed, and she kneeled to peer at an unsettling, hairy creature. He looked back at her with large round eyes and a nose that was too long for its small face. He crawled out from under the bed to stand in front of her.

The brownie was smaller than a mortal child, but Kelera knew better than to underestimate it. She had heard of the mischief they could cause. They were not to be trifled with, no matter how harmless they looked. He stuck his long nose in the air and huffed at her. "Spoilsport."

"I suppose my father has you to thank for the redecorating?"

His voice was hoarse as he spoke. "I was just havin' a little fun."

"You must be mad to risk your life here in broad daylight for a bit of fun." Kelera crossed her arms over her chest.

"No one would've caught me."

"I caught you."

The brownie thought for a moment. "Oh."

"You cannot be here. Especially not right now where you can be easily seen."

The brownie kicked at the dirt. "I know. But it looked like so much fun with all the colors. And I do so miss having fun."

"You can't have fun at home where you belong?"

The brownie looked at her with frightened eyes. "Oh no, milady. Tis not safe there right now. I thought it best to wait here until it all blows over."

Confused, Kelera asked, "Until what blows over?"

The brownie hesitated before answering, "Tis a nasty business, all of it. Trouble's a brewin' in the winter and I don' plan on bein' there whilst it's sorted."

"Winter? But it's summer..."

The brownie wheezed as it laughed. "You are fun. Would you like to help me rearrange the pretty blue tent next?"

Kelera inched closer to him and spoke as if she were talking to a child. "No, I would not. And you will be causing no more trouble here. If they find you, they will kill you."

He looked hurt. "Oh... that doesn't sound like fun at all."

"No, it doesn't. The lunch hour will be ending soon. You need to get out of here before then. Do you understand?"

The brownie nodded in understanding. He dashed to the other side of the tent. Kelera watched him to make sure he would do as she bid. He moved to lift the bottom of the tent so he could slip under it, but paused and flicked a cup off of the bedside table. It clattered to the ground, and she put a palm to her face in exasperation. The brownie snickered as he ducked under the tent and out of sight.

Kelera wasn't sure whether she should laugh or be horrified by the little beast. As she set her father's things back the way they were supposed to be, she pondered the unusual things the brownie had said. What was going on in Elfhame that would have him frightened enough to risk the mortal world? And what was all that nonsense about winter?

As she began her walk back to the grandstands, she couldn't make sense of any of it. It was going to be a struggle the rest of the day to be present in conversations with the other courtiers. She tried to convince herself that she had imagined the whole encounter. She spotted her father across the field tending to a wounded squire. *Ah, so that's where you were. Lucky for that silly little beast in your tent*, she thought with a laugh.

As she rounded the arena, she bumped into Cierine, who was talking with the tall knight from her household. Cierine beamed with excitement. "Kelera! Perfect timing. I would like to introduce you to Sir Jacome."

Kelera bowed her head to him in greeting. "It is a pleasure to meet you. Cierine has told me all about your accomplishments. It is very impressive."

Sir Jacome smiled and opened his mouth to say something, but stopped short. He shook his head as the smile faded. Then he took a step toward Kelera. He towered over her with his slender frame and looked down on her in disgust.

His horse snorted beside him and pawed at the ground. Sir Jacome sneered as he said, "Wait, I know who you are. Our society has no place for you, *halfling*." Sir Jacome spat the word at her as if he intended for it to sting.

Kelera's blood boiled, but she contained herself. Cierine raised her voice, "Sir Jacome, what in the world has gotten into you? You are completely out of line!"

He ignored Cierine and stared Kelera down with an intimidating glare. The prickling sensation of magic threaten to rise to the surface of her body. She needed to remove herself from the situation before it got out of hand. She stepped aside to walk around him, but he stepped in her path. Glaring up at him, she asked, "Was there anything else?"

Sir Jacome's armor creaked as he inched closer to her. "You're the girl who bested Lord Viktor in the training fields." His eyes roved over her in an attempt to size her up.

She balled her hands into fists at her sides. Who did this pompous ass think he was? She took a step back, putting space between them. "*He* challenged me."

"You had no right being on that field in the first place. These people here in the south may tolerate your presence, but make no mistake... you do not belong here." As offensive and unwarranted as this man's words were, it was nothing she hadn't heard before.

Kelera caught Cierine's eye. Her friend's face was bright red. Cierine was shaking as she said, "You, Sir Jacome, will be reprimanded for such horrid behavior." She grabbed hold of Kelera's arm, ready to pull her away.

Kelera was too busy focusing on suppressing the strange feeling of magic that was rising in her by the second, that she didn't notice the fury on Sir Jacome's face. She and Cierine turned on their heels, ready to escape this horrible man's presence, but he grabbed Kelera's arm and held tight. She felt something tingle along her arms in response to his rough touch. Heat rose to her face, and she warned him. "Unhand me."

His grip on her tightened as he leaned in to whisper, "I don't know how you did it, but you cheated in that match against Lord Viktor."

Her fury grew at the implication. "I did not."

Cierine tugged on her arm. "Ignore him, Kelera. My husband will deal with him later."

Sir Jacome still did not relent. "You Fae are all the same. You cheat and manipulate to get what you want..."

Kelera's rage was getting hard to contain as she imagined how satisfying it would be if his horse knocked him on his ass. As if summoned by her thoughts, a vision of ice and shadows flashed before her eyes. The voice from the training field echoed in her mind, *Stay your hand.* Kelera willed it to go away, but it continued. *Do not let them get to you.*

Her heart was pounding in her ears. "I'm not!"

As she shouted, the visions melted away. Sir Jacome opened his mouth to say something, but before the words could escape his mouth, his horse reared up. He dropped the horse's reins and leapt out of the way just as the horse's hoof came down into the dirt where he had stood.

Kelera felt a hint of joy at the shocked look on Sir Jacome's delicate face. His eyes were wide with panic as the horse reared once more. The prickling feeling of magic on Kelera's arms and hands drew her attention away from the scene. She had lived with magic lying dormant just under the surface for years. But she had not accessed that power since the night at the blackthorn trees when she was a young girl. Why was she having trouble keeping it locked away now?

Her breath hitched in her throat when she returned her attention back to the horse. It was still going wild, trying to strike anyone who came within its reach. Dark blue velvet robes caught her eye. King Tristan was attempting to help calm the out-of-control beast. But the horse was inconsolable. It rose on its hind legs and snorted.

One blow, and the King would be fatally injured. Kelera whistled loudly between her fingers. The horse's gaze went straight to her, and they locked eyes. For a moment, she could sense what the horse was feeling. He was angry. Just as angry as she had been when Sir Jacome was insulting her.

She put herself between the horse and King Tristan. The beast took a step back as it lowered itself to the ground. She inched closer. "Easy." Magic flowed from her like a whisper in the wind. The horse bowed its head slightly to her, and she caressed his large silken snout. She spoke softly, "It's okay, you're okay."

King Tristan's voice boomed over the noise of the crowd, "Lady Kelera has saved the day!"

The crowd was quiet for a moment, still stunned by how close their king had come to injury. Only after the king began to clap did they erupt into applause. Kelera wanted nothing more than to go back to her room and hide. She was still trying to process what had just happened, but it was difficult to do so with the entire kingdom watching her.

King Tristan's guard swarmed them, pulling their king away and back to the safety of the grandstands. Sir Jacome gave Kelera one more look of loathing before leading his horse away from her. She glanced around self-consciously, but by now the crowd had moved on, ready to return to the excitement of the tournament.

Cierine clung to Kelera's arm as they walked to the grandstand on unsteady feet. *What is happening to me?* She had used her magic without meaning to. That terrified her more than anything in this world. She knew the implications of being caught using magic would mean the end of her life at court—would mean exile for her and her father. And more than that, Kelera couldn't shake the impression that the mysterious voice was trying to help her. But why? Who would be trying to reach out to her and why now?

She no longer felt the buzz of magic on her skin, but she feared its return. As much as she tried to blend in with the mortals, to create a normal life for herself and ignore the Fae blood running in her veins, something deep inside her told her she could not wish it away. It was beginning to feel like everything was about to change. And not for the better.

Chapter Six

When Kelera returned to the palace, she could instantly tell something was wrong. The guards were bustling around in a frenzy while servants stood silently in the corners. They should have been preparing for dinner, but instead, they were all standing clustered in small groups. As she passed by a few of the footmen, she overheard them talking. "Did you hear?"

One of them scoffed, "Goes to show nothing good ever comes from the Fae." They quieted when they saw Kelera. Pretending she hadn't overheard, she quickened her pace. She was eager to leave them and their whispers behind.

Near the staircase, a few women were dabbing at their eyes with soft handkerchiefs while the men held their wives and daughters close. Kelera walked over to the kitchen maids with whom she often spent her mornings talking with. One of them, a woman she had known her entire life, shied away from her. Kelera stopped in her tracks, confused by the fear in the woman's eyes when she looked at her. Kelera asked, "What's wrong? What happened?"

The woman continued to stare at her as she leaned into her friends. She stuttered as she spoke, "E-Emma w-was t-taken." She let out a loud sob and took hold of her friends' hands as she hurried them away from Kelera.

Taken? Emma was one of the Queen's ladies' maids. She worked and lived here in the palace and rarely ventured outside of the palace grounds. The kitchen maids were clearly frightened. They had run away like skittish kittens. Kelera felt a pang in her heart. They were afraid of *her*. Did they think she had something to do with the kidnappings? All because of what she was.

Kelera bit the inside of her cheek. She needed to figure out what had happened. If the shadow-man had returned, and he was getting bold enough to come onto the palace grounds, then no one was safe. She thought of his promise, *another time then.* He had meant it. Every single book she had read about the Fae stated they couldn't lie. Did that mean he would return for her? The hairs on her arms stood on end at the thought.

She should talk to her father. Tell him everything about the shadow's encounter. Maybe he could help. She turned to the door, but one of the guards approached her with authority. "Lady Kelera, I need you to come with me."

Shocked murmurs filled the room. "Where are you taking me?"

The guard stepped to her side with his hand on his sword. "To the King."

She fell into step with the guard as he led her to the king's council chambers. He nodded to the door, signaling her to knock. She rapped her hand on the door three times before anyone answered. Viscount Landry, a plump and incredibly unpleasant man, opened it with a disdainful look. He looked offended that she had the nerve to show her face there. She didn't have the energy to deal with him and his prejudices, so she slipped past him and into the room.

Before she spoke, she curtseyed deeply to King Tristan. "Your Majesty, I was told you requested my presence."

King Tristan's angular face was bright red with anger as he paced around the room. He waved a hand toward a settee, and she sat. He continued to pace, and she moved her feet so she wouldn't trip him as he passed by her. He didn't bother explaining why she had been brought to the council meeting. Instead, his voice thundered in the chamber, "One of our own. Taken in plain sight. How did this happen?" One man stepped out of his path in the nick of time, bumping into one of the chairs. King Tristan shot him an annoyed look then continued, "Make sure the search party leaves no stone unturned. I want the intruder found."

The room was buzzing with nervous energy. They were all shaken by the revelation that the Fae were now bold enough to come into the heart of the palace.

Viscount Landry interrupted, "Why is *she* here?" He pointed his stubby finger in Kelera's face.

King Tristan took a deep breath and glared at him in annoyance. "Because, Viscount, she was a witness to the previous kidnapping. We must cover every detail—every base—if we are to stop this madness from continuing."

An argument broke out at the side of the room as men shouted that the only thing to be done was to retaliate. From the smell of them, she guessed they had been drinking heavily at the tournament. She scanned the room and spotted Alexander leaning against a wall near them. He gave her a small, reassuring smile. She returned it, then turned her attention back to the king.

He had called her there for a reason, yet it seemed he had no intention of giving her a chance to speak.

King Tristan raised his voice above the noise. "The men I tasked with investigating the incidents along the border claim that the kidnappings here over the last week have been conducted in a similar fashion." He ran his hand through his hair, leaving it in a ruffled heap. "I've kept the people in the dark for as long as possible... At least until we knew more."

Kelera folded her hands neatly in her lap, but her mind was racing. He had known all along. She didn't agree with his decision to keep things from his subjects, but she respected it. She couldn't imagine the weight that was resting on his shoulders as he made decisions for the good of his people.

Viscount Landry pounded his fist on one of the desks. "We need more iron. Put it over all of the doors... in every room. Have every single noble wear it on their person."

His council members began arguing loudly amongst each other once again. Kelera furrowed her brow as they listed off the many ways believed to ward off the Fae. What they were suggesting was nothing more than folklore passed down through generations. Iron had never hindered her before. It could be her mortal blood that protected her, but she doubted it. She had felt the shadow's magic firsthand. His power was immense. Iron would surely not do the trick on him, either.

Kelera tried to cut in, "If I may..." They either did not hear her or did not care about what she had to say as they continued to bark at one another like a pack of wolves. She gritted her teeth. She didn't belong here with these frightened, small-minded men. They had no desire to listen to what she—a female and a Fae—had to say.

Alexander caught her eye from across the room and she gave him an exasperated smile. He stepped forward, his voice rising above the noise. "Your Majesty. Lady Kelera would like to address the room."

The men were stunned into silence as Alexander gave them all a pointed stare.

King Tristan looked at her with his mouth gaping open, as if he had forgotten she had been there at all. She stood and curtseyed to him, speaking with as much confidence as she could muster, "Apologies for the interruption, King Tristan. It's just... You requested my presence because I was a witness to the aftermath of the attack at the reception. Wouldn't you like to hear my account?"

Viscount Landry sputtered at her, "The audacity. Young lady, do you have no etiquette what-so-ever?"

She ignored him and waited for the king to give her permission to speak. King Tristan's face softened into a charming smile. "Yes, Lady Kelera. We seem to have lost our manners." He raised a hand in warning to the other men in the room to stay silent so that she could speak.

"As I explained to the guards... Once Alexander... er... *Lord* Alexander," she corrected herself. It wasn't proper for her to address him so informally yet. Even if they did have a moment in the clearing together when he had kissed her hands. She thought of the way his eyes had darkened as he'd looked at her. No one had ever looked at her that way. The memory made her blush. She cleared her throat and continued, "Once he left to follow the screams, I was approached in the clearing."

Viscount Landry interrupted her, "By the bogies." He referred to the goblin-like creatures, whom they believed would lure children away from their parents.

Kelera clenched her jaw at the interruption, but continued to speak in a pleasant tone. "With due respect, Viscount Landry, it was not a bogie. It was something else. Something I have never seen."

The plump man scoffed at her. "We all know that it is the bogies who are responsible for the recent attacks." He puffed out his chest in confidence.

Kelera stood straight-backed in the presence of these men who had no real intention of listening to what she had to say. Their minds were already made up. She felt something spark within her as her frustration rose. She crossed her arms over her chest, trying to ignore the hint of warmth coursing through her veins. "I know what I saw. There was nothing goblin-like about this creature. He was... I mean, the *shadow* was... Something much more powerful." A few of the men mumbled something under their breath. Perhaps she had made a mistake in admitting that she could feel its power. But there was too much at stake to keep anything to herself right now. She continued, "I do not think iron horseshoes hanging on the walls will be enough to keep this thing at bay."

Alexander came to her defense, speaking with authority, "If she says it was something else... something more powerful, then I believe her. You would all be wise to do the same."

The men mumbled to one another and Kelera noticed a few nodding their heads in agreement with Alexander. She gave him a small, appreciative smile. She had not expected him to step in on her behalf, and it was nice to have someone on her side for a change. He patted her lightly on the arm and returned to his post against the wall.

King Tristan spoke now, "Then what will be enough? The attacks have been coming in more frequently. This kidnapping makes eight. Eight girls taken in the dark of night, right under our noses."

Viscount Landry stuck his button nose in the air. "Eight *commoners*."

King Tristan shot him a look of warning. "Eight of our people," he corrected him. "Innocent girls who are now being subjected to God knows what. Today it was my wife's maid. Tomorrow, it could be one of your own daughters." The Viscount's gaze dropped to the ground, and he didn't say another word.

They all knew it was true. Whoever was crossing over the blackthorn veil into Nevene had been bold enough to come into the palace. Unafraid of the guards that were around every corner. This shadow was a threat to servants and nobles alike. It was unlikely that it or any other creatures of Elfhame would care if it was noble or commoner blood running in your veins. Everyone was fair game.

King Tristan ordered his footmen to bring in every book on the Fae that they had in the library. Viscount Landry and his friends gathered in the corner and eyed Kelera with suspicion. Viscount Landry's eyes narrowed as he watched her. Drawing attention to herself was the last thing she wanted, especially at a time like this. She didn't want to be associated with the chaos that the shadow was causing, but she was afraid. With all the uncertainty and pressure, she would not be able to rest—not until she knew what was happening.

She stood in the middle of the room, unsure of whether or not she was allowed to leave. King Tristan called out to her and invited her to sit with him at the small tea table. He poured her a cup and handed it to her. Everyone in the room seemed to be holding their breath as they watched the scene unfolding before them. Surely, they were eager to have something to gossip about. Kelera tried to ignore them and focused on King Tristan instead.

He spoke gently, as if he was trying not to spook her. "I appreciate your help, Lady Kelera. The... shadow, as you call it, is a danger to us all. I fear that the maid..." He caught himself and corrected, "Emma. I'm afraid that Emma will not be the last. We have sent a search party out to look for her and I have commanded every guard to be on watch here in the palace. I do not intend to allow that monster on these grounds again." He took a small plate and topped it with a piece of strawberry cake. He handed it to her as he said, "I am going to do everything within my power to keep us all safe. You have my word."

His word. It did not comfort her as he had surely intended. What good was his word when he could not seem to get a grip on the situation? It had gotten so out of hand that the shadow had come into the heart of their country. It had come into their *home* and taken yet another girl. If it could slip past the guards, then no one was safe. Not even the king himself. But still, Kelera nodded graciously and gave him a small, encouraging smile. He patted her on the hand and stood. "If we need anything more from you, I will send for you." She rose as well, and he held a dismissive hand out toward the door. That was her cue to take her leave.

Before she made it to the door, King Tristan called to her, "By the way... You very well may have saved my life today at the tournament, Lady Kelera. I will not forget that."

Kelera furrowed her brow. It wasn't as if she expected a thank you, but even so, his expression of gratitude did not sound entirely sincere. He sounded almost cautious. As if she had an ulterior motive for stepping in to help. As she curtseyed to the king, she made note of the men in the room looking at her with suspicion. She didn't want to let them get to her, but the shame at being associated with the shadow was creeping in. Trying to shake it off, she turned and walked into the hall. The door slammed hard behind her, and she could hear a few of the men inside of the room snickering at her.

Perhaps they thought she was being hysterical. But it was easy for them to be blasé about the kidnappings when it was servant women being taken. They felt that their wives and daughters were safe. That *they* were safe.

And more than that, they were not the ones with Fae blood running through their veins. They would not face the brunt of the court's frustration and fear when they had no one else around to make pay for the crimes against their people.

Lost in thought, Kelera rounded the corner to her room and nearly collided with Drisella and her friends. The girls gasped dramatically when they realized it was Kelera. Drisella, however, didn't balk. She stuck her thin nose in the air and sneered at her as she spoke. "Lady Kelera. We did not think you would show your face after what happened this evening."

Kelera took a deep breath, trying to ignore the anger rising within her at the slight. "Surely, I do not know what you mean, Lady Drisella. I have been at the tournament, just as you have all day."

Drisella continued as if she hadn't heard Kelera, "Oh, poor Alexander. He must be beside himself."

Kelera knew she shouldn't take the bait, but she couldn't help herself. "Why is that?"

Drisella put a hand to her heart and feigned innocence. "Being trapped in an engagement to a Fae girl during such a terrible time such as this. I myself would just die."

One could only wish, Kelera thought bitterly as she imagined pulling Drisella's hair from her perfect updo. She imagined how satisfying it would be to place a toad in her bed or to turn her into a slug. Kelera shook the unwelcome thoughts from her head. Instead, she said politely, "He doesn't seem to mind. Now, if you will excuse me." Kelera veered around the group and continued down the hall, trying to ignore the whispers behind her as she left.

Kelera shut herself away in her room, trying to shake the voice inside her head that was telling her to make Drisella and her miserable friends pay for their cruelty. It was a constant battle Kelera had with herself. She often wondered if it was the Fae in her that made this darkness wash over her. She knew she could never act on the mischievousness that often called to her, but sometimes the urges were difficult to fight.

As she leaned against the door, trying to forget about Drisella and her minions, she felt a wave of magic wash over her. It was cold and hard. Like steel. Her heart dropped when the magic brushed against her. The same as it had been the night of Cierine's wedding reception; like a beating drum. She felt it along her arms and legs. If the shadow was there, then that meant she was in danger. She turned toward the door, but before she could take hold of the handle, something ran its fingers under her hair and along her neck.

The familiar smooth voice whispered in her ear, "Alone at last."

Kelera stilled and counted her breathing: *one, two, three, one, two, three.* Her thudding heart slowed, and she feigned confidence as she turned to face the intruder. "What are you doing here?"

The shadow wavered and for a moment she could see a handsome man's face beneath the dark shroud. He spoke softly, "I came to see you. I told you I would. And you know, we always keep our word."

"By we, you mean the Fae."

"Yes, the Fae, the darklings, the unholy... Call us what you will, but never call us liars." His hands had moved away from her, but he was still standing uncomfortably close.

"Do you mean to take me like the others?" Kelera wouldn't go down without a fight.

He thought for a moment before answering. "I considered it. But then I saw you in the hall with those half-witted women. They don't like you very much." The observation made Kelera want to strike him. She wondered if she could do harm to the shadow-man. He had touched her... Could she do the same to him? She dug her nails into her palms as she pondered the thought.

Realizing he was waiting for her response, she acknowledged him, "They are spoiled ladies of the court. It has occurred to me on occasion that they might not truly like anyone but themselves."

"An admirable observation. But you and I both know that's not it. It's because of what you are." His movement was too quick to stop as he flipped her long hair away from her ears. Kelera took a big step back and found herself pressed against the wall. The shadow followed, positioning himself dangerously close to her.

She could feel his breath on her lips as he leaned in and spoke, "The fun you and I could have, halfling." The promise in his words sent a shiver up her spine. Even if she put up a fight, she feared it wouldn't be enough to stop him from taking her if he chose to. Was this a game to him?

Her mind was racing as she tried to decide what to do. There was nowhere for her to go. She could scream for help, but she didn't know how the shadow would react. He could kill her before help arrived. Or would his magic be strong enough to kill the innocent guards who would rush to her aid? It wasn't worth risking, so instead she bared her teeth at him. "I have dealt with enough bullies in my life, and I do not intend to be insulted by the likes of you." She pushed back at him now, forcing him to take a small step back.

"You think I want to insult you? You are more naïve than I thought." He took a few steps back now, giving her the space she had been craving. Her magic began to bloom again. It was shocking to feel the heat of it after being so close to the cold shadows that were shrouding him.

"I am not naïve." She couldn't understand why she was arguing with him. He was a kidnapper. A criminal who preyed on young, vulnerable mortal girls. Every nerve in her body told her to run, but her mind wouldn't cooperate. He was toying with her, and it was causing her anger to cloud her judgment.

"Oh, no? I have seen the way you blush at your suitor. Perhaps you would like it if *I* made you blush." She could not see his eyes, but she could feel his gaze roving along her body like she was nothing more than a course he intended to devour. "I would very much like to hear you scream."

Kelera's skin crawled at his words. She couldn't understand what his fascination was with her or why he hadn't just taken her, if that was his intention. Before she could find out, there was a knock at the door. Kelera turned toward it, startled by the sudden noise. When she turned back to the shadow, he was gone. There was no sign that he had ever been there and not a hint of magic lingered in his wake.

Kelera opened the door with a shaking hand and let out a sigh of relief when she saw Cierine standing there. Kelera looked around the room again before inviting Cierine in. Even once her friend was inside, Kelera continued to search the dark corners of the room. She flitted about, lighting every candle she had, while Cierine took a seat on the bed.

Cierine bounced a few times before speaking. "I'm guessing you heard about what happened."

"Uh-huh." Kelera dropped to the floor to check under the bed. Surely the shadow had not given up so easily.

"Has anyone approached you on the matter?" Cierine sounded worried.

"Everyone is regarding me as if I were a leper. And I'm afraid I may have made a fool of myself when I was called to the King's quarters. I don't know what's gotten into me lately..." Kelera sat up on her knees and looked around in confusion. Would it be foolish for her to think the shadow had really left?

"I'm sure it's not as bad as all that." Cierine paused, then asked, "What are you doing?" She was watching Kelera with a raised eyebrow.

Realizing she must look like she had gone mad, Kelera stood quickly. "Nothing."

"It doesn't look like 'nothing.'" Cierine's eyes clouded with worry. "You know you can tell me anything."

"I just..." Kelera sighed. "Have you seen anything strange around here?"

"Other than my uncle's newly imported rugs... Not a thing." She laughed, but stopped abruptly when she noticed Kelera wasn't laughing with her. "Seriously, what is going on with you? Are you still shaken up from the incident with the horse? Surely you know that it was a freak accident. You should be filled with happiness right now. After saving my uncle, you will be a hero here at court."

Kelera groaned and flopped onto the bed. Suddenly, her dress felt like it was suffocating her. A vision of the way the horse looked at her flashed in her mind, and something told her that her problems would melt away if she tore the dress off and danced under the moonlight. She rubbed her temples. Visions like these had crept into her mind often when she was stressed. It would be so easy to throw off the mask she wore for the mortals at court and embrace the wild instincts that resided deep in her soul.

Cierine sat by silently, allowing Kelera to work things out in her head. Finally, Kelera spoke, "I think I spoke with the kidnapper."

"The shadow? You already told me about that."

"No. I mean just now. He was here. In this room... I think your knock might have just saved my life."

Cierine shot to her feet. "It was *here*? Why didn't you call for the guard?"

Kelera buried her face in her hands. Her voice was muffled as she spoke. "I don't know. I was so afraid. It's like my mind and body couldn't agree on how to react."

Cierine grabbed Kelera's hands and dragged them away from her face. "Did it hurt you?"

Kelera sat up. "No. It was just the things he was saying. I think he might try to come back." She bit her lip. "What if people think I had something to do with all of this?"

"I won't let that happen. We need to stay together. There is safety in numbers. And I'll have my uncle assign a personal guard to you." Cierine's voice was firm and Kelera knew there was no arguing with her.

That night Cierine stayed over, insisting that her husband wouldn't mind. He would be with King Tristan and the other members of the King's Council through the night. Cierine assured Kelera that the men would come up with a plan to stop the madness that was happening around them.

Even with Cierine's reassurances, Kelera couldn't shake the feeling that there was something unfinished between her and the shadow. As she laid awake in her bed, staring out at the full moon, she knew deep in her heart that this was only the beginning of things. And there was no doubt in her mind that she was not going to like what came next.

Chapter Seven

That night, the visions returned. In her dreams she found herself surrounded by a frost covered forest. The treetops were heavy with new-fallen snow and magic shimmered all around her. The very ground on which she stood was vibrating with it. The power she was feeling didn't strike fear in her heart like the shadow's had. It was more welcoming somehow.

She called out, "Is anyone there? I know you helped me at the tournament. Why? What do you want from me?" Whoever was responsible for the visions didn't feel like an enemy. The visions had seemed more like a warning than a threat.

No one answered. She turned, trying to figure out where she was. Snow glistened under the sunlight and long icicles chimed in the trees. The dream seemed all too real as the cold seeped through her nightgown and she shivered. Movement caught her eye behind the tree.

She wandered a little further into the forest, trying to get a better look. But as she came around a large hollowed out tree, something screeched and knocked her back. The creature was cloaked in shadows as it hissed, "Beware the veil."

Stunned by the attack, she awoke to sunlight peeking through her window. She was safe in her bed, but she could still feel the chill in her bones. She pulled the covers around her, then stretched out her stiff limbs and rubbed at her eyes.

A dream. That's all it was. If someone was trying to warn her to stay away from the blackthorn veil, then they were wasting their time. She knew better than to go near it. Relieved to be in the safety of her own bed, she let out a loud yawn and rolled over to ask Cierine if she wanted to get some breakfast. But instead of her friend, she was met with a small pile of bluish-black berries laid out carefully on a large green leaf. Her stomach lurched as she realized it was fruit from a blackthorn tree.

She sat up, terrified, searching for Cierine, but there was no sign of her. In a panic, she shouted for the guards. Three armed men burst through the door with wide eyes. They looked around for the threat, and when they saw none, they frowned at Kelera.

Still in her nightgown, she wrapped the blankets from her bed around her tightly. Her voice quivered as she asked, "Did the princess already leave this morning?"

The guards looked dumbfounded. One of them said, "No, Lady Kelera. No one has left or entered this room since we arrived last night."

Her head was spinning. If she had put her best friend in danger, then she would never forgive herself. She took a long, deep breath, trying to steady herself. It would help no one to become hysterical. Willing herself to stay calm, she said, "You need to sound the alarm. Alert the king immediately... I believe the princess has been taken."

The men nearly stumbled over one another, trying to leave the room. They hurried away to do as she bid, and Kelera took the opportunity to get dressed. She threw on the first thing she could find. It was a simple gown, not befitting an audience with the king, but she didn't care. The berries on the bed might not have caught the guards' attention, but it had hers. It was a message. One meant especially for her.

She took one last look in the mirror, hurrying to braid her hair messily on the sides so that it covered the tips of her ears when she pulled it back. Not wanting to waste another second, she leapt from the room and ran down the hall. Servants and members of the court stepped quickly to the side so they would not collide with her as she passed them.

By the time she made it to the king's council chambers, she was incredibly out of breath. Huffing for air, she knocked on the door repeatedly. It swung open to reveal an overwhelming number of bewildered faces. King Tristan had called in every important male member of his court and all of their eyes were on her now.

She gave the king a quick curtsey before being ushered into the room. She stood before King Tristan and linked her hands together in front of her. She had been in such a hurry, she hadn't taken a moment to think of what she was going to say. Cierine had gone missing under her watch. This whole thing was her fault and the guilt of that was overwhelming.

She felt a lump forming in her throat and did her best to speak clearly and elegantly, "Your Majesty."

"We need every detail. No matter how small." There was a hardness to King Tristan's tone as he commanded her. No more was the man who had served her tea and cake the day before. She didn't blame him. She was just as upset with herself as he must have been.

Trying to keep her voice steady, she explained, "She was there when I went to sleep. But when I woke, there was no sign of her." Kelera fought back the tears that were welling in her eyes.

"You're telling us that you saw nothing... Heard nothing."

"Nothing but a leaf of blackthorn berries on the pillow where she had laid her head." Kelera could hear the whispers from the crowd. Words like "Fae blood" and "halfling" were being thrown around. She did her best to ignore them. "I believe it was a message from the shadow."

King Tristan grunted in agreement. "Why the berries, though? What sort of message is it trying to send?"

Viscount Landry piped in, "Perhaps it is a clue. Pointing directly at the accomplice." He gave Kelera a pointed look.

Accomplice? She would never in a million years betray the people of this court, let alone her best friend. The others mumbled in agreement. They were turning on her, just as the witch in the poppy fields had warned. She hadn't wanted to accept it. After everything she had done to become one of them, it still wasn't enough. They were willing to accuse her without a second thought.

The viscount continued to goad the crowd, "Surely it is not out of the realm of possibility that the halfling could have had a hand in the princess' kidnapping. She could have been behind all of it. Who is to say she isn't the one who helped the monster into the palace in the first place?"

Kelera's temper flared. "Now wait just a minute. I had nothing to do with any of this. I have never had dealings with the Fae. All of you should know this. You have watched me grow up here in the palace. You know my father. You know *me*."

Viscount Landry took a bold step in her direction. He practically spat at her as he talked, "We know only what you want us to know. I see you. We all see you. Walking around here like you belong."

Alexander jumped in with a ferocity Kelera had never seen from him. "Hold your tongue, sir. Lady Kelera has done nothing to warrant your suspicion. She saved King Tristan's life yesterday for star's sake!"

King Tristan raised an authoritative hand to silence the vicious viscount before he could retort. Kelera felt dizzy and bit her lip as she tried to keep her composure. She had tried so hard for so long to belong amongst these mortals. And still, they thought the worst of her the first chance they got. Nothing she ever did would be good enough for them. Nothing would make her one of them.

King Tristan spoke loud enough for the entire room to hear, "I do not believe Lady Kelera played any role in Princess Cierine's disappearance. They have been lifelong friends and I trust Cierine's judgment over all others." He paused before continuing, "With that said. There is only one way to retrieve the princess from her captors. We must send soldiers into Elfhame."

The room erupted in argument. A ringing in Kelera's ears drowned out their shouts. A mortal army had never ventured into Elfhame. The histories were clear on that matter. Over a century ago, a treaty had been drafted between one of King Tristan's ancestors and the royalty who presided over Elfhame. The treaty clearly stated that no mortal was ever to step foot on Fae territory. In an effort to enforce that agreement, the blackthorn trees had been planted. Acting as a wall between their realms.

Truthfully, it was intended to also keep creatures of Elfhame from wandering north into mortal territory, but the occasional beast still slipped through the veil. Up until now, it had always been for harmless fun. They would play tricks on unsuspecting travelers or steal invaluable goods from bakers and the like.

What the king was proposing now could mean war. Kelera knew her opinion would not be welcomed in this room, but she couldn't stay silent when her entire world was falling apart. "Your Majesty, surely there is another way. You could send an emissary on your behalf to speak with the King and Queen of Elfhame. Urge them to stop the kidnappings and to return Princess Cierine and the other women who have already been taken. I am sure they would want to avoid war after nearly a century of peace."

The king's advisor, Duke Cunningham, stepped in this time. He was a lanky man who had spent his years behind a desk instead of amongst the people. Kelera had heard whispers about him from the servants. He spent his nights gambling and owed debts to menacing men around the world. He also had friends who were just as dangerous.

He reminded her of a snake in the way his eyes shifted around the room. "The Queen of the Seelie Court and the King of the Unseelie Court have never been a friend to this crown. They have ignored the treaty time and again by allowing their subjects to step foot over our border." He looked King Tristan in the eyes, ignoring Kelera now. "I will gladly put together a rescue party if it pleases your Majesty. One that will cut down anyone who stands in the way of retrieving the princess."

Cut them down? Have these men lost their minds? Kelera couldn't believe what she was witnessing. It was as if these men had forgotten their history. Before the treaty, the Unseelie King had wreaked havoc in the human realm. There had been nothing to stop him from stealing babies away from their cribs in the night. Nothing to keep insatiable goblins from feeding on their livestock. Nevene had a strong army full of capable men, but Elfhame had magic and a lust for chaos.

She looked pleadingly at King Tristan, praying that he would make the right choice. He stared back at her and ran a hand along his stubbled face. After a few moments, he made his decision. "Duke Cunningham, you will amass your rescue party. The problem that stands is that our men are unable to cross the threshold between our world and theirs. We will need to track down a wee one to use in the crossing." The duke looked elated and Kelera had to clench her fists before she spoke out of turn at him. This scoundrel was the last person she would trust with bringing Cierine home safely.

Kelera couldn't concentrate through the panic she was feeling. Cierine could be caught in the middle of a bloodbath if these men challenged the royals of Elfhame. This was all her fault. If she hadn't allowed Cierine to stay the night with her, then she wouldn't have been caught up in the middle of whatever was going on between Kelera and the shadow. She needed to fix this. Before she had time to second guess herself, she said, "I will go." The men fell into stunned silence. Kelera raised her chin, determined not to show fear. "I will act as an emissary." The men in the room looked scandalized, with shock painted all over their faces. She continued, "You said it yourself—only Fae blood can open the veil. Use mine. And let me plead with the leaders of Elfhame on your behalf."

But before anyone could voice their opinion, King Tristan asked, "You would do that? Put yourself in the midst of danger?"

Kelera held firm. "I would do anything for my friend."

Duke Cunningham narrowed his eyes at her as he looked her up and down. "But Sire, surely she would hinder the mission. And if she *is* working with them..." He was speaking as if she wasn't standing right there. She took a deep breath, trying to move past the affront and focused on what mattered. Cierine's safety.

King Tristan finished before the duke could continue, "Enough. Kelera has a point. There is a good chance the Fae will be more receptive if someone who shares their... lineage, speaks on my behalf. Your men will keep her safe on the journey into the Unseelie Court and bring her and my niece back safely." He walked over to a map that was laid out on a large wooden desk. It showed the territories between Nevene and Elfhame. He pointed to the Unseelie Court's territory, which was closest to their border. "The Unseelie King's lands are the closest in proximity to where the kidnappings have been taking place. My advisors agree that it is likely where the women are being taken. The Unseelie Court is notorious for its malevolent ways, so proceed with every caution."

He turned to Kelera, who was beginning to tremble. Visions of snow and the screeching monster lurking in the trees flashed in her mind. The warning rang in her ears, *Beware the veil.* She shook her head. She had to do this. There was no other way.

King Tristan stressed his point again. This time, the sharpness in his tone gave her pause. "You want to prove your loyalty? Prove that you belong here with us? Now is your chance. You will accompany the rescue party into Elfhame, and you will speak on behalf of the crown." He signaled for his guards, who stepped forward to flank Kelera as if he was worried she might try to run. Then he continued, "I will give you a chance to speak to the Unseelie King and make your case. If he does not agree to stop the assaults on our people—if he does not return Princess Cierine..." He addressed Duke Cunningham as he finished, "Then your men have my permission to do what needs to be done. Burn their world to the ground, if that is what it takes to bring my beloved niece home."

It didn't go unnoticed by her that until now, King Tristan had done nothing more than try to prevent more kidnappings. Soldiers had not been sent to retrieve the other women who had been taken. Wasn't it his duty to protect *all* of his subjects? Part of her worried, even now, that Duke Cunningham and his men wouldn't hesitate to leave the other women behind if it came down to bringing them or Cierine back. Would she do the same? Was she any better than these men when it came down to it? She was already beginning to doubt herself. And that was something that could very well get her and the rest of them killed.

Once King Tristan dismissed them, Kelera found herself walking through the halls between the two guards he had assigned to her. He claimed it was merely an escort to keep her safe, but she knew better. They were her jailors. The King might have announced publicly that he didn't believe she had anything to do with Cierine's disappearance, but it didn't change the fact that she was the only one who could open the veil that would allow his men to pass through to Elfhame.

They rounded the corner that led to her room, and she was surprised to find Duke Francis waiting for her at the door. He looked distraught. His curly hair was sticking out in different directions and the whites of his eyes were red, as if he had been crying. Kelera didn't know the duke well, but the way Cierine had talked about him made her think that he cared for his new bride deeply.

Even in this state, he was very handsome. His rich, brown skin was unblemished, and his hands were well manicured, signs that he had lived a life of luxury in the court. He tried to smile at her, but failed, as he said, "Is she really gone? King Tristan would not allow me to attend the meeting. He suggested it would be best if I went back to our chambers in case she returned."

Kelera's heart broke for him. Cierine would not return. Not unless she was successful in leading Duke Cunningham's men into Elfhame. The pressure weighing on her was building by the minute, but she was careful not to show it as she smiled softly at him and said, "King Tristan is doing everything in his power to bring her home to you." She glanced behind her at the guards, who were still and unmoving. They eyed her warily. Turning her attention back to Duke Francis, she explained, "I am to accompany a group into Elfhame. You have to keep faith. We will bring her back."

Duke Francis looked her up and down with a scrutinizing gaze. "Why you? You are but a lady of the court."

"Because of my ability to cross through the blackthorns and... because of my heritage. King Tristan is giving me the chance to plead with the Unseelie King. If I can convince him to return Princess Cierine, then we can avoid a confrontation."

Duke Francis didn't look comforted by the thought. Kelera didn't blame him. She had never been to Elfhame. Not since she was a baby on her mother's breast. Whatever had been plaguing her with visions over the last couple of days was trying to warn her. But warn her of what, exactly? Saving the best friend she'd ever had was surely worth the risk.

It was true that she knew nothing of Elfhame, save for what the books in the library and gossip in the court told her. But warnings or not, there was no other option. Helping the men cross the veil would be their only chance at saving her friend. And Kelera was willing to take any risk for Cierine.

Alexander approached them, coming from the direction of the grand staircase. Kelera was embarrassed that he had yet again had to stand up to defend her. He put a hand on Duke Francis' shoulder. "We'll save her. I will join them and see to it myself."

Kelera felt a weight lift off her shoulders at the offer. She didn't know what sort of men Duke Cunningham was gathering for the mission, so the thought of having Alexander by her side made her feel more secure.

Duke Francis relaxed his shoulders slightly. "Thank you, my friend." He embraced Alexander in a hug and whispered something to him. Kelera couldn't make out the words, but Alexander nodded at him before bidding him farewell.

Once Duke Francis was gone, Kelera was left alone with Alexander and the guards. He glared at them, and they turned to give him and Kelera some semblance of privacy. He took hold of her hands and said, "You are firm in your decision? You don't have to do this... we can find another way."

She shook her head. "For as long as I can remember, Cierine has protected and stood by me. She has defended me against cruelty and befriended me when not many others would. Please, Alexander. Support my decision?"

His eyes were clouded with concern, but he agreed, "Very well, but I will go with you. I have known Duke Cunningham since I was a boy. He is cunning but capable and I do not believe he will object to me leading the group down there. I will keep you safe. I promise."

He pulled Kelera in for a hug and she rested her head on his chest. She felt warm and safe in his arms. All the emotions that she had been bottling up in front of the king and his men begged for release. Her voice was muffled as she spoke into him. "It's all my fault. I let her stay with me last night because I was frightened. I shouldn't have put her in harm's way." A sob escaped her as Alexander ran a hand through her thick, wavy hair.

He continued to hold her as he comforted her with his words. "You are not to blame. Believe me when I say we will get her back." He pulled away from her slightly, taking hold of her shoulders and rubbing them with his thumbs. "We will return here with the princess, and she will have a front-row seat to our wedding. Everything will work out exactly as it's been planned. I promise."

Kelera wiped away the tears that were threatening to fall down her face. "I want to believe you."

"I must take my leave so that I can speak with the duke. Go and pack, and I will meet you with the others." He took her hand and turned it over so he could kiss her palm. His brown eyes lit up as he gave her one last smile.

Kelera parted with him and went to her room to pack. She left the door open so that the guards could keep an eye on her. She took a small canvas bag and stuffed it with clothes that she typically wore when she visited her father in the training yards. Pants, light linen shirts, and a leather vest he had given her for her birthday last year.

Then she took a moment to go behind the dressing screen in the corner so she could change out of her dress. The guards were watching her like hawks. She gave them a pointed look. They reluctantly turned toward the hall. Irritated with the unwanted company, Kelera quickly pulled on a pair of breeches, a long-sleeved linen shirt, and a leather jerkin. It was embroidered with fine details that wove their way around her waist. Once she laced it together in the front, she slipped on her boots and pulled her hair back tight.

She paused when her fingers brushed against the tips of her ears, wondering if she should bother to hide them. She had been chosen for this task because she was part Fae. Would it help her or hinder her if she displayed that fact proudly while in Elfhame? Or would the Fae also look down on her for not truly being one of them? Unsure of what the answer was, she relented and tugged at the sides of her hair, drawing it down far enough so that it covered her ears.

Now that she was ready, she followed the guards obediently into the large foyer of the palace. It was a grand room, decorated with ornate statues and paintings that had been imported from the kingdoms in the north.

Alexander and her father were there to greet her. Her father's face was beet red as he took his place by her side. He spoke in a hushed tone so that only she could hear him. "This is madness. It is too dangerous for you to be venturing into the enemy's territory. I don't know what the king is thinking."

"Careful, Father. You don't know who might be listening."

"I don't give a rat's ass who hears me." His voice rose, drawing unwanted attention their way. "You have done everything right. You have taken to your role as a lady of the court, have found a match, and have gone above and beyond everything that has been asked of you. Yet they still hold your mother against you."

Kelera put a calming hand on his arm. "There is no other way. I am the only one who can help them enter Elfhame. I must get Cierine back. I could never forgive myself if I didn't do all that I could to help."

Her father let out a frustrated groan. He had to know that she was right. As hard as he had tried to help her live a normal life amongst these mortals, they would never truly see her as one of them. Maybe if she could do this for them—if she could get her friend back and prevent a war—then she would still have a chance at the life she longed for. One where they accepted her and appreciated her for all the effort she put into making herself the perfect lady of court and an equal match for Duke Alexander.

She needed her father to support her on this. She added, "I am sorry to disappoint you, but this is something I have to do. My mind is made up."

Her father scratched at his goatee and relented, "Then so is mine. I am coming with you." He walked to the bag he had already packed and picked up the familiar sword, bow, and quiver that was sitting next to it.

Weapons he'd forged for her on her eighteenth birthday. He handed them to her and said, "Just in case."

Kelera took them gratefully and a mixture of relief and fear washed over her. She didn't want her father risking his life with her, but she would feel more capable with both him and Alexander there by her side. She strapped the weapons to herself, savoring the weight of them on her back and on her hip. Her father led her out of the palace door and into the yard.

Gravel crunched beneath her feet as she adjusted the pack on her shoulder and watched the rescue party gather around. They were a rough looking group of men. Scarred, dirty faces stared at her in curiosity, and she looked down at the ground to avoid making eye contact. Trust did not come easily for her, but these men made her especially uneasy.

Duke Cunningham took center stage and proclaimed, "You are all here for one thing: to bring back Princess Cierine."

Kelera's brow furrowed. "And the other women who were taken."

Duke Cunningham ignored her and emphasized once more, "*To bring back the princess*. Lady Kelera here has one chance to convince the beast that the Unseelie refer to as their king to release Princess Cierine. If that does not work, then you know what your orders are." He gave the men a pointed look, and they grinned in response. The hair on Kelera's arms stood on end. They were itching for a fight. How was she going to make sure they stayed their hands long enough for her to try the peaceful approach?

Kelera studied Alexander's face. He was unmoving as he stood amongst the savage group that Duke Cunningham had put together. The men were clearly not soldiers in their mismatched attire. She wasn't sure what barrel Duke Cunningham had scooped them out of. The only thing that comforted her was that the duke seemed to have agreed to appoint Alexander as their leader.

He whistled, signaling that it was time to go. Kelera's father put an arm around her shoulder and gave her a reassuring smile. He wasn't fooling her, though. She recognized the worry behind his eyes. They fell into step beside Alexander and walked in quiet anticipation past the towering stone walls that surrounded the palace grounds. To her right, Kelera could see the path leading to Princess Cierine's childhood home and the vast poppy fields that stood in between. The sight gave her a small boost of courage, driving her toward the veil. She had to take the risk. Cierine would do the same for her.

It didn't take them long to reach the tall blackthorn brush, and Kelera wished desperately that it had taken them longer to travel. She wasn't mentally prepared for what they were about to do. She was coursing with adrenaline and having trouble collecting her thoughts. She tried to get a grasp on them, thinking of her music lessons, and how she would focus on her breathing in order to play a symphony without error. This was a lot like that. She needed to move past her nerves and focus on one thing, and one thing only.

Magic strummed in her veins the moment she saw the blackthorns. She tensed at the overwhelming sensation. It called to her, drawing her in and begging for her to come closer like a lighthouse beckoning a ship home. The tree line was an impenetrable hedge of dark bark twining together. The blue-black berries on the ends of the black twigs caught her eye and her nostrils flared in anger at the memory of waking to find them next to her.

She took a bold step forward, taking the lead in front of the men. Alexander grabbed her arm and gripped it tightly. She was startled by the firm touch and looked at him in confusion. He loosened his grip and said, "We need to pass through together."

"Right. No, I know that." Kelera waited as the men lined up on either side of her. Alexander stood on one side and her father on the other. They were shoulder to shoulder with her as she reached out a hand.

She thought back to when she was a small girl. Her father had been so angry and terrified at the thought of her pricking her finger on one of the sharp thorns, and from that point forward, Kelera had known that these trees were off limits to her. Her nerve wavered. She hesitated and glanced at her father.

He nodded to the thorns. "I am here with you, my girl—always."

Reassured, she extended her hand until her fingers were lingering over the point of the thorn. An icy cold washed over her and her vision began to darken at the edges—another warning vision was coming. It filled her with dread, and she began to second guess what she was doing. What if it didn't work? What if she did something wrong, hurting her father and Alexander in the process? Trying to shut out the overwhelming fear, she closed her eyes tight, grabbed hold of the branch, and squeezed. The thorns sliced into her fingers and her palm, and she felt the trickle of blood run down her hand and wrist. She hissed in pain and the magic pulled her in.

It was like being sucked underwater. Panic struck her like an arrow hitting its mark. She couldn't breathe and the sounds around her were muffled. When she opened her eyes, she could see nothing but darkness and she reached out to grab for her father and Alexander. Her hands were met with only cool air, but she could hear their distant voices calling for her. She shut her eyes again and tried to turn around to go back. Thinking she was headed in the right direction, she leapt forward and fell to the ground.

She gasped, trying to catch her breath. Everything ached and she could still feel the immense magic pulsing around her. It was more power than she had ever felt before and her head spun with the sudden impact of it. Her hand stung where the thorns had cut through her skin, and she cradled it to her chest.

Kelera sat up and looked frantically around for the men. Instead, she was met with a stranger. He was staring at her with his head tilted to the side. Small bones were hanging from the hat he wore, and they clattered together as he took a step toward her. His face was coated in white paint, and she was having trouble making out his features, save for the pitch-black eyes that were studying her with curiosity.

Kelera scrambled away from the man. He chuckled as he spoke. "Well, that was interesting."

He advanced on her with remarkable speed. She crawled back further, feeling the cold hard ground dig into her wounded hand. The man gave her a vicious smile, revealing teeth that had been shaved into points. Before Kelera could scream for help, the man snapped his fingers, and her world went black.

Chapter Eight

K elera's ears were ringing when she regained consciousness. She rolled over on the wooden table she had been laid on. She needed to assess the situation. It hadn't even been a whole two minutes in Elfhame, and she had already been foolish enough to let her guard down. She wasn't sure if she was more frustrated with herself or the stranger who had knocked her out.

Her heart skipped a beat as she regained her bearings. Where had her assaulter gone? And where were Alexander and the other men? *Oh stars,* she thought to herself, *did I do it wrong? Did I leave them behind?*

She sat up slowly, careful not to make any sound as she moved. Out of instinct, she reached for her weapons and was relieved to find that she still had them. She climbed from the table and tiptoed toward the door. The room was small, with walls made of lumber. It smelled damp, and she had to dodge poorly crafted furniture as she crept.

She was having no trouble seeing in the dark space and her eyes darted around at the shelves that were lining the walls. Some were filled with liquids that shimmered in the firelight while others were filled with small animal bones and something that looked eerily similar to long human hair. Kelera didn't have experience with magic at this level, but she recognized the strange ingredients for what they were. She had read enough books to know that many magical creatures lived on the outskirts of both courts. Some of these solitary Fae were said to be friendly enough, whilst others posed a threat. She felt a lump in her throat. Would she be able to distinguish the difference between the two?

Before she could reach the door, it burst open. A gust of wind swept in, blowing stray wisps of Kelera's hair around her face. She stumbled back and suppressed a scream as she stood face to face with a wolf. It was bigger than the wolves she had seen in the wild before and had black eyes... Like the man.

The wolf bared its teeth like it was attempting to smile at her. It was disturbing to see. It continued to make the strained face as magic shimmered around it. Kelera took a few steps back, strategically placing a rickety chair between her and the beast. The magic flared with a bright white light and when it dissipated, the wolf was gone. In its place was the strange man from the veil with black pooled eyes.

He was naked from head to toe, causing Kelera to avert her eyes. Even through her fear, she blushed. This was the first naked man she had ever seen...

He chuckled as he said, "Apologies. I do not get a lot of visitors. You can look now."

Kelera returned her gaze to the man who had dressed himself in a large fur coat. He picked a hat up from the couch, and Kelera recognized it from before. Bones from small animals clinked together as he placed it on top of his head. He strolled carelessly over to the modest bed in the corner and sat on it.

Unsure if the man's carefree attitude was a trick to make her let her guard down, Kelera walked to the side of the chair, keeping it between them. It was not much of a barrier, but it was better than nothing. She had the urge to draw her sword, but waited. She wanted to avoid a fight, so it was best not to provoke the stranger.

Her voice was steady as she said, "The men I was with... Have you seen them?"

He furrowed his brow and leaned back against the pillows. His teeth, which had been filed into sharp points, flashed as he spoke. "Men? I did not see anyone but you."

Kelera's stomach dropped as her fears were confirmed. She whispered to herself, "It didn't work."

The man seemed intrigued by that and sat back up. "Oh, were you trying to bring *mortals* into Elfhame?" He shook his head. "Tough business. You'd have to be quite familiar with your magic to pull that off."

She should have known she wouldn't succeed. Once again, doing her best hadn't been enough. "I am such a fool." She racked her brain on what to do next. She knew she should go back to the blackthorns. But that would mean giving up her only chance to save Cierine... Something she couldn't do if she had gotten herself kidnapped. She returned her attention to the man. "What am I doing here?"

He picked at his nails. "You tell me. What *are* you doing here in Elfhame?"

This man was unbelievable. Through clenched teeth, she said, "Not Elfhame. What am I doing here, in your house?"

"Oh that." He chuckled. It sounded like bones clacking together and made Kelera shiver. He whistled and said, "You looked quite helpless there on the ground. I thought I would bring you here before anyone found you. It can be rather dangerous in these parts."

He couldn't be serious. She huffed, "You *knocked me out*. Seems like a strange way to help someone."

He waved a dismissive hand in the air. "I admit it was not the most admirable thing to do. But just imagine if a flesh hungry goblin had happened upon you." He smiled broadly, flashing his razor sharp teeth at her. Every instinct in her body told her to get as far away from him as she could.

She proceeded cautiously, "Then I am free to leave?"

"Leave?" His eyes shifted around the room nervously, then landed on her weapons. "Where would you like to go?"

"I am on official business and need to get to the Unseelie King's palace."

His mouth dropped open in shock. "You want an audience with the king?"

"He... His people took something from me. I intend to get it back."

The man whistled. "That's a terrible idea." He clucked his teeth three times as he looked her up and down. "You won't last a minute at court."

Kelera straightened her jerkin and raised her chin. She had never met a challenge that she couldn't overcome. She had taught herself the arts, been top of her class in the girls' school, and had learned how to fight like a knight... She had perfected ballroom dancing, for star's sake. Surely, she could do this. "I do not know why you really brought me here, but I will be taking my leave now. I appreciate your... hospitality, but I am needed elsewhere." She nearly cringed at her words.

The man stood abruptly and Kelera reached for her sword but did not draw it. Her hand lingered over the hilt as he wandered away from her and over to the shelves. He kicked aside a basket of women's dresses. Dresses like the women in the southern Nevene villages wore... simple and roughly woven. She had a strange feeling in the pit of her stomach at the sight of them.

He searched the bottles as he spoke, "My name is Vazine. You can call me Vaz. Though you so rudely did not ask."

Kelera stifled a retort. He was the one who knocked her out and dragged her to his peculiar little abode, yet he was calling *her* rude. "I'm sor—"

He spun on his heel. "Careful now, dear. You do not want to finish that sentence." When she stared at him in confusion, he asked, "Do you know anything about this realm?" Without giving her a chance to answer, he continued, "It would seem not. How irresponsible of you."

Kelera had had enough of this. She ran to the door and tried to open it. To her horror, it wouldn't budge. Vaz laughed from behind her. When she turned to face him, he dangled a bottle of glittering green liquid in front of her face.

With a sleight of hand, he made it disappear before speaking, "Rule number one: never say you're sorry. *Pardon me. Apologies.* Both are acceptable. But never sorry. Sorry would indicate that you owe me some sort of debt. And trust me, we Fae always collect." He drew the last words out as he eyed her curiously. Kelera listened with interest as he continued. "Rule number two: listen carefully. We Fae cannot lie. But that does not mean we cannot twist the truth." The bones dangling from his hat swung as he tilted his head. "Got it?"

She nodded her head in understanding and gripped the doorknob behind her tightly. "Anything else?"

Vaz took a step closer to her. His face was thin and sunken, and he looked as if he were in need of a meal. "Yes. Stay away from the Princes of the Night."

"A-are you a Prince of the Night?" Kelera desperately wanted to escape this strange man and all of his rules.

He laughed at her, causing her to blush in embarrassment at her ignorance of this world. His pitch-black eyes bore into hers and his voice was low as he replied, "No. The nobles of this realm are what you would call, High Fae. An irritating, pompous bunch." His eyes narrowed as he studied Kelera's face. "I'd say you've got some of that in you. High Fae, I mean."

Kelera's curiosity was peaked. "How can you tell?"

"High Fae do not possess the more animalistic qualities like the rest of us. They have an unearthly beauty about them. No horns, or fangs." He winked, and she couldn't tell if he was joking or not. He was still uncomfortably close to her as he said, "But the thing that sets them apart the most is the magic they wield. Potent magic passed through the strongest bloodlines of our realm. Powerful and ancient magic granted to them by the first elders."

Kelera thought of her mother. If Vaz believed she was High Fae, then that could only mean that her mother had been a part of one of these bloodlines. It was too much to take in. She shook her head. She couldn't get distracted. What she needed in this moment was to escape this man, whatever he was. She realized he still hadn't told her. "And you?"

Vaz gestured to his eyes. "Lesser Fae. I am what they call a *Vedmak*." When she stared blankly at him, he elaborated, "A warlock. One of the solitary Fae. I live here," he gestured around the room, "alone. Wow, you really don't know anything, do you?" Kelera fought the urge to retort. Vaz added, "Typically, I use my gifts for the greater good, but tonight I'm feeling naughty." He wiggled his eyebrows at her as he made the jar appear in his hands once more. "I would like to give you a gift. Would you like that?"

"I cannot accept." Kelera didn't trust Vazine as far as she could throw him and knew better than to accept a gift from the Fae. It often came with dangerous strings attached. She had heard rumors of farmers accepting livestock from the Fae, only to find that they were infected with an illness that caused the rest of their herd to meet a fatal end. Another rumor was of a woman who had accepted a wedding dress from a handsome stranger, only to find that once she took it, she had also unwittingly accepted the man's proposal. She hadn't been able to marry the man she loved as a result and was left to grow old and die alone.

Annoyance flashed in Vaz's eyes, but he continued to smile politely at her. "Are you certain? Surely you will need something to help you if you are to get your friend back."

The hair on Kelera's arms stood on end. She hadn't mentioned Cierine to him. "How do you know about her?"

Vaz shrugged his shoulders. "Word travels fast in Elfhame. One of the Dark Princes was bragging about the great prize he had stolen away in the night. Everyone knows the only prizes the princes like to brag about are of the feminine variety."

"This Prince... does he shape shift like you?"

"A man of no imagination, that one. He likes to use shadows as a glamor. Never made any sense to me. Why be practically invisible when you could be a great and powerful beast?" Vaz's nose crinkled in disapproval.

He continued to babble about all the things he disliked about the Unseelie King's sons and their escapades, but Kelera wasn't listening anymore. She was too focused on the revelation that the shadow who had taunted and threatened her was a Prince of the Unseelie court. That was a hurdle that she wasn't sure she could jump.

She interrupted Vaz's ramblings. "Does the King know what they're doing?"

Vaz scoffed at her. "If anything, he has likely encouraged it."

Kelera thought for a moment. There was a battle raging inside of her. She might not be able to take on someone as dangerous as the king's son. But she also couldn't leave Cierine to spend the rest of her life as a plaything for the immoral beast. She had to do whatever it took to save her. She made her choice as she asked, "What does the potion do?"

Vaz grinned at her and dangled it in front of her face. "It will incapacitate the one who drinks it."

"For how long?"

"Just long enough for you and your friend to make your escape." He winked at her.

Kelera reached out a hand, ready to accept the gift. It could be her only chance. Before her fingers met the glass jar, she paused. "Why are you helping me? What will I owe you in return?"

Vaz hesitated. Before he could answer, there was a loud crash from outside. He dropped the vial, and it tumbled on the floor unbroken. The alarm on Vaz's face told Kelera that something was wrong. He shoved her aside and put his ear to the door. She leaned against it, trying to listen with him. She whispered, "You said you lived alone."

He hissed at her, "I do." He opened the door slowly, then took a step back and held an arm out to keep her away from him. "Stay here. Do not make a sound. There are worse things than me lurking in these woods." Before she could object, magic sparked to life around him and he shifted back into the large, dark wolf.

He bounded from the room into the night and Kelera debated on what she should do. This was her chance to escape, and she needed to take it. But it was the middle of the night, and she had no idea where she was going. As she took a step forward, she heard the clink of glass against her boot.

Looking down, she saw the jar of green liquid that Vaz had offered her. She bit her lip. Stealing went against everything she had trained into her brain. But stealing would beat the alternative to owing anything to the strange warlock. Would he come after her if she stole it? The little voice inside her head, which she typically ignored, said, *Who cares? Take it.*

She picked it up and shoved it into her pocket. Somewhere along the way, she had lost her pack and didn't want to waste any time looking for it. She slipped out through the door and into the brisk night. There was no sign of Vaz or the intruder. Kelera spotted a small clearing in the trees and prayed that it was a path. If she could find a road, it would surely lead her somewhere. And it beat wandering aimlessly in the forest.

She kept her pace slow as she walked, trying not to draw attention to herself. There was another crash near the cabin and a wolf howled. The howl was cut short with a yelp and then it was silent. Kelera was shaking now as she paused to listen. It sounded like Vaz had been hurt. If that were the case, then it meant that something more dangerous than a shape shifting warlock was lurking somewhere nearby.

To hell with being careful, Kelera thought as she broke into a run with every intention of leaving the cabin and the strange encounter behind. Dead leaves crunched under her feet and the trees up ahead were shedding their fall foliage. It was midsummer back home, but here it looked and felt like autumn. The Unseelie Court was split into two smaller courts: Autumn and Winter. *This must be the Autumn Court's territory.* It occurred to her that she was far more unprepared to venture into Elfhame than she had thought. Trying to shove aside her doubts, she continued to barrel into the woods and onto a dirt path.

She looked back the way she had come to be sure that she wasn't being followed. She slammed into something hard and fell back onto the path. She felt the arrows in her quiver snap and her head slammed into the ground.

Her vision went blurry from the fall. Blinking rapidly to regain her sight, she scrambled to get up. Before she could rise, someone was on top of her.

Moonlight shone through the trees onto her attacker. His body was pressed against hers and she struggled under his weight. She caught a glimpse of his delicately pointed ears and realized that he was Fae. Her heart thudded in her chest as he grabbed hold of her chin with one hand and held a finger to his lips with the other.

Kelera yelped, "Get off of me!"

The man let out an irritated snarl and pressed his hand against her mouth. She struggled under his hold as he spoke. "Do not make a sound. I am saving your life. Do you understand?"

She didn't understand, but she would say anything to get out from under him. She nodded slowly, and he pulled his hand back from her mouth. He smirked at her as he got up.

Kelera scrambled back and then leapt to her feet. She heeded his warning and kept quiet, waiting for him to speak. Her vision had returned, and her heart skipped a beat as she got a better view of the man.

He was utterly beautiful, with striking green eyes and black hair that curled at the nape of his neck. A long scar cut across his face, reaching from the top of his eyebrow to his prominent jawline. Small scars also graced his neck and his strong hands. Signs of a violent life.

She put a shaking hand to the hilt of her sword, and he raised his eyebrow in amusement. He opened his mouth to say something but stopped short as a low growl cut through the quiet forest. Through clenched teeth, the man commanded her, "Move aside. And do not get in my way."

She did as he said, just in time as the wolf pounced. The wolf and the man collided. The wolf, whom Kelera could only assume was Vaz, snapped its teeth at the Fae man. His teeth nearly connected with the man's throat, but a blast of magic knocked Vaz back. He rolled as his body hit the ground and the Fae held his hands out.

Kelera had never seen magic wielded like this before. He had so much control over his power that it was hard for her to take her eyes off him. He threw the magical blast at Vaz, skidding him further down the path.

Kelera was ready to flee but didn't want to go back in the direction that she had come. With Vaz and the man blocking her path forward, she was stuck. She continued to watch the altercation, unsure of who she wanted to win the fight.

Bright magic flooded the clearing as Vaz shifted back into his human form. He was naked once again, and Kelera had to fight the urge to shield her eyes. She didn't want to miss her opening if they moved out of the path.

Vaz shouted to the man, "Just because you are High Fae, you think you can steal from me?"

The man teetered on arrogance as he responded, "I do not answer to the likes of you." He spat on the ground.

Vaz looked at Kelera, but this time, any semblance of friendliness he had shown earlier was gone. Did he know that she had stolen from him? She shifted uncomfortably under his glare.

The Fae man noticed it too and took the opportunity to taunt Vaz, "Alright, then. I will return your wine."

Wine? All of this was over wine? Kelera looked between the two men in disbelief. They were insane.

The man reached into his pocket and withdrew a large leather flask. He held it out in front of him, and Vaz took a step forward, eager to accept it. Before he could come any closer, the Fae man added, "I will return your wine in exchange for the girl."

Kelera was distraught. "What?"

The men ignored her. Vaz addressed the Fae, "She is not mine to give."

The Fae raised an eyebrow. "You and I both know of the high price a healthy mortal woman goes for in these parts... and one with halfling magic to boot."

Vaz looked as if he had been caught in a lie. He looked at Kelera as he spoke to the Fae, "How much are you willing to pay?"

The Fae man tsked at him. "As I said before, the wine for the girl."

Vas thought for a moment, and Kelera could not believe what she was hearing. He had never intended to let her walk out that door. He had been toying with her the whole time with his advice and his "gift." She drew her sword, causing both men to look at her in alarm.

"I will not stand here to be traded like a sheep at the market. I am leaving and the two of you are going to stand aside as I do." She swept the sword around in one fluid motion, trying to drive her point home. She had underestimated the dangers of this world, but these men would be wise not to underestimate her determination to save her friend and herself.

Vaz advanced on her with a snarl. She took a fighting stance, ready to defend herself. He did not make it more than a few steps before he was hit with the Fae man's magic. It hit him with a force so strong that it nearly knocked Kelera over as well.

When the magic settled, Vaz was lying on the ground in a pool of his own blood. Kelera held the sword out in front of her, aimed at the Fae. Her hands shook, and she cursed silently, angry that she was showing weakness.

He made no move to grab her, instead he tucked the wine into his jacket. There was amusement in his voice as he said, "No need to thank me." His tone changed, becoming more serious as he added, "Now you would do well to return to where you came from. Do not go looking for more trouble." He gave her a small bow and turned back toward the cottage.

Stunned, Kelera stood there for a while, gripping her sword tightly. His warning caught her off guard. Sweat beaded on her brow as she expected the Fae to change his mind and return to claim her as his prize. The wait was agonizing, but she was too afraid to turn her back on him. Afraid that he would change his mind and attack her, she stayed ready. When he didn't return, she let out a sigh of relief.

Exhaustion flooded her senses as the events of the day and night caught up with her. Finally, she sheathed her sword and sidestepped around Vaz's lifeless body. Walking down the path, still unsure of where she was going, she felt a tear fall down her cheek.

She felt a pang in her heart as she assessed her situation. She was utterly alone and unless King Tristan could find another Fae to open the veil successfully, no one was coming to her rescue. Both her own life and Cierine's hung solely on her shoulders. With an agonizing sense of defeat, she thought that despite her efforts to mold herself to perfection, it might not be enough to get her happy ending.

Chapter Nine

A rustling in the trees woke Kelera from a restless slumber. She wasn't sure how long she had been asleep, and it took her a moment to remember where she was. Every muscle in her body screamed as she shifted against the sturdy tree she had fallen asleep against. She could see her breath in the frosty morning air and rubbed her arms to warm herself.

Something moved around in the leaves behind her again and she froze, worried that the Fae man might have doubled back to take her after all. She was having trouble getting him out of her mind. He was a thief and had acted as if he were interested in taking her as his hostage. But once he had been given the chance, he hadn't acted upon it. It made little sense why he had left her alone.

More leaves crunched under the weight of her visitor, and she held her breath in anticipation. Willing whatever it was to pass, she pressed her back against the rough bark of the tree. The large, black snout of a horse peaked around the tree trunk, making her jump in surprise.

It sniffed in the air, sensing her presence. Kelera scrambled to her feet as it wound its way around the tree to face her. She relaxed as she realized it was just a wild pony. There was a soft magic emanating from it, but she saw no threat as it nibbled at a patch of brown grass.

Something about the midnight black pony called to her and before she knew it, she reached out to touch it. It didn't move away from her, so she ran her fingers through its long, tangled mane. She spoke softly to it—afraid she might spook it. "You're a curious creature, aren't you?" It looked up at her with knowing eyes. "Can you understand what I'm saying?"

It gave her a curt nod. This was remarkable. She wondered to herself if all animals in Elfhame had a hint of magic to them. It occurred to her that this could be a glamor like Vaz had used. The thought made her lower her hand and back away a few steps. She couldn't afford to take any unnecessary risks.

She turned to leave, but as she walked, she heard the clunking of hooves close behind her. When she looked back, she saw that the pony was following her. Each time she snuck a glance at it, the pony would stop and look away as if it were not stalking her through the forest. Perhaps it was just a curious creature. There was no hint of evil magic here. Instead, she felt comforted by the slight buzz in the air. Smiling to herself, she continued toward the path. Still, she could hear the persistent pony's footsteps.

When she reached the small dirt path, she turned back again, to find that she was face to face with the curious creature. She put a hand on its velvet nose. "You are very cute, but I have to get to the Unseelie Court."

She paused and then asked, "Do you know where that is?"

The pony snorted in response. Kelera ran her hand along his cheek and scratched softly. It seemed too good to be true, but if he could take her there, then she would save precious time. It could take days on foot and that was if she could even find it on her own. Navigating the forest was bad enough, but she wasn't sure if she was even headed in the right direction.

"Can you take me there?" She gave him a hopeful smile.

The pony snorted again and knelt on its front legs. Kelera watched in fascination and walked around to its side. Carefully, she swung her leg over his wide back and grabbed hold of his mane. He stood and before she could kick at his sides to signal him to go, he took off through the forest.

Immediately, she regretted her decision. She had always considered herself an exceptional rider, but she had never been reckless enough to mount a horse she wasn't familiar with. The pony was faster than he looked. He jumped over fallen trees and dodged large stones that were protruding from the ground. Kelera had no choice but to hold on to his mane. She tangled her fingers in it, as it was the only lifeline she had to the wild beast.

As the unruly pony ran, Kelera dodged branches that dangled dangerously close to her head. The further they ran, the colder the air became. Soon the pony was galloping on freshly fallen snow. Now the branches she had been dodging were glistening with ice crystals. It would have been beautiful if she had not been hanging onto the wild pony for dear life. The bitter wind bit into her cheeks as the pony picked up its speed. Kelera shouted at him, "Stop! Woah!"

The pony didn't listen to her as he bounded from the woods and into a snowy clearing. Her body bounced relentlessly, and she thought she would fall off at any moment if he kept this up. He didn't slow his pace until a foreboding, towering palace came into view, and even then, he didn't slow completely. Kelera wrapped his mane around her hands, still holding on as well as she could.

They neared a snowy field that separated the forest from the palace. It was like nothing she had ever seen before. The palace's towers reached so high that she couldn't see the tops through the dark clouds that circled it. The stone was sleek and black, with dying vines tangling themselves along the stones. It was a startling contrast to the stark white snow on the ground around it. Kelera's stomach sank as the realization settled in. She had made it to the Unseelie Court. Cierine could be locked in one of those towers at this very moment.

The pony continued to run at full speed toward the palace. Kelera shouted to him again, "Slow down, you ghastly little thing!"

They were approaching an icy creek, and Kelera wondered if the small pony would be able to make such a big jump. She braced herself for the leap, but the pony dug his hind legs into the icy ground, sliding as he came to a halt. The sudden stop threw Kelera from his back and over his head. Right into the creek.

Ice cracked and water filled her nostrils as she went under. Her body slammed against the shallow bottom. The wind was knocked from her, and she pushed herself above the surface, gasping for air. She sat up with the water sitting just at her waist and pushed her wet, matted hair from her face. She glared at the horrid pony, and it snickered. The noise sounded unnatural coming from him and she squinted her eyes. Magic shimmered, and through it, she could see a smaller face with beady eyes and long, hairy ears.

She recognized it from one of her favorite childhood books on lesser Fae in Elfhame. *A pooka! How could I have allowed myself to be tricked so easily?* Kelera chided herself as she realized the pony had been a glamor. She had willingly taken help from a pooka, a creature notorious for tricking unsuspecting travelers. *Well, at least he got me here...* she laughed to herself.

She splashed the freezing water in the pooka's face, and it snickered again as it spun on its hind legs and galloped away. The whole scene would have been comical if it had happened to anyone else. Instead, it had happened to her, leaving her cold and alone as she climbed from the creek onto the other side. Shivering uncontrollably, she limped toward the palace. She adjusted her sword, bow, and quiver of snapped arrows and listened to the squeaking of her sopping wet boots as she walked.

She spotted a small opening in the wall that surrounded the palace and peeked underneath. Her teeth chattered as she peered around for anyone lurking nearby. She spotted a group of people lingering near a small stone house at the side of the palace and watched them curiously.

The women were dressed in identical moss green gowns and the men wore jackets in the same color. All with rounded ears—mortals. To Kelera's disappointment, there was no sign of Cierine and her fiery red hair. She watched the humans carefully. Were they prisoners? It would be strange for them to be free to move around the palace as they wished. It wasn't at all what she had imagined when she thought of the Unseelie Court.

More curious were the masks that they wore. They were intricate and made of delicate silk, covering their eyes and the tops of their noses, but leaving their foreheads and mouths exposed. The masks looked like something one would wear to a masquerade ball and were at odds with the simple clothes they were wearing.

Kelera watched quietly, hoping to learn more about them. Without Alexander and her father by her side, she wasn't confident that she could get an audience with the king. Even if she did, without Duke Cunningham's men, there was no one to make sure he allowed her to leave when it was all said and done. She would have to do this quietly. She needed to find a way into the palace without drawing attention to herself. The masks would be the perfect disguise if she could just figure out how to get her hands on one.

A tall, incredibly elegant Fae man walked into the yard, approaching the group of masked mortals. She studied the difference between him and the others. His ears were pointed in a telltale sign that he was Fae. There was something otherworldly about him. This must be what Vaz had meant when he spoke of the High Fae.

He snapped his fingers, and the group stood at attention. A few of them cowered as he approached them. He looked each of them up and down with a smug look on his face. It was as if he was inspecting them. He wove his way around each individual and sneered anytime he found something not to his liking. Kelera clenched her hands into fists. He had no right to subject them to this sort of scrutiny.

He ran a hand through his frost-colored hair and groaned. "Back to work, you miserable lot." The group took that as their dismissal and went their separate ways. They scattered like mice.

The man paused, and Kelera ducked behind the wall before he looked in her direction. After a few minutes, she braved another peek around the wall to find that he had left. With a sigh of relief, she unbuckled the sword from her hip and removed the bow and quiver from her back. She tucked them behind the bushes that lined the outer wall. An armed girl wandering around the palace would draw too much attention. She would have to come back for them.

The hole here in the stone wall would be the perfect place to escape, avoiding anyone standing guard at the main entrances of the palace. If she could find Cierine, then they could slip through the hole and make their way covertly to the blackthorn veil. That was if they could make it that far. Or if she would be able to successfully cross with Cierine. Things had gone horribly wrong with the rescue party. She would need to focus her magic when the time came... or at least try. But she didn't have time to worry about that now.

Waiting until she knew for sure that she was alone on this side of the palace, she crept across the yard to the modest stone house. It had no windows, forcing her to take a risk as she opened the wooden door. Stepping inside, she was relieved to find that she was alone. It was a cramped space with small slabs of wood topped with dirty blankets and small, flat pillows.

There were at least ten slabs and only two trunks. She knelt before one of the trunks and unlatched it. Lifting it slowly, so that it wouldn't make any noise, she found a pile of neatly folded jackets and trousers to match. She closed the trunk and pushed her hair from her face as she tried the next one.

Jackpot, she thought as she found a pile of moss green dresses and, beside them, masks. She threw off her boots and wet clothing and stuffed them behind one of the wooden slabs, praying that no one would find them. She squeezed into one of the dresses, disappointed that it was a little tight around her wide hips. It would have to do for now.

She tied her damp hair back with a leather strap she had brought with her, careful to keep enough hair pulled down to cover her ears. It would do her no good to give herself away as Fae when she needed to pass as a mortal servant. Once she was satisfied with her hair, she placed the mask over her face. She would need to keep her head down to avoid making eye contact with anyone. Her ringed eyes would be another giveaway that she had Fae blood.

In an effort to go unnoticed, she slipped from the house and hurried to the servant's entrance on the side of the palace. It was a small door that led to a tiny corridor. There was a hallway that led into the first level of the palace and a stairway that led to the second story. With no idea about where she was heading, she paused.

She closed her eyes, trying to focus on planning her next move. As she did, she could feel the steady pulse of magic coming from the hallway. With no hint of magic coming from the stairwell, she made her decision and began to climb the steep stairs.

Her footsteps echoed on the stone as she ascended them. The palace was cold and eerie in the silence. King Tristan's court was always alive with the sound of music and courtiers. Even the servants back home could be found laughing together and gossiping around every corner, or singing as they did their work. She suddenly felt terribly homesick.

When she reached the top of the stairs, she could see a dim light. There was no sound coming from the room and Kelera thought her luck might be changing for the better. She slipped into the hallway and stifled a cry as she came face to face with a group of the masked women. Their eyes were wide as they took her in.

Kelera's heart was hammering in her chest. Were these the women the shadow had kidnapped? Her thoughts raced as she tried to figure out if she would be able to get them all out on her own. If it came to choosing between saving all of them or saving only Cierine, she feared the choice she would make.

One of them balked at her and said, "What on earth? Where did you come from?"

Kelera scrambled for a lie. "I-I was just brought in." She thought of the Fae who had overseen them outside and added, "By your master with the silver hair."

The women looked at one another with concern. It was obvious that they were doubting her lie. The mousey one who had spoken to her, bit her lip as she said, "It is not safe for you here."

Kelera knew it was a risk to trust them, but she saw no other options. So she told them the truth, "I am looking for a girl. She has brassy red hair. She is about my height, but very slim... Please, have you seen her?"

The woman, who looked a little older than Kelera, thought for a moment. Kelera prepared herself, worried that the woman was going to call for a guard. Instead, the woman twirled her dull brown hair around her finger anxiously and said, "She is the property of Prince Samael." She whispered his name as if the mere mention of it might conjure him from thin air.

Kelera's temper flared at the word *property*. "Is he the one who glamours himself as a shadow?" She was sure of the answer. She knew it deep in her bones. But she asked all the same.

The woman gave a small, frightened nod of her head and clasped her hands tightly together in front of her. Kelera looked past them, down the long corridor. The hall was carpeted with a long dark red rug that resembled the color of blood. Everything about this place made her uncomfortable. From the dark, foreboding halls to the very magic that hummed around her. Cold magic that burrowed down into her marrow. It was everywhere she turned—there was no escaping it.

When she turned her attention back to the woman, she grabbed her by the arms. Gripping them to allow the woman to know just how serious she was, she said, "Take me to her."

The woman tried to pull away. "I can't. If he catches us, he will send us to the pits."

"The pits? Is that a dungeon?"

Another girl piped in. She looked like she was in her teens, with the plump cheeks of adolescence. "Worse. It is where they send deserters to fight. It is King Cyrus' favorite entertainment..." Her lower lip quivered with fear.

Kelera released the woman she had taken hold of. These women were terrified into submission to the king and his court of nightmares. She couldn't ask them to risk their lives for her. "If you cannot take me to her, can you point me in the right direction?"

The young girl nodded nervously. "Follow the hall until you come to the turn. Keep your right hand on the wall. The palace has a mind of its own and shifts. When you turn, you will know where to go."

A shifting palace? Kelera took a deep, steadying breath. Right hand. Follow the turn. Simple enough. "But how will I know where to go?"

Each of the women looked away, avoiding eye contact with her. Finally, the woman she had grabbed said, "You will hear the screams..."

Kelera clenched her fists. She needed to hurry. Without a word of thanks to the women, she pushed past them and placed her hand firmly on the wall. She could feel it vibrate with magic against her palm and fingertips. They no longer stung from the wounds inflicted by the blackthorn.

She followed the hall at a steady pace, praying she wouldn't run into anyone else. The palace was still quiet. It was strange to not see courtiers bustling about their business for the day. Kelera wondered if they were all sleeping. Perhaps this court was the opposite of King Tristan's in more ways than just the appearance. Then again, what else had she expected?

Her heart raced as she came to a turn in the hall. Bracing herself, she turned the corner, careful to keep her hand on the wall. As soon as she rounded it, her ears were flooded with the screams. It was terror inducing as she listened to the cries of agony coming from a room at the end of the hall. She didn't let the terror flooding her stop her from putting one foot in front of the other as she made her way toward the red door painted with black vines. This was too important. She couldn't lose her nerve after she'd come this far.

When she reached it, she released her hold on the wall and pressed her ear to the door. The only sounds she could hear were men and women moaning and screaming to be freed. It was impossible to distinguish the different voices amongst the symphony of anguish. Her hand shook as she took hold of the handle.

Before she could turn the knob, she felt a sense of dread wash over her. This was a bad idea. Who knew what, or who, was on the other side of the door? She thought about turning to walk back the way she came. Maybe she could bide her time amongst the servants until she found Cierine... *No*, she thought, *Cierine would be brave. If the roles were reversed, she would stop at nothing to help me.* She knew it in her heart.

She turned the doorknob and was met with darkness. She pushed the door open so the light from the hallway would light her way. The wailing didn't stop as she stepped into the room. Instead, they grew louder and more urgent. Shadows masked the people being kept deep within the room. It was like looking into the abyss.

A loud scraping noise made Kelera jump back. She bumped into a table, knocking its contents onto the floor. She bent down to pick them up, but paused when she got a closer look. She ran her finger along one of the steel blades. It was finely crafted and shimmered like an icicle.

She stood carefully, still holding the blade, and someone chuckled. It sent a shiver up her spine, and the blade slipped from her hand, clattering to the ground. She spun on her heel to face the open door. Standing between her and the only path out of the room was a dangerously handsome man with a wide grin on his dimpled cheek. His stark white hair was braided back with wisps escaping at the side. He was shirtless, revealing a pale, scarred chest, and he was panting heavily. He blew a strand of hair from his face and greeted her in that same familiar honeyed voice, "So we meet again."

Chapter Ten

P rince Samael stepped aside as shadows reached around Kelera. They tore her from the room and pushed her out into the hall. He followed her out of the room, letting the red door slam behind him. Grabbing Kelera roughly by the arm, he dug his fingers into her flesh and dragged her with him. She struggled under his hold as he pulled her down the hall and away from the room where she worried Cierine was being held. She was kicking herself for not having a better plan. And for allowing herself to fall into the clutches of the very man she needed to stay far away from.

He laughed. "I knew you'd come. You just couldn't resist, could you?"

Kelera snarled at him. "You took my friend! How did you think I would react?" She tripped as he dragged her.

"So that's the only reason?" The suggestive tone made her want to claw his eyes out. She certainly hadn't come for *him*.

Prince Samael was focused on the hall ahead, so Kelera took the opportunity to strike. She kicked him hard in the back of the knee, sending him tumbling to the floor. Then she ran. He yelled out at her, "You *bitch!*" And before she could get far, he shot his magic at her. Shadows wrapped around her ankles and sent her face first into the carpet. It burned as her cheek skidded against it.

The shadows bound themselves tighter around her legs, preventing her from getting up. Prince Samael stomped over to her and grabbed her by the hair. He leaned down and growled into her ear, "Stupid halfling. You have no idea what you've just gotten yourself into."

He lifted her by her hair, wrapping it around his hands so that she could not pull away from his grasp. The shadows on her legs released her so that she could walk. She scrambled to her feet, and he dragged her down the hall, refusing to let go of her. They came to a grand staircase that led down into a dark ballroom. She tried to pay attention to her surroundings, memorizing the route they were taking and looking for any exits to make her escape.

It was all a blur of rich tapestries and glittering chandeliers. Not a soul was around to witness the scene she was making as she fought against Samael's grip. Her feet slipped on the slick marble floors as they crossed the dance floor. Prince Samael said nothing more as they walked to the double doors. The silence was almost as maddening as his harsh words had been.

"Where are you taking me? And where is my friend?"

He ignored her, dragging her out the double doors and through long, winding hallways. The palace shuddered as Prince Samael stormed them through it. It was like the palace was reacting to his sour mood. Kelera regretted kicking him. Perhaps if she had been compliant, he would have been easier to persuade.

They exited through a large glass door that was covered in hand-crafted bronze vines and into what barely passed for a garden. It was filled with broken statues and thorny bushes. The sun had nearly set over the horizon. Kelera could see men sitting around a stone table up ahead with refreshments in front of them. The man in the middle was broad, with a clean-shaven face and hair as white as Prince Samael's. He wore a crown of dark metal that resembled long, twisted horns. At first glance, it looked as if they were protruding from his head. The two men sitting beside him looked strikingly similar but were devoid of horned crowns.

Kelera pleaded with Prince Samael, "Please, I only came for Cierine. The berries... you left the berries for me to find. Surely you wanted to talk to me again. Can't we keep this between the two of us?"

Prince Samael snarled at her, "Don't you worry. We will have plenty of time for that." He used the grip on her hair to turn her to face him. Her scalp screamed in agony. He grabbed her chin with his other hand and squeezed. "But, first, you must be presented to the king." He looked her up and down in disapproval. "We'll have to do something about your attire later."

Before she could plead her case to him, he pulled her over to the men and threw her to the ground. Rough gravel dug into her hands as she caught herself. She hissed as pain shot through them. Prince Samael walked around her and tore the mask from her face.

She looked up reluctantly at the men staring down at her. There was amusement on their faces as they took her in. Prince Samael introduced her, "King Cyrus, allow me to present to you Lady Kelera of Nevene."

King Cyrus sat forward with interest as he commanded her, "Stand."

Kelera, knowing she had no other choice than to do as he bid, stood. She smoothed out the rough green dress and met the king's eyes. They were the color of winter, with rings of varying shades of light blue around the pupils, like Prince Samael's. He didn't look much older than his sons. Though she knew from the history books that age didn't progress the same in Elfhame as it did in the mortal world, it was shocking to see firsthand.

He looked her up and down like he was inspecting a vase he wished to purchase in the market. Kelera glared at him. King Cyrus' voice hinted at approval as he said, "Wide hips, large breasts... A pleasant addition, son." He mused. "She looks strong enough for the pits." The men sitting around the table muttered in agreement. The king raised an eyebrow as he asked, "But are you certain of her abilities? Your brothers have voiced their doubts." He nodded to the men beside him.

Vaz had let it slip that there was more than one prince of the Unseelie Court. She counted four here, including Samael. How many more were there? She fought back the bile rising in her throat at the thought of being subjected to whatever games these men liked to play.

Prince Samael answered his father with certainty, "I have had my eye on her for some time now. It seems she has no control over her power yet, but give her time and the right motivation..." Prince Samael smiled suggestively at Kelera.

King Cyrus waved a dismissive, jeweled hand in the air. "Go ahead. Add her to your collection. Just keep her away from the mortal servants. Mortal blood may taint her veins, but she is still High Fae and traditions must be upheld." His voice was stern as he added, "And Samael, I warn you. Keep her under control. Halfling magic can be volatile. I will not have her causing trouble in the court."

Halfling magic. Kelera had no idea how to use her magic. The only time it ever seemed to show up was when her emotions were getting the better of her. Something that resembled hope bloomed in her chest. If she could access that magic, then perhaps she could use it to her advantage. *Stop*, she warned herself. That would mean abandoning everything she had been taught. It would mean unleashing her true nature... She couldn't let them destroy the life she had worked so hard for.

Prince Samael, satisfied with the king's response, bowed deeply. He grabbed Kelera by the arm and attempted to drag her away. She fought to stand her ground. "Your Majesty, please. I am here on behalf of King Tristan of Nevene. He asks that you release his niece and the other mortal women who were taken. The treaty—"

King Cyrus stood abruptly, knocking his glass from the table. It shattered on the icy ground. The shards of it twinkled under the rising moon. He spoke slowly and calmly, "Damn the treaty to the fiery pits of hell." He smiled viciously. "I am the King of Unseelie. Ancient magic strums in my very soul. I will not answer to mere mortal men. *Princess* Cierine will stay exactly where she is until we tire of her."

Arrogant fool. That's what he was. What point was he proving by standing his ground on this? There was nothing for him to gain by having Cierine and the other mortals in his custody.

"But King Tristan—"

"King Tristan holds no authority over me and my sons. What sort of father would I be if I did not allow my boys a little fun every century or so?" Two of the men beside him grinned and toasted each other with their glasses. King Cyrus sat back casually in his seat. "You are dismissed."

Samael grabbed her by the sleeve of her dress and dragged her away. Before they returned to the palace, she took one last chance to look back at the man who had just condemned her. King Cyrus waved merrily at her and laughed at something one of his sons said.

⚜

"Where are you taking me? And where is Cierine?" Kelera had to jog to keep up with Prince Samael.

He turned on her and she knocked into his bare chest. His skin was ice cold to the touch. But it was his voice that was like frostbite in her ears. "You do not ask questions here. You do as I say." He backed her into the wall. The stone pressed into Kelera's back and she shifted uncomfortably. Prince Samael's demeanor changed as he noticed her discomfort. Now he practically purred at her as he spoke, "You are *mine* now, halfling. You will go where I say and do as I bid." He trailed a finger along her cheek until he reached her jawline. She flinched at his touch, revolted by the hunger in his eyes.

Then, as quick as he had been upon her, he backed away. Kelera didn't offer a retort. If he wanted obedience, then she could give that to him. She would be the perfect prisoner. And then, when the moment was right, she would strike. She would be sure that he did not see it coming.

She lowered her eyes to the floor in submission and he walked ahead, satisfied. To Kelera's relief, she recognized the halls from before. But just as they came upon the turn in the hall that led to the red door, magic shimmered in the air. In the blink of an eye, the hall no longer turned to the left, but to the right. Kelera's direction was thrown, and she was having trouble processing the change. Prince Samael humored her, "The palace is an entity in and of itself. A spell you can thank my great-great-grandfather for."

Kelera felt deflated. Any hope she'd had of memorizing her way around the palace to aid in their escape was gone. How could she navigate a maze that she couldn't memorize or predict? They rounded the corner and came to a long hall lined with red doors. Each was identical with golden knobs.

Prince Samael walked to one of the doors and held his hand over the knob. A cloud of dark magic flared to life under his fingertips, flowing like shadowy tendrils, and the lock clicked. He threw the door open unceremoniously and gestured for Kelera to step inside. She walked quietly into the room.

It was smaller than she expected. With a simple bed lined with soft furs, a tall bureau, and a small writing desk by the window. Kelera stood awkwardly in the middle of the room, taking it all in. There were very few decorations in the room. A simple painting of a naked woman bathing on a smooth rock by a waterfall, and several candlesticks on golden holders.

She turned to Prince Samael, who was watching her like a hungry dog ready to feast. She pursed her lips. "I am here as you bid."

He almost looked annoyed by her obedience. Had he hoped that she would disobey him? To what end? Kelera folded her hands in front of her. Her time at court had taught her how to act with men like him—men who expected a woman to know her place and who thrived on the power they felt in that.

Realizing she would say nothing more, Prince Samael said, "This will be your room."

"You mean I won't be sleeping with the servants?"

"I'll forgive the question... No. You will not. You are a lady of high standing, and as my father so elegantly pointed out, though you are but a halfling, you are still High Fae. Our customs stand firm in that regard. But do not make any mistake. You are still my prisoner. You will not be emptying our chamber pots, but I have many other ideas on how I may use you."

The relief she had felt thinking that being High Fae would keep her from being subjected to Prince Samael's whims blinked out of existence. She was no servant, but she was still a prisoner. From his veiled threats, she worried that this might be worse.

She felt as if she would be sick. He turned to leave, but paused and spoke over his shoulder, "The fun starts tomorrow."

Before she could say another word to him, he shifted into the shadows and shut the door behind him. The lock clicked in place, sealing her fate. She had been Cierine's only hope, and she had failed. It was only then, once she was sure he was gone, that she wept.

Chapter Eleven

The sky was still dark outside when Kelera was awakened by servants bustling around her room. She
had no idea what time it was, but her body told her
it wasn't yet time to rise. She pulled the furs over her
to cover the undergarments she had slept in. One of
the servants, wearing the familiar moss green gown and
mask to match, lit a fire in the hearth. While another
set a tray of breakfast on the writing table. The third
woman, one she recognized from the previous day,
gave her a sympathetic smile as she laid out Kelera's new
wardrobe.

It was a blood red dress with black lace along the
sleeves and bodice. Beside it, the woman set down a
matching mask. Kelera ran her fingers over the lace that
outlined it and then gave the woman a puzzled look.
"What does this mean?"

The woman cleared her throat before she answered, "It means you belong to Prince Samael." She gestured to her mask. "Green is for the servants, black for the King's personal entertainers... and red for Prince Samael. Each prince has his own. It makes it easier for the court to know which of us belongs to who." She patted Kelera's leg sadly and walked away.

The masks, though beautiful, were barbaric. A way for the royal family to remind their prisoners of their inferior status here at court. Worse, it was a way for them to take away the individuality of those they lorded over—Kelera included.

The woman signaled for the other two servants to follow her, leaving Kelera alone in the room. She flung herself back onto the feather down pillows. She rubbed at her temples, trying to get her bearings before she did anything else. First things first, play the role she was expected to play. Stay poised, keep control of her temper, and do not cause any trouble. The less the Fae of the Unseelie Court noticed her, the better.

Cinnamon wafted from the plate on the writing desk, and Kelera's stomach growled. She couldn't remember the last time she had eaten. Surely Prince Samael would not poison her before he'd had the fun that he had promised her. She went to the desk and sat in the chair.

The plate was topped with a warm, twisted dough that was coated with whipping cream and cinnamon. The blue-black berries on the side caught her eye, causing her irritation to rise. She took the fork in her hand and pushed them aside. Prince Samael must have thought himself very clever to have included the blackthorn berries with her breakfast. She poured herself a cup of tea and savored the warmth as she sipped it.

Stars twinkled through the window to her room, and she would have thought them beautiful if she were not facing such perilous circumstances. Elfhame had been everything she had feared it would be. Dangerous, terrifying, and lonely. But what she had not counted on was how her heart swelled at the sight of those stars. When she was very young, she would sneak out of bed to peek out her window. It was when the pain of being without her mother hit the worst. She would wonder if her mother was somewhere out there looking up at those same stars. Now here she was—in her mother's homeland.

Kelera set the teacup gently on the delicate, dark blue saucer and sighed. She hadn't thought about her mother much since she was that little girl looking at the night sky. She had watched the women at court dote over their daughters. They would buy them beautiful dresses and brush their hair. Being the only girl without her mother had been yet another thing that made people whisper about her. Some would be vicious, saying things loudly about her mother being a Fae whore, while others would give her pitying looks as they passed her in the halls.

Being here, in her mother's land, made her wonder if she was still alive... out there somewhere staring up at the same starry sky. She slumped in her seat unceremoniously. After a moment of wallowing, she regained her composure. Standing with all the grace she could muster, she walked into the small washroom attached to the bedroom. She took a moment to wash herself from the bowl the servants had left for her, then made her way over to the bed and grabbed the red dress. She took her time fastening the buttons and tying the ribbons that held the bodice together.

To her surprise, it fit her like a glove. The craftsmanship of it was remarkable, and she admired the way it accented her waist without suffocating her. She grabbed the mask next and tied it in place around her face. It was softer than the green one had been. Its delicate silk caressed her skin.

She picked up the vial she had stolen from Vaz and turned it in her hands. If she could find Cierine and slip the potion into Prince Samael's drink, then it would be their ticket out of there.

She went to the door and tried to open it, but it was locked from the outside. She rubbed her thumb along the detail on her necklace, trying to quell her nerves. Would they keep her trapped in here like a princess locked in a tower? Perhaps that would be better than the alternative of spending the night with Prince Samael.

She flopped back onto her bed and tried to smooth out her gown. She ran her fingers along the red fabric. Fabric that looked like the blood that had dripped from her hands when she cut them on the blackthorns. She groaned. Things had gone so terribly wrong. Her father and Alexander must have been beside themselves when they realized she had crossed the veil without them.

She laid back and closed her eyes, trying to imagine Alexander's charming smile. If she could get herself out of this situation, then she could return home to that smile. She imagined cheering crowds as she walked through the palace doors with Cierine at her side. King Tristan's court would never be able to doubt her again. They would see how truly loyal she was to the mortal realm. It would be like the happy endings she'd read about in storybooks...

She wasn't sure how much time had passed. Without the sun, there was no way to tell. Just when she thought she would burst with restlessness, a knock at the door startled her. Prince Samael didn't strike her as the type to knock, but just to be safe, she tucked the potion between the mattress quickly and called out, "Who is it?"

The man on the other side cleared his throat. He sounded nervous as he answered, "Prince Gadreel. I... er... I am here to escort you to lunch."

Kelera suppressed the urge to groan. It had to be well after midnight by now. She should be sleeping, not sitting down to lunch with these lunatics. Instead of voicing her disapproval, she opened the door and forced a smile at the Fae Prince standing before her. It was the same man she had seen inspecting the servants outside.

His facial structure was similar to Prince Samael's, but his smile was genuine, bright with laugh lines at the edges. His eyes were even like Samael's, but with deeper tones in the rings around his pupils.

He held his arm out to her, and she paused before taking it. Once she took hold of it, there was a look of relief on his face as if he had expected her to resist. As much as she would have liked to put up a fight, it would do her no good until she was able to find Cierine.

When they reached the end of the hallway, it shifted again. The magic shimmered in the air to reveal a grand staircase. This one led them down to the palace foyer, and Kelera looked longingly at the large double doors that could lead to her freedom.

Prince Gadreel had to lean down to whisper to her. "Brace yourself."

Kelera looked at him in alarm, but before she could ask him what he meant by that, he led her into a large dining hall. There was a long table centering the room and green-clad servants standing in a line on either side against the wall. They were wearing their signature masks and looking down at the ground.

The table was lined with a feast befitting several kings. There were meat pies, roasted duck, and fountains of sapphire liquid. King Cyrus raised a finger, signaling one of the servants to step forward. The woman grabbed the glass that was in front of the king and tipped it into the small fountain. The servant allowed the sapphire liquid to pour into the glass without spilling a drop. She set it in front of the king, who did not bother with thanks, and stepped back into her place.

The room was cold, clashing with the ornamented decor. The table was the most elaborate of all, with its vine carved legs and deep red table liner. Prince Gadreel motioned for Kelera to follow him to her seat. She sat on the left side of the king, across from a stunningly beautiful pale blonde woman. She stuck her thin nose up at Kelera and turned her attention to the man sitting on the other side of her.

He leaned in intimately and whispered something in her ear. She laughed, and it sounded like wind chimes. Kelera watched them curiously, wondering if they were lovers. The man was beautiful, like the rest of the High Fae. He was massive, and muscular, much like Dodger. He caught her staring at him and gave her a dazzling white smile. His pale eyes crinkled at the corners when he did.

He had an arrogant way about him as he sat back and put his hands behind his closely shaven head. His voice was almost sensual as he spoke. "Like what you see?"

Kelera blushed and the woman across from her snickered. Gadreel sat on the other side of Kelera and chimed in, "Ignore him. Kane's just mad that father canceled the fights later tonight."

Kane, whom Kelera could only assume was one of the other princes, snarled at Gadreel. "You have a lot of opinions on the fights for someone who isn't man enough to step into the pit."

Prince Gadreel opened his mouth to retort, but the man sitting on the other side of Prince Kane stopped him. He was almost as tall as Gadreel and nearly as broad in build as Kane. He looked like the perfect mix between the two. Sitting forward in his seat, with a hand raised in the air, he said, "That's quite enough. Kane, you will get to brutalize some poor mortals tomorrow. And Gadreel... I do believe you are in Samael's seat."

Prince Samael's smooth voice came from the doorway, "Why, Ammon... I had no idea you cared. I'm touched."

Prince Ammon sat back in his chair and shot a withering glare in Samael's direction as he strode over to the table. Ammon took on an air of indifference in his presence. "I don't care. But I also do not want our lunch ruined over a petty squabble."

Samael strolled over to the table and Gadreel moved quickly to take the next seat over. Kelera wished he had stayed where he was. There was kindness in his eyes and in the way he had escorted her to the dining room without the poor treatment that Samael seemed to prefer. Though she wasn't foolish enough to trust anyone here, Gadreel seemed to be the only decent one out of the lot of them. And she had felt safer by his side than anyone else's.

The chair made a loud scraping noise as Samael pulled it back. Once he was firmly in place, he leaned over and kissed Kelera on the cheek. Instinct made her pull away from his touch, and Kane bellowed out in laughter from across the table. Samael summoned his magic in response and sent his shadows catapulting over the roasted duck and directly into Kane's chest.

Kane's chair toppled backwards with him in it and the wood cracked underneath the fall. When the brutish prince rose, his eyes were ablaze with anger. Silver magic drifted from his fingertips, ready to pay Samael back for the attack. Kelera held her breath, waiting for him to unleash it.

"Enough." King Cyrus' voice echoed loudly through the cold room. "Kane, sit. Samael, if you attack your brother again, I will have you strung up."

Both men obeyed and turned their attention to their plates. Kelera clenched her jaw in disappointment. It would have been satisfying to see Samael get a taste of his own medicine. Servants stepped forward, piling food high in front of each of the royals. They served Kelera and the blonde woman last. Once they stepped back to take their posts at the wall, the men began to feast.

Kelera picked nervously at her food. She was still full from the breakfast plate Samael had sent to her room and, with the display she had just witnessed, didn't have much of an appetite. She studied the brothers who were sulking as they dug into their lunch. In all her time around nobility, she had never seen an altercation like that before. No lord of the Nevene court would deign to act so barbarically, especially not men of royal blood. She chose to take a sip from her glass instead. The sapphire liquid was cool and sweet on her tongue.

She felt eyes on her and looked up to see that the blonde woman was watching her closely. When she met Kelera's eye, she said, "So you were raised in the mortal court, yes?"

Kelera set her glass down. "I was."

"Is it your mother or your father who is Fae?"

Kelera looked around to see that everyone's attention was now on her. It was the last thing she wanted. Trying to busy her hands, she picked her napkin up and placed it on her lap before answering, "My mother."

The blonde woman raised an eyebrow. "Interesting." She took a sip of her drink and then said, "It is uncommon for a mother to abandon her child, even in a world as wild as this one." She gestured around her, then sneered at Kelera. "She must have seen something quite distasteful in you."

Kelera tensed at the slight. She gripped the napkin sitting on her lap. Anger clouded her judgment as she snapped, "Or maybe she thought I would be better off being raised away from the likes of you."

Prince Kane spat his drink out as he laughed. The woman's face blushed with a deep red, making Kelera regret her words. It wasn't wise to offend the very people who held her life in their hands. She usually worked harder at holding her tongue, but she hadn't been able to stop herself this time. Maybe it was exhaustion. But it was as if all the times she had wished to stand up for herself in the mortal court had caught up to her. She twisted her fingers into the fabric of the napkin to try to hide the fact that she was shaking.

Prince Ammon spoke up now. "You must forgive our mother, Lady Kelera. She does not like beautiful women. And though you are not what we in Elfhame would consider bewitching... You do have a certain quality about you that is hard to ignore."

Their mother? She, like the king, didn't look a day older than any of their children. It was still surprisingly difficult to wrap her head around the revelation. The royal family sitting at the table could be hundreds of years old without looking a day over thirty.

Offending the queen. Definitely not a good idea. Kelera dipped her head at the Queen Consort. "My apologies, your Grace."

The queen simply scoffed at her and returned her attention back to her drink.

Finally, King Cyrus spoke, acting as if he had not heard anything any of them had just said. He directed the question at Prince Ammon. "Where is your brother?"

Ammon shrugged his shoulders. "How should we know?"

With a mouthful of food, Prince Kane added, "Hasn't been around for days."

King Cyrus looked displeased at that as he grabbed hold of the meat on his plate and tore it apart with his bare hands. Kelera tried to hide her disgust. She took a small bite of the mushroom mixture on her plate. The food was divine. Like magic in and of itself.

The family around her began to discuss mundane matters of state. They talked of gossip in the court, and how well the crop was doing in the Autumn Court. It seemed that the Unseelie Court spent a lot of time throwing lavish parties as Queen Beatrix began listing off the many items she would need for the events of the month. King Cyrus didn't say much as he ate. From time to time, he would grunt in approval, or growl in disapproval when something they said displeased him.

Listening to them talk reminded Kelera of home. It was not at all what she had expected, based on her recent experiences in Unseelie. There was no talk of torture or kidnappings, though Kelera listened closely for it. She still had no clue where Cierine was being held, or what being under Prince Samael's control truly meant.

She was so wrapped up in her thoughts that she did not notice that she had been asked a question. She looked up from her plate and found everyone waiting for her to answer. She set her fork down. "Apologies. I was lost in thought."

King Cyrus snarled. "I said 'where did you get that?'" Kelera followed his gaze to the locket around her neck.

"My mother. It was all that she left me with when she..." Kelera trailed off, not wanting to share the intimate details of her life with any of them.

The king gave her a curious look and grunted. He didn't press the issue further as they finished their breakfast. Kelera wanted to ask why he was interested in a trinket, but she refrained. King Cyrus was a man of few words, and something told her he wouldn't appreciate being interrogated by her anyway.

When the family finished, King Cyrus stood. He extended a hand to his wife and left without saying a word to his sons. Prince Kane wiped his face with the back of his sleeve and wiggled his eyebrows suggestively at Kelera. She wrinkled her nose and looked at Prince Samael. He was watching her over the rim of his glass. What plans did he have in store for her?

Prince Ammon tossed his napkin onto the plate and said, "Well, some of us have duties to attend to. I am headed to the Seelie Court to meet with the queen's advisors about the trade agreement."

Prince Gadreel perked up at that. "Is the queen not meeting with you as well?"

"Her advisors say that she is under the weather."

Samael raised an eyebrow. "I do hope it is nothing serious." The sly smile on his face said otherwise.

Gadreel ignored him and directed his question at Ammon, "Would you like me to accompany you?"

Ammon turned up his nose. "You have matters to attend to here."

Samael added, "Yes, I will be going back out to the border soon. You will need to have things ready for the delivery when I arrive."

Delivery? Could they mean more kidnapped mortals? She listened intently in hopes that they would reveal more.

Instead, Gadreel's eager smile faded away. "Yes, of course."

Gadreel and Kane stood and followed Ammon from the room, leaving Kelera and Samael alone. He leaned in close to her and ran a finger along her collarbone. She wanted to shudder at his touch, but sat firmly in place. He cooed into her ear, "Alone at last... What shall we do with our time?"

Kelera didn't answer and his jaw twitched. If she refused to take the bait, then maybe he would grow tired of the game he was trying to play. She could tell he was attempting to get a rise out of her. Her anger had gotten the best of her many times. Even now, she could feel the buzz of magic in the tips of her fingers. But she didn't trust herself to use it intentionally. She took a deep breath and willed the feeling to go away. If she could fight the little voice in her head that told her to act on her feelings, then she could also fight the impulse to offend and fight him.

When he stood, he reached down to grab her under the arm. He jerked her up with a force that nearly made her fall from her seat. Without a word, he led her out of the room and into the hall. Kelera looked back at the dining room to see the servants hurrying to clear the table. She almost envied them. The royal family paid little attention to them. And she would give anything right now to be in that position.

Chapter Twelve

S amael dragged Kelera unceremoniously through the endless halls winding throughout the palace. She had lost all sense of direction as they took the twists and turns, watching the palace shimmer and change shape as they went. She had no idea how Samael could navigate his way through it, but still, he walked on with confidence.

Images of the room behind the red door flashed in her mind. Was that where he was taking her? To his room of nightmares where blades were left sharpened on the table, ready to inflict pain on whomever he wished. Prince Samael was unpredictable. And not knowing what he had in store for her was torture in and of itself.

She was breathless as she asked, "Why am I here, your Highness? The berries on my pillow were clearly a message of some sort."

"I prefer to think of it as a love letter. You see, I need you."

If this was his idea of a love letter, then he was more twisted than she thought. And she was nothing more than a half mortal girl. There was nothing she could give him that he couldn't get elsewhere.

"Why me? What could I possibly have to offer you? Because of the magic you claim I have? Allow me to save you the trouble. There is no magic," she lied. She couldn't imagine what he would want with her magic when he had his own. But she wasn't about to help him, so instead, she would play the naïve mortal if that's what it took. "I inherited nothing from my mother save for these damned pointed ears and frightening ringed eyes."

He slammed her against the wall and hissed through his teeth, "Liar." His pale eyes blazed like ice when the light hit it just right.

Pain shot through her back, and she struggled to get away from him. "Are you going to torture it out of me?" It was a genuine question, but the moment the words left her mouth she regretted it. It sounded like a challenge. And without control of her magic, she couldn't afford to challenge Samael and the power that he wielded.

He raised his eyebrows and Kelera feared whatever idea had just dawned on him. He pulled her from the wall and led her to the end of the hall. She could hear screams coming from behind the red door at the end. The hair on her arms rose, but instead of leading her into the foreboding room, he turned to the right, where another door awaited them. Magic shimmered as he held his hand over the lock and turned the knob. Kelera got shivers as she followed him in.

Candlelight filled the room, giving air to the romantic quality of it. Floral wallpaper decorated the walls, and a soft quilt was laid out neatly on the bed. It was not at all what Kelera had expected, and it took her a moment to get her bearings. She had expected a torture chamber, not a woman's bedroom.

"Kelera?" Cierine's voice sounded suspicious. Kelera turned to find her dressed in a pink gown that clashed with her copper hair. Relief flooded her as she looked her best friend over, realizing that she was unharmed. She moved to embrace her friend, but Cierine stepped back, knocking into the small writing table she had been sitting at. She turned on Samael with cold, angry eyes as she accused him. "Another one of your tricks."

Samael leaned against the wall and picked at his nails carelessly. "No trick. Your friend here thought herself to be a white knight. She has come to save you." He paused to look Kelera up and down in disdain. "As you can see, she failed."

Cierine's face softened, and her eyes began to well with tears. She wiped them away roughly before they could fall down her face. "What are you going to do to her?"

Samael pushed off of the wall and walked over to Kelera. He circled around her like she was a horse at a sale. "I haven't decided yet. I could introduce her to my room of shadows... but I have a feeling she would wear that irritating little mask of indifference, thus resulting in no fun for me." He stopped circling and pushed her hair away from her ear. "I could put her in the pits..."

Cierine took a step forward and Kelera worried about what would happen if she acted against Samael. She gave a small shake of her head, stopping Cierine in her tracks. Kelera was finding it difficult to breathe. He was playing with them both, and if they were not careful, he would win the game.

He continued, "I admit I am curious as to how she would fare in the pits. It is clear that she has a fighting spirit. But she refuses to acknowledge what she is." He grabbed Kelera by the shoulders and turned her to face him. "Would you continue to deny the power in your Fae blood, or would you die stubbornly pretending that it does not exist?"

"I have no power." A lie again—one she would continue to tell him... One that she had been telling herself for twelve years.

"All halflings have power. Did your mortal father tell you nothing of your lineage?"

Kelera shifted on her feet. Hearing Samael speak of her father made her frustration rise. "I know enough. I know that my mother left me alone in a world that did not want me. I know that my father, the most admirable man I have ever met, did everything within his power to make sure I had a good life. I know that if it weren't for you, my best friend and I would be home right now preparing for my wedding. I know that I never asked for any of this. And most of all, I know that my hatred for you is growing every moment of every day!" She shouted the last part without thinking. As she did, an almost painful heat sparked at her fingertips and she looked down, afraid that she would see fire dancing on her skin. But there was no visible sign of her magic.

She caught her breath and waited for him to punish her for her insolence. Instead, he laughed. "There she is." He raised her chin as he said, "You have suppressed your Fae nature for far too long. And I think it is about time it broke free." He gave her a vicious smile and raised his hand. She flinched, expecting him to strike her, but instead he snapped his fingers in Cierine's direction. Cierine fell to the ground with an ear-piercing scream.

Kelera leapt for her, but twisting shadows pinned her against the wall. Tears were pouring down Cierine's face and her eyes were wide as she stared straight ahead. She whispered, "No. Please, don't."

Kelera couldn't see who she was talking to, but there was no mistaking the utter terror Cierine was in. She continued to beg for mercy and Kelera shouted at Samael, "What are you doing to her?" He was leaning lazily against the wall with one hand in the air. His fingers moved like a conductor leading a symphony. Kelera screamed at him again, "Stop! Prince Samael, stop!" Cierine was in agony and Kelera was helpless to stop it. Tears streamed down her face as she watched her friend suffer on the floor.

There was a hint of amusement in Prince Samael's voice as he said, "I am weaving her nightmares together. It is quite easy to do, especially when that person is already filled with fear."

Bile threatened to rise in her throat. What nightmares of Cierine's could he be bringing to life with his magic? She fought against the shadows keeping her back from Cierine, and the buzz of her magic bloomed to life, threatening to reveal itself. Cierine cried out as she tried to get away from the nightmarish vision Prince Samael had brought to life. Kelera watched with horror as her best friend tried to crawl away from the vision. She clawed desperately at the floor, leaving streaks of blood from her fingernails.

Kelera could stop him. If she could just take hold of the magic her own body was offering her now. With a shudder, she reached for it. She hated Samael for what he had done to them. He had taken so much from her already and now he was going to break her friend's mind right in front of her. She clenched her fists and closed her eyes. Embracing every ounce of hatred and anger she had toward him, she felt the magic pool within her grasp.

"There she is." The way he said the words was almost sensual.

Kelera's heart skipped a beat. *This is what he wants.* As the revelation hit her, the magic slipped from her as quickly as it had come. He was clever, going after the person she was willing to risk everything for just to get what he wanted. Her anger was replaced with resolve and any hint of magic she'd felt went with it.

Samael closed his fist and lowered his hand in one swift motion. Cierine gasped. She was breathing heavily, but the agony on her face was gone. Samael withdrew his shadows away from Kelera, releasing her from his hold. She ran to Cierine before he could change his mind and stop her. She embraced her friend and rocked her as Cierine sobbed into her shoulder.

Samael went to the door and his hand lingered over the doorknob. "The magic is there, Kelera. And I *will* have it one way or another." He opened the door and sighed. "Even if I have to break the two of you to do it." He slipped from the door and the lock clicked in place behind him.

Cierine's face was pale. "Kelera, what are we going to do?"

Kelera wrung her hands in anticipation. The sun would be rising in a few short hours, and Samael still had not come for her. Once Cierine had recovered from the horror Samael had inflicted on her, she had told Kelera everything. She explained how the shadow had come into Kelera's room to steal her away silently. He had brought her here to the Unseelie King's palace and locked her away in the flower walled room to wait.

Cierine had whispered through tear-filled eyes, "At first, that was the worst—the waiting. The only people I saw were the mortal servants who brought me food throughout the night. But then the visions started." She had gripped Kelera's hand tightly as she described the nightmares that Samael liked to torment her with.

Kelera wouldn't have been able to imagine the pain Cierine had been in if she hadn't just witnessed it with her own eyes. She had no words for the sorrow and guilt she felt as she listened to her friend's account.

They had sat like that in silence for quite some time. Holding one another and sharing in the comfort that they were reunited, even if only for a little while. But now Kelera was growing restless. They were sitting ducks. They needed to get out. As she paced the room, she asked Cierine, "Has there been any sign of Emma? The lady's maid that he took before you?" If Kelera could save them both, then she would. She would try to save them all.

Cierine shook her head sadly. "I asked one of the servants when I arrived. They say they haven't seen her and that it may mean she is locked away behind the red door." Her eyes were red from crying. It broke Kelera's heart. In all their years together, she had never seen Cierine cry like this. Being in the Unseelie Court was breaking her friend's spirit.

Cierine stood and clutched Kelera's hands tightly as she said, "I can't believe you're really here. After all the time he's been toying with my mind, I was convinced I'd never see you again. There have been so many times where I was sure you or Francis had come to my rescue. It seemed so real. But each time when I let hope creep in, you would disappear. I'm scared Kelera."

"I know. And I'm going to get us out of this. I have a plan. We just need to stay safe a little while longer."

"You don't understand. He threatened you with the pits. He pushed you tonight to see how far he could go before you gave into him. If he sends you to that barbaric place..." Her voice broke, "The servants talk. I have heard of the horrors that take place in the pits. Mortals and even the Lesser Fae are brutalized..."

"Then for once, it is a good thing that I am not mortal." Kelera's expression hardened with determination. She would do everything she could to avoid that path, but Cierine was counting on her strength now. It was her duty to fill her friend with hope, even if she herself was lacking in it.

Cierine took a deep, steadying breath. "Even so, you cannot go. The servants say that the princes are warriors through and through. They have been bred in the blood of the innocent—violence is in their very nature. The Unseelie royal family will stop at nothing to get what they want. You will not be able to survive them all."

The room was eerily silent as the girls sat together. The fire was dying down, sending a chill through Kelera. She moved closer to Cierine and pulled the covers over them. It reminded her of the nights they had spent in Cierine's room at Rose Manor.

Cierine's voice broke as she asked, "Do you think my uncle will be able to get his men through the veil?"

"I think it would not be wise of us to count on it. The odds of him finding someone with Fae blood who would be willing to bring a hunting party through are slim. We cannot rely on anyone to save us but ourselves."

Cierine pulled away to study Kelera's face. Her brow was furrowed as she mused, "Something is different about you."

"What do you mean?"

"I can't put my finger on it. Maybe it's the way you antagonized Prince Samael. You have more... fire. It reminds me of when we were children." She gave Kelera a small smile.

You mean when I wasn't afraid of my Fae nature, she thought bitterly, but didn't say it out loud. Kelera stood abruptly. She couldn't allow this place to change her. To destroy the person that she had worked so hard to become. She went to the fire, poking and prodding at it to bring the flames back to life. They flickered in the dim light of the room. She could almost feel the shadows dancing along her face.

She didn't want to think about the ways that this world could change her if she let it. She had to admit in the short time she had spent in Unseelie, she had been brazen and rash. She had done things she never would have dared to do when she was back in Nevene. And yet, if she was being truly honest with herself, she didn't feel sorry for it. Furthermore, she wasn't embarrassed. If anything, her short temper had been well received by the royal family.

Again, Cierine cut through the quiet. She sounded very small, like a child, and not at all like the fiery woman she was. "We're going to die here, aren't we?"

Kelera's heart felt like it was breaking. Cierine's life was in danger because of her. Because Samael had known that Kelera would come for her. Her mind tried to grasp what he could do with her magic. What made her power so special?

She didn't voice her questions out loud. It was too difficult for her to admit out loud that she was the reason her friend's life was in peril. Besides, she needed Cierine to stay the course. If she could make it through the night and return to her room, then she could grab the potion and enact their escape plan.

She knelt in front of her friend. "Listen to me carefully. I have a plan and I will get us out of this. I need you to trust me."

"Of course..."

Both girls jumped at a soft knock on the door. Kelera braced herself to come face to face with Samael again, but instead saw the frightened face of a young woman. She recognized her from the hall when she first arrived at the palace. The girl slipped through the door with a bundle of freshly washed blankets in hand. Her slender face was rosy as she scurried to the bed like a mouse and dropped them on the mattress. She was so utterly mortal with her light brown hair and small stature. It made Kelera want to weep for the innocence lost to the madness of Elfhame.

Looking around for any sign that they were being listened to, she whispered, "We know what you're planning. And we want in."

Kelera was careful to wear her mask of indifference. "You want *in*?"

The girl let out a small, frustrated breath. "We know you are here to rescue Princess Cierine. Take us with you."

Kelera bit the inside of her cheek. She had every intention of helping as many mortals as she could. But getting Cierine and herself out of Elfhame was challenging enough. Add a group of frightened mortals into the equation... it would be next to impossible. Though her decision to help them had wavered, it had not changed.

Still, she wasn't sure who she could trust. She asked carefully, "How many of you are there?"

"Six that will be brave enough to make the journey." The girl held her chin high. She had a fighting spirit. Kelera hoped desperately that she could get them all through the veil. What if it didn't work? What if she left them behind like the rescue party? She couldn't think about that now. One step at a time.

"There are far more mortals being kept here than that." She thought of the poor souls trapped in Samael's room of shadows.

The girl's eyes shifted between her and Cierine as she admitted, "Not all are brave enough to take the risk."

Kelera could understand that. She couldn't force anyone to put their lives on the line if they weren't ready. If she could get the mortals who were willing to come with them through the veil, then she could bring the rescue party back through for the rest.

King Cyrus had made it clear that negotiations were out of the question. And after what Kelera had witnessed in her short time here, she wouldn't stand in King Tristan's way if he wanted to storm into Elfhame. She only hoped his men would be strong enough to stand against the power of Unseelie. Nausea washed over her. This was all too much.

Putting her faith in the young woman, she said, "Fine. But I need you to get something from my room first."

The girl gave Kelera a wicked smile. "Consider it done."

Chapter Thirteen

"She's been gone too long. What if someone caught her? Or worse. What if she's betrayed us?" Kelera paced around Cierine's room like a tiger in a cage. "She probably went straight to that bastard to tell him what we were up to."

Cierine was lying on the bed with one of her arms over her face. She didn't look at Kelera as she said, "The servants here are treated like they are less than nothing. There is no way she has betrayed us."

Kelera's arms prickled with the heat, though she was nowhere near the fireplace. Ignoring it, she nearly shouted, "Then where is she?"

The door cracked open, and the girl peeked her head into the room. "I'm right here. You didn't think I'd run off with this, did you?" She poked her arm through the door. Vaz's vial was in her hand. Its shimmering liquid felt like a light in Kelera's soul. *She did it. We can go home.* Kelera regretted every bad thought she'd had about her.

The girl slipped into the room, shutting the door quietly behind her. Kelera took the potion from her gratefully. "Thank you..."

"Mira. My name is Mira." She gave Kelera a small curtsey.

Kelera hadn't noticed it before, but Mira had the accent of someone who lived in one of the southern villages. She wondered how long ago the girl had been taken, and how much pain she had endured during her time in the Unseelie Court.

"Thank you, Mira." Kelera turned to Cierine. "Time to get up, Princess. We have a shadow prince to thwart."

They had a plan. That was what mattered in this moment. Now whether or not that plan would work... First things first, Kelera needed to get Samael alone. If the potion inside the vial did as Vaz had claimed, then it would incapacitate the shadow prince long enough for the women to make a run for it. It wasn't much, but it would have to do. Mira had already gone off to gather the servants brave enough to flee from Unseelie captivity. Meanwhile, all Kelera and Cierine could do was wait for Samael to return. The wait was maddening.

The sun was beginning to rise over the wintery horizon, casting an orange glow through the curtained window. Cierine let out a loud snore. For the first time since coming to Elfhame, Kelera laughed. The sound escaped her lips, and she put a hand to her mouth in surprise.

"Well, that wasn't very lady-like, was it?" Samael stepped out of the shadows. He had foregone his black jacket and there was blood on his white linen shirt. It was fresh. Still wet and soaking through onto his lean chest.

Kelera snapped at him. "You're one to judge. What sort of *prince* uses his position and power to terrorize and inflict unimaginable pain?"

"There it is again." He moved toward her with a sly smile on his lips.

"What?" She stepped away until her back was pressed against the wall. He leaned into her, pinning her in place.

"That fire that you try oh so hard to suppress. Come on. Let it all out. Think of the fun we could have." He trailed a finger along her collarbone, sending a revolting shiver through her body.

He wanted a rise out of her, but she couldn't give him the satisfaction. She needed to keep her temper in check. She averted her eyes from him. He slammed a hand on the wall beside her head and she flinched. He pushed himself off of her and walked to the window.

Kelera's hand drifted to her pocket, where the vial was waiting patiently. Her fingers gripped the smooth glass. *On second thought, perhaps we should play his game.* She thought to herself.

She looked over at Cierine to see her staring wide-eyed at her from the bed. Kelera shook her head softly and Cierine laid back down on the pillow, closing her eyes to feign sleep. Kelera walked over to the desk, where a decanter of wine was waiting. Mira had brought it in earlier with dinner.

She poured two glasses. Then, glancing back at Samael to be sure he was not watching her, she slipped the vial from her pocket. She emptied the contents of it into one of the glasses, watching the shimmering liquid merge with the red wine. It brightened, making her heart skip a beat. If he saw, it would be her death sentence.

Samael spoke from the window. "It will all be mine one day, you know. The whole bloody kingdom. Of course, Ammon thinks he still has a shot because he is the eldest. And then there's my sordid, bastard half-brother to deal with. But in the end, it will be I who prevails."

Kelera half-listened to his self-centered ramblings, too busy praying that the potion would turn red with the wine. She stalled. "And what is it that you will do with your newfound power when it comes?"

He chuckled, "I will make this world in my image."

The venom in his words irked her more than she expected. This was not her world. What did it matter what happened to it once King Cyrus was gone? She owed the creatures of this realm nothing. Her own mother had seen to that when she had left Kelera in the mortal realm.

Her father had not known what her mother was when he took her to his bed. It had been a reckless night of fun during a fall festival. Glamoured, her mother had ventured over the blackthorn veil. So taken with the young knight she came across, she had allowed him to take her under the stars. Only to find herself pregnant with a halfling. Less than a year later, on a warm summer night, she had dropped the babe on his doorstep and never looked back.

Why should Kelera not do the same? She would cross the blackthorns one last time and never think of this dangerous world and the royals who ruled it with reckless abandonment again. She studied the glass in her hand and saw the shimmering die down. With a quiet sigh of relief, she turned to Samael.

"A drink then. To the future king." She extended the spiked glass to him.

He eyed her suspiciously, and she did her best not to show her fear, giving him a small half smile. Finally, he accepted. She held her breath as he raised the glass to his lips. Stopping short, he let his gaze fall to the wine, and swirled it in the glass.

Samael drinking the potion was their only ticket out of there. She inched closer to him, taking a long sip from her own untainted drink. "What will you do first?... As king."

As if amused by her sudden interest, he looked her in the eyes and taunted her with his words. "I will tear the blackthorn trees from the earth... and burn them."

Kelera suppressed a shudder. He would open the veil. She wasn't sure why it came as such a shock. Samael did not value mortal life. The screams coming from his room of shadows made that abundantly clear. But that also changed things. If he planned on making it open season for his minions in the mortal world, then her people would face more danger than the odd kidnapping.

Time was precious, and she needed him to drink. But she couldn't help but ask, "Why go after the mortals? Why not go about your business and rule Elfhame as you see fit?"

He answered without hesitation, "Because it is fun. Because my people have been held back from their true potential for far too long. The Autumn Court and the Winter Court that fall under Unseelie rule could be unstoppable if given the chance. We are superior and, as such, we will rise above all others. Your beloved mortal court included."

Her hands were cold and clammy. "But the kidnappings—"

"Are simply a way for me to give that imbecile king of yours a taste of what's to come."

He was evil. Truly and purely evil. All he wanted was power, and he would stop at nothing to get it. Kelera steadied her breathing, but she knew the hatred she felt for him was plain on her face. There was no hiding what she thought of him now. He must have gotten joy from that look, because he raised the glass to her in a toast and pressed his lips to the rim. She watched as he downed the wine, drinking every last drop.

This was it. The moment she had been waiting for. She braced herself, waiting for him to fall ill or into a deep slumber. His face went pale as he tried to catch his breath. A panicked wheeze escaped his throat as he snarled at her, "You little bitch. What have you done?"

He grabbed hold of her dress, tearing the arm of it from her shoulder as he fell to the ground. Kelera wasted no time. She snagged the bag that she and Cierine had stuffed under the bed. Mira had packed it for them. Rations of food and warm jackets awaited them inside. All they would need to make it through the wintry landscape and into the Autumn Court.

Cierine was already at the door. Samael mumbled something from the floor. Kelera was sure that he was spouting meaningless threats at her for poisoning him, but she paused to listen. His voice was muffled as he groaned with pain, "Spring will turn to fall and summer to winter. The queen will spout a fountain of blood under the hawthorns." He let out another groan.

The queen? She couldn't make sense of his words. Cierine tugged on Kelera's arm. "We need to go. Now!"

Samael began to pull at his hair. He growled and then laughed. "There is no heir." Through the laughter, he continued to speak nonsense. "No heir." He fell into a fit of coughing and then began to cry. "Just me. Just me. I must bring winter upon them all." He was descending into madness before her very eyes.

Cierine pulled on her arm again. "Kelera, what are you doing?"

Snapping out of it, she turned toward her best friend. The door was open. Their freedom was waiting for them. It was time to leave this nightmare behind. It was time to go home.

It felt as if they were running through a maze. The halls were constantly shifting before her eyes, making it hard to tell which direction they were headed. Mira had been clear in her instructions. Keep your right hand on the wall and follow it until the red carpet ends.

Footsteps pounded behind them in the direction of the room they had left Samael in. His shouts still echoed through the halls. Soon the guards would put the pieces together and realize Kelera and the others were making a run for it.

Kelera cursed at the wretched palace under her breath, "Damn you. Get us out of here." Heat rose again on her arms and hands, and anger fueled her forward.

The halls suddenly ceased their shifting. Cierine stopped ahead of her. "Did they just—"

"Obey me?" Kelera's voice was filled with awe. "Yeah, I think they did." There was no time to linger on the question of why. Shouts were coming from down the wing, headed in the direction of Cierine's room and Samael's screams. "Let's keep moving."

Cierine nodded, sending her wild red hair flying into her face. The girls continued to race down the hall until they came to the door to the stairwell Kelera had come through when she first arrived. Six women, Mira included, were standing on the solid wood floor where the red carpet ended.

They were dressed in heavy furs and Kelera allowed herself to wonder for a moment where they had gotten them. Perhaps these women were more resourceful than she had given them credit for. Mira stepped forward, pulling her coat closer to her face. "Ready?"

Kelera gave her the go ahead. "You have no idea."

She followed Mira and the others down the stairwell and out of the palace. The morning sun was shining brightly, but the air was bitter and cold. The wind nipped at Kelera's face. It stung, but she ignored it as they raced across the yard to the hole in the wall.

Kelera stopped to grab her sword from the bush where she had stashed it before. She hoped she wouldn't need it, but something told her King Cyrus wouldn't let them escape so easily. Cierine and Mira stopped to wait, but she shouted at them, "Keep going!" They did as she commanded, running across the snow-covered ground in the direction of the forest.

She could hear shouts coming from the palace. The king's men would be closing in on them soon. She took hold of the familiar steel and thought of her father. He'd had the sword made especially for her—had taught her how to use it. *So you will always have the means to defend yourself,* he'd said as he placed it in her hands. *You are special, my girl. It is not your mortal or Fae blood that defines you. It is what's in your heart. Never apologize for who you are. And cut down any who try to make you.*

As one of the king's guards slipped through the broken rocks in the wall, she held onto his words. *I'm not sure this is what you had in mind, Papa,* she thought as she stood ready to defend the women running across the icy field.

The Fae soldier reached through the wall, taking hold of her dress. It tore as he pulled her back to him. She tried to pull away, but he grabbed hold of her leg, sending his magic into her. It was like hundreds of icy splinters shooting through her skin. Desperate to escape the pain, she descended on the Fae soldier. He didn't see her sword coming as he tried to climb through the hole while still holding tight to her. She sliced through his neck in one swift motion. His head rolled on the ground and landed with his lifeless eyes staring up at the clear sky.

Bile threatened to rise to her throat. She had never killed anyone before. Already, her soul felt a little darker for it. But this was a matter of life or death. It had come down between the two of them and she had done what was needed. Without another moment of hesitation, she ran.

The shock of what she had done was wearing off by the time she caught up with the others. Her hands were trembling so much that it was difficult to hold her sword. The mortal women weren't faring much better. Out of breath and terrified, they were moving at a dangerously slow pace. One of the women tripped on a branch. Kelera stopped to help her and gave Cierine an annoyed look. As much as she wanted to help these women, now that they were in the moment with the king's men hot on their heels, the instinct to help her friend was stronger.

The woman thanked Kelera for her help and fell back into step with her friends. Kelera grabbed Cierine's hand, holding her back. "We're not going to make it. Not with them to worry about."

"You can't be suggesting that we leave them." Cierine's look of shock sent a wave of guilt through Kelera. Is that what she was suggesting?

Before she could respond, an ear-splitting screech like the one she had heard in her dream sounded through the trees. It was followed by more screeches. They were coming from all directions. The bitter winter wind whipped Kelera's hair into her face. She grunted as she lifted her sword. Her exhaustion was at odds with the new adrenaline that was coursing through her. She was no match for whatever it was that was lurking beyond the shadows of the forest. Guilt ate at her as she stood side by side with the women that she had allowed to be dragged into this.

The screeching continued to cut through the trees, growing closer with every passing second.

Cierine's voice trembled as she asked, "What is that?"

Maia answered, "The King's Night Riders. Wraiths... men that are neither living nor dead. Men who dared to stand against the king in the past. So driven by greed and hate that the king used a spell that caused them to go mad. They are sentenced to serve him for eternity."

Kelera held her sword close. The fact that the sword would be the only thing standing between these women and the king's monsters made her dizzy. Kelera turned toward Cierine and the others. "You need to keep moving."

Cierine's eyes were red rimmed and bloodshot. She pulled the coat around her tightly. "We cannot cross without you. Whatever it is you are about to do, it will all be for nothing if we can't get through the veil."

She was right. They needed her to get over the threshold. She nodded to Cierine, and they began to run. She kept pace with the slower women, ready to defend them against the creatures that were hot on their tail.

Kelera tried to focus on her breathing, but her chest was tight from the cold. She tried desperately to remember how far she had traveled on the pooka and prayed to the stars that it wouldn't be long now before they reached the Autumn Court. Her legs burned from running in the deep snow and judging by the way the women were panting, they wouldn't be able to go on like this for much longer.

Another inhuman screech came from behind them, causing the hair on her arms to stand on end. One of the women began to cry. "We can't outrun them."

Kelera shouted to her over the wind. "We keep moving. Stopping means certain death... or worse." By now, the king's men would have found Samael. It would not matter if he were alive or dead. She had attacked a prince—a man of royal blood. Had stolen servants—*property*—of the Unseelie Court. There would be no mercy for any of them if they were caught. Kelera would rather die fighting than face that sort of wrath.

Mira pointed ahead to a break in the trees. Beyond it, Kelera could see fields of browning grass and sunlight. The Autumn Court. Just a little further and...

One of the women ahead of them let out a scream. Kelera watched in horror as a monstrous winged beast trampled over her. Kelera could hear the sickening crunch of bone as the horse-like creature stepped on her mortal body. The other women screamed in terror and stumbled back a few steps, but Kelera stood her ground.

The beast sitting on the horse's back looked at her and let out a low crackling sound. Its face was shrouded in tattered black robes so she could see nothing but shadows where its face should be. Its horse was nothing but bones and rotten muscle beneath spiked metal armor that matched its rider's. The steed's smokey gray eyes looked weary. It was a wonder that it was able to stand at all on its decaying body, let alone hold the incredibly tall rider.

Kelera looked from the rider to Cierine, who was standing dangerously close to the dead mortal woman's body. She needed to put herself between her friend and the monster. She could feel the rider's eyes on her, though she could not see them. This wasn't a time to show weakness. If this was her final stand, then she would make it count. She raised her voice so it could hear her. "You are standing in the way of us and our freedom. That is your mistake."

The rider's voice hissed in her mind as it spoke. "You are the one mistaken. We do not care about these vile creatures. We have our orders." More screeching filled the trees. It was like nails on glass. The rider wasn't alone, and it seemed it wanted Kelera to know that. The horrid creature raised its hand. The armor looked like skeletal bone as it pointed at her.

"Then come and get me." Kelera took a fighting stance and raised her sword. She shouted to the women standing around her. "Go!" When she met Cierine's eyes, years of friendship and trust passed between them. Cierine nodded in understanding and led the women north, headed for the blackthorns.

The rider laughed bitterly, its voice still inside of her mind. "Stupid girl." Without another word, he advanced on her. His horse's hooves trumpeted on the frozen ground. He pulled a sword from his scabbard. The metal scraped as it was drawn from its place hold.

Kelera felt her fear rise to record breaking heights. This was more than she had bargained for when she had crossed that veil. She wished more than anything that her father and Alexander were by her side right now. Without them, she was just a lady of the court playing the hero. But even if she couldn't convince herself, she would need to convince the rider.

She roared as she ran head on into him. She ducked, rolling on the ground as he swept his sword at her. As she righted herself, she spun around, slicing her own sword through the steed's leg. It did less damage than she had hoped. The horse didn't even cry out as it limped away from her.

The rider turned his horse back to face her. He readied his sword once more. Kelera pushed the hair from her face as she asked, "Why do this? Why carry out the whims of a madman and his sons?"

"You have much to learn. And learn you will." He spurred his horse roughly, and it galloped in her direction.

Her heart raced as she braced herself for another defensive move. As she did, heat flooded her. It was overwhelming. Like a fever hitting suddenly in the night. It didn't feel like the other times that her magic had awakened. This was more than she could handle. There was no grasping at it as it consumed her entire being. She became dizzy as sweat beaded on her brow. Her vision blurred. *I am my own undoing*, she thought to herself as she felt the ground falling toward her.

Chapter Fourteen

S he was drowning. At least, that's what it felt like. Like she was trapped underwater and could not swim to the surface no matter how hard she tried. She gasped for air, but instead of warm water, she was met with ice. It burned as it filled her lungs. She opened her eyes.

When she did, she was faced with a cloudy, wintry sky. Snowflakes fell gracefully onto her face, sticking to her lashes. *The rider.* She sat up, sure that a sword would meet her flesh as she did. Nothing came. The clearing was empty. There was no sign of the rider or the nightmarish steed on which he rode.

She scrambled to her feet. Disoriented, she walked toward the warm glow where the tree line split. Each painful step she took brought her closer to the green-ish-brown grass that awaited her in the Autumn Court. Her vision was no longer blurred when she reached it. It was then that she broke into a run.

She ran at a break-neck pace until she arrived at the blackthorn trees. When she made it to the tree line, Cierine met her with tear-streaked cheeks and bloodied hands. The blood trickled from her fingers and down her wrists. "I couldn't break through. I tried but...."

Horrified by her friend's pain from her failed attempts at clawing her way through the thorny brush, Kelera embraced her. "It's okay. I'm here now."

Mira's voice trembled. "What happened back there?"

Kelera answered her honestly, "I have no idea. One minute, th-that *thing* was attacking me and the next..." she trailed off, unable to find the words. It didn't make sense to her. One instant, she was at the mercy of that monster and the next she was engulfed in heat.

Mira gulped. "No one has ever defeated them."

Did she defeat the beast? She had no memory of what happened. The last thing she remembered was the overwhelming intensity of power and the certainty that it would consume her in one fell swoop.

Mira pried. "How did you do it?"

Kelera swallowed her irritation. "I don't know. And I don't think this is the time or place to discuss it." Mira eyed her suspiciously. Something about the way she was looking at her made Kelera nervous. Mira seemed to know more than she let on. And she'd offered no help when Kelera had stayed back to sacrifice herself. It wasn't fair to blame her, though. You couldn't judge someone for their actions when staring death in the face.

Kelera looked around at the frightened women. "Let's go home."

Cierine waved a hand at the women, urging them to follower her toward the brush. Before they could move, a stampede of hoofbeats came their way. Kelera turned to find that she and the others were surrounded by the Fae. The men were heavily armed with swords and axes, all dressed in expensive armor. It had to be the king's guard.

Kelera felt a breeze as an arrow flew past her face and into the neck of one of the mortal women. The woman fell to the ground and she gasped. Her first instinct was to protect Cierine. She held her sword out with unsteady hands.

The crowd of guards parted as a man's voice rose above the women's screams, "Come willingly, and no more blood will be shed."

Kelera gripped her sword tightly as she tried to get a better look at their leader. "Somehow I doubt that."

The man rode forward until his horse was a few yards away from her and the helpless women. He smirked as he met her eyes. Kelera's jaw dropped in recognition. It was the same smirk she had seen in the forest mere days ago. The Fae man's striking green eyes bore into hers and she felt a shock run through her. There was no mistaking that this was the same man who had saved her from Vaz, with his midnight black hair and the scar that graced his beautiful face. He had been her savior that night, but the man she was looking at now was certainly no white knight who had come to save a damsel in distress.

On his jacket, he wore the crest of the royal family of the Unseelie Court; a crown surrounded by blackthorns. A lifetime around royalty told Kelera what she desperately wished was not so. This was a prince of darkness... The bastard prince of the Unseelie court.

The chaos Kelera witnessed as the prince barked at the guard, "Grab them," was like nothing she had ever witnessed before.

It was a frenzy. The women fought against the hold the king's men had on them. Kelera was quick to put herself between the oncoming guards and Cierine. Their advance was pushing the girls away from the tree line. Kelera could see now that there was no way to save them all. The guards were brutal, cutting down the unarmed women where they stood. They would take no prisoners. She couldn't save them, but she could save her friend. She *would* save her friend.

Kelera watched as one of the women fought on the ground against a relentless guard. She slammed the heel of her boot into his face. Blood poured from his nose and onto her green dress, staining it brown.

Mira slipped from the grasp of one of the guards and scrambled toward Kelera and Cierine. She gestured to Kelera's sword. "I'll hold them back while you open the veil." Kelera hesitated. Opening the veil was the key to their survival. If Mira could hold back the guard long enough... She handed Mira the sword and the three of them backed toward the blackthorns. Just a little further and she could leave all of this behind.

The prince dismounted his horse with a sigh. There was a scowl on his handsome face as he pushed the guards and servant women aside, never taking his eyes from Kelera. He was coming for her, just as the Night Rider had been.

She was surprised when he spoke. "Mira, you have upheld your end of the bargain. You are free to go."

Kelera ached with the stab of betrayal. "You told them what we were planning. You led them straight to us," her voice shook with anger. She stared at Mira, waiting for her to deny it.

Mira shook her head regretfully. "I'm sorry. Truly, I am."

Kelera bared her teeth at the traitor. She had trusted her. And because of that trust, Kelera had put Cierine's life at risk. She grabbed Mira roughly by the collar of her dress. "What have you done?"

Mira looked genuinely afraid. Her lip trembled. "I did what I had to." She raised the sword and pulled away from her grasp. With the tip of the blade pointed at Kelera's heart, Mira took a few careful steps back before turning and running east.

Kelera barely had time to process the revelation that the young girl had sold them out. She turned toward the blackthorn trees. The only thing standing between them and their salvation. She grabbed Cierine tightly by the arm and pulled her toward the thorns. She could hear the women's cries behind her and the footsteps of the advancing prince.

Cierine cried out, "We're not going to make it!"

"No. *We're* not. But you are." She grabbed hold of the thorns, biting her lip as they tore into her flesh. *By the stars, please let this work.* Blood dripped from her hand. Then, picturing rose manor in her mind and re-membering all the days spent in the sunshine with the scent of newly bloomed poppies, she pushed Cierine. Magic shimmered to life as Cierine's body disappeared through the tree line.

The relief nearly brought Kelera to her knees. But the journey wasn't over yet. She moved to follow Cierine, but a hand gripped her arm. She was yanked back, hitting the chest of the prince. She slammed into him, knocking them both away from the trees.

His arms were wrapped around her and the alterca-tion drew stares from the guards. They eyed the two of them as he snarled loud enough for everyone to hear, "It was reckless of you to steal from the Unseelie Court. A debt is owed. And you, little thief, are the price."

She fought against his hold. "You *bastard.*"

"Call me Adrastus." He put a hand to her temple and her vision went black.

Chapter Fifteen

S he was dreaming. There was no other explanation for what she was seeing. A million little stars shone around her. Brilliant and bright against the dark backdrop of her mind. She reached her hand out to touch one, but as soon as it met the light, the star blinked out.

What is happening to me? She thought to herself as she spun around, looking for any sign of the tangle of blackthorn trees or the prince whose grasp she had fallen into. She was met with nothing but the twinkling starlight.

A voice beckoned to her in the depths of her mind, *Time to wake, little thief.*

Kelera gasped as she was pulled from the stars and back to reality. She was disoriented to find that she was on horseback with the prince holding tightly to the reins behind her. Ahead of them, she could see the familiar tall, and foreboding palace. He had brought her back to the Unseelie court.

She struggled under his hold. "The dreams... the visions. That was you."

His breath was warm on her ear as he said, "You should have heeded my warnings."

"Why did you send them? Why try to protect me?"

He scoffed. "This isn't about you. This is about keeping power from my brother's greedy hands."

Her magic—that is what this all boiled down to. "You let me go in the woods when Vaz attacked..."

"Because I was naïve enough to believe after the encounter that you would head straight for the blackthorns—that you would go home, where you belong. *Not* into the heart of more danger."

His frustration caught her off guard. She could think of nothing else but to beg him, "Then please, let me go now. Show me that mercy once more. You do not have to take me back."

There was a hint of regret in his voice as he said, "I'm afraid I cannot do that. You have much to learn about this realm. A debt to the crown cannot go unpaid." He looked around cautiously, and Kelera followed his gaze to the blood-soaked guards. None of the women had been taken. Instead, their bodies were left to rot at the border, so close to what should have been their salvation. Kelera's guilt for her part in their fate brought tears to her eyes.

She would not befall their same fate. Not without a fight. Resolve overcame her. Kelera slammed the back of her head into his face. He fell from the horse, pulling her down with him as he went. He took the brunt of the fall as Kelera landed on top of him. She clawed at the snowy ground, trying to escape him, but he grabbed her dress. He pulled her back to him as she fought to break free.

The guards that had ridden in with them stepped in. They grabbed her by her arms and dragged her to her knees. The snow around Prince Adrastus was splattered red with his blood. Kelera didn't take her eyes from it as he got to his feet.

He groaned, putting a hand to his nose to stop the bleeding. He sounded impressed as he said, "You have a spark in you. That's good. Hold on to it in the days ahead." Without another word, he turned away from her and walked into the palace. Kelera shook uncontrollably. She wasn't sure if it was from the cold, or if it was from the fear that was flooding her heart and soul.

The guards pulled her roughly to her feet and took her into the palace. The double doors were opened wide, allowing two more guards to flank them. When they reached the foyer, the royal family was waiting alongside a large group of high Fae. There was no sign of Samael or Adrastus.

The courtiers stood tall and proud, looking down their noses at Kelera. She knew their type. She had been surrounded by those same judgmental gazes all her life. If they thought it would be enough to rattle her, then they were terribly mistaken. What she was more concerned with was the look that King Cyrus was giving her. His eyes were ablaze, his jaw was set—he looked absolutely murderous.

She tried to stop herself from trembling. Showing weakness would only fuel him. If there was ever a time that she needed to wear that mask of calm, it was now. She breathed deeply and the smell of herbs filled her nose, along with the tang of something else. Something potent. Like magic. It was coming from the drawing room to the left of her.

She turned her gaze to the room, trying to get a glimpse of what was inside. King Cyrus' voice snapped her attention back to him. "You look at me. And me only." He walked toward her slowly. Each footstep felt like a blow to her heart. She had no idea what the penalty was for what she had done, and it was the not knowing that was the worst torture of all.

He took hold of her chin when he reached her. His touch was surprisingly gentle as he raised it. "You poisoned my beloved son. You stole our property. And you killed one of my faithful riders." Kelera furrowed her brow. The rider in the forest... How could he possibly know it had been her doing? King Cyrus studied her face as he continued, "I want to know how."

Kelera took great care not to stutter as she gave him an honest answer. "I don't know."

His eyes flashed with anger. "You would do well not to lie to me. I have been gracious during your time here." Kelera nearly laughed in his face. He'd given his son free rein to do what he wished with her and Cierine. He is the one who sent his monsters after her and allowed his guards to slaughter the mortal women at the border. If that was his idea of playing the gracious host, then she wasn't ready to find out what it meant to have him as her jailer.

She spoke carefully, "Honest, I don't know." He needed to believe her. She had felt her power when she faced the rider, but she had no clue how she'd defeated him with it. One minute she was at that thing's mercy and the next, it was gone. Banished to oblivion.

King Cyrus was thoughtful for a moment, but his brow wrinkled in concern as he said, "I believe you." He released her chin and gestured to his court. "However, these things cannot go unpunished." He rejoined his family and turned back to her again. "Three offenses. Three debts. That is what is owed."

Queen Beatrice grinned beside him, flashing her sparkling white teeth. There was malice in her eyes. Even in all her beauty, Kelera saw her for the hateful creature she was. If it were up to her, Kelera guessed that she would have been killed before gracing the palace steps again.

King Cyrus spoke loudly as he gave his sentencing, "I am a merciful man."

We have very different definitions of that word, Kelera thought to herself bitterly.

"Your fate, as I have decided it, will be three hundred years of servitude to the royal family." As he spoke, Kelera sensed magic circling her. It was like ice on her skin. She cried out as it settled into her, right down to her very veins. The pain was excruciating, sending her to her knees. King Cyrus continued to speak, "Under which time, you will obey our every command. Should you try to run or rebel against us again, you will find that there are fates worse than servitude... and far worse than death." The crowd murmured in response to the proclamation.

The magic he had forced upon her felt like a tether keeping her bound to the royal family. She could feel it in her soul. Kelera glared up at him. If this was his idea of mercy, then he was more a monster than he looked.

Three hundred years? How was that even possible? Even if she could live that long, by the time her sentence was up, her father... Cierine and Alexander... everyone she had ever known and cared about would be gone from this earth. She looked around at the courtiers helplessly. There wasn't a soul there to speak up for her. No one to save her from this nightmarish grave she had dug for herself.

Queen Beatrice grabbed hold of the king's sleeve. "My dearest, she does not deserve to walk the same halls as us. Surely death by the pits would be more satisfying for us all."

He shook her off of him. "Tread carefully, *wife*. This halfling girl destroyed one of my fiercest riders today. Samael was right. She may not know how to control it, but there is power in her. Power that we can use to our advantage." Queen Beatrice opened her mouth as if to argue, but thought better of it. Kelera held on to the satisfaction she felt at seeing the king chide his hateful wife like a child in front of the court.

Queen Beatrice clasped her hands together in front of her, and Kelera watched as she dug her nails into her own skin, splitting it open. It was clear that the queen did not like being talked down on in such a manner in front of the court. She was raging inside.

King Cyrus addressed the guards that were still holding Kelera. "Take her to her room. See to it that the remaining servants give her a black dress and mask. She is to serve me directly until Samael is healed. Then I will allow him to deal with her as he sees fit." His tone was final. The courtiers dispersed, off to bed for the day.

Kelera was taken up the stairs and back to the room Samael had given her. She held back her tears as they ushered her into the room and shut the door behind them as they left. Kelera sat on the bed with a hand to her chest. She struggled to breathe as her situation sunk in. She was to be the property of the Unseelie Court for *three hundred years*. Three offenses and three centuries to pay for them.

How was she going to get through this? Time was different here, so perhaps three hundred years would not be the same as it was in Nevene. She clutched tight to the hope that when this was over, she may see her father again. But in order to find out, she would need to apply all of her years of self-control, and wear a mask of obedience beneath the lace mask that taunted her from the bed. If she could do that, then she stood a chance of staying alive in the Unseelie Court long enough to find a way to break the spell keeping her here. She refused to accept that she would never see her father again.

A servant slipped into the room carrying Kelera's new wardrobe. She set it gently on the bed beside her. There were tears on the girl's face. She paused in front of

Kelera. Her voice was a frightened whisper as she asked, "The others... did they..."

Kelera shook her head sadly. "They did not make it. The king's guard slaughtered them at the veil. Mira was the only one who escaped." Kelera was too ashamed to admit that Cierine was the only one who she had been sure to save.

The girl stifled a cry and nodded in understanding. She turned to leave but Kelera stood and grabbed her hand. "Prince Samael?"

The girl's lip trembled as she said, "Alive. They have him in the drawing room with a healer from the Spring Court. Whatever potion you gave him nearly shattered his mind. The healer is attempting to pull him out of it." Before Kelera could ask anything more, the girl pulled away from her and fled from the room. She shuddered to think of what Samael would do to her if the healer was successful.

Alone now, Kelera walked to the window. The sun was bright in the sky. She prayed that Cierine was strolling in the sunlight of Nevene, heading to the safety of their home. The flicker of hope at the idea that her father and Alexander would find a way to her dimmed a little. Even if they found a way through the veil, there was no way King Cyrus would give her up now. Nor did she believe King Tristan would risk a war for her.

She drew the curtains in, darkening the room, and left the window. After finding a simple cotton nightgown in the armoire, she climbed into the bed. Her bed. She held her hands out in front of her and turned them over. Would her power be enough to break the spell King Cyrus had cast on her? She took a deep breath and tried to call on it, but it wouldn't come. There was no spark, only the chill surrounding her in the isolating room. She gave up and pulled the covers over her aching body, snuggling into the deep feather down pillows.

Sleep did not come easy but when it did, she dreamed of Nevene. She was standing in the field of poppies between Rose Manor and the palace. The sunlight was warm on her face, and she breathed in the sweet floral air. She could hear footsteps rustling in the field behind her. When she saw her guest, she smiled. "Alexander."

He returned the smile and held his hand out to her. "Are you coming?"

"Yes, of course." She reached out to him, grasping his strong hand with her own. But when he pulled her in close, it was no longer Alexander. Blond hair was replaced with black hair as dark as the midnight sky. Dark brown eyes were replaced by brilliant green ones as vibrant as the forest in springtime. *Adrastus.*

Kelera awoke with a start. The dream had seemed so real. She wiped the tears from her eyes and pulled the heavy quilts in closer to her. They were the only shield between her and the new life she would soon have to face.

She could see the night sky between a break in the curtains. It seemed the creatures who resided in the Unseelie territory preferred night over day. She would need to get used to that. There was a soft knock on the door, but before Kelera could answer, two servants slipped inside. They said nothing as they entered and Kelera wasn't sure if she should rise from the bed or wait for them to give her direction.

One of the women took a tray to the writing desk and opened the curtains to reveal the starry sky. The blanket of twinkling lights reminded her of the ones she had seen when she had been unconscious under

Prince Adrastus' arrest. The other woman took a steaming bucket into the small washroom and began to fill the tub. She went back to the hall to bring in another and then another until the tub was full to her liking.

She motioned for Kelera to follow her into the washroom. Still, she did not speak. Instead, the woman gestured to her clothes, pretending to remove them. Then she pointed to Kelera and nodded her head vehemently.

Kelera looked at the other woman for help. She explained, "Ditra wants you to remove your clothing so she can wash you."

"I see." Kelera slowly began to remove the nightgown. She covered her bare breasts with her arms as she climbed into the lion claw tub. The water was remarkably warm, and her muscles relaxed as she sank in. Ditra did not waste a second as she began to scrub at Kelera with a soft bristled brush. The soap smelled divine and Kelera found herself grateful. She smiled at the woman, "This is very kind of you, though unnecessary. I can wash myself."

Ditra ignored her as she got to work on Kelera's matted hair. She coated it in a soft salve and weaved her fingers through until the tangles came undone. The other woman lingered in the doorway. "Ditra isn't much for conversation. She is mute."

"Oh, I'm sor—I mean, that must be very difficult."

The other woman sat on the floor with her legs crossed. "It was her punishment for speaking ill of Queen Beatrice."

"Punishment?" Kelera looked at Ditra. The woman narrowed her eyes in hatred at the mention of Queen Beatrice.

The other woman spoke for her. "They took her tongue."

Kelera's stomach turned in disgust. She was glad she had not eaten breakfast yet. She sat forward, splashing water onto the floor. "How am I to survive here?"

There was sympathy in both of the women's eyes. Ditra shot the other woman a look that only she seemed to understand. Noting the look of despair on Kelera's face, she answered, "With our help. We will guide you through life here at the Unseelie Court. You have mortal blood in your veins. And you tried to help the servants who were bold enough to attempt their escape. For that, we will stand with you as your ally."

Kelera appreciated the sentiment, but it didn't bring her as much comfort as she wished. The servant stood and Ditra followed suit, handing Kelera a fresh towel. The woman went to the door to get the empty buckets for Ditra. As she did, she said over her shoulder, "My name is Robyn."

"I appreciate your help. Both of you." Kelera stepped out of the tub and dressed herself in the black gown. Putting on her prisoner's uniform was more difficult than she had anticipated. Every silk tie she fastened was like another dagger in the heart.

The women went to work emptying the tub. They were quiet as they worked.

Her stomach growled, reminding her of the breakfast waiting for her. She walked to the writing desk and sat. The plate was heaping with strips of fried venison and sweet bread slathered with cream. Blackthorn berries rested in a neat pile on top of the cream. Kelera's heart skipped a beat at the sight of them. "W-what is this?"

"It was a special request. From Prince Samael."

Chapter Sixteen

S amael had come out of the madness Kelera's poison had plunged him into. It was crazy for Kelera to have thought that getting through her first day at court would be her biggest worry. She had been foolish to hope that the healer from the Spring Court would fail in nursing the prince back to health while she had slept.

How was she to act as the perfect prisoner if Samael was there to draw out the worst in her? He was cruel, possessive, and now he would be looking for revenge. She'd made a fool of him when she escaped. She'd hurt him physically, but she knew men like him were more angered when it was their pride that was wounded.

As Ditra and Robyn led her down the halls, the fear of what Samael would do to her consumed her entire being. She felt faint by the time they reached the drawing room. Robyn whispered to her, "Keep your head down and choose your words carefully. Nothing will

get you maimed or killed faster than offending them."
She patted Kelera's arm in reassurance. "You will get
through this."

She pushed Kelera gently through the door and disappeared back into the hall. Kelera was on her own now.
The drawing room was crowded. There weren't enough
lounge chairs to hold everyone, so they stood scattered
around with drinks in their hands. She looked around
at the unfriendly faces of the courtiers, realizing she
would find no allies here. What they didn't know was
that this was how it had been often for her back home.

She stood at the door awaiting orders from King
Cyrus, who sat by the fire. Prince Gadreel, Prince Kane,
and Prince Ammon sat in chairs scattered around the
room. They were lost in conversation with the courtiers
and paying no mind to her. Only Queen Beatrice
watched her with cold eyes. She was likely hoping Kelera would make a mistake worthy of punishment at her
own hand. A punishment like the one she had doled out
to poor Ditra.

Kelera jumped as fingers trailed along her neck. A
shadow crept into her view and shifted into a familiar
face. Samael's nostrils flared as he leaned in, only inches
from her. "My, my. Black really does not suit you. Does
it, Father?"

King Cyrus grunted in response as he read silently to
himself from a parchment in his hands. After a thoughtful beat, he looked up at Samael. "Dress her how you
like, but remember, Samael, she is not to be harmed.
Her power is far greater than you let on and if she can
be of use to us, I want her left in one piece." He turned
his attention back to his reading.

Samael pulled her into him. His body pressed against
hers as he said, "Don't worry, Father, I do not have any
intention of harming her. Not yet."

A few of the courtiers snickered at the promise in
his words. Kelera fought the grimace that threatened

to show itself on her face. Instead, she gave him a look of neutrality. Annoyance flickered in his eyes, quickly replaced by a charming smile. He had masks of his own, and she feared what would happen when he decided to remove them.

King Cyrus stood and the courtiers around him scrambled from his path. He looked every bit the malevolent king that he truly was. With all his grunts and dismissive waves, it was easy to forget that this was the man who had raised someone as vicious as Samael. His voice was firm as he said, "Do not let your ambitions cloud your judgment, Samael. It is I who have decided to let the halfling stay under your charge." Black magic rose around him like mist in the forest at night. Kelera could feel it like smoke in her lungs. Instinct told her to get as far from it as she could. King Cyrus continued, "But make no mistake, I will take her from you just as quickly. You will unleash her magic for *my* benefit, not your own."

The king's frightening show of power was the only thing keeping Kelera's temper in check. They were talking about her as if she was nothing more than a tool to be left at their disposal. They weren't keeping her comfortable at court because she was High Fae. They were only allowing her to walk amongst them and their court so they could keep her close. Close enough to manipulate the magic they wanted.

Samael didn't take his eyes from the power emanating from his father, as if he was worried it might lash out at him any second. Kelera watched with interest. It was good to know that some things in this world frightened him.

Samael gave King Cyrus a shallow bow. "As it pleases you, Father."

He led her from the room without a word of goodbye to the courtiers or his family. The atmosphere in the palace had shifted significantly since the last time she had been dragged through it. The halls were brightly lit and buzzing with courtiers and servants. Everyone had a role to play, and they played it well. Kelera found comfort in that, knowing that she could find routine in daily life while she was here. If she could do what they expected of her, then maybe they would drop their guard. If she was patient, then she could find her window of escape.

A male servant walked by them, and Samael grabbed him roughly by the collar of his shirt. "Have the maids gather reds for her. I want them delivered to my quarters." The man gripped the tray he was carrying tightly and gave a curt nod to Samael. Samael pushed him away, causing the man to stumble and the glasses on his tray to rattle. It was an unnecessarily cruel way to ask the man to do something. Could he not just give the verbal command? Or did he find joy in being a bully?

They walked up the grand staircase, and Kelera felt the palace vibrate with magic. The walls shifted when they reached the top to reveal the hallway lined with red doors. To Kelera's relief, she heard no screams coming from behind the doors as she had before. Samael hovered his hand over one of the doorknobs and the lock clicked.

Once inside, Kelera looked around in awe. His quarters were the size of a small manor. There was a large sitting room with numerous velvet couches and small oak tables. She wandered into the room as Samael disappeared into the bed chamber. She ran her hand along the rough-cut wood of the bar that stood to the side of the room. Behind it, there were shelves lined with bottles of fine wine, rum, and whiskey.

Samael still hadn't returned. Unsure of what he expected her to do, she took a seat on one of the couches. There was a book sitting on the table in front of her, so she picked it up and flipped to the last read page. It was titled *Histories of the Seelie Court*.

She had always been curious about the Seelie Court, though she hadn't had the opportunity to learn much about it. The books back home spoke of old wives' tales and accounts from men claiming to have gone into Elfhame. Nothing felt substantial to her. In the books of the Unseelie Court, she had read of a place of grotesque creatures who fed on the flesh of one another. Though she had witnessed the atrocities of Unseelie firsthand since crossing the veil, she knew that the books had not been entirely accurate. There was no anarchy here. They had rules and etiquettes. Though they delighted in violence, High Fae ran a civilized society in their own way.

But what was Samael's interest in the histories of Seelie? His thirst for power over the territories in Unseelie was adamantly clear. He wanted his father's throne and judging by the tension she had just witnessed, he hadn't done a very good job of hiding it.

But what of his interest in the Seelie which ruled over the Spring and Summer Courts?

She flipped through the pages of the book in her hands and read a passage that caught her eye:

The Royal Line

Queen Mabine of the Seelie Court has ruled with a generous hand throughout her time on the throne. Her people have long awaited an heir to present itself, yet the Queen has not had success in this endeavor. Should the Queen not produce a blood heir within her lifespan, then it is left to the court council to appoint one through the blood rites. The safety and prosperity of the Seelie Court relies on this. For many would give all they have to ascend.

The Seelie Queen. Prince Ammon had mentioned that the queen was feeling ill... *The queen will spout a fountain of blood.* Those had been Samael's exact words when he had taken the poison. Did he mean to take Seelie for himself? If he was willing to bring down the mortal world for his own powerful gains, then it wasn't out of the realm of possibility that he would want Seelie as well. And if there was no heir to stand in his way... Kelera shut the book with shaking hands. She was in over her head. Kings and queens, heirs and thrones—these were things she had respected but had never involved herself in. Her place was to serve the court as a lady. To uphold traditions and etiquettes. She wanted a quiet life, not one filled with plotting and grabs for power.

"Learning anything worthwhile?" Samael interrupted her reading. She had been so engrossed in her thoughts that she hadn't seen him return. He fastened the buttons on his black linen shirt, leaving the top two open to reveal his bare chest.

Kelera set the book down on the table and folded her hands neatly in her lap. "I was curious, that's all."

He sat on top of the table and picked the book up. Flipping it open to the passage she had been reading, he asked, "Do you know what happens when a kingdom is left without an heir?"

"The next of kin takes the throne. If not a child of the king or queen, then a sibling, or a cousin..."

"Ah, perhaps in the mortal realm that is how it works. Here in Elfhame, we delight in the fight. Should the king or queen not have a direct blood heir—a child—then claimants of the throne step forward and take part in the blood rites. A battle to the death. Only then will the worthy rise."

"I see." She did see now. He would spread his darkness throughout the entire world if given the chance. No one would be safe from his wrath.

He shut the book and tossed it on the table with a thud. "You hold magic deep within you, though you have never been taught to use it. I am willing to keep you alive and well, long enough to see if that power will be of use to *me* when the time comes. My father realizing your magic is more powerful than I let on does pose a problem. He'll be keeping a more watchful eye on us. But I have my ways of dealing with him."

Kelera clenched her hands together on her lap, trying to focus on them and not on the anger that was rising in her. Samael wanted to weaponize her. But he would be sorely disappointed. She had spent so long suppressing it, that it only came now when she was losing control of her emotions. If she had no control, then there would be no way for her to keep him from taking hold of it. She regretted ignoring her power all these years. If she had known it would come to this, then she would have learned all she could to keep her and her father safe. To keep them all safe. But it was too late for that now.

Samael was looking down at her hands. She couldn't let him see that he was getting to her. Keeping the subject on his father, she said, "King Cyrus seems to be in good health."

"Though I do not exercise it often, I do have patience." Samael went to the bar and poured two glasses of whiskey. "As for you. If you do as I say—if you give me what I want—then perhaps you will have the chance to see your father again. That is what you want, is it not?"

He would have her trade her magic for her freedom. But if he had his way, then her father would lose the world he had dedicated his life to protecting. She wouldn't betray her father's legacy by giving into Samael. She shuddered. She had to find a way to stop him. She took the whiskey as he offered it to her, wrapping her fingers around the cold glass, and sipped at it. It burned in her throat as she choked it down. Samael downed his own in one gulp and wiped his mouth with the back of his hand.

He shrugged on his jacket that donned the king's crest. "I have business to attend to. In the meantime, Gadreel will attend to you. He will show you what is to be expected of you." He reached down and took her by the hair. He was inches away from her face as he warned, "This is my gift to you. Be grateful that I am not resorting to less pleasant methods."

He released her and she held her hand up to where he had pulled at her hair. Gadreel was a far better alternative to Samael, so she made no argument. He gestured for her to join him at the door. Taking her chin in a firm grasp, he gave her one final warning, "I mean it, Kelera. The magic my father holds binds you to the royal family and to *me*. Do not do anything foolish. I may not be able to kill you yet, but I assure you I can make you *beg* for death should you cross me again." His fingers dug into her face.

Steady, she replied, "As you command, Prince Samael."

Satisfied, he swung the door open to reveal Gadreel waiting in the hall. His eyes darted between Samael and Kelera with open curiosity. Samael strode past him. "Keep her in line." Then he was gone. Off to enact whatever plans he had for the future of Elfhame.

"I'd like to say he hasn't always been like that. But thus, I cannot lie." Gadreel gave a small hopeful laugh. Kelera didn't return the good humor. Her chin still hurt from where Samael's fingers had held it tight. And she couldn't shake the feeling that she was caught up in the beginning of a political war.

"What makes him so special? In your father's eyes, I mean. It seems to me he favors him." If Gadreel was willing to talk to her and answer her questions, then this could be her only chance to gather as much information as possible. Information that could prove useful in both her survival and the well-being of the ones she cherished most.

Gadreel lowered his voice and the smile on his face reminded Kelera of the court gossips back home. Maybe getting information wouldn't be as difficult as she thought. He whispered, "He is the spitting image of Father. Cruel, powerful, and determined. I think that makes it easy for my father to love him." They rounded a corner and the palace halls shifted. Kelera worried she would never be able to memorize the palace layout.

She studied the paintings on the walls. They were at odds with the malicious nature of the court. Beautiful portraits of women with soft smiles on their lips and scenes of people dancing naked under a starry sky lined the walls.

They would be nearing their destination soon, so she took the opportunity to press Gadreel further. "Are your brothers not all of those things as well?"

Gadreel chuckled. "Ammon is the oldest. He fancies himself the best choice as father's heir. Many at court love and respect him, but I personally do not see the appeal. He's an arrogant ass, if you ask me."

"And you? Would you not want to be king?"

"No. I would not." Something in the way he said it told Kelera not to push him to elaborate on why.

That explained why Samael had enlisted Gadreel in helping. He could trust that Gadreel wouldn't use take Kelera's magic for himself. She pressed on, "And Kane?"

"Kane is Mother's favorite. He is a brute and an imbecile. Father would never choose him as heir, and he wouldn't have the wits to take the crown from our brothers."

"So, it comes down to Prince Ammon and Prince Samael." The idea of Samael taking control of the Unseelie Court made her stomach roll. He clearly had no respect for the treaty with the mortals... and his talk of wanting all the courts for himself made her uneasy.

"Yes, it will come down to them... and our half-brother, Dras. You remind me of him, you know."

"After my recent run in with him, I am inclined to take that as an insult." She said it jokingly, though she couldn't imagine how being compared to any of the dark princes could be taken as a compliment.

Gadreel laughed again. He was different from the others in that aspect. He laughed easily and wholly. There was something lighter about him than his brothers. She walked beside him as they maneuvered their way through courtiers and servants. The High Fae bowed to him as they passed. He spoke softly so he would not be overheard by eavesdroppers. "I suppose you should know as much as you can if you are to be sentenced to a life in our court." He sighed. "Dras has always taken the brunt of our brothers' brutality. He is strong. Both in strength and in power. Something that wins him favor in Father's eyes. And he is well liked by the people of our realm. My brothers have always been jealous of his abilities. So, they lean on his weaknesses."

Kelera's ears perked at the mention of weakness. If she could learn each of their weaknesses, then she could use that to her advantage. "Which are?"

Clueless of her intent, Gadreel continued, "He is kind. You saw my father's idea of mercy. But Dras truly is a merciful man. He tends to the Lesser Fae when they are in need... cares for them in a way that not many Unseelie rulers have in the past."

"That doesn't sound like weakness to me." They had reached their destination. A large library with a vast collection of books. It was unlike any other she had ever seen. There were balconies rising high above them, with more rows of books and ladders leaning against the shelves. She walked over to one of the large desks and laid her hand on the solid wood.

Gadreel followed, taking up one of the chairs across from her. He propped his feet lazily on the table. "Here in the Unseelie Court, it is."

Kelera sat in the chair across from him and rested her hands on the table. Between Gadreel's trusting nature and the books in the library, she wondered how much information she could access. A loophole in the spell that bound her here to the royal family perhaps...

She wanted to keep him talking while they were still alone. "You said half-brother... who is his mother?"

Gadreel leaned back in the chair, resting his hands behind his head. "Some unlucky maiden of the Seelie Court, though there are more scandalous rumors." He gave her a pointed look. "That is Dras' greatest weakness of all in my brothers' eyes. Tainted blood." He looked at her apologetically. "I didn't mean that as an insult to you."

Kelera shook her head, genuinely unoffended. "Don't worry yourself. I'm used to it. It seems to be a mindset that both the mortals and Fae share."

Gadreel studied her face, then changed the subject. "Are you curious as to why I've brought you to the dustiest room in the palace?" He spread his arms wide, gesturing to the library.

Kelera thought that in another life, she and Gadreel would have been fast friends. He was easy to talk to and not so quick to pass judgment. He was a lot like Cierine in that aspect.

"Consider me intrigued." She leaned forward, propping her elbows on the table so she could rest her chin on her hands.

"This is where your training begins. My father believes it was your magic that caused the blast in the forest that led to the demise of his beast. A beast who, by the way, had it coming. Dreadful creatures, the lot of them."

"Prince Gadreel, I am being truthful when I say that I do not know how to wield magic. Even if it were running in my veins, I would still have no way of intentionally tapping into it."

"Not yet. And just call me Gadreel, please." He rose from his seat and grabbed a stack of books from one of the other desks. He dropped them in front of her. A cloud of dust tickled her nose, and she fought the sneeze that threatened to come. Taking his seat once again, he gestured for her to look through them. "High Fae are taught how to control their magic from a young age. You, sadly, did not have that luxury. So, we start with the basics."

Kelera stared at the stack of books. She had always excelled in her lessons at school. Driven by her need for acceptance in the mortal world, she had learned everything she could about it. From the histories of Nevene, to mathematics, writing, and the like.

Though she doubted her power, she didn't doubt her ability to learn. But could she do it in a way that kept Samael and King Cyrus from using it for their own gains? Doubt was clouding her judgment. She felt like a pawn in a game she hadn't been asked to play. With no other options in front of her, she picked up the book. It was time for her to make her first move.

Chapter Seventeen

K elera had been nose deep in the books for hours. The enormous fireplace that sat centered in the library crackled with heat. Her mask lay on the table to the side, taunting her with the memory of Samael's threats of what would happen if this didn't work. The lace details on the mask had been driving her mad all night and Gadreel had been kind enough to suggest that she remove it.

It was night two of learning magic in the library with him and by now she had read every detail about how it worked in Elfhame. Yet, irritatingly enough, she still couldn't make sense of how to claim it for herself. According to the histories of magic, each Fae was born with a gift bestowed upon them from the very land in which they had been born. A gift of magic weaved together by the elders—an ancient race of Fae who ruled over Elfhame since the beginning of time.

Lesser Fae, like the bogies and the pooka, only had access to minuscule power. They were able to summon small tricks and spells, but never anything that could be matched with the magic that the High Fae held. Gadreel explained it to her in layman's terms. "Magic in Elfhame is tightly woven with the elements. Night is the Unseelie Court. The High Fae here can access elements such as wind and ice. Those of us who are of the old blood, the strongest in our land, can also access the mind. Some can shift into the shadows like Samael. Or control your dreams like Dras."

Kelera thought of the dream she'd had the other day. Alexander's face had turned into Adrastus'. Was that his doing? And the stars she had seen when he'd pressed his palm to her face by the veil...

Gadreel stretched out in his seat and stifled a yawn. "Then there's the Seelie Court, of course. Delighting themselves in Day magic. They wield fire, earth, and water. And the strongest in their ranks can heal with sheer force of will. Though the Lesser Fae and their witches are quite gifted at healing potions in their own right."

"Earth." Kelera half whispered it to herself, remembering when she was a child. She had drawn the roots up from the earth to grab onto the bogie. Something stirred within her, as if her own heart was telling her she should voice what she had known all along.

"Earth?" Gadreel tilted his head in confusion.

Ignoring his question, she asked one of her own, "Gadreel, what sort of magic does your father suspect I have?"

He grinned. "I wondered how long it would take you to ask." His eyes crinkled at the corners as he smiled at her. "Seelie magic."

Kelera grabbed onto the locket hanging from her neck. Her thumb grazed the familiar carvings in it. That would mean her mother was Seelie. Had she known deep down all along? Since coming to the Unseelie Court, there had not been a moment where she could have imagined that these were her people. That this malevolent place was where she had come from. It made sense now.

And the blast in the clearing when she had faced off with the Night Rider. Had that been fire magic? With dots beginning to connect, she felt a small hint of elation. Not enough to rid her of her doubts completely, but it was something.

She raised her hand above the candle sitting on the table between her and Gadreel. She closed her eyes and tried to imagine the flame growing.

Gadreel's voice was steady as he encouraged her, "Welcome the sensation of the fire and latch yourself to it. You are the master, and it is your subject."

Kelera tried to embrace the warmth coming from the candle. She imagined it growing tall and strong, but that's all it was. Her imagination. When she peeked up through her lashes, she saw no change. She felt no change. Frustrated, she pulled her hand away. She hated being out of control.

Gadreel tried to reassure her, "It takes time. Give yourself some grace."

She opened her mouth to tell him it was hopeless, but a knock on the wall beside the open door stopped her.

Gadreel pushed the mask over to her. "Quick, put this on."

She sighed and did as he bid. The servant waiting at the door looked more relaxed in Gadreel's presence. He calmly said, "I am to summon you both to the night's festivities."

Reluctantly, Kelera walked side by side with Gadreel down the hallway. She hated to leave the safety of the library, where they had not been disturbed for hours. As they walked now, she sneaked a sideways glance at the prince beside her. If she didn't know better, she would have been surprised that he was related to Samael at all. His demeanor was softer, though she could still feel the power that he held.

She was almost afraid to ask, "Where are we going?"

"I should have prepared you. For that, I must express my deepest regret." He clenched his hands together, making Kelera nervous about what she was walking into.

A roar of cheers erupted from double doors at the end of the hall. Kelera's heart began to race as they walked down a dark hallway flanked by tall Fae guards. They refused to meet her eye as they stood staring straight ahead.

The pits, she realized with a start. It took every ounce of self-control not to turn and run away.

"Gadreel... am I in danger?" She turned to look up at him so he would be forced to acknowledge her. "Please be frank. Do not twist your words."

He was thoughtful for a moment before answering her, "For the time being... no. You are to be a spectator of tonight's events, not a participant."

Relief washed over her like a cool waterfall. He had chosen his words carefully, though. Samael would not send her into the pits this time. But that didn't mean he wouldn't change her mind, especially if she failed to produce the results he wanted.

She walked obediently beside Gadreel. Tonight, she would observe the horror that took place in the pits. She would watch and learn. So, if the time came, she would know how to survive.

Kelera was stunned into silence. They had walked down into the depths of the palace and come out into an enormous room with a deep cavernous floor made of hard packed dirt, like in her father's training arena.

Her heart began to race uncontrollably the moment they stepped into the crowded stadium. That was when she felt the rush of magic hit her. It was more overwhelming than anything she had felt before, like being caught in the middle of a hurricane. Since she was a child, she could always sense the magic of Elfhame from the creatures who had wandered into the mortal realm. But here she was, engulfed by it. She looked around the stands that surrounded the arena. They were filled with both Lesser and High Fae who stood shoulder to shoulder whooping and shouting with blood lust.

Gadreel led her up to a private box where the royal family was waiting. They were isolated from the rest of the crowd, but Kelera could still see them clearly on either side and across from them. King Cyrus sat lazily on a cushioned chair with a drink in his hand. He ignored Kelera and Gadreel as they took their seats beside Ammon.

Kelera leaned forward to get a better view of the pit down below. It was empty, save for a rack holding various weapons. She spotted a broad sword immediately and took a moment to admire its size. Beside it, she could see axes, throwing knives, and even a whip. Sweat started to bead on her forehead where the red mask was pressed against her face. She itched at it, feeling the anger creep in again at being subjected to something so dehumanizing.

A tray was dropped behind her and Queen Beatrice's high-pitched voice rang in the air, "You stupid little twit!" She slapped the mortal servant who had dropped the tray of hors d'oeuvres. The girl sank to the ground, crying as she picked the food up with her trembling hands. The queen reared back to strike her again, but before she had the chance, Prince Adrastus stepped into the room. He put himself between Queen Beatrice and the servant.

"I believe you've made your point, stepmother." He didn't bend down to help the servant girl, but still stood firmly in place so that Queen Beatrice could not punish the girl further.

"Adrastus," Queen Beatrice practically spat his name out, "how nice of you to join us. What with your busy schedule and all." She put a hand on her bony hip. "Out playing with the riff-raff again?"

He smirked at her, unphased by her spiteful tone. He ignored her and instead addressed King Cyrus with a bow. "Father."

King Cyrus grunted and raised his hand in acknowledgment before holding his glass out for another servant to fill. Adrastus chuckled and walked over to join his brothers. Kelera couldn't take her eyes from him as he took the seat beside Ammon. He was possibly the most handsome man she had ever seen. Even with the scar reaching across the side of his face, he was like the men in the picture books her father had read to her as a child.

She continued to watch him, taking only a moment to sneak a glance in Queen Beatrice's direction. The Queen Consort was staring daggers into Adrastus, though he didn't seem to notice. Queen Beatrice clearly didn't like him. Kelera wondered if it was because of Adrastus' mother, or if the tension between them ran deeper than that. She was interested to see how the other princes were going to behave around him.

Gadreel nudged her in her side and stared at her wide-eyed. "Try not to draw more attention to yourself than necessary."

"I'm not."

"You're staring at him like a love-struck puppy."

Kelera was horrified. "I am not!"

Gadreel snickered and sat back in his seat with his arms crossed over his chest. "I wouldn't blame you. I myself love tall and dark, handsome men, too."

Kelera whispered so only Gadreel could hear her. "In case you've forgotten, *he* is the reason I am sitting here, bound to you and your family."

Gadreel pressed his lips into a thin line and nodded in understanding. He said no more on the subject. Kelera tried her best to return her attention to the pits, but she couldn't shake the feeling that she was being watched. She shot a careful sideways glance in Prince Adrastus' direction and caught his eye. He was watching her with a raised eyebrow and chuckled to himself.

Kelera's blood went hot. There was nothing amusing about her situation. How dare he laugh at her? She clenched her hands together in her lap and refused to look his way again as the crowd erupted in applause.

The doors lining the pit opened to reveal warriors dressed in scant leather armor. Their pointed ears and ethereal appearances told Kelera that they were Fae. Two of the men stepped forward into the pit and threw their arms up, reveling in the cheers from the crowd. The royal family watched silently from the private viewing box. The silence in the small space gave Kelera a chill.

The men below wasted no time in advancing on one another. Ignoring the weapons that were sitting ready for the taking, the men went at each other with brute strength. The way they each anticipated the others' moves was entrancing.

One of the men called upon his magic, summoning a wind so powerful that Kelera could feel it where she sat, though she was high above the pit. It whipped itself into his opponent, knocking him from his feet and into the hard earth. The impact left the man dazed.

Kelera's breath caught in her throat. The precision with which he wielded his magic was remarkable. There was beauty in that sort of power and control. The man performed effortlessly. What if she could do the same?

She sat on the edge of her seat as the Fae who was controlling the winds advanced on his opponent. Not willing to give his challenger the chance to stand again, he called up a dust storm from the ground. He focused it around the other man's head, spinning it like a tornado. The opponent choked as the dust and sand suffocated him.

Before he lost all ability to breathe, he raised a hand in the air. The dust storm stopped as suddenly as it had begun. The match was over, but Kelera could see the blood lust in the eyes of the man left standing. He would have ended the other man's life without a second thought.

She couldn't process the adrenaline she was feeling. She was impressed by the man's skill and had wanted to see how far he could take it. Did that make her a monster? She sat back, ashamed of herself.

A slow clap came from the viewing box entrance. "Splendid. Just splendid." Kelera spun around to see Samael grinning at the gory scene below.

King Cyrus scoffed, "I've seen better." His words were drawn out in a sure sign of his drunkenness.

Samael took the seat on the other side of Kelera. Instinctively, she leaned away from him. He ignored her as the next round began in the pit. This time, it was a man in tattered robes. His ears were pointed, but he did not have the same noble quality about him as the Fae Kelera was currently sitting amongst. There were small spikes protruding from his shaking hands.

To Gadreel, she noted, "He is not a warrior."

Gadreel looked solemn. "No. He is not. He is a Lesser Fae. Brought in from one of the villages in the Autumn Court."

She almost didn't ask because she had a feeling that she already knew the answer. "Who will he be matched with?"

Just as she voiced the question out loud, Prince Kane stepped out from the door. He brandished a long sword. He smiled at the frightened man before him and when he did, magic shimmered along the blade. Kelera watched in sickening fascination as ice crept along the glittering steel. A frost of smoke emanated from it as Kane went after the man.

Kelera was furious. There was no honor in this match. The odds were stacked heavily against the Lesser Fae. She hissed at Gadreel, "This is no match. This is an execution."

Gadreel agreed, "Yes."

"What was his crime?" The man looked harmless enough. She couldn't imagine what he could have done to warrant such a brutal punishment. He didn't stand a chance against a warrior like Kane.

Samael answered, "He offended my mother."

Kelera's eyes narrowed. "Offended her, how?"

"He did not pay tribute to her when we went into the village."

Anger flooded Kelera's senses. She fought the urge to turn her glare on the queen sitting behind her. If that was all it took to offend her royal highness, then Kelera needed to tread more carefully than she thought.

By the time she looked back down at the unfair match, it was over. The man's lifeless body lay on the ground at Kane's feet. It struck Kelera odd that the crowd had not erupted in applause as they had before. An uncomfortable silence filled the air until Samael rose from his seat. He stepped forward so that the observers could see him clearly. "Weakness does not belong in Unseelie! Thank you, brother, for claiming yet another victory for our people!"

Kelera was appalled by the speech. Even worse was when the citizens of Unseelie responded to it. They began to clap and hoot. She wasn't sure if it was from fear of the royal family or if they truly believed the ugly words Samael said.

He returned to his seat beside Kelera. "No applause?"

Kelera chose her words carefully. "I'm just taking it all in."

"You do not agree with our methods." He said it matter-of-factly.

His mood shifted when she didn't respond. He sat back in his seat, throwing back drink after drink as new matches came and went. He was sulking like a child. Kelera couldn't understand why he cared what she thought of it all. She was nothing more than a new toy to him.

He was deep in his cup when he spoke again. "You are no better than us, you know."

Kelera scoffed in response to the ridiculous accusation. "I do not bully and beat my way through life."

"I watched you. After we met that first night. I saw what you are truly capable of—the hatred that resides deep within your heart. You would have killed that man in your father's training field and would have unleashed your wrath again when that knight confronted you at the tournament, had my bastard brother not interfered."

Kelera narrowed her eyes at him. "You were there when those men confronted me both times?"

"Oh, my darling little pet." He leaned in close. His eyes were glazed over, and she could smell the stench of ale on his breath. "I am the reason why they confronted you." He leaned back in his chair lazily. "It was simple, really. Their fear of you was already so close to the surface. Ripe and ready for me. I only had to tug slightly for it to make them lash out at you." He tugged at the air with one of his hands.

He was bragging. Kelera felt heat creep along her skin. She could feel the magic surrounding her in the arena intertwined with the magic strumming through her veins. Magic that threatened once again to overpower her. She had spent the last couple of days longing for her magic to make an appearance and it chose *now* to do so? The moment when she was closest to the very man who wanted it for himself. She tried to push it away before Samael took notice. Closing her eyes, she thought of home. Of her father's smile. She focused on the way Alexander's lips had felt on her hand when he kissed it.

The heat of her magic remained still, begging to be released. She thought of the life she and Alexander could have if she could just survive this. Would it be enough? That quiet life she'd dreamed of. She had been adventurous once upon a time. And even just now, in this dark, enchanted place, part of her had enjoyed the fight in the pits between the well-matched High Fae.

The traitorous thoughts caught her off guard and she felt the magic flow to her fingers. The distraction wasn't working. Not until her thoughts shifted away from Alexander to the way Adrastus' body had felt on top of hers when he'd tackled her in the forest. The way he had pressed his hand firmly against her mouth to keep her quiet... And with those memories, just like a candle being snubbed, so too was the magic threatening to give her away.

When the final match ended, Kelera was drained mentally and emotionally. She was trying to grapple with her view of the pits. At first, it had been thrilling to see the High Fae wield magic at one another. But on the other hand, she couldn't rid herself of gruesome images of the mortals and Lesser Fae that had been brought in on occasion. It was sickening to think that they would inflict the pits on those who didn't have the means to defend themselves in them. Even as she walked beside Samael to the drawing room, the stench of blood and sweat lingered in her nose.

The only thing she took solace in was the absence of the overwhelming magic she had felt coming off the crowd in waves. Calmer now, she took a seat on the couch beside Gadreel. Kane and Queen Beatrice sat across from her. They leaned into one another, whispering. Kelera watched the intimate way the two of them acted with one another. Queen Beatrice laughed at something Kane said and put a hand on his chest. She caressed it with her long, well-manicured fingers, making Kelera look away uncomfortably.

A smooth, deep voice came from behind her. Adrastus leaned down near her ear as he said, "He's her favorite."

"I don't envy him." Kelera's eyes went wide as the words slipped from her mouth. To her relief, no one else in the room seemed to notice.

Adrastus rounded the couch to join them, taking the seat beside her. His weight shifted the cushions, causing her to fall into him slightly. She righted herself and glanced over at Samael. It had been clear to her from the beginning when they gave her the red mask that he didn't like his things to be played with by others. He paid her and Adrastus no mind, though, as he focused on a heated discussion with Ammon and King Cyrus. The three of them sipped from crystal glasses near the fireplace. Occasionally, they would begin shouting at one another before falling back into a calmer tone.

She moved over to give Adrastus more room. Surprising her, he leaned in close to whisper, "I hope you're being careful."

"I don't see why that's your concern." She looked at him in accusation. *Pompous ass,* she thought to herself. If he had let her go, she would be home with Cierine right now.

His nose flared, and he spoke low. "They may not be treating you like a servant, but you *are* their prisoner. Do not let them lure you into a false sense of security."

"I can take care of myself." She didn't need him or his warnings.

He laughed and leaned back with his hands behind his head. "Well, you've done a marvelous job of it so far." He propped his feet up on the ancient oak coffee table and dropped the subject. Turning his attention to Gadreel, he asked, "How was your day, brother?"

Gadreel turned to answer, putting his arm on the back of the couch behind Kelera. She was all too aware of how close the men were to her. At home in King Tristan's court, men and women would separate for the evening to drink and play cards. It was much more informal here. She couldn't deny, though, that she was glad none of the courtiers had joined them. It struck her as odd, but at the same time, she felt a sense of comfort. There were no eyes to watch her aside from the royal family, and as long as they were occupied with one another, she wouldn't have to make meaningless small talk.

She sat idly by as Adrastus and Gadreel talked of their day. It wasn't until Gadreel asked Adrastus where he had been that her ears perked up at the conversation. He shook the question off. "I was just helping out a friend."

Gadreel scoffed, "Father will not like it..." He took a long drink from his glass.

"Father does not have to know." Adrastus smiled broadly at Gadreel, but Kelera didn't miss the threatening tone in which he said it.

Gadreel shrugged and walked away to stand closer to the fire. He held his hands out near the flame. Kelera watched in fascination as he molded shapes from it. Small animals began to dance around, casting shadows on the walls. Kelera envied the way he could turn something as dangerous as fire into something so beautiful.

Adrastus turned his attention back to her. "It's incredible, isn't it?"

She looked down at her hands placed neatly in her lap, embarrassed that he had caught her staring. "I suppose it is rather impressive."

He rolled his eyes and threw back his drink. "Do you always do that?"

"Do what?" She looked at him now. His eyes bore into hers, and she was mesmerized by the rings around his pupils. They were vibrant, with three shades of green. The same eyes from her dream, like looking at a forest in the springtime.

He elaborated, "Work so hard to say the right thing. Granted, in your short time here, you've let your temper get the better of you. But it doesn't take magic to see how much you beat yourself up for it. Why allow yourself to wallow in your shortcomings? Nobody can be perfect all the time."

"I can." It was a faint whisper, and she wasn't sure why she had said it. It was a lie. She was far from perfect. But it was embarrassing to admit, when she had spent her entire adult life trying to say and do all the right things.

"What a tiring existence." His feet hit the floor, and he set his glass on the table with a thud before walking away.

She wanted to be angry with him for judging her, but she couldn't muster the strength for it. A small part of her agreed with him. But what other choice did she have? Being the perfect prisoner would keep her alive here in Unseelie. Being the perfect lady would maintain her position at court in the mortal realm. Both required her to sacrifice a piece of herself. But both were necessary. Someone like Prince Adrastus would never understand.

Chapter Eighteen

"**A** gain." Gadreel waved one hand at her and pressed the other to his temple as he paced the library.

Sweat beaded at Kelera's brow. She could sense the presence of her magic, but it was just out of reach. It was like walking in the rain and trying to grab the raindrops. Angry with her eighth fruitless attempt, she swiped the book of spells from the table. "It's not working! We've been at this for days and have yielded no results. Face it. I do not have the sort of power Samael and your father believe I possess."

She was past frustration at this point. As hard as she tried, she couldn't summon the magic on command. There were times when she could sense it, like now, sitting just beneath the surface. A tingling heat that strummed in her veins. But here, in the library, it was always out of grasp.

"You need to try harder. *Feel* it. Not in the sense that you recognize that it's there. Rather, you need to become one with it. Imagine that it is an extension of you. Like another limb..." Concern clouded Gadreel's eyes. He was nervous, though he wouldn't voice it out loud. Kelera knew King Cyrus and Samael were pressuring him. She had overheard them arguing just that morning. Just after Samael had broken a vase in her room. He wasn't going to wait forever for her and Gadreel to figure this out. She feared that soon he would make good on his threats and use other means of getting what he wanted out of her.

"I'm afraid." It was the first time she had said the words out loud, but it was the truth.

Gadreel stopped pacing. "You cannot afford to let your fear hold you back. Keeping your power hidden away in the mortal court may have been the right thing to do... but here, you need to embrace it." He crossed the room until he stood in front of her. "Listen to me carefully, Kelera. There are forces at play that threaten not only this realm, but the next."

She clenched her fists at her sides, thinking of Samael's plans. "You mean the mortal realm." How much did he know? Gadreel loved his fair share of gossip and she wondered what whispers he'd heard amongst the courtiers as a result. Did any of them know just how far Samael was willing to go to get what he wanted?

Gadreel's jaw twitched as he said, "If you are to survive long enough to help your people, then you will need your magic."

"You and I both know that King Cyrus and Samael only want my power for their own gain. If they can take it from me, then they can do whatever they want with it." That was what frightened her most of all. She was already their captive. She couldn't allow herself to become their weapon as well.

Gadreel lowered his voice. Even though they were alone, it always felt as if someone were listening in the shadowy corners. "That is precisely why you need to learn to control it. So that no other may ever be able to control *you*. My father and brother are a lot of things. They are callous, cruel, and ambitious. But they underestimate you. They believe if you can open the door to your magic, then they will be able to force you into obedience." He chuckled softly. "You do well at appearing to be the compliant and poised lady, but something tells me that there is more to you than meets the eye. It is *my* belief that if you can get a grasp on all of this, then you will be a force to be reckoned with."

His candor was disarming. He had a way of making her feel less alone here in the Unseelie Court, but could she consider him an ally?

She put a hand on his arm. "I am trusting you, Gadreel. I hope you know I do not give this trust easily."

He patted her hand. "I am not the only one looking out for you. You may not see it yet, but not all here in the Unseelie Court are like Samael. Some of us believe in a better world. One that doesn't involve his vision of violence."

Wordlessly, Kelera picked up the book she had thrown on the ground. Tears welled in her eyes. "I've spent so much time denying my Fae nature. It is not something I can easily let go."

"Fae nature is no different from human nature, Kelera. The only difference, aside from the magic, is that humans try to be what they think others *want* them to be when they should just be themselves." He gestured for her to sit with him, and she did. He wiped away the tears that had slipped from her eyes and continued, "If the mortals blame your downfalls on your 'Fae nature,' then it is only because it is a way for them to explain what they do not understand. They are superstitious fools."

Kelera laughed and dried her eyes with her sleeve. "So, you're saying I should just be myself?"

He sat back with a satisfied grin. "Precisely."

"What if I don't know who I am anymore?"

"Then, my dear friend, it is time for you to figure it out." He reached across the table and poured her a cup of tea. "Let's take a break. Tell me about this fiancé of yours."

Kelera's heart skipped a beat. "How do you know about him?"

He slid the teacup across the table, and she sat down to accept it. "Samael has a big mouth. Now, tell me, do you love him? This lord who you have agreed to be tied to for as long as you both shall live?"

"You sound as if you disapprove." She raised an eyebrow as she sipped her tea.

"The eternal magic of Elfhame allows us Fae to live a long time. To commit yourself to one soul for eternity is a very serious thing. Most Fae have several great loves in their lifetime."

"I admit, I care for Alexander. And I believe I could love him one day."

"One day," Gadreel mused. "But not today."

"I didn't say that." It felt disloyal to talk about Alexander this way. Their betrothal meant she owed him her allegiance. Admitting that she didn't love him yet to an Unseelie Prince, even if he was becoming her friend, gave her a strange feeling in the pit of her stomach. Deciding to turn the tables on him, she asked, "And what of you? Have you experienced any of these great loves you speak of?"

He winked at her. "Perhaps."

Brilliant green eyes flashed in her mind, and she asked, "What of Adrastus?" She regretted the question as soon as it escaped her lips. The pit in her stomach grew twice as big. To be thinking of Adrastus at all seemed like another act of disloyalty to Alexander. But there was something about that particular Prince of Darkness that wouldn't allow her to shake him from her mind.

"He is the youngest of us. Though we all hold on to our youth for centuries, Adrastus is indeed as young as he looks. He's your age, actually. So, no. He has not found his first great love yet."

Kelera set her tea down. "Well, it is fortunate then for him that he has centuries to find it."

Gadreel eyed her as he finished his tea. "Yes, indeed."

Kelera stabbed a pea with her fork. She was too consumed by her thoughts to eat or to pay any attention to the banter at the dinner table. Each day had been the same. Breakfast at nightfall in her room. Topped with the dark berries that Samael liked to taunt her with as a cruel reminder of who was in charge.

Then lessons with Gadreel. She found solace in her time spent in the library. They would comb through the dusty books, eat lunch together, and exchange trivial small talk. Their time spent there was pleasant enough.

It wasn't until the late hours of the night that the dread of her situation would set back in. Dinner with the royal family, followed by whatever festivities the king had planned. The nights in which the pits were the main event were the worst. The matches between the High Fae were interesting enough to watch, but they were always most certainly followed by mortals or Lesser Fae being set upon by warriors like Prince Kane. Those poor souls didn't stand a chance and Kelera saw no sport in it.

Samael was also growing more restless. He delighted in brutalizing the servants for Kelera to see. Each time his eyes would meet hers in a look that said *I can do the same to you.*

She rubbed her temples. She had a blistering headache and wasn't sure if it was from her failed attempts at magic or the looming festivities of the night. Tonight, she had been promised the party of a lifetime.

The King's Revel. It came once a week. A grand feast in which every creature of the Unseelie realm was welcomed into the palace for hours of drinking, dancing, and general debauchery.

Kelera felt Queen Beatrice watching her from across the dinner table. She and Prince Kane were already drunk and finding amusement in toying with the help. One of the servant girls sat on Kane's lap while feeding grapes to the queen. Kelera focused on the plate in front of her. It was difficult to watch the way in which they treated the mortals.

When they weren't punishing them for every little mistake, they were stringing them along like playthings. King Cyrus, as usual, paid hardly any attention to his family. With a glass of wine in hand, he shuffled through a stack of parchments. Occasionally, he would grunt in acknowledgment when one of his sons said something to him.

Adrastus was the only one missing each night. She hadn't seen him since the night in the sitting room. But his family didn't seem to mind his absence as they ate together. She pushed the roasted potatoes slathered in a dark gravy around her plate. The herbs and spices smelled divine, but she was too lost in thought to eat.

Adrastus was infuriatingly difficult to figure out. An outcast amongst his own family, her savior in the woods, and the one who doomed her to his father's sentencing. At least she knew where the other members of the royal family stood. She knew what they wanted and had a vague idea of what they were each willing to do to get it. He, on the other hand, was a wild card. That made her uneasy.

A servant stepped between Samael and Kelera to fill their glasses. As he backed away, he knocked into Kelera's glass. The dark red wine spilled along the table and onto her red dress. The servant gasped and grabbed one of the napkins with a shaking hand. He dabbed at the table as Kelera wiped at her dress.

She tried to reassure him. "It's fine, no harm done."

But the man screamed in agony. Kelera felt sick as she watched Samael dig his fork into the servant's hand. The man screamed again as Samael pulled it back out. With an air of superiority, he said, "You are dismissed for the night."

Kelera stared down at the tablecloth, now stained with wine and blood. Through gritted teeth, she said, "That was unnecessary. It was an honest accident on his part." She tried to steady her rapid breathing as she glared at Samael. She could feel the buzz of her magic. Had she been alone with Gadreel, she would have welcomed it gladly. But not here, where Samael and King Cyrus could see.

"You do not tell *me* what is necessary."

Kelera had to hold her tongue. If he saw that drawing out her anger was also drawing out her magic, then all of her hard work at controlling it would be for nothing. The family was watching them now in anticipation. She wouldn't give them the satisfaction of giving Samael any reason to punish her as well. She stared back down at her plate, trying to avoid looking at the dark stains on the table beside her.

King Cyrus gave the signal for them to disperse once they finished eating. Kelera followed Samael through the halls. The palace was more crowded than usual as guests began to arrive for the night's event. The servants bustled around them in preparation. They expertly executed their details, having perfected their routines after years of performing the same duties.

When they reached his quarters, he barked at her, "Get in." When she didn't move fast enough, he shoved her through the door. "Put it on." She went to the box he was gesturing to on the table and opened it. Her eyes widened in surprise when she saw the dress inside. It was midnight black with glittering red jewels gracing the sheer bodice. She had worn many beautiful gowns throughout her life at court, but none compared to this. She lifted the dress out of the box and started toward the washroom so she could change.

"Here." Samael's voice was firm. "Put it on, here."

Kelera's nose flared in anger. He would subject her to humiliation, and she would have to obey or risk the wrath she witnessed at the dinner table. With her back to him, she unlaced the red gown she wore. As she undid the ties at the top, it slipped to the ground, leaving her standing vulnerable in nothing but her silk undergarments. She held her breath, praying to anyone in the universe who was listening that he would do nothing more than watch her.

"The slip too," Samael said from behind her.

Reluctantly, she let the only thing covering her body fall to the ground. She stood naked and at his mercy now. Quickly and with trembling hands, she pulled the black gown on.

The bodice was sheer, showing her naked skin beneath. She held her breath as Samael stepped forward to fasten the ties in the back. His hands were like ice as they brushed against her. He tightened it, pulling the red jewels taut across the front of her. They were numerous and glittering, trailing along her chest all the way down to her hips where the bodice met the skirt. To her relief, they prevented anyone from catching a true glimpse of her breasts and torso.

Samael turned her to face him. "Tonight, the most influential leaders of the realm will be attending. You will play the obedient lady." He stalked to the bar and poured them each a glass. "Something that should be easy for you." There was a hint of annoyance in his tone. "And you will not breathe a word of what you know." He handed her the glass. As she took it, he grabbed her by the wrist. "For if you do, I will do more than watch you undress. Are we clear?"

She met his gaze with her own challenging one. "Why tell me anything at all if you are worried I will repeat it?"

"Because you are a survivor. You do what you must, in order to stay safe. And if you want to continue spending your days safe in the library with my weakling of a brother, then you will do as I say."

Kelera could see in the way his hungry eyes roved over her that he was thriving on the knowledge that he was in control. He seemed confident that she wouldn't risk stirring up trouble for herself. He had cleverly given her a taste of safety by allowing Gadreel to oversee her magic lessons, so she would know that he could just as easily take that sense of security away. It was manipulative and made her hatred for him grow.

Once he finished readying himself for the party, he led her down to the grand ballroom. The marble floors were sleek and shining under the light of the golden chandeliers. A band of strange horned creatures played a lively tune. Kelera stared at their pale blue skin, wondering what sort of Fae they were.

Courtiers mingled with one another, drinking, and laughing without a care in the world. Meanwhile, Lesser Fae she had never seen before danced with wild abandonment. They linked arms with one another, rejoicing in the revel their king had thrown in their honor. How easily they forgot of their neighbors who were plucked from their homes and slain for entertainment in the pits.

Samael left her in the corner to speak with two High Fae with tanned skin, dressed in bright gowns. They stuck out amongst the dark tones that the court of Unseelie favored. Gadreel joined her with an offering of refreshment. She wrinkled her nose at the bronze liquid in her glass. It shimmered with the signs of magic.

"Don't worry. It's not poisoned." He winked at her. "It's a special recipe of mine, meant to enhance the senses. Colors will become more vibrant, and you will feel the music within your very marrow. It's fun. You'll see."

Kelera had never been one to lose control to drunken inhibitions. She held the drink in her hands, unsure if she wanted to take the risk of drinking the potion. She changed the subject without taking a sip. "Who is Prince Samael talking to?"

"Emissaries from the Summer Court. Seelie residents visit from time to time. An effort on the Seelie Queen's part to keep up relations between our court and hers. And after all, who can resist a good party?" He grinned at her before leaving to join a gorgeous man with golden brown skin and rich auburn hair. The man pulled Gadreel to the dance floor, and they lost themselves in the song. Kelera was entranced by the way they moved together in perfect harmony to the rhythm of the music.

"You do not want to share in the ecstasy of the occasion?" Adrastus' voice came from behind her. He stalked around her, taking in the gown that slinked along her curves. He didn't look half bad himself, dressed in a stunning midnight blue jacket with silver stars embroidered on the cuffs.

She tried to avert her gaze, but struggled as she said, "I don't like to lose control."

He scoffed, "That much, you have made exceedingly clear. But you should know, the drink in your hand does not have the same effect as alcohol. It simply acts as an enhancer to what is already around you. It can be quite divine under the right circumstances."

"And is this the right circumstance?" She raised an eyebrow at him as he circled around her.

He leaned in close. His breath was hot on her neck. "I prefer to save it for more... intimate occasions."

A shiver crept down her spine, but it was not in the way that Samael brought shivers to her. Adrastus didn't make her uncomfortable. Rather, she wondered what it would be like to feel *his* hands on her back.

She banished the thoughts away when she noticed Samael regarding them with curiosity. "Your brother is watching. Are you trying to make trouble for me?"

Adrastus pulled away from her and said, "No." The band slowed to a soft melody. The Fae on the dancefloor fell into a graceful waltz. "But surely he would not object to one little dance." He offered his hand to her. She met Samael's eyes from across the room. She gritted her teeth. It was not worth the risk.

"I appreciate the offer, but I think I would rather stay here."

Adrastus growled in frustration, surprising her at the sudden change in his demeanor. "Could you stop that for just one moment?"

"Stop what?" She knew she shouldn't take the bait, but she could still feel Samael's eyes on her, and it was unsettling.

Adrastus drew her attention away from Samael as he stepped into her line of vision. There was an edge to his voice as he said, "Stop pretending."

"I am not pretending." Kelera's own words did not even convince herself.

"Do not lie to me, *little thief*. You have been flutter-ing around this castle like a delicate butterfly for days. Obediently taking your magic lessons, sitting through dinners with my wretched family, and witnessing the atrocities they inflict on the mortal servants. Do not act as if you are content to spend centuries living like this. You may be able to fool them, but you do not fool me. You're holding back because you are afraid."

Had he been watching her? Her voice sounded small as she asked, "Why do you care? As I've said before, you had your chance to help me, and you threw it away."

A dark strand of hair fell into his face. He pushed it back and turned without another word. Kelera stood by as he grabbed the hand of a tall, beautiful woman and led her to the dance floor. In his absence, Kelera felt empty.

She wandered aimlessly through the revel, hoping that it would soon come to an end. The princes were occupied with the guests, leaving Kelera to her own devices. She approached a group of young Fae from the village. Their appearance was not much different from the courtiers apart from the blue pallor of their skin and the smooth horns protruding through the tufts of dark hair on their heads.

They were huddled together, snickering. Kelera inched closer to them, wanting to know what had them all so amused. She pretended to admire a large oil painting nearby. The snickering turned to outright laughter, and she heard one of them say, "The man was downright gullible! 'Twas his own fault for thinkin' an icicle would be a cure all."

Another in the group, shorter than the rest, caught her eavesdropping. There was cheer in his voice as he said, "Are you as gullible as the rest, milady?"

Kelera's cheeks turned red at being caught listening in. She tugged at the mask on her face self-conscious-ly and stepped into their fold. "I've been called many things, sir, but gullible has never been one of them."

The group of men barked with laughter. It was strange not to feel as if they were laughing *at* her, but rather *with* her. The shorter man nudged her in the arm. "Our loss!"

A servant came around with a tray of drinks and one of the taller men graciously handed one to her. She smiled at the gesture, happy to be included instead of snubbed as she had been so many times in King Tristan's court.

The man asked, "How've ye been enjoying yer time here in his majesty's palace?"

Kelera took a long drink from her glass, buying herself time before giving an answer to the bright-eyed group of men. "It has been... an education."

The men eyed one another knowingly. The short one held his hand out to her to shake. It was so pale that it was almost blue, with long nails that looked frighteningly close to claws. She paused before accepting. He beamed up at her. "Name's Gilby, milady. That there's Tobias." He pointed to the taller one who had been telling the story about the icicle. "And the rest o' the lot ain't important enough for introduction."

The men he was referring to laughed haughtily before dispersing to grab hold of the women standing on the sidelines of the dance floor. They dragged them out and began dancing to the lively music. Gilby and Tobias remained with Kelera.

She was curious about the good-natured creatures standing before her. They weren't at all what she expected of the residents of Unseelie's Winter Court. "You are from the village?"

"We are!" Gilby puffed out his chest proudly. "Grown up in these parts. The two of us are well respected members of the community."

Adrastus came up from behind. "And here poor Kelera thought the Fae couldn't tell a lie."

Tobias snorted as he laughed and clapped Gilby on the back. "Dras has got ye there!"

Kelera was puzzled. "Is that not true?"

Tobias smirked. "It is not within our customs to lie. But that doesn't stop cheeky buggers like Gilby here from twistin' the truth from time to time."

Gilby held his hands up in defense. "Well, you lot respect me, do ye not?"

Adrastus chuckled. It was a pleasant sound that made Kelera's heart skip a beat. He nodded in agreement with Gilby. "Aye, my friend. We respect you."

Tobias rolled his eyes. "Oh, now ye've done it. His ego is sure to grow three sizes." He poked at Gilby's chest and said, "Come now. Let's see if we can find some women to deflate it."

Kelera laughed as they went to join their friends on the dance floor. Adrastus stepped closer to her. "They're harmless, really."

She raised her chin. "I can see that for myself."

"Ever the keen observer, aren't we?"

She turned her head to find that he was studying her face thoughtfully. She straightened. "Yes, well, learning from one's surroundings can keep them out of trouble if done right."

"Of course. You wouldn't want to stand out." There was sarcasm in his voice.

"Standing out is exactly what will put me in danger." She thought of the Seelie magic that Samael hungered for.

"Or it could very well be the one thing that can protect you."

She turned, ready to ask what interest he had in whether or not she could protect herself, but he was already gone. Not interested in taking part in the indulgences as the others were, Kelera wandered around the room aimlessly. She admired a large tapestry with an interesting scene of a woman rising from an ice-covered lake. The sword she held in her hand was nearly as long as she was. And a soft smile graced her beautiful face.

A young boy, no older than fifteen, joined her. He was frail and coughed before he spoke. "The lady of the lake. Tis' one of my favorite tales."

Kelera welcomed his company. "She is certainly beautiful."

"Legend says she rose from the lake to give the King of Unseelie the gift of strength and the Queen of the Seelie Court beauty."

Kelera was about to ask him more, but another boy bumped into him. He fell into a fit of coughing as he tried to right himself. The boy who had run into him sneered. "Watch it, weakling." He sauntered away to join his friends, barking with laughter at something they said.

Kelera called for a servant to get the boy some water. "Are you alright?"

"Fine, milady. I'm used to it." A blush formed along the bridge of his nose.

"No one should have to be used to cruelty." She placed a comforting hand on his arm. "There is nothing wrong with being different."

"Weakness of any form is not welcome in Elfhame, milady. Especially not since the princes opened the pits..." He trailed off, and Kelera noticed a few courtiers listening in. He gave her a small bow and then scurried away.

Kelera bit her lip. She understood the boy's situation all too well. The people of Unseelie, the villagers, were not the monsters she had feared. But that seemed to only put them in danger when the royal family believed in an infallible court. As she scanned the room, she saw them laughing and embracing one another. Dancing and sharing drinks with lighthearted smiles spread across their strange faces.

Melancholy befell her as she thought of her mother. Did she attend revels like this in whichever court she hailed from? Did she embrace the good of her people while overlooking the bad, just as Gadreel did? It was hard not to think of her mother here in Elfhame. Three hundred years was a long time for a half mortal girl. Would their paths cross at some point in that time? Even if they did happen upon one another, Kelera doubted very much that they would even recognize each other.

She was moving on to look at a different tapestry when there was a shout from across the room. The young Winter Fae she had just spoken to moments ago was lying on the floor with blood trickling from his mouth. Kelera's heart skipped a beat, and she felt her palms begin to sweat. Samael was standing over the boy with a fierce look on his face. He shook out his fist, bruised from striking the boy.

Gilby pleaded with him, "Please, your Highness, he didn' mean nothin' by it."

Samael raised his voice. "Stay out of it, or join him on the floor." He turned his attention back to the battered boy. "You think the pits are distasteful? You would have the strongest of us cower like you?"

Kelera gasped. The courtiers must have overheard them talking. But even so, he hadn't said anything to warrant this sort of brutality. It was her fault the conversation had come up at all. She felt sick with guilt.

Adrastus strode past her, and she followed quickly, running to catch up with him. The party goers in the room were giving Samael a wide berth. Gathered just close enough to see, but far enough that they were safe from the flurry of the dark prince's wrath.

Samael reared his foot back as if to kick the boy while he was down. Guilt drove Kelera, and she stepped forward before anyone else had the chance. She blocked Samael's path. "Hasn't he had enough?"

Samael's eyes went wide with amusement. "Ladies and gentlemen. I give you Lady Kelera. Gallant hero of the fools." The crowd laughed at the jest, and Kelera crossed her arms defensively.

Adrastus stepped in. "That's enough, brother."

Samael bared his teeth. "Oh, I'm just getting started." He gestured grandly to Kelera. "You see, the halfling standing before you in my colors, came to court to play savior to the mortals. But now finds herself subjected to the very same ridicule and shame as they were." He looked Kelera in the eyes. "Tell me, was it worth it?"

Kelera thought of Cierine. Safe on the other side of the blackthorn veil, no doubt in her husband's arms as they spoke. *Yes,* she thought, *it was worth every moment of this.* But out loud, she said nothing. Frustration flashed in Samael's eyes. A warning sign that he had wanted her to rise to the bait.

The room fell into an uncomfortable silence. All the good cheer that had filled it moments ago was now gone. Samael stepped forward and grabbed her by the arm. Through gritted teeth, he said, "Step aside, or be cast down with him at my feet." When she didn't move, he pushed her so hard that she fell onto the floor beside the bleeding boy.

Queen Beatrice interjected. Signaling for the guards, she commanded, "Six lashes for the boy's offense."

Kelera looked around at the party goers, but none spoke up in the boy's defense. Their shoulders were hunched, hoping to shrink away from the situation entirely. Their eyes were wide as they watched the guards take hold of the boy. He begged them, "Please, yer Highness, I didn' mean nothin' by it. I didn', I swear it!"

The royal family had gathered now around Samael and Queen Beatrice. All except for Adrastus, who was standing between the guards and Gilby's group of friends. They were seething with anger and clenched their fists as they watched the boy being forced onto his knees.

Adrenaline coursed through Kelera. She pleaded with the King and Queen, "He's just a boy! He did nothing to deserve this punishment."

Queen Beatrice looked down on her in disgust. "The sooner you realize we do not need a cause to rule as we see fit, the better."

A tall guard stepped forward. His footsteps sounded like thunder in Kelera's ears. He unwound the long whip in his hands and struck the boy with a blow so powerful that it echoed through the room.

Kelera felt bile rise in her throat at the sight of the welt forming on the boy's back. She had to stop this. The boy was a villager. And a sickly one at that. How could he survive the conditions of a hard day's labor in the cold if he was carrying six lashes on his back?

The guard hit him again, drawing gasps from the crowd. The ladies of the revel held their hands to their hearts and mouths in horror. Even the men's pale skin looked ashen as they stood by and watched one of their own receive the unfair punishment.

The boy had taken three lashings now and Kelera could see his eyes rolling as if he would lose consciousness soon. Would they stop this madness if he did? Or would they beat his lifeless body to a pulp?

Something came over her and as the guard drew back to give him another lash, she shouted, "I'll take them!"

Samael held a hand up, stopping the guard from striking the boy again. There was a hint of amusement in his voice as he asked, "You'll what?"

Her voice shook as she spoke. "Take the rest of the lashes. I'll take the remainder of the boy's punishment if you'll give me your word that it will be the end of it. He'll be free to go home to his family unharmed any further." She wasn't sure she herself would survive the lashings, but the boy looked so broken after the first three, she could not sit by and watch him come to further harm.

Samael shouted to the guard, "You heard her! She would take the punishment in his place and I for one would be very amused to see it."

Adrastus growled in warning from where he stood. "Samael."

Their eyes met in a challenge. But Samael did not balk. "Would you step in then?"

Adrastus began to remove his shirt in acceptance and stepped forward. But Queen Beatrice stopped him, "Do not take another step, *Adrastus*. It is mine and your brother's sentence to dole out, and I do not consent to *you* taking the boy's place. Kelera thinks herself the hero of this story. Let her see where that gets her." She nodded to the guards.

They shoved the boy aside and pulled Kelera into his place. Gilby and the others helped the frightened boy to his feet as tears streamed down his face. Gilby and Tobias were looking at her with sorrow filled eyes as the guards untied the ribbons on the back of her bodice. They moved it to reveal her bare back.

Her eyes met Adrastus' just as the first crack of the whip cut into her skin. Kelera held in a scream as the agony of it washed over her. Adrastus shouted for them to stop and rushed forward but something blocked him suddenly. He roared in pain as shadows twisted around him.

He was on his knees now, held in place by the shadowy magic coming from Samael. She didn't break her hold on Adrastus' eyes as the second crack of the whip tore through her. She bit the inside of her cheek as she struggled to stay quiet. She wouldn't give them the satisfaction of crying out. The metallic taste of blood pooled in her mouth and tears threatened her eyes.

One more. Only one more to go. She braced herself as the third and final snap of the whip met her back. The pain was accompanied by a flood of heat, and light began to seep from her fingertips. She clenched her hands into fists trying to hide her magic, but the searing agony was too much. As her vision went black, she heard Adrastus call out her name.

Chapter Nineteen

Cold hands poked and prodded at Kelera. Someone dabbed at her face with a cool cloth, breaking
through her fever. Searing pain shot through her back
as she tried to move. She fell face first into the pillow
and screamed into it as someone touched her wounds.
The pain was like fire, but soon cooled as the salve they
placed on her began to do its work.

Robyn's voice was sympathetic as she said, "There,
there, Lady Kelera. You must hold still while he does his
work."

Kelera cried into the pillow, "My magic. He knows. He
saw it."

More salve met her torn skin, and she buried her face
further into the pillow, wishing she could escape this
nightmare. Robyn stroked her hair gently, tucking it
behind Kelera's ear. "There, there, deary. It's all going
to be okay."

A man spoke softly, as if trying not to frighten a wounded animal. "I'm almost finished. I promise, it will feel as if it never happened." He came around to where her head was and knelt beside her. She was shocked to see that it was Adrastus holding up a jug of wine. He insisted, "Drink. This will help speed up the healing."

What was he doing here? She tried to remember what happened after the last lash, but couldn't. She had felt her magic. A vision of light flashed in her memory. But all she could recall was the worry in his voice as he called out her name. It was embedded in her mind.

Kelera reluctantly accepted the drink, allowing him to put the jug up to her lips. She drank deeply, willing to do anything he said if it would make the unbearable pain go away. The wine burned her throat as it went down and warmed her belly once it settled. Slowly, the pain from the lashes began to ebb away.

Once it was no more than an ache, she braved sitting up. A loose strand of hair fell into her face and Adrastus reached out to move it, but stopped himself short. His eyes were full of regret as he said, "This is my fault. I should not have allowed you to involve yourself."

Kelera tucked the hair behind her ear. For the first time in a long time, she didn't move her hair to cover the tips of her ears. She tried to force a smile but failed as she said, "It was foolish of me to think that I could help the boy without consequence."

Robyn cleared her throat. Kelera had almost forgotten she was there in the room. She gripped the skirts of her dress as she said, "Speaking of the boy... He is waiting in the hall."

Kelera sat up straighter. "Is he okay?"

Adrastus stood. "He is. Thanks to you."

Robyn added, "And thanks to Prince Adrastus. He healed him as well."

Adrastus shrugged. "It was the least I could do. I should have stopped Samael as soon as I realized what he was going to do."

Robyn patted him on the shoulder before leaving to fetch the boy from the hall. Kelera eyed Adrastus curiously. "You stood against them... openly. Won't there be repercussions?"

"My brother and stepmother already despise me. But there is nothing they can do to me with my father there to keep them in line." His voice wavered as he said it. Something told Kelera he didn't believe what he was saying.

She felt sorry for him. He was isolated in his own home. That was something she was familiar with. He started to stand, but she put her hand out to stop him. "My magic... did he see?" What would Samael do now that he had seen her magic with his own eyes?

Adrastus' voice was firm as he said, "Let me deal with my brother." He opened his mouth to say something more, but Robyn returned with the boy in toe. Adrastus gave Kelera a small bow. "This is where I must take my leave." He paused and chuckled softly as he said, "You know, this isn't what I had in mind when I told you that standing out might be the thing to protect you." He sighed and added, "Do try to stay out of trouble." He smiled, but his tone was serious.

The boy bowed to Adrastus as he made his exit. Then he followed Robyn to Kelera's bedside. He scratched at the horns that twisted slightly above his head and stammered, "I canna... I canna thank ye enough, milady."

"Please, do not thank me. I only regret that things went as far as they did to begin with. No one should be subjected to such brutality."

"Hasn't always been this way, milady. The Winter Court really can be a beautiful place if ye give it a chance. Ye'll see."

Robyn ushered the boy away. "Come now, Ferden. Lady Kelera needs her rest, and so do you. Let us get you back to your mother."

Ferden glanced back once more when he reached the door. "I mean it, Lady Kelera. I am in yer debt."

Robyn shut the door behind them, leaving Kelera alone in her room. The fire was burning brightly, casting shadows along the wall. Outside, she could see the beginning glow of the morning light. She supposed that was her cue to get some sleep. She reached behind to her back, half afraid of the wounds she would find. Instead, her fingers met unblemished skin. She ached as if she had been sleeping on a barn floor, but gone were the open wounds that had been inflicted on her by the guard's whip.

It was remarkable. She had never seen healing magic, let alone experienced it firsthand. Her studies with Gadreel in the library had taught her that healing magic was very difficult to wield. It was something that the High Fae of the Seelie Court were able to master after extensive training. It said much of Adrastus' power that he was able to heal both her and the boy.

She laid back on her pillow, relishing in the comfort it brought her. She would be safe for the day as the rest of the palace slept. She shut her eyes, hoping to find peace, but instead she could hear the crack of the whip and Ferden's cries as they struck him. In her dreams, she could see nothing but Adrastus' eyes staring helplessly into hers as he was held back by his brother's magic.

When night fell, she awoke to arguing outside of her door. She sat up and pulled the covers around her protectively. Had Samael returned to finish what he had started at the revel?

The whispers were heated as one of the voices said, "You and that greedy mortal made a deal. And you broke it when you brought her here."

Samael replied bitterly, "I do not answer to *mortals*. Whatever deal I made with those varmints was null and void the moment I found a halfling with ancient magic living amongst them. How convenient that they failed to mention it months ago when we first met with them."

Kelera couldn't believe what she was hearing. *Mortals* had made a deal with the Prince of the Unseelie Court? She sat up on her knees and crawled to the end of the bed, hoping to hear more.

The man arguing with Samael hissed. "We need the Nevene army distracted if we are to go through with this plan. But we very well cannot have them sending search parties here to Elfhame. It will draw too much attention from Seelie. Be smart, Prince Samael. Do not let a girl with a pretty face make you lose sight of the important work we are doing here."

Samael snarled. The sound sent the hairs on Kelera's arms standing on end. There was a thud on the door as something slammed against it. Samael warned the man, "You overstep. I do not care for the halfling. I seek the power she holds. With her Seelie magic at my fingertips, I will be able to infiltrate the Spring Court with very little to stop me. Do not mistake my interest in her for anything other than that." Kelera couldn't hear the man's response as he mumbled.

The doorknob began to turn, and she leapt back under the covers just in time as Samael strode in. She rubbed at her eyes, pretending she had just woken up. He ignored her as he went to the curtains and flung them open to reveal the starry sky.

She waited quietly in the comfort of her bed. It was strange for him to wake her. Usually, Robyn and Ditra were tasked with bringing her a breakfast tray and preparing her for the day. Samael finally looked at her with disdain. "You will find no sympathy here. You see, the creatures of this realm have much to learn before I ascend the throne. I have no patience for insolence, as you learned firsthand last night."

Kelera's back ached with thoughts of the previous night. Before she could respond, he was looming over her. His face twisted in malice as he spoke down to her. "You made a mistake dropping that mask of yours last night. I now know what to do to awaken your power."

Kelera glared up at him. He, too, had shown his true nature. He was nothing but a sadistic, twisted man. Willing to do anything it took to be the most powerful man in Elfhame, and ready to destroy anyone who stood in his way. He needed her magic—he needed *her*. And that gave her the advantage she would need.

She played into his game as she asked, "And what is it exactly that you believe will awaken my magic?"

He grinned at her through the shadows that the fire was casting along his face. "You will find out soon enough."

The threat in his words struck a blow to her heart. The real games were just beginning. But would she be strong enough to be the player left standing?

Gadreel called from the hall. "Kelera! Let us not keep them waiting. I would not like a repeat of last night."

Kelera struggled to pull the shining metal armor over her cotton dress. She huffed in frustration, trying to buckle everything in place without the help of the servant women. After Samael's visit, it seemed that she was not to speak to anyone in the palace aside from Gadreel, who had just recently shown up after she'd finished eating her dinner.

Samael had been *oh so* gallant enough to have dinner laid at her door, alongside an ornamented trunk of red and gold. She had grunted as she pulled the heavy trunk into her room and opened the lid. Inside, she had found a faded red cotton dress and several pieces of armor.

It didn't take a genius to realize what this meant. Samael would, after all, subject her to the pits. She had defied him in front of the court and their subjects. A mistake that could have very well cost her her life, if it were not for the magic that he and his father wanted.

Gadreel sighed loudly through the closed door. Kelera adjusted the gorget that would protect her neck and chest in battle, and shouted, "I'm ready!" She tugged at it uncomfortably. She had never worn armor like this before. At home, with her father and Dodger, she was never truly in danger when they matched with one another. The worst she had ever walked away with were a few bumps and bruises. This would be different. This could cost her everything.

She flung the door open to find Gadreel staring wide eyed at her. His jaw dropped, and he searched for the words. "Wh-what in the world? What in the stars' name are you wearing?"

His disbelief only frustrated her more. She shook her arms, trying to adjust the weight of the pauldrons on her shoulders. "A gift. From your brother."

Gadreel's face went ghost white. "From Samael..." Kelera watched as the understanding clicked in his mind. "He means for you to fight in the pits."

Kelera grabbed hold of Gadreel's hands. "Tell me what to do. Please."

Gadreel shook his head. "I didn't think they would go through with it."

"You knew this would happen." It was more a statement than a question. As kind as Gadreel had been to her, he was still one of them.

"I've tried my best to dissuade them. But after your display at the revel..." He truly looked sorry as he elaborated. "They believe that the way to unlock your magic is to make you feel as you did last night. Like you did that day in the clearing with the Night Rider."

"So either... I call on the magic that I still have not had full control of since I was a child, or else I face certain death."

Gadreel shook his head solemnly. "Not death. Samael will push you to the brink of death. He will make you long for it, but he will not kill you. He can't." There were more guards than usual in the halls as they began to walk. He whispered to her, "Listen to me. You cannot unleash your power in that pit. Whatever anger or fear you're feeling, you need to let it go. If your magic appears at its full strength, then there will be nothing to stop Samael from binding it to his own power."

She whispered back in anger, "I have been trying to take control of it. You've seen me."

"I've seen you trying to do everything by the book. But now I need you to do something else. I need you to forget the lessons in the library. Forget about what everyone else is thinking about you when you're out there. Just focus on what you're *feeling*. Not what you're thinking. If you can take hold of your emotions, then you will take hold of your power. You will be able to contain it."

That's easy for you to say, she thought bitterly as they continued past the guards. Gadreel was a prince. His place in the world had been secured from the moment he first opened his eyes. It was different for her. She had been abandoned. Unwanted in the world she was born into and forced to change herself to remain in the world she had been left in. She took a deep, steadying breath.

There were so many things she wanted to say, but she held her tongue. There was nothing Gadreel could do for her now. She dug her nails into her palms and felt sweat beading on her back.

They descended a dark stairwell. She placed a hand on the cool stone, concentrating on her footing. They approached a set of large double doors, and her heart skipped a beat. The guards stepped forward to open them with grave expressions on their angular faces. As soon as the doors opened, Kelera could hear feet pounding on the ground and a loud applause rising. Her heart raced as she stepped forward at the guards' signal. She glanced back at Gadreel one final time, and he gave her a small, unsure smile.

Kelera bit the inside of her cheek, trying to use the pain as a distraction from what she was facing. The fighting pits. As Samael had promised. The Fae gathered here tonight were ready to watch a fight, and Kelera feared that she was the main event. They whooped and shouted high above in the stands. She could feel their magic pulse above her like an electric storm.

Scanning the crowd, she spotted King Cyrus and Queen Beatrix standing in their large, boxed area that separated them from the common crowd. Prince Ammon was there too. His face was flushed with excitement, and he was whispering to a courtier who stood beside him. Gadreel stepped into the box, and Kelera's eyes met his worried gaze. His thin face was red with anger, but he stepped into place silently beside his brother.

One of the guards shoved Kelera from behind, forcing her further into the arena. The crowd was hysterical with excitement as they took in the sight of their newest fighter. She looked around the arena, hoping to catch sight of her opponent, but she was alone.

The doors behind her opened again, and Kelera turned to watch Prince Kane emerge from the hall. His bare arms and chest were glistening with sweat and blood. Even his face was splattered with red. He raised his hands to the crowd and bellowed, "Friends and foe! It is time for our main event." They went wild in response, stomping on the wooden stands and shouting to see blood. *Her* blood.

Kane turned to her, and she thought for a terrifying moment that he was going to be the one to fight her. He grinned; his eyes still wild with bloodlust from whatever match he had just come out of victorious. He made a show of taking a turn around the arena, then strode back toward the double doors. Kelera was dizzy with relief as she realized it wouldn't be him who she was matched with.

The guards opened the doors at his signal, revealing Samael in his fighting gear. This was worse. Much worse. He wore dark leather armor over his shirtless torso and bracers on his arms. He sneered at her as he sauntered into the arena.

The crowd began to chant his name, no doubt happy at the opportunity to bet on one of their own princes. A prince who was sure to win the match against a curvy, seemingly harmless, half mortal woman. She could see money exchanging hands in the stands as she circled away from Samael.

He shouted over the sounds of the audience, "The time has come, halfling! It is time for you to prove your worth."

Kelera tried to reason with him, "Prince Samael, have I not done everything that has been asked of me since receiving my sentence?" The crowd fell to a hush as she spoke. "Last night was a moment of weakness. I am not yet used to your ways, but I can learn. It was not my place to step in and I have learned my lesson at your behest." *A lie,* Kelera thought to herself. But in this moment, she was willing to say anything to make him rethink this path.

Samael saw through her well thought out words. "Your mortal blood allows your tongue to spit lies like venom."

Kelera felt heat rise to her cheeks. Was it embarrassment? Or was it the early signs of the magic she held, deciding to show itself in her moment of peril? "I ask that you do not call me a liar." With the heat, she could feel anger raging beneath the surface of her elegant facade. Was this what he wanted? For her to challenge him. Did he really think she would make it so easy for him?

Samael held his hands out in front of him. Kelera watched in horrid fascination as ice began to crystalize above them. He snarled, "But isn't that what your entire life has been? A lie? Hidden truths beneath your courtly pretense and polite smiles. I see it. My brothers see it. And last night, the entire revel saw it."

Kelera took an alarmed step back as the ice formed into sharp icicles. With a flick of his wrist, Samael shot them in her direction. She ducked to the ground, hitting her knees on the hard dirt. It sent a jarring shock through her legs, and she groaned in pain. The icicles hit the guards who had been standing behind her. They cut through the men with an impact so hard that it pinned them to the solid wood doors. When the ice melted away, the guards sank to the ground lifelessly.

No cheers came from the crowd as they had in the countless fights Kelera had witnessed during her time at court. She raged at him. "What do you hope to gain from this? You think you can bully me into accessing my power, but what happens when I do? Surely, even you are not arrogant enough to believe that I will do your bidding!" She was left breathless when she finished.

"What I want is to be *entertained*." He gestured widely to the audience. "I am the Dark Prince of Elfhame. The Prince of Shadows. I want power. I want allegiance. And I want *you*."

His power came to life again, but this time, Kelera could feel the chill of it before she saw it. It was like a bitter wind nipping at her neck and face. She tried to back away, putting distance between her and Samael's magic, but it surrounded her in a white flurry.

Samael laughed and began to taunt her. "Fight, little lady of the mortal court. My people want to be entertained." The crowd continued to stare down at them, and Kelera sensed a change in the atmosphere. Something inside of her told her they were frightened. Though if it was for her safety or their own, she wasn't sure.

The magical flurry of snow began to close in on her, forcing her to inch closer to Samael. He looked almost triumphant as he said, "You're not fooling anyone with your decorum. Fight back!" The flurry hit her hard from behind, sending her face first into the dirt floor.

Sand filled her mouth, and she choked and spat until it was out. She glared up at him but made no move to fight back. She would not access her magic for *him*.

Samael's lip curled in annoyance. "Strike me down, halfling. You know you've wanted to since the first moment we met. When that imbecile you call 'fiancé' was unable to save the girl from my clutches." He kicked the dirt in her face. Her eyes stung as it met its mark. Relentlessly, he continued, "I know your type. You care so deeply about how others perceive you. Afraid that they will think you are a monster if you show your true colors."

He advanced on her, and she scrambled to her feet. Her throat burned as she argued, "I have only ever wanted security. I will not be ashamed of that."

He clenched his teeth, then snarled, "You want people to stop whispering about you? To stop judging you? *Make them.* Go ahead! Fight!" He struck her hard in the face and she felt blood trickle from her eyebrow.

This time, the heat rising in her chest was not from embarrassment. There was no mistaking the prickling sensation underneath the surface of her skin. "I would rather die than allow you to use me as you please." Her magic crackled in her veins like flint on a fire. She focused on the noise of the crowd instead of the fear and anger building inside of her and felt it die down.

Samael howled as he shot a freezing wind at her. It sliced into her face. When it faded, she put a hand to her cheek and found blood on her fingers when she pulled them away. She heard a commotion from the royal box but didn't bother to look. There was nothing Gadreel could do for her. Nothing anyone could do for her. Not here. Not in this place of shadows and ice.

Someone shouted for Samael to stop, but the owner of the voice drowned out as Samael gathered another wind. His eyes looked as if they were glowing with the intensity of his power. This went far beyond wanting to be entertained. She had resisted him when no other ever had. For that, he was going to make her pay. His power flared as he threatened her. "You made a mistake in coming here for your mortal friend. And it will be your last." As he continued, the air around her became wilder, blowing her hair all around her face. "When I'm done with you, you will be nothing but a pretty, broken shell."

Kelera bit back a scream as fire burned from inside of her. Confused, she looked at Samael for any sign of fire magic. Still, only the blue-silver light of his power was coming from him. This wasn't his power she was feeling. It was her own. She turned to get away from him but was blocked by the powerful winds.

Samael advanced on her. "Your father should have better prepared you for coming here. I suppose it falls to me now to teach you the lesson." He reached out and grabbed her by the hair. He pushed it aside to reveal her pointed ears. "You may be the great pretender all you want, play the role of a lady of the mortal court. But the world is cruel, and your efforts will never be enough. *You* will never be enough." He pushed her to her knees and grabbed her by the throat. She struggled under his hold and felt tears come unwillingly to her eyes.

Samael was voicing every insecurity she had ever had out loud for all the Unseelie Court to hear. And he wasn't finished. He roared in her face, "You wanna survive? Fight me. Unleash your magic on the world. Or do you want to run from yourself like you always have?"

When she made no move to call upon her magic, he shrugged. "So be it." His hands on her throat went ice cold, and it felt as if she were freezing from the inside out. Her very being grew heavy, like it was being turned to ice.

"I will die before I help you." She meant it. Just as she closed her eyes, ready to accept her fate, Samael's hold on her broke. She opened her eyes to see him skid clear across the arena, leaving a mark in the sand where his body had been thrown through it. Smoke was rising around her as if a blast of fire had erupted. She looked down at her hands, wondering if it was as it had been in the clearing with the Night Rider. But she hadn't felt anything. It couldn't have been her.

She looked back up at Samael with wide eyes. Adrastus was there, and he looked murderous. He was gripping Samael's armor. He lifted him high enough from the ground that he was able to connect his fist to Samael's face. Adrastus dropped him and took a few steps back. He lifted his hands up. Rising from them was a golden flame of light. *It was him. Adrastus just saved me.*

Samael raised his hands in defense. Though his forehead was wrinkled with worry, his voice did not waiver as he said to Adrastus, "You've no right to interfere!"

Adrastus smiled viciously. "I have every right, *brother*. Or do you forget yet again that I, too, am a prince of this court? Her sentence was to the royal family. That includes me, does it not?"

Samael spat at Adrastus' feet. "*Half* brother. Or do *you* forget?"

"Very well. If we are to play it that way, then perhaps a challenge is in order." Adrastus turned toward the royal family's box. "Father, what say you? The first of us to draw blood shall win the lovely Lady Kelera as their own."

King Cyrus stepped up to the balcony. He studied his sons as he thought. Showing only mild interest, he smiled slightly before declaring, "So, let it be binding. The first to draw blood will control the girl. But make no mistake, my boys, should her magic present itself, it will fall to *me* to decide what is to be done with it."

Kelera didn't know where to go. She wanted to put as much distance between her and the fight that was about to commence, but the doors were still locked shut. Her back hit the solid wood that lined the arena. She pressed herself to it, praying it would be enough to keep her out of the way of what was to come next. She could feel the magic building in the arena, emanating off of the two Unseelie Princes.

Adrastus circled around Samael as he pushed himself from the ground. Samael dusted himself off as Adrastus removed his shirt to reveal scarred skin. At first, they looked like simple blemishes, but as Kelera's eyes adjusted to see through the glamor, she could see that they were battle scars. He was like the statues in King Tristan's courtyard of warriors from long ago. He was not as broad as their brother Kane, but there was power in his body in the way he moved so effortlessly.

Adrastus readied himself as Samael circled the arena. Samael put on a show for the Fae in the audience. They were reluctant at first, after the display he had put on with Kelera. But now, with a fair match, they were riling up. Samael threw his hands up to the crowd and aimed up bursts of snowy drifts, causing them to delight in the showcase.

Meanwhile, Adrastus crossed the arena to meet Kelera. He blocked her body from the crowd and took her hands in his. Her body tensed until he rubbed his thumbs along her knuckles. She felt herself relax and stared up into his eyes. The intensity of his gaze reminded her of their first encounter in the forest. He had protected her then... and he was protecting her now.

His voice was low as he said, "Whatever happens, stay against the wall." Kelera nodded, but he was persistent, "Promise me, Kelera."

It was the first time he had used her name when speaking directly to her. She swallowed back the uncertainty she was feeling. "I promise, Adrastus."

Satisfied, he released her hands and turned back to his brother. Samael was glaring at the two of them. If he had witnessed the small exchange between her and the brother he seemed to despise, then it would only fuel his eagerness to win. In all her time in the Unseelie Court, she had yet to see Adrastus take his place in the pits. It felt as if her stomach was full of stones. It surprised her that she was so worried about him.

But she didn't have time to dwell on the thought. Silence fell over the crowd as they waited for King Cyrus to announce the beginning of the match. He stepped forward with a black flag raised high in his hand. In one short breath, he dropped it. It fell to the ground, like a bird plummeting from the sky. Kelera clenched her fists as it touched the ground in the arena. She knew in her heart that she would never forget how small and harmless that piece of cloth looked laying in the dirt. For it was that one act by the king that would set her destiny in motion.

Chapter Twenty

F ire and ice collided as Samael and Adrastus commanded their magic at one another. Time seemed to slow as the brothers fought for their claim over Kelera. Samael maneuvered his way around Adrastus like a predator circling its prey. His shadows slithered across the ground only to be met with a blaze of fire. They shrank away from the heat and back into Samael's hands.

He hissed and shook his hands out. Adrastus stopped him before he could raise them to call on his power again. His magic lunged out like a blade. It slashed across Samael's chest, striking where his armor left him exposed and vulnerable. Blood seeped out from beneath the steel plate. He bared his teeth and glared at Adrastus.

King Cyrus clapped loudly. "Well done, Adrastus. You prove yet again that you are a warrior worth your title."

He gestured to Kelera, who was trembling against the wall. "Claim your prize."

Adrastus crossed the arena and grabbed Kelera by the arm. But before they could make it to the door, Samael shot a shadow out. It took hold of Adrastus, tearing him away from Kelera. She slunk back against the wall again as she watched Samael descend upon him.

He maneuvered his shadows, covering Adrastus' mouth. King Cyrus was shouting at the guards to stop the two of them, but they didn't listen. The men stood by, stunned by the brothers who had disobeyed the agreement. Blood had been drawn. The match was over. But it appeared Samael wasn't ready to give up.

Adrastus summoned sparks of fire from thin air, burning away Samael's dark shadow magic. Samael stumbled back with fear-filled eyes. Before he could summon his magic again, Adrastus tackled him. He tore into Samael's face with his bare hands, beating him relentlessly.

The only thing holding Kelera in place against the wall was the determination not to allow her magic to reveal itself. As she sat by and watched, she heard King Cyrus roar. The lanterns lighting the arena went out suddenly. A darkness fell over them and the crowd went silent. Kelera felt like she was lost in a deep void, with no hope of ever escaping. Time seemed to slow. And it wasn't until Adrastus' grunts stopped, that the blanket of darkness lifted.

Kelera looked up to see King Cyrus pulling the darkness back into his hands. It flowed effortlessly to him. His face was neutral, but Kelera caught the twitch in his jaw as he stared down disapprovingly at his sons. "I said *enough*." Then, without another word, he turned and left.

No one in the crowd moved. It looked as if they weren't even breathing. Kelera found that she herself had been holding her breath, too. She slumped against the wall. It was the first time she had witnessed the full force of the Unseelie King's power, and it was something she wished to never experience again.

Adrastus walked to her and helped her up. He pulled her with him to the door. As the guards swung it open to let them pass, Samael called out, "This is not over, brother!"

The only response he received was a grunt from Adrastus. Once they were in the hall, the guards secured the doors shut. Kelera could hear cheers behind them. It appeared the crowd had recovered, and the night was not over for the rest of the court.

***

Adrastus was pacing Kelera's new rooms. She had been given chambers in his wing of the palace. They were much more spacious than the room Samael had given her. Befitting of someone with noble blood, not the prisoner that she was.

His body shook, and he continued to clench and un-clench his fists. It appeared he had still not come down from the adrenaline of the fight. There was still blood on his face and his knuckles. Samael's blood.

The sight of him like that in her room without his shirt stirred something inside of her. Though her situation was still a dire one—trapped in the Unseelie Court, bound to the whims of one of its unruly princes—she felt safer being under Adrastus' control than Samael's. But he was still a mystery to her.

She could try to persuade Adrastus to do the right thing and to allow her to return home. She wanted so badly to trust him. What if he could help her break the spell that tethered her to the royal family? What reason could he have for keeping her there? As for King Cyrus, perhaps they could come up with a story as to how she escaped...

This could be the opportunity she'd been waiting for. She cleared her throat before asking, "Prince Adrastus, may I speak freely?"

He grunted at her in response as he poured himself a drink.

She spoke with as much confidence as she could muster, "I don't belong here, and I think you can agree with that. It's only a matter of time before your father tires of showing me any semblance of hospitality. And when he does..."

"No one would dare touch you now." He threw his drink back and went to the tub of water one of the servants had brought in. He scrubbed furiously at the blood and grime on his hands.

She could see that he had a lot on his mind. Trying to hold on to her courage, she continued, "If you want to protect me, then sending me home is the only way to—"

He slammed his hands on the table, startling Kelera into silence. Water splashed from the small tub and onto the lace tablecloth. "I am not your champion, Kelera. I have a duty to the throne, and I will not risk it all for some mortal girl who was ignorant enough to get herself into this mess!"

His words stung, but Kelera didn't balk. "*Half* mortal. And let us not forget that you played your own role in getting me into this mess." It was he who had stopped her from crossing the veil with Cierine, but he had also saved her from Vazine, had tried to step in to stop the lashings at the revel, and tonight he very well may have saved her life. Even if she couldn't fathom the reason for it all, it didn't change the fact that he had aided her before, and he was the only one who could aid her now. She stood tall with her chin raised. Brushing her hair behind her ear, she said, "I know that there is more going on than you are willing to share with me. I know that there are mortals working with Samael to kidnap innocent women all so he can distract King Tristan. I need to go home to *warn* them."

"The mortal realm is not my concern, just as Elfhame politics are not *yours*."

"But surely you, of all Fae, are powerful enough to stand in Samael's way. Think of the lives you could save. Both Fae and mortal alike." Kelera was overstepping, but she needed to see how far she could go with him. She needed to know, right here, right now, if he was her enemy or her ally. When he said nothing, she tried appealing to his emotions. "There was a moment in the arena between us. Will you deny it now?"

When Adrastus turned to look at her, her stomach sank. He narrowed his eyes at her and balled his fists so tightly that his knuckles were turning white. Had she gone too far? But how could he act as if he had not just risked his own well-being, his own relationship with his family... *for her*? She fumbled to find the words, but none came.

Adrastus was the first to break the silence. "You forget yourself. I challenged my brother so that I could *claim* you and keep him from binding himself to you. Not to set you free. And certainly not to take the mortal realm's side in any sort of tension between them and my family. My only concern is Samael and the destruction he can bring upon my people. And I am willing to do whatever it takes to keep that from happening. There is no line I won't cross. I am no hero, like it or not. I am just another monster in this fairytale."

Kelera took a cautious step toward him. "You're wrong. You are not like your brothers."

He snarled at her, "You know nothing about me." He pushed her against the wall, and she cried out in surprise. He caressed the cuts on her face, and she stilled. Heat flowed into her cheeks as he ran his fingers along the side of her face. The wounds began to heal, and she was relieved to find that they no longer stung.

Distracted by the relief, she leaned into his touch. He pulled back as if she had burned him and stared at her nervously. She tried again, "Please, your Highness, let me go home."

The anxiety on his face was replaced with one of anguish. She could read people well enough to see that a battle was raging within him. He narrowed his eyes at her as he leaned in. His breath was warm on her lips, and she thought for a moment that he might kiss her. He had the same bite in his voice as Samael as he warned, "As I said before, I claimed you for myself. I have no intention of letting you go."

Was he trying to frighten her? Kelera bared her teeth at him. "I am a lady of the mortal court who has been subjected to the malevolent ways of the Unseelie Court. What is it that *you* would do to me that has not already been done?"

Adrastus pressed his body against hers, pushing her hard against the wall. She had never in her life been this close to a man. Not even Samael had invaded her space in such an intimate way. "Choose your words carefully, little thief. There are still a few Unseelie tricks you have not yet experienced."

He *was* trying to frighten her. But she couldn't understand why. She had witnessed his kindness toward others many times since coming. He was more like Gadreel than he was like Samael and the others. But it was clear now that he wanted to scare her. Calling his bluff, she dared, "Then what are you waiting for?"

He grabbed her by the wrist and raised her hand to his face. "You know nothing, little thief. You need me to *show* you who I am?" Magic shimmered as he dropped his glamor to reveal the same handsome face he'd had before. Only now, it was marred by additional scars strewn about in uneven lines. They ran down to his neck, intertwining with the scars on his chest that he didn't bother to hide.

She gasped as he ran her fingers along them. Her voice shook as she said, "*This* does not make you a monster. Only your actions can do that."

Her breath hitched in her throat as he ran his hand along the small of her back and around her waist. She was warm and tense all over. It was an intense feeling, one that she had not experienced before.

His voice was husky as he said, "My actions are my concern. You will do well to remember that you are still bound to the royal family, even under my hold. You will be more careful from here on out. No more sticking your nose in where it does not belong. If I must choose between you and my people, the choice will not be in your favor."

"Adrastus." His name came out as no more than a whisper. "Please. If you are working against Samael, let me help." Tears welled in her eyes.

She could help him if he would trust her. He had saved her. Was it truly just so he could keep an eye on her magic? Only so he could keep it from Samael's clutches? Her mind told her that it was a good enough reason for going through so much trouble, but her traitorous heart refused to believe that it was the only reason. He leaned in closer to her and she held her breath as she waited for his lips to meet hers. She knew she should turn away. Push him. Anything to uphold the promise of betrothal she had made to Alexander. But the memory of Adrastus defeating Samael in her name flashed through her mind.

He still smelled of blood and sweat and it felt as if it were awakening something inside of her. Something that had long since been locked away, hidden from the rest of the world. What would it be like to give in and let herself feel something other than fear for once? She leaned forward. Their lips met like the flutter of a butterfly's wing. Then he pulled away from her, cursing under his breath. In one swift movement, he took a step back, leaving her shivering in his absence. Her body ached in betrayal.

She put her fingers to her lips. She couldn't believe she had done that. It was her first kiss. And it had been with a man who wasn't her betrothed. Had she really changed so much in her time in Elfhame? What frightened her most was that she wasn't sorry. Somewhere deep down, she wanted to do it again.

All of this for a man who was refusing to help her save her people. She was a traitor. As he licked his lips, she shot him a look like daggers and then left her alone in her new room. She cursed at herself once she was alone. Her body and her heart were responding to him in a way that shook her to her core. She had made a mistake just now giving into her desire and emotion. He had said everything he could to convince her that he was still her enemy. Her captor. And if he wasn't going to help her save herself or her people... if she couldn't control her feelings when she was around him, then she would have to do all she could to keep him at a distance.

Chapter Twenty-One

S he had to admit it was much more comfortable being Adrastus' prisoner than Samael's. The midnight blue dress he had sent to her by way of Ditra and Robyn was elegant but practical. It had fur lined cuffs and another remarkably soft lining of fur around the collar. To her joy, she found no mask to accompany it. She was finally free of the lace that had scratched at her face daily since coming to the Unseelie Court.

When she left her room, she was greeted by Gadreel. He embraced her in a hug that overwhelmed her. He was the closest thing she had to a friend here, and she felt tears threatening to fall as he squeezed her. He pulled back, holding her shoulders firmly. "I could find no other way. It was all I could think to do."

Kelera wrinkled her brow. "What do you mean?"

"Dras... I had to ask him to step in. I had no idea how far Samael planned to go, so I turned to Dras to save you."

And now she was Adrastus' prisoner... because of Gadreel. She didn't blame him, though. She patted him gently on the chest. "You saved my life, Gadreel. Though I have traded one jailor for another, I am honored to have *you* on my side."

He smiled warmly at her and offered his arm for her to take. "I am glad to put my neck on the line for my friends." He nudged her with his shoulder. She looped her arm through his and they started down the hall. The foyer was filled with courtiers going about their daily business. They stared at her unmasked face with surprise and interest. Gone were the disdainful looks she had grown used to. They studied her as if she were some mythological beast that they wished to reach out and touch.

She leaned into Gadreel and said, almost under her breath, "Why are they looking at me like that?"

He covered the smile that crept across his face with his hand and whispered back, "Dras has never kept a servant. Neither mortal nor Fae. Last night's events have been all anyone in the palace can talk about." He led her to the large doors, and the guards bowed to him before opening them. As she and Gadreel stepped out onto the palace steps that led down to the large courtyard, he added, "And the absence of a mask tells them that Dras holds you in high esteem. Not as a faceless servant or prisoner."

She thought of his warning the night before that he was not her ally and the kiss that contradicted his words. She scoffed, "And does he?"

Gadreel gave her a puzzled look. "Does he hold you in high esteem?" He gestured across the courtyard to where Adrastus waited with two horses. "I suppose that is something the two of you will have to figure out for yourselves."

Adrastus looked dazzling in his thick black jacket, contrasting against the pure white, snow-covered ground. He greeted her more reserved than he had been when he'd left her. "Good evening, Lady Kelera." Her name sounded formal coming from his lips, and she was surprised to find that she preferred the rather insulting nickname he had given her before. Something about the way he said *little thief* with a mixture of admiration and fascination made her eager to hear him call her that once more.

Something had shifted between them last night, but it seemed he was keen to forget it all. In turn, she acknowledged him politely. "Prince Adrastus."

"I thought you might like to get out of the palace for a while and see one of the villages."

It sounded wonderful. She hadn't had the chance to explore the Winter Court yet. And she was curious to see how the villagers reacted to Adrastus' presence.

He held out a gloved hand and led her to the midnight black gelding he had chosen for her. She rubbed its velvet nose and thought of the mischievous pooka who had thrown her into the stream. She almost laughed at the memory of the cheeky creature, but held back, keeping her composure.

Adrastus circled around to make sure the horse's saddle was firmly in place. The horse stood patiently, pushing his snout into Kelera for more affection. She gave it freely, enjoying how friendly the towering creature was. He was strongly built, and his coat was full for the winter. She wondered if he ever even shed it, considering he lived in the icy terrain full time.

Curious, she asked, "What is his name?"

Adrastus motioned for her to come to the side. He held his hands out down low with his fingers interlocked. Kelera placed her booted heel in his hands and used them to boost herself into the saddle. She patted the horse on the neck affectionately.

Adrastus tightened the sinch on the saddle as he answered, "His name is Chance."

"Interesting. Most men name their horses after kings or the great heroes."

Adrastus chuckled as he mounted the slightly smaller white horse beside her. "I guess I'm not like most men." He was serious as he added, "Would you consider that a bad thing?"

Kelera shifted uncomfortably in the saddle. "I suppose that is something I shall have to wait to find out. I do have 300 years to do so, after all." His face fell slightly, as if she had hurt his feelings. She gave him a small lighthearted smile.

He twisted at the reins in his hands. "About last night..."

Kelera bit her lip. "Don't. It was foolish of me to ask you to risk yourself for me anymore than you already have." She didn't mention the kiss. She wasn't ready to talk about it when she still wasn't sure what it had meant to her.

He gave her a curt nod. Then, clearing his throat, he declared, "We'd best get going. I had Robyn pack gloves in your saddle bag. Night will fall soon and with it, the chill from the mountains will come."

Kelera dug into the pack behind her and found warm moleskin gloves. They were stark white with fur inside and warmed her hands immediately. Adrastus was certainly more attentive than Samael was. It was refreshing. It also made it hard not to compare the brothers. Like day and night, they were different in many ways. And though Adrastus claimed to be as bad as the rest of them, there were moments where she saw glimpses of Gadreel. It only complicated her feelings about him more.

They began their ride through the countryside. The snowy ground glittered beneath the setting sun, and Kelera stared in awe at the beauty around her. She had not yet explored the Winter Court and welcomed the excitement that came with getting out of the palace, even if it was only for a little while. She spotted mountains on the horizon. They were snow capped and treacherous, yet there was a powerful beauty to them.

Adrastus caught her staring. "We don't visit the mountains often. Only a few times throughout the year to check on the villages in the valley. Gadreel visits most often, to bring them necessary supplies; things they can't get on their own."

"That's kind of him."

"He's the best of us all." There was no mocking tone in his voice as he talked about Gadreel. Had they always been close? Or were they forced into a brotherly alliance because of the way their family treated them differently?

Things were quiet as they rode on. They followed a path from the palace, allowing the horses a reprieve from trekking through the deep snow. The silence was not at all uncomfortable. For a brief moment, Kelera wondered how far she could get if she made a run for it. What would happen if she fought against the magic tying her to the royal family? She was considering the risk when the first village came into view.

Adrastus led the way on his white horse and soon they were in the middle of a town square. The sun was nearly set, and the moon was beaming through the clear sky. One of the villagers, a tall man with a burly beard and kind eyes, came out to greet them. "Welcome, Prince Adrastus! We've got a table set up for ye in the tavern. Though I canna promise ye the good ale. Gilby and Tobias got in early. By now, I fear the place may be as dry as the sands of the Summer Court."

Adrastus, already dismounted from his horse, came around to offer a hand to Kelera. She shook her head gently, and he lowered his hand, allowing her the room to dismount on her own. With the kiss from last night fresh on her mind, she was wary about the feelings that might come with feeling her hand in his. She smoothed out her dress and moved to pull her hair down around her ears. Noting the points on the villagers' ears bustling around them, she thought better of it and tucked the hair behind her ears instead. It was freeing to be able to show them off without worrying about anyone whispering or treating her differently because of them.

Adrastus patted the man heavily on the back. "As always, Therin, you outdo yourself with the hospitality."

Kelera handed Chance's reins to a village boy and followed Adrastus to the tavern. Therin bowed slightly to her as she passed, and she gave a small curtsey in return. His eyes widened for a moment at the gesture, and she worried she had done something wrong. She picked up her pace, falling into step beside Adrastus.

His voice was soft as he said, "They are not used to being treated with such dignity from courtiers."

"Ah, but I'm not a courtier here, am I?"

"Maybe not at the palace, but here it is different. You rode in on my personal steed, you wear no mask to indicate servitude, and you are clearly High Fae judging by your appearance."

"Therin is not High Fae?" He looked ordinary as far as the Fae went.

"You'll get used to seeing through the glamors. Using magic to make themselves appear more like the High Fae is what I suppose the mortals would call *fashionable* in their realm."

"Gilby and Tobias don't use glamors... and I see nothing wrong with their appearance."

Adrastus raised an eyebrow at her. "Nothing at all?"

Kelera thought for a moment. "I suppose it took some getting used to at first. I have not spent much time with Fae in my life, aside from the occasional run-ins with pixies and bogies. And I did meet a brownie recently..." He was listening to her intently, and she hoped she wasn't embarrassing or offending him with this conversation. "I guess I just don't see why they should hide who they are amongst their own people."

"Seems to me it is a shared experience." He gave her a pointed look. They stepped up to the tavern door. Lively music was playing inside and the light shining through the windows was bright. It illuminated Adrastus' face as he paused and turned to her. "We all hide at some point in our lives. Whether it's from others or ourselves. There is no shame in that. But until we can accept the truth of who we are, we can never truly be happy."

"Funny, Gadreel recently said something similar." She studied Adrastus' face. He was more open today. More relaxed. She wanted to chalk it up to the tension of last night's events in the pits having worn off. He had warned her not to step out of line, but already, he was treating her as an equal and not as a prisoner.

He reached for the door, but Kelera put a hand on his arm to make him pause. She could see her breath in the cold night air as she asked, "Why was there no mask sent with my dress?"

He looked like he would reach for her with his free hand, but paused. "Something tells me you were wearing a mask of your own making long before you came here. Don't you think it was about time you rid yourself of them altogether?"

Kelera was stunned by the conviction in his words as he opened the door and strode inside. She took one last look at the village behind her, coming alive with the villagers who were rising for the night, and then followed Adrastus inside.

Warmth hit her instantly and suddenly the fur lined dress felt stifling. Adrastus held out a chair for her across from the men she'd had the pleasure of meeting at the revel. Gilby and Tobias were deep in their cups and in good cheer.

Gilby raised a cup to her in cheers and a loud hiccup escaped his throat. "'Bout time ye graced us poor unfortunate souls with yer presence!"

Adrastus poured Kelera a cup of ale and then one for himself. She had never been much of an ale drinker, but she thought, *Why not,* as she took a swig. Gilby and Tobias nodded in approval as they downed the rest of theirs.

Gilby hiccupped again before asking, "Will ye be visitin' Grace while yer here? I know she'll be eager to see ye."

Kelera snuck a glance in Adrastus' direction at the mention of another woman. She could see why he would be a highly sought-after commodity, and she had no business judging his love life. She blushed, remembering the taste of his lips on hers.

"That's the plan. I thought I'd show Lady Kelera around a bit first." Adrastus leaned back to make room for the tavern keeper as she brought them bowls of stew. Steam rose from it, along with the most wonderful aroma of vegetables and venison. She leaned over her bowl, breathing it in and letting the steam warm her face.

Tobias grinned at her over his own bowl. "This tavern's got the finest food in the land, and no one will convince me otherwise." He shoved a heaping spoonful into his mouth and Kelera followed suit. He wasn't exaggerating. It was almost magical. The thick gravy was like nothing she had ever experienced, even at the palace. It was as if the meal warmed you to your very soul.

Adrastus laughed and shook his head as he dipped into his bowl. They ate silently, too focused on the delicious meal in front of them to make any sort of small talk. When they finished, Kelera was so satisfied she couldn't imagine leaving the table to go back out into the bitter frosty night.

Patrons of the tavern took opportunities to pay respects to Adrastus as they passed by. They exchanged pleasantries with Gilby and Tobias, as well. Kelera was enjoying herself. These were not the monsters from the storybooks in King Tristan's library. They were warm and welcoming. A little odd at times, but Kelera didn't mind that. She laughed and joked with the small group at their table until they had their fill of food and ale.

Adrastus stretched out and sighed. "We'd better be on our way." Tobias and Gilby said their goodbyes without rising from their seats. It was a stark difference to the way Kelera had seen Princess Cierine treated at the mortal court. Instead, there was a familiarity between Adrastus and the subjects of the Winter Court. And surprisingly, she found that she preferred it this way. Skipping all the pretense and not feeling the need to overthink every little action and the consequence that they would hold was liberating.

When they walked outside, she found that the village had been lit with lanterns that stood tall on posts, lighting everything below them on the streets. The houses were tall and sturdy, made of beautiful white stone. The villages in Nevene were humble in comparison with their wooden frames and straw roofs. She and Adrastus followed a walkway that had been cleared of snow and made small talk with the villagers that they passed along the way. Adrastus greeted each and every one of the citizens with familiarity as he asked after their families, livestock, and crops.

He smiled proudly as he asked Kelera, "What do you think?"

She answered honestly, "I think it's incredible. I'm almost ashamed to admit that it's not quite what I expected."

"I see. You expected hovels in disrepair. Or perhaps monsters living in caves."

Kelera let out a loud laugh. "I wouldn't go that far. But if I'm being honest, I expected something... *less* than this." She gestured to the houses and the tall lanterns that lined the streets. "It's so..."

"Advanced?"

She shot him an apologetic glance. "Yes." They rounded the corner and came to a slightly smaller house than the rest. There were wooden boxes under each of the windows with beautiful white bowl-shaped flowers resembling roses. "Are all the villages like this?"

"Not all. Though I would like them to be. The mountains are a hazardous place to live, and it can be difficult to get them the supplies they need. They don't mind it though, as they prefer the old ways." He stepped up to the door but did not knock yet. "Then there is the Autumn Court... they're detrimental for harvesting trees and some of our crops, yet my father tends to neglect them. 'Out of sight, out of mind' seems to be his motto."

"And what of the Seelie Court?"

"I've not spent as much time there as I'd have liked. Gadreel is in charge of trade relations there, so I've been a few times with him. The Spring Court is very lively. And the Summer Court tends to keep to themselves."

Kelera felt almost silly having to ask any of this. She had, after all, been born in Elfhame. She supposed she'd been ignoring the bitter feelings that came with being abandoned by her mother. Maybe that was why she had been content learning what little she did about Elfhame from the outdated, dusty history books the Nevene libraries held.

According to those very books, the residents of Elfhame were primitive and dangerous. Though one could still argue the dangerous part, it was clear that they were far more progressive than they were given credit for.

Adrastus knocked again and this time a woman answered. She was slender and beautiful with silver hair that glimmered under the light escaping her home. Smiling broadly, she wasted no time ushering them into the house. It was warmly decorated with soft throw pillows and hand-crafted rugs. The scent of cinnamon and cloves wafted in from the small kitchen in the back. This was more than just a well-built house... it was a home.

Kelera felt a tug in her heart. She had never known a home like this. She and her father had always lived in the palace. It was his firm belief that as the commander of the king's knights, it was his duty to live in the heart of the king's land. Not that she blamed him. She never imagined what it might be like to live anyplace other than court. It had always been her goal to belong there so that she would always have the security that it offered her.

But now, standing in this cozy abode, she saw that security could be found in many places. Places she had never considered giving a chance. She joined Adrastus on one of the sofas and waited for an introduction to the incredibly perfect woman sitting in front of her. Who was she to Adrastus? Kelera felt a sliver of jealousy, imagining the two of them as an item.

Adrastus handed Kelera a cup of tea, then remembering his manners, he said, "Lady Kelera, this is Grace. Grace, this is Lady Kelera... The woman who shared in your son's punishment so that he could be spared from the sum of his lashings."

Kelera choked on the tea she was drinking. Regaining her composure, she set the cup down on the table in front of her. She had misread the relationship between them. He had brought her here to meet the woman whose son she had tried to help. Grace's eyes were filled with tears. She placed a hand over her heart and bowed her head to Kelera.

Her voice reminded Kelera of a songbird. It was soft and sweet as she said, "I can never repay you for the kindness and mercy you showed to my dear Ferden." She moved from her seat and came over to Kelera. Kneeling on the floor in front of her, Grace vowed, "No matter where you go in this world, know that you have a friend here in the Winter Court." She dipped her head near Kelera's knees and then stood.

Kelera was touched by her actions and words, but couldn't think of anything she could say in return to such a declaration. She had not stepped in to help the boy so that she could call forth a debt from him and his family later. She had only wanted to spare him the pain and humiliation that he didn't deserve in the first place.

She raised her hand to the locket and ran her fingers along the engravings as she tried to think of the right response. "That is very kind but—"

Adrastus put a hand on her knee, interrupting her mid-sentence. "But Lady Kelera is not used to our customs and traditions yet. She accepts your declaration of friendship and extends her hand to you and your family as well."

Kelera felt like she should be paying close attention to the words he was saying, but all she could concentrate on was his hand on her leg. Her heart thudded in her chest and she felt a blush creep across her face. It was bold of him to touch her like this, and it reminded her of the night before when he had pressed her against the wall. He removed his hand as quickly as he had set it on her and stood. Kelera followed suit and Grace led them to the door.

Kelera tried not to tense as Grace pulled her into a hug. Other than Cierine, the people of the mortal court had never been comfortable enough around her to touch her so freely and openly. She relaxed her shoulders slightly and returned the embrace.

Grace pulled away and smiled brightly. "Well then, I send you off with blessed wishes." She turned to Adrastus. "Both of you."

"We accept them with thankful hearts." Adrastus put an arm around Kelera to lead her out the door.

Grace stopped them just as they crossed the threshold. "Oh, I almost forgot. The wine you brought from the Autumn Court—it did wonders for the child. She will live, thanks to you."

Adrastus dipped his head and turned away, leading Kelera back to the stables. She pulled her gloves onto her hands as she walked and said, "The wine she mentioned... is it the wine you stole from Vaz?"

"It was." He winked at her. "He was always as bad as a dragon hoarding treasure. And a friend of mine was in dire need of healing, so I helped myself."

"I feel guilty now for thinking you were a common thief." Kelera was half joking, but she couldn't deny that she did feel bad for thinking the worst of him.

He grunted in response, reminding her briefly of his father, whose general response to most things was a grunt or a growl. They rounded the corner of the street and came to the large stables. Chance began to prance around at their return, eager to get out of the restricting stall holding him.

Kelera patted Chance on the forehead as she studied Adrastus. "You risked your life against the warlock so that you could give it to the villagers. So they could heal one of their children." He could claim to be just another monster in her story all he wanted, but time after time, his actions proved otherwise. When he said nothing, she pressed further, "Why hide your compassion? If you would just—"

Adrastus' jaw twitched. He took a deep breath, then turned to face her. "Aside from Gadreel, my family would not be able to name one person in this village. I do not agree with their ways and anything that I do to contradict them is done in secret. But if you are going to appeal to me again on behalf of your mortals, you are wasting your breath."

Kelera's frustration got the better of her. She swung open the stall door, hitting Adrastus with it. "I was only trying to understand the kind of man you are. Nothing more." She stomped out of the barn with Chance following at her heels.

They rode back in the direction of the palace in silence. Adrastus wore the look of a scolded child, and Kelera felt a bit guilty for snapping at him. She had no business talking to a prince like that, not in any realm. It was not her place. And she *had* asked for his help the previous night. Could she blame him for thinking she would try again? Or that she had any other motive than getting free of her punishment and rushing over the blackthorn veil to warn her mortal king of the conspiracies within his own court?

She didn't want Adrastus to be suspicious of her. She would need to choose her words more carefully from now on if she was to get him to keep his guard down. If she wanted any chance of escaping or any opportunity to figure out which mortals had made a deal with Samael to carry out the kidnappings, then she would need to do everything within her power to go unnoticed at the Unseelie Court. Her mind was spinning. Would it be wise to make a run for it when she still didn't know who the traitor was? And would it be worth the risk to stay just to figure it out? She felt a headache coming on.

He broke the silence as he asked, "Do you have any memory of your mother?"

The question caught her off guard. "I used to dream of her. But the older I got, the more the memory faded away."

"And do you think of her now that you're in Elfhame?" He studied her face with genuine curiosity.

"I've thought of her a few times. Wondering how close in proximity we might be. Or if she would know who I was if she saw me..." She threw her head back to look at the stars twinkling in the sky. "It's silly of me, I know."

He halted his horse, and she met his eyes. "Not at all. I too grew up without my mother. When my father found out about my existence, he decided he would not have a son raised amongst the Seelie. He sent his Night Riders to collect me in the dead of the night. They tore me from her arms, and I have been without her since."

"That's heartbreaking."

"That is the reality of my father and his rule."

They quieted after that. Lost in thoughts of love lost and childhoods forever altered. Kelera rode on, trusting Chance to walk the path that was familiar to him, when a cackle of laughter interrupted them. Adrastus halted his horse immediately and jumped down. Kelera started to swing her leg over the saddle, but he held a hand up to stop her. He pressed a finger to his lips, reminding her of the moment they first met. This time, she did as he bid without a second thought. Creatures that were unknown to her lurked in the darkness here, and she was not willing to risk either of their lives by being stubborn.

The laughter came again, but this time it was from several directions. Whoever, or whatever, was out there had surrounded them.

Chapter Twenty-Two

T he first attack came from behind. It was swift, nearly dropping Adrastus to his knees. Another one of
the attackers descended on Adrastus in the blink of an
eye. Moving so fast that it was a blur in the darkness. The
white light of magic burst from Adrastus, knocking both
of the creatures unconscious. Now that they were on the
ground, unmoving, Kelera could make out a better view
of them.

They were as pale as the snow they were laying on.
She moved Chance a few steps closer so she could get
a better look. As she inched closer, she could see that
the tips of their ears and fingers were black with intense
frostbite. There were patches of it along their exposed
necks as well. Kelera covered her mouth in disgust and
looked away.

Adrastus fought off another one of the creatures.
Where were they coming from? Her heart was racing

as she squinted into the darkness, trying to catch sight of any more attackers. Chance danced around the hard packed snow, and she pulled the reins tight. This could be her chance to make a run for it. Adrastus was distracted, and she was confident that he knew how to handle himself. It would give her the perfect head start. She turned Chance toward the tree line and kicked hard.

She made it only a few yards before she felt something tighten around her neck. She dropped the reins and reached for her throat. Nothing was there, yet she was still gasping for breath as it began to strangle her. She fumbled for the reins and pulled them back, stopping Chance from running any further. Her vision blurred as she turned him back the way they had come.

As soon as she came within view of Adrastus, the hold on her throat loosened. She sucked in the cold winter air, welcoming the sting of it. She wiped away the angry tears in her eyes. Adrastus was still struggling with the Fae who had ambushed them, and she realized it couldn't have been his magic that had nearly strangled her. She clenched the reins tightly between her hands. So now she finally knew what King Cyrus' sentencing spell meant. And it broke some of the hope inside her.

She was relieved to see that Adrastus was still faring well against the attackers. But they were still coming. Several of the rotting Fae were slain, staining the snow red. She turned her head just in time to spot movement in the shadows. It was headed straight for Adrastus.

She shouted, "To your left!"

Before the attacker could reach him, Adrastus called on his magic. The same white light as before burst from him at all angles, but this time it was accompanied by icy blue power. It was magic that she had seen Samael wield. It intertwined like a web, utterly consuming the attacker. The Fae writhed on the ground, trying to pull the strands of power away from his body. But it was to no avail. Adrastus held strong to the power, tightening it around the man's body.

"You attacked the wrong rider tonight, *rouge*." Adrastus snapped a finger and the man's eyes turned black. "You prey on the weak. Scaring them into submission to get what you want. Let's turn the tables, shall we?" The man let out an ear curdling scream and Kelera watched in horror as he clawed at his head. He tugged and pulled at his hair as tears pooled down his cheeks.

Kelera jumped from the horse. "He's had enough! Adrastus!"

He ignored her, focusing solely on the man at his mercy. She ran to them and grabbed hold of Adrastus' arm. His face was devoid of emotion. She looked down at the man to find blood running from his nose and eyes. She tugged on Adrastus again.

"Please, Adrastus! Arrest him. Put him in the dungeons. Just, please, stop!"

Adrastus turned on her, grabbing her by the hair, and she yelped in surprise. The rage in his eyes disappeared at her cry. He released her immediately and took a step back. He avoided her eyes, looking down at the ground like he was ashamed.

The attacker was still on the ground, whimpering in pain. Without another glance in his direction, Adrastus mounted the white horse and began to ride away. Kelera looked back at the man one last time, conflicted on whether or not to help him. He was in pain, but how many countless others had been hurt at his and his friends' hands? Perhaps this was justice.

She huffed as she pulled herself back into the saddle and allowed Chance to trot in order to catch up to Adrastus. She was nervous as she asked, "Are you alright?"

"I'm fine," he replied, though he didn't look like it. Had he noticed her escape? Her body shook with adrenaline.

"You don't look fine." She watched his chest rise and fall in quick breaths.

Adrastus let out a heavy sigh. "I should not have allowed myself to merge it."

She thought of the streams of magic she had watched interlace around the man. "You mean your magic?"

He slowed the horse and looked at her for the first time since the attack. There was shame and regret on his face as he explained, "I am the bastard prince of the Unseelie Court. I am both night and day. It is unnatural and volatile to mix the power. It... *I* become unstable when I weave it together." He ran a hand through his raven-colored hair. "I could have hurt you..."

"But you didn't." He had scared her, but he had not hurt her. And she felt deeply that he needed to hear it said out loud. She could see he was shaken in the way his hands trembled as he held the reins.

"That rogue Fae was not so lucky." Adrastus raised his face to the sky. The stars were exceptionally bright tonight, blanketing the sky like millions of diamonds above.

"You told him you would turn the tables on him. Make him feel the fear that he made others endure at his gain... What was it that you did exactly?"

He clicked at his horse to pick up the pace again. The palace was in their line of vision now, and Kelera felt an ache in her heart at the thought of being cooped up in it again. Before the attack, she had been enjoying herself.

Just when she thought he wouldn't answer her question, he said, "I dug into his mind, calling forth his greatest fears. Like a nightmare that he could not escape until I allowed it."

Her voice trembled as she asked, "Do your brothers possess that same ability?"

"Not exactly. Dream magic is of the Seelie Court. A gift from my mother, whoever she was. But mixed with my Unseelie magic, it becomes something more sinister. Allowing me to pull forth nightmares instead of dreams."

Kelera thought about the dreams and visions warning her about her return to Elfhame. Those were nothing like what she'd just witnessed. She thought of the nightmarish vision Samael had given to Cierine when he first tried to pry Kelera's magic out from her. How easily she forgot that the two were cut from the same cloth. That Adrastus was just as dangerous as the rest of them. She whispered, "Like Samael."

"But worse. Samael is able to pull forth fears, and with the help of his shadows, he can make those fears feel every bit as real as you and I are. Mine goes further than that, though, burrowing its way into the deepest corners of their minds." Servants from the palace met them at the gate, taking Adrastus' horse first. His boots hit the ground hard as he dismounted. "Will you excuse me? I just... I need a moment. I will call on you later." He bounded up the stairs, leaving Kelera behind. She jogged up the palace steps, but as soon as she made it to the door, Gadreel stepped in her path.

She nearly slammed into him, and he furrowed his brow at her. "Where are you rushing off to in such a hurry?"

Kelera peeked around him, trying to see where Adrastus had gone, but he was nowhere to be seen. She shook her head. "Nowhere, I guess."

"Good. Because you're coming with us." He looped his arm around hers and turned her in the direction of the stairs.

She groaned as Gadreel led her through the halls. "Where are we going? To the library?"

The tall, handsome Fae that Gadreel had danced with at the revel fell into step beside them. "So, this is the lovely little halfling that's been wreaking all the havoc between your brothers?" The way he said halfling didn't sound as demeaning as when Samael said it. She studied the Fae man's face with interest. He was slender, but he carried himself with a quiet strength. Much like the knights under her father's command. He was dressed plainly this time without the bark-colored armor and sash.

There was admiration in Gadreel's eyes when he looked at him. "Kelera, may I have the pleasure of formally introducing you to Oliver, emissary and renowned warrior of the Seelie Court."

Kelera shot them both a puzzled look. "Is it safe for you to be here?"

Oliver shrugged carelessly. "Why wouldn't it be?"

Gadreel was kind enough to explain, "My father is, at times, barbaric, but he follows the ancient rules of etiquette. Oliver works closely with us in regard to court relations." He nudged Oliver in the side. "Plus, he likes to live a little dangerously from time to time. What better place to do that than here?" He gave Kelera a sly wink.

Kelera followed them through the halls and past the library. *I guess that means no lessons today,* she thought to herself. She considered trying to find Adrastus to make sure he was okay, but part of her feared what would happen when the rush of the ambush wore off. She had tried to escape. It had been reckless, and she hadn't considered the consequences of what would happen if she failed. Perhaps it would be best to give him space. Besides, Gadreel seemed eager to bring her along with him and Oliver.

They reached a hall filled with deep purple doors adorned with small yellow suns. While Gadreel fiddled with the lock on one of them, Kelera turned to Oliver. "So you come here to the Unseelie Court for danger and excitement?" She teased, "I'm not sure if that makes you brave or reckless..."

He smirked at her. "I could say the same about you."

Kelera burst into laughter. Gadreel turned to look at her in surprise just as the lock clicked and the door opened. "You're in good spirits today. Hold on to that." He came around to cover her eyes from behind and guided her into the room. Normally, being led blindly into any room of the Unseelie palace would have made her feel uneasy, but it was different with Gadreel. She trusted him.

Once they were in the room, he uncovered her eyes. "Welcome to the main event." Candlelight blazed to life around the room, revealing an intimate setting filled with pillows and colorful veils scattered across the floor. There were trays of food and decanters of glittering drinks set up carefully around each of the sitting areas. The scene spilled into the other rooms of Gadreel's quarters as well. It was like stepping into another world.

Shadows danced on the walls, taking on shapes of rabbits and hounds. They chased the poor creatures around the room, fading from view and then popping up again when Kelera least expected it. She was utterly awestruck at the detail that went into such a beautiful setting.

She ran a hand along the bead embroidered pillows. "And what sort of main event might this be? Certainly, one more comfortable than the pits."

Gadreel chuckled, "Much more. I figured now that you are free of Samael's clutches, we should celebrate. Besides, you could use some fun." He held his hand over one of the decanters, allowing magic to flow from his fingertips. The blue liquid inside of the glass turned to a sea-foam green. Gadreel nodded in satisfaction. "You see... we have spent all of our time together trying to awaken *your* magic, yet I have not had the pleasure of showing you what mine can do."

Kelera thought of the shadow figures he had played with when she'd had drinks with his family. She had assumed his powers were similar to Samael's, but perhaps instead of shifting into the shadows, he could control them.

Oliver poured three glasses from the decanter and handed one to Gadreel. The two men clinked glasses and then raised them to their lips. They drank deeply, closing their eyes in pleasure as the glittering liquid drained from their glasses.

When Gadreel opened his eyes, his pupils had become significantly dilated. Oliver danced over to the door, moving his body smoothly without any music playing. Gadreel offered the third glass to Kelera. She hesitated, but Gadreel assured her, "It will not impair, only enhance. As I promised the other night."

She took the glass. "And if I'm not sure I want to partake?"

"Then you are free to watch." He signaled for Oliver to open the main door that they had come through earlier. Courtiers poured into the room. Some were familiar faces and others were new. They strolled in without a care in the world and began eating and drinking. The room grew noisy with chatter and music, and Kelera had to step closer to Gadreel to hear him. He took a bite from a large purple fruit and explained, "You see, my friend, we all have our gifts. I just happen to excel at the arts of ecstasy." He tilted his head to her glass.

She would have been surprised if she had not grown so used to Gadreel's uplifting spirit and encouraging attitude. It made perfect sense that someone like him would devote their powers to the pleasure of others. "I am very impressed." She handed him the glass. "But I think I'll take you up on your offer to just watch."

Gadreel shrugged his shoulders. "As you wish." He walked away to join Oliver on a pile of cushions. He settled into the crook of Oliver's arm as they both leaned back to watch the shadow scenes play out on the walls. Others followed suit, lounging together in tangled limbs while enjoying the show. Kelera sat on a set of cushions off to the side. The shadows on the wall changed from animals into riders on skeletal horseback.

It reminded her faintly of the Night Rider she had encountered during Cierine's escape. But there was something more noble about the shadows on the walls here. There were a number of the riders, all galloping in perfect unison on top of what looked like shadowy stars.

There was a small group of Fae sitting within earshot of her, and she heard their excited whispers. "The Wild Hunt!" they gasped as the shadows gave chase to what appeared to be knights on a battlefield. They were fleeing from the riders in the sky and Kelera could make out the shapes of their swords, sharp and swift as they plunged them into any soldiers standing in their way.

She listened to the group near her talking in hushed tones, "Someone in the Autumn Court swore they spotted them the night she came through."

One of them argued, "I heard Prince Adrastus was there, too. Who is to say it was not his presence that awakened them?"

Another scoffed in response, "The Wild Hunt has not been seen for centuries. Surely a mere halfling would not have awakened such ancient beasts. But a prince of both Unseelie and Seelie blood..."

Kelera's heart sank as she realized they were talking about her and Adrastus. She could feel eyes on her now and did her best to concentrate on the shadow show, pretending she couldn't hear them. She had played this part many times before, keeping her face neutral as King Tristan's court gossiped about her while in the same room.

She watched the shadows dance on the walls and thought back to the history books. The Wild Hunt was an ancient tale that outdated almost every other story she'd read. Sightings of them were rumored to have warned of oncoming war and radical change. She couldn't fathom what that would have to do with her specifically.

The first Fae spoke again. "King Cyrus believes she killed a Night Rider. Aren't you curious about the power she holds? Or who her mother might be?"

A third Fae chimed in, "Answers King Cyrus will no doubt ascertain as quickly as possible."

The second Fae chuckled. "If he doesn't, Prince Samael will."

Heat rose to Kelera's cheeks as the others laughed. She risked a glance in their direction and caught the eye of the Fae who had spoken first. Her silver hair was cut short, a strange style for the court, as other women seemed to prefer their hair longer. She gave Kelera a small, kind smile and nodded in acknowledgment. Kelera returned the gesture, then went back to watching the shadows.

It was some time before anyone in the group spoke again. The scene had once again changed. This time into a love story. From what Kelera gathered, it was a woman forced to choose between two lovers. The men were engaging in a battle for her heart, and Kelera thought of Alexander for the first time in a while. It was painful to think of him. She had been gone for weeks now. Was he out there looking for a way to get to her? Would he come to claim her like the man in the shadow show, or would he move on? His father had been clear about his disappointment in the match. Perhaps this would be Alexander's chance to bow out of the engagement gracefully.

The word *mortal* caught her attention as the group of Fae began to whisper again. Kelera immediately pushed her thoughts aside and listened in as one of them continued, "Prince Samael told me himself." The tone of the group changed, and no one laughed as he said, "The mortal always meets him on the western side of the veil. He is well respected in their idiot king's court, so no one suspects a thing!"

"I hear he's a nasty one."

Someone snorted. "Must be, if he's willing to betray his own."

Kelera's fast beating heart drowned out the murmurs from the group. Someone in King Tristan's court had betrayed them. She had known that much. But who would be traitorous enough to make a deal with the devil himself? What did he gain from it? She thought of Lord Cunningham. The man who had put the hunting party together. He was a greedy man and a gambler. Rumors floated around often about the money he owed to collectors for his gambling debts. If Samael had offered him riches in exchange for helping him, then it wouldn't be out of the realm of possibility that he had accepted...

The shadow show stopped as the men in the story plunged swords into each other's hearts, leaving the love of their lives to mourn them. Once it was over, the candle flames grew, lighting up the room. The group lost interest in the subject as the music tempo picked up. Kelera was lightheaded. Unsure if it was the smell of the plant some of the Fae in the room were smoking, or the news she had just overheard, she decided she needed to get out of the room.

No one had told her to stay put, so technically leaving would not mean breaking any rules. She looked around to be sure no one was watching her. For a split second, she wondered how far she would get if she tried to escape through the forest again. On her own, she would likely stand a better chance. And with the spell still tying her to the royal family, it would no doubt mean death. She would need to think of another way to get a message to her father about the snake living amongst them.

For now, her bedroom would have to do. She could lay down for a bit and wait to be summoned for dinner. It was her first day under Adrastus' supervision and it seemed he, like Samael, was content with letting Gadreel handle the burden of watching her.

She wondered if she should just tell Gadreel she was going to her room. She scanned the quarters and spotted him through the open door to one of the rooms. He and Oliver were engaged in an intimate act with a small woman who had intricate tattoos along her back. Kelera's jaw dropped. She had never seen such an open display of passion. Their naked limbs were tangled as they moved together in harmony. Blinking a few times in disbelief, Kelera turned away. Gadreel would most definitely not miss her. Without a word, she slipped silently out the door.

She backed into the hallway, closing the door as gently as she could so she would not draw attention to herself. She blew out a breath of relief. Proud of her stealth, she turned on her heel and smacked right into someone. She looked up at an amused Adrastus and gasped. "Your Highness! I was just..."

"Trying to escape my brother's scandalous soiree?" He chuckled softly. "They get more and more outrageous every year. I stopped going ages ago after one of the curtains caught fire and nearly burned the whole room to the ground."

She eyed him warily, wondering if he would bring up her attempted escape. Trying to keep the conversation light, she said, "Oh. It actually seemed rather relaxing..." Kelera hadn't thought it to be that wild, aside from the carnal scene she had caught Gadreel in as she'd left.

"Had you waited any longer, you would have found yourself naked amongst a pile of very flexible courtiers."

Unaccustomed to such unrefined talk, she felt heat rush to her face. Adrastus looked apologetic. "Apologies. That was crude of me." He leaned against the wall with his arms crossed. "Since you clearly do not plan on going back in there, how about a game instead?"

Cautiously, she asked, "What sort of game?"

"Chess." When she only stared at him questioningly, he added, "You have it in the mortal realm, no?"

He really meant chess. This was not a trick. She nodded, feeling silly for the second time that night. "Yes, of course. My father and I played often when I was younger..." She trailed off as the longing for her father hit her. It was like stones being piled in her stomach. She hoped he wasn't driving himself mad at the loss of her.

Adrastus tilted his head, waiting for her to respond. She was caught between the urge to put distance between them and having the chance to get more answers out of him. If the courtiers knew about the mortal traitor, then maybe Adrastus knew who it was. And realizing that she had no good reason to give him for saying no, the latter won out. She nodded, accepting the offer. He held his hand out to her.

She looked from his hand to his face with a furrowed brow. He raised an eyebrow at her. "It is not a trick."

"Where I come from, it is not proper for a man to be so forward with an unmarried, unchaperoned woman."

"Ah, yes, the uptight law of man in the mortal lands." He rolled his eyes, but did not retract the offer of his outstretched hand.

Kelera sighed and took it. Her breath caught the moment his fingers laced around hers. It felt more intimate than she had expected. She thought of the men and women engaging in carnal pleasures on the other side of the purple door beside them. What would it be like to let go of it all? To embrace the freedom that others enjoyed in Elfhame. To feel Adrastus' hands on her and not just wrapped around her fingers.

"Shall we?" Adrastus was staring at her intently.

Kelera jumped. "Shall we?"

"Shall we go play?" He smirked at her, "Chess?"

Relieved he couldn't read her mind, Kelera nearly shouted, "Oh! Yes, yes please."

She tried to get her bearings back as Adrastus led her down the hall and away from the purple room of pleasures.

Chapter Twenty-Three

Her father was going to be so disappointed in her. At least, he would be if she ever made it home. Kelera had now been in countless rooms, alone, with men who were not her fiancé. It would have been quite the scandal in the mortal court. And after the kiss, she wasn't sure she could trust herself to be alone with Adrastus. She paced the room as she waited for him to return from his bedroom.

They were in his private chambers. She stopped pacing for a moment and looked around at the large room. It was more modest than Samael's was. A simple set of sofas and nice, polished wooden furniture was placed with careful precision around the room. There was no bar, but instead a lovely stack of bookshelves beside a roaring fireplace.

"Can I get you anything?" He had returned from his bedroom and was wearing only a linen shirt and his breeches. He made her nervous. Not in the way she was nervous with Samael. There was no mistaking that Adrastus was every bit as dangerous as his brother, but she didn't feel the same sense of dread when she was with him. Instead, it was almost... thrilling.

Her palms were sweating. She wiped them on her dress. Not a lady-like thing to do, but here in this court, she couldn't be sure that she was a lady at all.

Life in the mortal court felt like another lifetime. It was as if everything she had taught herself to do had been left at the veil. All her perfections, now mocked by the Unseelie who thought her silly for trying to fit in when she could stand out.

Adrastus pulled a seat out for her at the small table near the bookshelves. Her hand brushed against his as she walked over to take her seat. There was something in the way he looked at her as he pushed her chair in. Something that spoke of the things he would do if her heart would give him permission.

Her hand was still warm from where it brushed against his. She folded her hands in her lap, waiting for him to begin the game. He bit his lip and raised an eyebrow at her before he said, "You ran."

This was it. The moment she'd been anticipating. There was no point in denying it. "I did."

There was pity in his eyes as he said, "You had to have known you wouldn't get far."

"I had to try." She could still feel the magic trying to strangle her as the horse took her farther from Adrastus.

He grunted. "I was grateful for your help back there. If you hadn't returned when you did, then that rogue might have gotten the jump on me."

"I didn't have much of a choice." She watched his hands as he poured them each a drink from the decanter on the table. She recalled the way they had felt on the small of her back and she felt a heat rising in her that wasn't from her magic.

He shrugged as he handed her a glass. "You might not have had a choice in returning, but you didn't have to help me."

He had a point. "I suppose I owed you one."

He chuckled. "I suppose you did." He grabbed a pawn and made his first move, then looked up at her under his heavy lashes. "Your move."

Her move indeed.

He was good, but she was better. They'd been going at this for hours. Game after game, they had bested one another. But as of now, Kelera was in the lead.

"Check mate," she said, as she took his queen.

Adrastus slumped in his seat and rubbed at his face with the palm of his hand. The first time she had beaten him, her body had tensed, anticipating his reaction. In her experience, men did not enjoy being bested by a woman. Who knew what a dark prince of the Unseelie court would do? But instead of finding anger on his face, she had looked up to find an amused smile playing across his lips. "Well done, little thief." He had used the nickname, making her stomach flutter with unwelcome excitement.

Now, his leg brushed against hers as he sat back up. It slid from her knee to her inner thigh and her breath caught in her throat. Adrastus smiled knowingly, then retreated his leg away from hers.

Spending time with him alone like this was dangerous. She had to keep reminding herself that he wasn't her ally, or her friend. But when he smiled at her like that, it was difficult to hold her resolve. And she had to admit, she was enjoying herself. She folded her hands in her lap while he set the board again. "You're quite good at this," she said.

"I'm inclined to attribute that to a life at court. As I'm sure you can agree, considering how we've been forced to manipulate and maneuver our way through it our entire lives." His hair fell into his eyes as he looked up at her with a lopsided smile. Kelera made the first move, sending her pawn into the field. Adrastus took his turn, speaking as he did so, "You and I are alike. Both trapped in a court that we don't fully belong in."

"Do not forget the part you played in trapping me here. Had you not stopped me, I would have been through the veil with Cierine." She wasn't trying to start a fight with him, but it was a fact.

"He would have found another way to get to you."

"I've heard that excuse before."

"Yes, and I'll continue to remind you until you believe it." Adrastus stared intently into her eyes, holding his pawn above the board. He didn't move to play it. Instead, he continued, "In you, he saw someone that he could manipulate. Someone he could bring here and mold into his image."

Kelera scoffed. "We all see how that worked out."

Adrastus sighed. "He saw how you shaped yourself for the mortals. But what he did not take into account was that you hate being what others want you to be."

Kelera snatched the pawn from Adrastus' fingers. Rolling it over in her hand, she mused, "Perhaps you're right. But what choice do I have except to become what everyone else needs me to be?"

He took the pawn back from her and made his move on the board. "There is always a choice, little thief."

"And what of your choices, your Highness?" She made her move, capturing his pawn.

"My choices keep myself and the people I care about safe."

"Like the child in the village?"

Adrastus stilled. His jaw twitched as he said, "I do what I can for them."

Maybe it was the wine, or maybe it was the fact that she was tired of treading carefully that made her push him with her words, "Yet you still let your brothers conduct their brutal fights. You allow them to carry out unjust punishments and only step in when you think they may go too far." Adrastus' face turned red, but Kelera kept going, "You are right, I am not the only one who has maneuvered her way through court. And I would go so far as to say you have been wearing a mask just like me."

Adrastus' demeanor shifted into something darker. "Careful."

"What if I am done being careful? You act as if you are willing to sacrifice anything to keep your people safe, yet here we sit, playing chess in the comfort of your palace." If only she could call on her magic to remind him that she wasn't a damsel in distress. If she could just take hold of it, she could make them all see.

His eyes darkened as he looked at her. "You don't understand."

She sat forward and challenged him, "Then *make me*."

He swept his arm across the small table, knocking the chessboard to the ground. The pieces scattered to the floor with a clatter, and Kelera jumped back in her seat.

His glamor faded in the heat of his frustration. He lunged at her, stopping with his hands on either side of her chair. His knuckles turned white as he gripped the wood. The sudden outburst shook her, but she didn't flinch as she looked up at the scarred skin covering his handsome face.

Surprise flashed across his eyes as if her courage struck a chord with him, but it was quickly replaced again with irritation as he said, "You are once again on dangerous ground. You know nothing of my sacrifices." He paused to run his fingers along her unblemished face. She froze, wondering if he would take her right there if she gave him the chance. He leaned in closer, his breath hot on her face.

"And whose fault is that?" she asked. He was the one who refused to see her as anything other than a helpless woman who had to be protected from his brother. He acted like she had nothing else to offer. Maybe he was right. But it didn't mean she wasn't willing to try to help.

She raised her chin, looking into his eyes. As terrified as she was, something more primal inside of her wanted to see how far he would take it. What would it be like if she just let go of everything that had been holding her back? If she turned her back on everything that she had worked so hard for. What if they could let go together? Who would they become? True, as a prince of the Unseelie Court, he was an enemy to her people. But in here, at this moment, Kelera wanted to know what it would be like to belong with someone. Anyone. Even if it was him.

The frustration on his face was replaced with desire as his lips lingered over hers. She leaned forward, flinching in surprise as her lips brushed against his. He pushed her hair away from her ears and tangled his fingers in it. His icy, shadow magic brushed against her neck as if illuminating from his hands. It didn't frighten her though. She leaned into the kiss, hungry for more, but the image of Alexander flashed in her mind. Guilt washed over her like a tidal wave, and she pulled back quickly. She put her fingers to her lips and shook her head.

"I—I'm so sorry. I don't know what came over me." She shoved her seat back, nearly knocking it over.

Adrastus straightened with a look of confusion on his face. "Kelera, I—"

Before he could say another word, she turned and fled from the room. She crossed the hall of dark blue doors and found her bedroom. Slamming the door shut behind her, she slumped against it. Sliding down to the floor, she brought her knees to her chest and buried her face in them.

What is wrong with me? He is my enemy. Bitter tears spilled from her eyes. Every moment she enjoyed with Adrastus, every moment she spent admiring the village—or the Fae who lived there—was just another moment that made her a traitor to her people. They were in danger, yet here she was attending pleasure parties and kissing one of the king's favored sons over a game of chess. He had no intention of helping her save them. Not if she had nothing to give him in return.

She was losing sight of what was important here. Young mortal girls would continue to suffer if she kept on going the way she was. She would not allow that to happen. A week. That is the amount of time she would give herself to get the information she needed and find a way to use her magic to break her out of the Unseelie Court.

It was a huge risk. One that could kill her if she lost control of the magic. One that could mean giving Samael the chance to take her power. But it didn't matter. She would face the wrath of King Cyrus and his sons. Her loyalty belonged to the mortal people. To King Tristan... and to her father.

Every moment she spent in the Unseelie Court was another moment that would allow her to change into someone she didn't recognize. It was another moment for her to lose everything.

Chapter Twenty-Four

It was strange how used to waking at sunset Kelera was becoming. Spending her days sleeping and her nights awake felt as natural as anything else. Each night when the moon rose, she found herself looking forward to seeing the bright starlight streaming through her window.

What did not feel natural, however, was the way things had ended between her and Adrastus the night before. Trying to understand the sort of man he was, drove her mad. It was like trying to solve a puzzle at knifepoint.

The men in her life had always been very black and white. Her father was a man of noble nature. He was a knight through and through, and he acted accordingly. Alexander, though they had only a short time together, seemed to be a man of high sensibilities.

Samael, of course, was easy to figure out. He was ruthless and arrogant. Adrastus, on the other hand, was like a smorgasbord of all these men. He cared for his people but was hesitant to show it to his family. And it seemed he extended that same hesitation toward her, keeping her at arm's distance. It was like he was afraid if anyone got too close, then they might see that he was, in fact, a heroic soul. And would that be so awful? If others admired him? Why was he so intent on making her think he was like his father and brothers?

Tired of stewing on these questions, Kelera got ready for the day. No breakfast had been brought to her room, so she wandered out in search of nourishment. Adrastus didn't lock her in her room, but she wasn't sure if it was because he knew she couldn't get far with the magic restraint his father had placed on her or because he trusted her.

She reached the end of the hallway when it shifted suddenly. She could see the stairs to the ballroom. *Seriously?* She thought to herself. Out loud, she said, "I just want some food." *Well, that's it. I've finally lost my mind. I'm talking to a palace.* She groaned and leaned with her back against the wall. Magic swelled in the hallway and Kelera fell onto the floor.

The wall she had been leaning on was gone and there was a new entryway in its place. The smell of fresh baked goods wafted toward her. The palace had listened to her again. It was so strange. She couldn't recall hearing any of the courtiers or servants give it commands. Why was it listening to her? Thinking it was best not to question it, since the important thing was that it had taken her to the food, she walked on. She was practically drooling by the time she made it to the end of the new hallway. She pushed gently on the heavy wooden doors in front of her to reveal an empty kitchen.

Grateful that the palace had listened to her, she said, "Thank you." When she made it home one day, Cierine would never believe all the things she'd have to tell her. That is, *if* she made it home. She reached a hand to her throat where King Cyrus' magic had tightened around her like a noose.

She shook off the helpless feeling and stepped into the kitchen like a mouse snooping where it shouldn't. Then, looking around, she saw no servants to stop her, so she helped herself to the savory rolls on the counter. Next, she poured herself a heaping cup of something black. It was bitter with notes of cinnamon and nutmeg.

Pans clattered to the ground behind her, and she jumped, spilling the hot drink on her hand. She hissed and spun around to see what had caused the commotion. "What in the stars' name?"

A familiar small creature with eyes and a nose that were too large for its small face stared back at her. The brownie scratched at his wild, hairy head. "I didn' mean for that to happen."

Kelera looked around, nervous that the kitchen staff would walk in and find the mess. She bent down to pick up the pots and pans. "What are you doing here?"

"I followed the whispers." He clenched his hands together and took an eager step toward her.

She inched away from him cautiously. "What whispers?"

"That the sunshine was here to melt the ice." He rang his hands together and looked around nervously.

Kelera huffed in frustration. She was tired of riddles. She reached out to him, careful not to spook him, and set her hands gently on his shoulders. Speaking softly as if she were talking to a child, she said, "When I found you in my father's tent at the tournament, you said you were waiting for the trouble to pass in winter. You meant the Winter Court, right?" He nodded. Relieved to be getting somewhere, she pressed on, "But you came here because of the sunshine?" He nodded again. Good. She continued, "Who is the sunshine?"

He gave her a puzzled look and tilted his head. "You are the sunshine, silly."

Kelera bit the inside of her lip. The sunshine was here to melt the ice... She gave his shoulders a small squeeze. She needed him to focus. "Am I the sunshine because of my Seelie magic?"

"Yes!" He sounded exasperated, like he'd been waiting a long time for her to catch up. He put one of his small, clawed hands on her cheek. To her surprise, she didn't flinch. His eyes bore into hers as he said, "So, will you do it?"

Kelera put her hand on his. It was wrinkled and soft under her touch. "I'm not strong enough to take on Samael."

He pulled his hand away and tears welled in his eyes. "Then we are all lost."

Before she could stop him, he slipped away and scurried onto a table. Plates fell to the floor in his wake and shattered on the ground. Kelera called out to stop him, "Wait! Please, if you know anything else..." But before she could finish, he slipped out of the window and into the snowy night.

Kelera rubbed at her temples. She hadn't even had a chance to ask how things were in Nevene. She shouldn't have wasted time with his riddles. Angry with herself, she swung the kitchen door open and stepped into the hall.

The palace shimmered with magic and shifted to reveal rows of blue doors. The color blue had never comforted Kelera before, but it did now. She ran her fingers over the smooth paint and took a deep breath, relishing the safety she felt here in comparison with Samael's quarters.

She rested her forehead on one of the doors. She had experienced the anxiety that came with everyday life, but she had never felt such an overwhelming burden. She was letting everyone down and all because she couldn't trust herself—couldn't trust her magic.

"Admiring the carpet?" Adrastus asked from behind her. There was a hint of amusement in his voice.

She hadn't heard him approach. Surprised, she spun around to face him. His face was once again glamored to cover the scars, aside from the one he didn't bother to hide. His lovely green eyes were staring into hers. Her cheeks grew warm in embarrassment. "How long have you been standing there?"

"About as long as you." He kicked at the ground nervously. "Look, I was just coming to find you to... apologize for last night. It's difficult for me to talk about my brothers. From the moment I was brought to the palace, they have treated me as less than them."

"I can relate to that," Kelera offered. It was true. She had been teased and talked down to and she knew what sort of invisible bruises that could leave on a child.

He opened the door beside them and motioned for her to step inside. His fireplace was already lit, and the room was warm. She took a seat on a blue velvet chaise, and he joined her.

He turned to face her and took a deep breath as he said, "It's more than that. My brothers hate me because I am a threat to their claim to the throne. They've known it since we were little and have done everything within their power to remind me that I am not truly Unseelie—that I am tainted with Seelie blood."

Kelera leaned forward and rested her hand on his arm. "They fear you because you are stronger than they are. And because the people of this realm can see that."

He placed his hand on top of hers and caressed it gently. Her stomach fluttered with what felt like butterflies, but she held steady, careful not to give her feelings away. He was solemn as he said, "Cowards are not strong. And that's what I've been. I didn't want to admit that you were right when you said those things about me standing by and only stepping in once they've gone too far."

He ran his hand through his hair and shut his eyes tight, like he was having trouble talking about this with her. She waited patiently, allowing him the time he needed.

He gripped her hand tight. "I have to be careful when it comes to my brothers. I've stood against them in the past and it's only brought pain and misery. You might not understand my actions, but I need you to understand that they will not hesitate to put me down. And that fear has kept me from trusting myself."

"But surely your father can protect you. You are a prince with the same rights to the crown as them."

His voice was husky as he said, "My father prefers to stand on the side lines. He believes that only the worthy will survive a fight for his throne." He dropped his glamor and waited a moment. Kelera studied his marred face. When she first saw him in the forest with Vaz, she had known that this was a man who had lived a violent life. But she couldn't have fathomed how right she was.

Adrastus raised his chin. "My brothers did this to me. Samael said I was too pretty because of my Seelie blood. He said that they needed to remind me I was no better than they were. Kane and Ammon held me down while Samael sliced into me. He took his time and smiled as he did it. I'll never forget that smile." Kelera's heart felt like it was breaking in two. How could they do that to their own brother? All because of where his mother had been born. Adrastus gave the final blow to her heart as he finished, "I was eight years old."

A tear fell down Kelera's cheek. She wiped it away with the back of her free hand and did not loosen her grip on his arm with the other.

"Why are you telling me this?"

He tilted her chin up to look at him and then wiped away her new tears. "Because you're holding back and it's going to get you killed. Like me, you are afraid of trusting yourself and believing that you are strong enough to stand against the storm. I understand your need to be what others want you to be. I do not judge you for it. And I need you to do the same for me. I need you to understand why I have chosen to do things the way I have." She nodded in silent understanding. Then he added, "But after last night, I've realized something. We do not need to pretend with each other. I think it might be nice to have someone in this world with whom you can show your true self to."

She wanted to say yes. To say she was tired of being afraid of doing the wrong thing. She wanted to explain that she understood and that deep down she knew her heart had always been searching for someone that she could share these moments with. She had hoped and prayed that this was what it would be like with Alexander. Though she had never admitted it to herself, she had wanted him to take her for who she was. Not who she was masking herself to be.

As badly as she wanted to tell Adrastus that she could be that person for him, she couldn't. Not if she was going to get home to warn her father and King Tristan. And she could not break her promise to Alexander.

"Adrastus, I—"

The door swung open to reveal Gadreel. He was breathing heavily, and his eyes were wide as he said, "Brother, come quick. It's Father."

Kelera stumbled unsteadily through the halls after Adrastus and Gadreel. The palace was shifting so quickly it was hard to keep up. Gadreel's face was even paler than usual, looking as white as a wraith in the winter forest.

They reached the king's quarters to find the rest of the royal family and a few of the higher ranked courtiers. Kelera felt strange being there, knowing that she was not a member of the court, even if Adrastus was giving her more freedoms than Samael had.

She stood off to the corner while Adrastus followed Gadreel and the others into King Cyrus' bedroom. The courtiers lingered close to the door but did not dare to enter his room uninvited. Kelera watched their faces carefully.

One of the courtiers caught her eye. It was the small woman Gadreel and Oliver had been with the night before. Her large doe eyes brightened when they fell on Kelera. She nodded her head in a show of respect, and Kelera did the same.

The exchange caught the attention of a few of the other courtiers, and they too, nodded to Kelera. Her heart warmed at the attention. They weren't mocking her or avoiding her. Each one of them seemed to genuinely welcome her presence. One of the king's footmen came around the room with refreshments in hand. He stopped in front of Kelera.

She stared at the tray presented in front of her and gave him a small smile as she took the glass. She thought of the rude server at Cierine's reception who had snubbed her and refused to serve her.

Feeling more comfortable amongst the courtiers than before, Kelera found a seat to the side of the room. Small murmurs could be heard throughout the room. No one seemed to know exactly what was wrong with King Cyrus, but most of them were tense with worry. He seemed beloved enough with courtiers often trying to win favor with him. But with the way he allowed his sons to run wild through the kingdom, Kelera had doubts that everyone agreed with his ways.

She listened in intently.

"Poison from the Seelie Court, no doubt," one courtier whispered excitedly.

"Poison from the mortal court! For the girls that Prince Samael has stolen," another argued.

Others were claiming it was a simple cold and nothing to get worked up about. A few thought it was a curse for the blood spilled in the pits. Whatever it was had doctors rushing in and out of the room like madmen.

Kelera's nerves grew as she thought of what King Cyrus' death could mean. If he didn't recover, then the crown would be left for one of the princes to claim. She believed Adrastus could take it for himself. But Samael would be a formidable opponent. And she knew she would be caught in the middle.

Kelera turned her attention back to the king's bedroom, where she could hear Queen Beatrix barking orders. She couldn't make out the words, but she knew some poor soul was in for it now. Something clattered to the ground, and a man came running from the room with a bloody nose.

For star's sake. Someone needs to teach that horrid woman a lesson, Kelera thought. Queen Beatrix was a miserable creature, hell bent on making everyone else as miserable as her. How someone could be so unearthly beautiful and act as dreadful as she, Kelera would never understand.

Ammon and Samael were the next to leave the room. Kelera looked down at the ground as they passed her, hoping they wouldn't direct any frustration they were feeling at her. After a moment, she realized the rest of the family was planning to remain in the room.

Kelera slipped from the couch and backed into a shadowy corner. The two of them had to be up to no good. Why else would they leave while their father was on his possible death bed? If they were plotting something, then someone would need to warn Adrastus. And she still needed to know who it was that Samael was working with in Nevene. There were a number of men from court who it could be. It would have to be someone greedy. Someone who didn't despise the Fae. At least not so much so that he would be willing to help them.

Someone needed to follow them. She looked at the bedroom door. Adrastus and Gadreel were inside, and she couldn't call for them without drawing attention. Fearing she had no other choice, she slipped from the room and started down the hall.

There was no sign of Ammon or Samael. Adrastus had warned her to tread carefully where it concerned his brothers. His scarred face was evidence that there was no line they wouldn't cross, but her determination overrode her fear. She couldn't sit on the sidelines any longer. She closed her eyes and took a deep breath as she whispered to the palace, "Take me to Prince Samael." Magic folded itself around her and she watched the halls shift direction through the shimmering power. Her heart pounded in her chest. She was outside of the ballroom now and she pressed her ear to the servant's entrance and listened.

Ammon sounded like his usual self-righteous self as he chided Samael, "You need to tell me what is going on, brother."

"I don't have to do anything, Ammon. Are you forgetting who is in charge here?"

"Just tell me, are you going to meet with the mortals?" When Samael didn't answer, Ammon scoffed, "You're unbelievable. Father is sick and you're gallivanting off to play your games! You know, it is only a matter of time before they realize you have no intention of following through with your bargain."

Kelera gasped at the mention of the mortal traitor.

Samael laughed carelessly. "The imbecile doesn't suspect a thing. He believes me to be his greatest ally. Greedy fool."

"And what happens if Father dies? What happens when you control both of the courts? Will you keep your word to keep our people out of their borders, only allowing our people to wreak havoc in the northern countries?"

Samael tsked at Ammon. "I only said we would give Nevene the respect it deserves."

Ammon made a sound of disgust. "Why any of you would desire to pillage and run wild in the mortal realm, I will never understand."

"All *you* need to understand is that my plans are in motion. And unless you want to end up on the losing side of this war, you will do as I say."

Ammon lowered his voice, making Kelera press herself closer to the opening of the door so she could hear. "And what of Adrastus? If father dies, he will not stand aside and allow you to take the throne without a fight."

"He'll never see it coming. He's so distracted with his little village visits and now, with the halfling, he won't see me coming until it's too late."

Kelera steadied her breathing. Whatever Samael was planning, it involved hurting Adrastus. That bothered her more than she expected.

Ammon paused before saying, "Gadreel says the Seelie Queen's condition has worsened. And there have been whispers from the elders of the fabled lost heir rising to take their place. I know you've thought as I have that it could be—"

Samael slammed Ammon against the door on the other side and Kelera jumped back. Samael's voice was murderous as he said, "Adrastus is not... *cannot* be the heir."

"You can't know that. His power increases every day. I saw what he did to the rogue Fae coming back from the village. He shattered that man's mind. What if Father was lying when he said Adrastus' mother was a Seelie maid? What if she was of the royal line? Magic like that only manifests in the old families. If Adrastus is the lost heir as the prophecies foretell, then you must admit to yourself that it will make things more difficult for you."

Samael's voice was calm... too calm, as he said, "I will be the High King of Elfhame. No bastard prince of Unseelie is going to stand in my way. By the night's end, *I* will be king."

Kelera's heart sank. He didn't think King Cyrus would make it past sunrise.

Ammon's voice trembled in a mixture of fear and anger as he said, "Father's sudden illness... It was your doing."

Samael, in his usual careless attitude, replied, "All that matters is it won't be long now."

Ammon was more furious than Kelera had ever heard him as he shouted, "Fuck! You really are out of your damn mind! What if someone finds out you've poisoned the fucking king? Your own father."

"Who's going to say anything?" The room grew so cold that it crept out to Kelera. She could see her breath frosting in the air. Samael's voice sounded as if it were made from ice itself as he warned, "You chose your side. You bound your magic to me. There is no going back now. Once Kane binds himself to me, then I will be powerful enough to take the halfling from Adrastus."

Kelera's stomach dropped at the mention of her. Ammon's voice shook, "With all of that power, why do you still need her? She is nothing."

"She has the potential to be powerful. My contact in the mortal realm insists he can help me to make her more agreeable. She cares for her father. If I have to, I will bring him here." It sounded more like Samael was thinking out loud to himself than talking to Ammon still.

Ammon interrupted, "You did not answer my question, Samael. Why do you want *her* power so badly?"

"I need *Seelie* power if I am going to stand against Adrastus and if I am to make the Seelie Court kneel to me."

"What makes you think she will bind herself to you?"

"Because, you fool, she is a *halfling*. Her magic is volatile, and she has no idea how to control it. She'll have no choice but to bind her power to mine once I break her."

The hairs on Kelera's arms stood, and she felt the heat rise to the surface of her skin. Her magic. Just there at the surface. *No. Not here. Not now.* If Samael thought for a second that she could access her power, then he would not hesitate to tear her away from Adrastus' protection.

She backed away from the door. She had heard enough. What she needed now was distance from the two horrid men in the ballroom.

The conversation between Samael and Ammon was a lot to process. Did Adrastus know that their oldest brother had given up his claim to the throne to stand beside Samael as he took it for himself? Kane would no doubt side with Samael as well. They were two sides of the same malicious coin.

That left Gadreel and Adrastus. Would they be enough to stand together against the other three brothers? She needed to get to Adrastus to warn him of his brother's treacherous plans. She turned to leave, but the door to the ballroom opened behind her and something wound itself around her ankle. She fell face first into the ground, hitting her head on the stone floor. She felt blood trickle down her face and tried to regain her blackened vision.

Samael's voice rose like a snake in the grass behind her. "Seems you've picked up a few Unseelie habits here in my father's court. Surely, ladies do not eavesdrop in the mortal realm."

Kelera put her hand to her head to stop the bleeding. She didn't have time for his games. "You know even less about mortal women than I thought."

Samael grabbed her by the neck and raised a hand to strike her. Ammon cleared his throat, making him pause. "Samael, she is still under Adrastus' keep." Kelera nearly breathed a sigh of relief, thinking he would help her. The feeling was short lived, though, as he continued, "If you harm her here for anyone to see, then you risk setting things into motion too soon."

She glared at the men as Samael pulled her to her feet. He ran his fingers over her bloodied head and put them to his lips. He smiled at her as he licked her blood from his fingers. "Then let us find someplace more private."

The palace was eerily quiet, with everyone attending to King Cyrus. The halls did not shift this time as they walked. Instead, making her and Samael walk the long way to his quarters.

Kelera pleaded with Samael as he dragged her down the hall, "I heard nothing of significance. I was only trying to get back to my room, but the damned walls kept shifting. I swear it, Samael!"

"All of you mortal women have dirty, lying mouths. Would you like to see what I do to mortal tongues when they lie to me?" He swung her around him so that she was facing the red door at the end of the hallway.

Ammon followed them, trying to reason with Samael. "If Adrastus finds that she's missing, he'll kill us."

Samael ignored him and pushed Kelera toward the red door. It was the only thing standing between them and his room of shadows. Where screams could be heard at all hours of the day and night. Dread overwhelmed her. "Prince Samael, you do not have to do this..."

"Of course not. But I want to." He slammed her hard against the door, and her head throbbed in response. "I have wanted to take you to my room since the moment I first saw you. I admit, as much as your tainted blood disgusts me, I am intrigued by your spark. If it wasn't for the Seelie fire magic that killed my father's Night Rider, I would have surely thought your mother hailed from the Unseelie Court." He kissed her neck and her entire body revolted. She wanted to claw at him. To slap his face and tell him never to touch her again. He ran his tongue from the base of her neck to her ear and whispered, "It's too bad, really."

Kelera closed her eyes, willing him to go away. Instead, she heard the click of a lock as the door opened. Samael pulled her in by the arm. Hesitatingly, she opened her eyes. Ammon followed closely, shutting and locking the door behind the three of them.

The room was dark. So dark that it felt as if the entire chamber was made up of one large shadow. She squinted but couldn't see walls or furniture.

No. There was nothing frightening within sight. But that wasn't the problem. The problem was the ragged sound of breathing coming from several directions. Terror crept through her as Samael led her deeper into the room.

She wasn't sure how far they had walked, but it felt like miles. Her feet were beginning to ache and every nerve in her body was on high alert. The heavy breathing in the darkness around her began to mix with muffled cries and groans of pain. It was difficult to tell how many people Samael kept in here. It was likely that even he had lost track.

She stumbled down a small staircase. "Where are you taking me?" Her voice echoed in the room.

"I have reserved my favorite spot for you." He called on his magic and the room lit up with dozens of ice-covered crystals. They glowed bright, shocking Kelera's eyes, which had grown accustomed to the dark.

She gasped as she took in the cavernous room. Its walls were slick with black stone and crystals hanging all around in colors of blue and purple. Had she not been in the company of Samael and his victims, she would have thought it was one of the most beautiful things she had ever seen.

Ammon lingered in the opening of the cavern with visibly shaking hands. Was he regretting the side he'd chosen, or was he afraid of getting caught? Kelera glared at him, willing him to feel the hatred she felt for him and his brother.

She shivered as Samael led her to a black stone chair in the center of the room. The lights seemed to cast only on her and Samael, leaving the rest of the room blanketed in pure darkness. She still couldn't see the other captives, but she could hear their frightened cries.

Samael circled around her like a cat toying with a mouse. She stared up at him in defiance. "Do what you will with me, but you will not *bind* me."

He raised his eyebrows in surprise. "So, you *have* been listening in?" He kneeled on the icy ground in front of her and trailed his fingers along her arms. "Do you know what binding means?"

"I've gathered that it has something to do with being able to use someone's magic."

His hands moved to her thighs. "Smart girl." His grip on them tightened. "I'll admit, it is easier done with spouses or blood relatives. But I think with the proper motivation, you will agree to the risk."

His fingers dug into her, and she tried to pull away but found that she was frozen in place. It was as if he had placed magical restraints on her arms and legs. Her words were venomous as she said, "Do your worst. I will not help you destroy innocent lives."

He stood abruptly. "Do you mean that of the mortals you were raised alongside, or the Fae that you have come to know and like?" He laughed. "Don't look so surprised. I've had my spies keeping an eye on you. I know about your little holiday in the village. Of course, *you* would appreciate the weakest lot of our people. Like calls to like."

She spat at him. "Weakness is using poison to get what you want. Weakness is sneaking around in the shadows."

She saw the blow coming. Samael slapped her hard, rocking her back in her seat. Her wrists stung as the magical restraints held them tight. He scoffed at her as he said, "I don't need your approval or respect. Once we are bound, I will have control."

She licked the blood from her lip and glared up at him. "You poisoned the Seelie Queen. What happens when the Seelie Court hears of it? The treaty—"

"My father and his father before him have always been content to rule the Unseelie courts. Satisfied with their hold on the Winter and Autumn territory. I, however, know that we are more powerful than the Seelie. When I take the throne, I will not be content with half of Elfhame." He flashed his teeth at her. "I want all of it. Winter, Autumn... Summer and Spring. With her impending death, the court is nervous. I will not hesitate to strike when the chance arises."

"And the mortal courts? Where do they come into all of this?"

"Interesting that you ask. They have, after all, abandoned you."

"Liar." Kelera was seething with anger.

"I cannot lie, remember? And why would I? My ally in the court has made sure to hold off the search party. He is rather good at getting them to do what he wants."

Could she have been right to suspect Lord Cunningham? He was, after all, in charge of the search party that had come to the veil with her. And he was both greedy and influential.

She shook her head. Even with the mortals on his side, it couldn't be enough. Not when his own people realized what he'd done. "That may work, but the Unseelie will not follow you when they find that you've poisoned the king. Your own father!" Surely, they wouldn't follow a man who had committed patricide and regicide in one fell swoop.

He flicked his wrist at her, and icy pain shot up her spine. She screamed in agony. Her vision went white, but she could still hear him talking. "That is where my baby brother will finally be of use to me. Imagine, a bastard prince so afraid to lose his chance to claim the crown that he is willing to do whatever it takes to secure his place in the world. Even if it means killing the man who took him in and raised him as an equal to his other sons."

Her vision was slowly returning. "They'll never believe you."

"They don't need to believe me. They only need to doubt him." Samael laughed. She could make out his shape now as he reached up to the cavern ceiling and grabbed something. She heard a snap and then footsteps as he crossed back over to her.

Kelera felt hot, angry tears welling in her eyes. Samael had thought of everything. The poisonings, framing Adrastus, and taking her power in order to finish him off. She breathed deeply, doing everything in her power to keep her magic pushed down deep inside. She couldn't let him get his hands on it.

Ammon's voice echoed as he warned, "Samael."

Samael brushed him off with a careless wave of his hand. He stalked over to Kelera. His voice was cool as he said, "I would like to say this will be quick... but after my bastard brother humiliated me to win you, I feel some retribution is owed."

Kelera's vision cleared in time to see Samael bring a razor-sharp icicle up to her face. She turned away wanting to escape him, but she was still frozen in place—completely at his mercy. There was nothing she could say to stop him. Begging would only bring him sick pleasure.

He ran the ice down her neck. It was as sharp as a sword's edge. One wrong move and he could slit her throat...

He ran it down her chest until it came to her breasts. "I've seen the way Adrastus looks at you. There's something about you that appeals to him unlike any other woman we've had here at court. It's rather fascinating."

Kelera spat at Samael. "You will not beat him."

Fury flashed in his eyes. "Oh, but I already have. The Seelie Queen and my father will fall to the same poison, leaving both courts ripe for the taking. Once I break you, I will have Seelie power just as he does. I will carry out his execution in the name of our father, and then I will be unstoppable."

Someone shouted from across the cavern. It had a domino effect, causing Samael's captives to call out for rescue.

Ammon shouted to Samael, "We need to get out of here!"

Samael swore under his breath. Kelera squinted her eyes to try to get a look at who was coming through the room in the dark. She called out, "Help me, please!"

Someone yelled something to her, but she couldn't hear it. Searing pain tore through her face as Samael took the icicle and cut her from the outer corner of her eye to her jaw. The pain was unbearable, and her vision began to go fuzzy again.

She could barely make out the shape of a tall man standing face to face with Samael at the edge of the darkness.

The man roared with rage, "Release her. Now!"

Kelera recognized that voice. She sobbed with relief. Adrastus had come for her.

Chapter Twenty-Five

C onsciousness wasn't a thing she could grasp. Not with the icy cold pain ripping through the broken flesh on her face. Blood dripped down onto her blue dress, leaving dark red spots on the delicate fabric. She blinked rapidly, struggling to regain her bearings. Samael's magic still held her in place, wrapping itself around her arms and legs.

Samael and Adrastus were shouting threats at one another. She shook her head, trying to get a grip on her situation. *Focus. You can do this.* She focused on the heat of her magic that had risen when Samael had sliced into her. Calling it up from the depths of her soul, she concentrated on the feel of it just at the surface of her skin. She concentrated on her fingertips, willing the magic to move to them. She tried to imagine a warm blanket around her arms and her legs, beckoning the warm heat of her magic to spread throughout the rest of her body. It did as she wished, thawing herself of the magic that Samael had been using to keep her in place.

Her face still throbbed, and she looked down to see blood pooled on her gown. She reached up to touch the wound and hissed as her fingers met the deep gash. She stumbled out of the chair, trying to get to Adrastus.

Ammon was shouting at them to stop, but they were too lost in the hunger for blood and retribution. Adrastus and Samael were oblivious to her presence as they continued to fight with one another. Samael raised his hands, ready to attack his brother. Blue sparks mixed with shadows as he combined his ice power with the darkness.

Adrastus readied his defense. His magic blazed to life around him like a shell of bright red flames intertwined with shadows and ice. A deadly combination. Though Kelera hadn't finished her magic lessons with Gadreel, she knew that only the most powerful High Fae could wield several elements at once.

Adrastus grunted under the power he was commanding. If he called on both his Seelie and Unseelie magic, then there was the risk of it becoming unstable. She knew weaving it together was a danger to him.

Samael didn't seem to realize the danger his brother was in by his own hand. Kelera could see Samael's fear in his eyes and in the way his jaw was set. Still, he didn't retreat. He held fast to his power, blasting it into Adrastus' shield. If Samael's magic broke through to Adrastus, it would kill him. She couldn't allow that to happen. She was so sick of feeling powerless. Of sitting by and waiting for someone to come to her rescue or to tell her what she was supposed to do. This time, she allowed the fear to drive her.

Magic bloomed to life in her hands like a million tiny stars pressed together. It lit the cavern up and drew everyone's attention to her.

Samael's jaw dropped. "Look who's decided to embrace her true self." He threw his hand out, shooting shards of ice in her direction. They swept past her. All except for one. It embedded itself in her side, sending a chill through her. She struggled to call on her magic, but her body shuddered.

Her breath was coming in shorter spurts now. It was getting increasingly more difficult to stand up right. She tried to get to Adrastus, but stumbled to the ground. She opened her mouth to call for help, but she was too weak to speak. There was blood on the floor and her adrenaline rushed when she realized it was hers. How deeply had he cut her?

Adrastus shouted her name, "Kelera! Don't give up!"

Samael bellowed with laughter. He was enjoying every moment of this. "Surely you don't still want her now that she's ruined. Or perhaps you'll enjoy having someone around who is as scarred as you."

Samael took the opportunity to bring the ice down on them. Adrastus dodged the broken shards, but Kelera was not so quick. They sliced into her arms and legs. Icy pain shot through her entire body. She screamed in pain.

Samael laughed again but was cut short as Adrastus attacked him. He was no longer using his magic. This time, he was relying on his bare hands. Kelera tried to rise from the floor. On shaky legs, she went to Adrastus and Samael.

Adrastus was on top of his brother. His hands were gripping Samael's neck so tight that his face was turning blue. If he held on much longer, he was going to kill him.

Kelera's instincts told her to stop him. But she held back. After all the pain Samael had put her and countless others through, it seemed a poetic justice for his life to end there in his room of nightmares.

Samael struggled under Adrastus' hold, clawing at his arms until he drew blood. But it was no use. Adrastus' eyes were filled with bloodlust as he stared down at the brother whose life he was about to end.

Kelera counted her breathing, *One, two, three...* On three, the light in Samael's eyes began to dim. She waited for the relief that would come with his death. But before Adrastus had the chance to finish him, a blast of magic hit him like a snow flurry. He rolled across the room, just out of Samael's reach, and Kelera turned to see it had been Ammon's magic that had stopped Adrastus.

Ammon gulped when Adrastus stood, regaining his balance and ready to finish what he'd started. Kelera desperately tried to reclaim her magic, attempting to pool it into her fingertips, but she was trembling. What if she wasn't strong enough?

Ammon's voice shook as he announced, "Adrastus, youngest prince of the Unseelie Court, you are under arrest for the attempted murder of the king."

Adrastus' eyes narrowed in confusion. "You think *I* murdered our father?"

Kelera's breath was coming in quick bursts as she tried to call on her magic. Through her concentration, she shouted to Adrastus, "They mean to frame you!"

Ammon stuttered, "D-did you say murdered? Father is dead?"

Samael rose from the ground. He spat blood out on the floor and wiped his mouth with the back of his sleeve. "It's mine now." A wide grin spread across his face, revealing blood covered teeth. "Surrender now, brother, and perhaps I will allow your little village friends to live. Unless you would like them to stand beside you as I take your head."

Adrastus turned red with fury. "You murdered him. I knew you were willing to cross lines, but I never imagined this."

Samael laughed. "Face it, brother, I've won." He shouted over his shoulder to Ammon, "Grab the girl!"

Ammon took hold of Kelera's arms before she could defend herself. She watched in horror as Samael lifted his hand and clenched his fist. A blanket of shadows wrapped themselves around Adrastus and began to tighten. He struggled to catch his breath, and Kelera's heart dropped.

She had to do something. She thought of what Adrastus and Gadreel had told her. They wanted her to stop being afraid—of others and of herself. If she was going to get them out of the room of shadows alive, then she needed to accept that she could never escape who she truly was. She was Fae. She had magic in her veins, and she needed to embrace it.

Adrastus' eyes began to flutter shut. He was on the brink of losing consciousness. Kelera cried out, "No!" and with her scream came a powerful blast of magic. It slammed into the walls of the cavern. Ammon was thrown from her, into the wall. The ice melted away leaving heaps of puddles on the ground.

The room was eerily silent. She could no longer hear the sounds of Samael's hidden victims. All she could hear was her heart pounding in her ears. She looked across the room to see that Samael had been knocked out from the blast and Adrastus was kneeling on the ground gasping for air.

She turned to check on Ammon, making sure he couldn't make a grab for her again, but he wasn't moving. Blood was pooling on the ground under him. A lot of blood. She inched closer to him, and with shaking hands, she turned him over. His eyes stared lifelessly up at the ceiling reminding her of the Unseelie guard she had slain in her escape with Cierine. She stumbled back, horrified. *Oh, stars. What have I done?* Her magic flooded her then. It felt like she would burst. As she stepped back, away from the prince she had killed, little fires began to spark to life around her.

With every panicked, ragged breath she took, her fear rose and with it so did her magic. She was a murderer. She had finally embraced her power, but she still couldn't control it. She cried out as Samael moaned in pain. He was waking up. They needed to get out of there.

She ran to Adrastus, leaving small fires in the wake of her footsteps and tugged on his sleeve. "We need to go." White searing pain tore through her side as she tried to pull him to his feet.

She reached down to touch her side and pulled back to find her hands covered in blood. Dizzy from the blood loss, she collapsed on the floor. Adrastus rushed to her side, pulling her onto his lap. He cradled her in his arms and rocked her. "It's okay, you're going to be alright."

Kelera tried to pull away from him. They needed to run. But her body wouldn't respond. She writhed in pain and listened to the comforting sound of Adrastus' voice. "I've got you, Kelera." It was the last thing she heard before she drifted off into the void.

Chapter Twenty-Six

K elera had never known pain like this. She screamed in agony as she regained consciousness. Gadreel was there now. Where had he come from? She tried to recall how she had gotten out of Samael's room of shadows, but couldn't. Gadreel grunted as he lifted her arm over his shoulder. Adrastus swung her other arm over him, and they urged her to walk.

Gadreel sounded frightened as he said, "It doesn't look good, Dras. She's losing a lot of blood."

Kelera's heart swelled at the sound of Gadreel's voice. Her friend. She was glad he was here, even if his voice was quaking with fear. She wanted to tell him everything was going to be alright. But for some reason, her voice wouldn't come. Pain tore through her side and her face again.

Adrastus sounded as worried as Gadreel as he said, "You didn't see her. She's stronger than we ever could have imagined. She's going to pull through." It sounded like he was trying to convince himself more than Gadreel. "She has to."

Her magic had answered her call. They had been right all along. She'd just been too afraid to admit it to herself. She could still feel it buzzing in her veins, ready to unleash fire into the world. *Sunshine was here to melt the ice.* Just as the brownie had said. But she was not sunshine. She was a raging fire. One that couldn't be contained. The smell of smoke filled her nose. Was she still setting fires as she went?

She struggled to stand on her own, but the men on either side of her wouldn't let go. They didn't understand. She was a danger to them. She was stronger than anyone had ever guessed. Some feral side of her thought it felt good to admit it. But at the same time, she didn't want to hurt anyone else.

Gadreel was panting by the time they made it to the end of the hall. "The palace isn't shifting. We're going to lose our advantage of a head start."

Adrastus growled. "It's her magic. It's blocking the palace out."

Sweat beaded on Kelera's forehead and she could barely hold her head up. She felt bile rise in her throat as another round of pain tore through her. Raindrops began to fall from the ceiling and she thought she was hallucinating.

But Gadreel called out, "It's too much power for her. She's getting out of control, Dras. We need to get her out of here before she brings the palace down around us."

"The servants' entrance. It's up ahead. We can cut through—"

Samael's voice bellowed through the palace, "Find them! I want them brought back alive!"

Terror flooded Kelera at the sound of his voice. Why wouldn't he die? Why couldn't it have been him instead of Ammon?

As they descended the very stairs that she had gone down during her escape with Cierine, her world went black. All she could hear in the void was Adrastus' reassuring voice. "Don't give up, Kelera. I can't do this without you."

Sunlight kissed her face. She hadn't felt warmth like this in such a long time. It reminded her of summers at Rose Manor, running through the gardens with Cierine—it reminded her of home.

Adrastus' voice echoed like a beacon, bringing her back to the real world. Her eyes fluttered open. Her journey wasn't over yet. Her head spun as she sat up.

Adrastus had a hold of her in a split second. "Easy. Here, drink this."

Gadreel smiled at the other side of her and handed her a flask of water. He watched her warily as she gulped it down. Was he afraid of her because of her magic? She looked away, unable to bear the thought.

She handed the flask to Adrastus, and when he reached out for it, she gasped. His hands were glowing like starlight. He explained quickly, "Healing magic. I'm still weak from the fight, but I was able to stop the bleeding. I'm sorry I couldn't—I wasn't able to..." He gestured to her face.

She tentatively touched her cheek, afraid of the searing pain she expected to come. Instead, she found the wound had been closed. She could feel raised, puckered skin where it had been deeply opened up.

Adrastus frowned. "I couldn't heal it fully. I tried... but I wasn't strong enough after the fight with Samael and after healing the more fatal wounds on you. I'm afraid you'll be forced to live with the scar."

Kelera's resolve hardened. So be it. It would serve as a reminder to her that she would not cower to anyone ever again.

She looked at her surroundings for the first time. Gadreel was sitting by with a soft, sad smile on his face. He ran his hands through the sand they were sitting on. Sand? Kelera realized with a shock that they were no longer in the Winter Court.

"Where are we?" She looked out on the horizon. The sun was high in the sky and there was an ocean in the distance. A warm breeze carried through the air, blowing her hair around her face.

"The Summer Court." Gadreel reached out to take her hand. "It is not safe for either of you in Unseelie. Our father is dead," he hesitated, "and so is Ammon."

Kelera felt a stab of guilt in her heart. Ammon was dead because she had lost control. Adrastus took her hand in his. "We had no choice but to run."

Gadreel nodded in agreement. "Even so, the two of you running only solidified Samael's claims that Dras is the one who killed our father. The two of you will be hunted for treason. But we have a plan." He patted Adrastus gently on the back. "Oliver will meet you at the Spring border."

Kelera looked pleadingly at Adrastus. "Can't we just go to the blackthorns? My father will protect you."

Adrastus shook his head. "Samael will have the strongest Unseelie soldiers placed along the veil. We need to go where they would least expect. We have friends in the Seelie Court who can protect us for the time being. Until we figure out our next move."

"We?" Kelera wrinkled her brow.

Gadreel answered for Adrastus, "Dras and I have been working together for years to keep Samael from gaining enough power to ascend the throne."

Guilt crept in as she thought of the way she had accused Adrastus of not doing enough to protect his kingdom. He had been fighting for it the whole time, like he said. Indifference was just a mask he'd been forced to wear so no one would suspect him.

Gadreel handed Adrastus a large pack. "I've included everything you need on your journey. Use your supplies sparingly, though. And you need to keep a low profile. Samael will no doubt put a bounty on your heads. Both Unseelie and Seelie alike will be looking to collect."

Adrastus nodded and then turned to Kelera. "Do you think you can walk?"

With his help, she got to her feet. The pain she had been feeling was minuscule now. "I can walk."

Gadreel pulled her in for a hug and she winced at the discomfort at her side. He pulled back quickly. "Good luck, Lady Kelera. It has been a pleasure."

She stood on her tippy toes and kissed him on the cheek. "You have been a true friend, Gadreel."

"Until we meet again." He waved to them both as he walked toward a snowy tree line in the distance. They weren't far from the Winter Court border, which meant they were in grave danger the longer they lingered on this part of the beach.

Kelera followed Adrastus across the golden sand. She was slow moving, but did her best to keep a good pace. She didn't want to slow him down any more than she already had.

Her nerves were nagging at her as they made their way over a dune. "How much did you know of what Samael was planning?"

"Not enough. I had no idea he would go to such great lengths to get his hands on the crown. I didn't think he would make his move until he had your magic and even then, I never expected that he would kill our own father. I thought we had more time."

The buzz of Kelera's magic lingered just under the surface. The overwhelming feeling of it was gone, but she knew she couldn't stop it from wreaking havoc if it was called on again. Bitterly, she said, "I should have heeded your warnings and stayed away. If I hadn't come here..."

"Then Samael would have dragged you through that veil himself. When word came back of a girl with a Seelie locket and ringed eyes, I knew he would stop at nothing to take you. When I found you at the veil trying to go back to the mortal realm, I panicked. I thought if I could bring you back, then Gadreel and I could keep you safe."

"You were doing what you thought you had to in order to keep my magic out of Samael's hands." He had kept her safe because he was doing what he needed to protect his people. Maybe it was exhaustion, but part of her felt a pang of disappointment at the idea that it might not have been for something more.

He offered a hand to help her down the sandy slope. She stumbled into him, and he caught her at his chest. Holding her close to him, he confessed, "You know that's not the only reason."

Kelera was a hurricane of mixed emotions. But after all they had been through over the last few weeks, she couldn't deny her feelings toward him. Admiration, appreciation, respect... and something more unspoken.

Not ready to explore those feelings when they were still in danger, she asked, "What now?"

"Dark times are coming to Elfhame. I'm sorry that you've been dragged into it, but that is the hand you have been dealt. I need your help—"

Kelera held up a hand to stop him from going further. "I will not abandon my people. With Samael wearing the Unseelie crown, the mortal realm is in imminent danger."

"I was going to say... and you need mine. Together we can ensure that the treaty the old rulers of Elfhame created in order to uphold peace between our courts, as well as the mortal ones, still stands. But the only way to do that is together. Your magic is unstable. You need to find a way to control it."

He gestured behind them. She turned to find that roots had sprouted from the sand where her footsteps were. The small branches were full of sharp thorns. Her heart skipped a beat. Her magic didn't feel out of control, yet it was acting without her knowledge.

Ammon's lifeless eyes flashed in her mind. She hadn't meant to kill him. She hadn't meant to do any of this. How could she trust herself to keep her father safe if she had to worry about protecting him from her own magic?

She turned to Adrastus, overcome with helplessness. "If I go home, no one will be safe from me." He nodded sadly, and the truth of what he was suggesting dawned on her. She furrowed her brow at him as she asked, "You want me to bind myself to you?" She pulled from his arms and stepped away warily.

"My brother may have the Unseelie crown, but he still needs you." He gestured to her locket. "You are Seelie. With our magic bound, I can help you control your power and in turn, you can help to balance mine. With your Seelie magic tied to my own, the scales will be tipped, and we can use it to defend us against my brother. And more than that... Samael will not be able to bind you to himself. Once done, the binding cannot be undone." He stepped toward her, and she backed away. A look of hurt flashed across his face, but he didn't give up as he said, "The answers about who you are and where you come from are all within your grasp. We are safer and stronger together. We can unlock the secrets of your power and together we will survive this. Though there have been moments when I could not protect you as I should have, I promise you now that if you bind yourself to me and I to you, I will not make that mistake again."

Warm tears fell down her face. "I want to trust you..."

He reached up and touched her cheek gently. His thumb grazed over the scar that she would carry with her as a reminder of what it meant to deny her Fae blood. A reminder of the cost of being what others wanted her to be.

Her voice was determined as she said, "I will not be a pawn in this. If I bind myself to you, then it is as your equal."

He kept his hand on her face as he vowed, "I will be as bound to you as you are to me. I will protect your people—mortal, and Seelie alike. You will be my equal in every way."

Kelera took a step back, so she was out of his reach. "Tell me what we need to do."

They waited until the sun set and the moon was at its fullest. The stars were as magnificent here in the Summer Court as they were in the Winter. But every little sound and movement around them put her on edge. Who knew what creatures would be lurking in the shadows?

Samael wouldn't waste any time trying to capture them. They needed to act fast and bind themselves if they were going to keep moving. Kelera shivered as a cool breeze blew in from the ocean. Would Samael send the Night Riders after them? Or would he come for her himself?

Adrastus was building a small fire and her nerves began rising again in anticipation of the ceremony. "Samael said it's dangerous to bind your power to one another if you're not already bound by matrimony or blood."

Adrastus responded with confidence. "He was right." Kelera stared at him wide-eyed, and he chuckled. "Don't worry, we will instead rely on the power of the full moon and the healing properties of the sands here in the Summer Court. I believe we will be well protected."

Kelera thought of Alexander. Though she was not marrying Adrastus to make the binding ceremony safer, she still felt as if she were betraying her fiancé in some way. Binding her magic to Adrastus meant having a deep connection with him for the rest of her life. There would be no going back.

He removed his boots and walked over to her barefoot. He sat in front of her so that they could take hold of one another's hands. Her palms were sweating, and she was having trouble hiding the fear she was feeling. She tightened her hold on Adrastus' hands using him as an anchor of strength.

He tried to comfort her as he said, "You've proven your strength time and time again. You risked your life coming for your friend. And proved it again when you took those mortal servants to the border with you." He ran his thumbs along her knuckles, and the tension faded from her shoulders. "You fought for the Fae when it wasn't your fight. The moment that you stepped in to take the punishment for Grace's son was the moment that I *knew* you were someone special. Not for the way you carried yourself with the grace of a lady of court. Not because of your magic. But because of your *heart*. And I am honored now to share the sacred connection of our elders with you."

His magic spurred to life in a ribbon of golden thread intertwined with shadows and icy blue power. It wrapped itself around their hands and remained. Then he nodded to Kelera. It was her turn.

"I came to Elfhame to save my friend. All my life I have strived to be the perfect human, thinking that it was the only way to find security. When I crossed that veil, I never in my wildest dreams thought that I would find my strength here. That I could be myself and the world would not crumble apart because of it. I want to save my people —the mortals. But I also want to save yours. You have shown me that there is beauty here in Elfhame. And that the Fae are worth fighting for, as well as the mortals. I, too, am honored to share the sacred connection of the Fae elders with you, Prince Adrastus of the Unseelie Court."

Magic breathed life into her hands, flowing out in a ribbon of golden light and silver flames. She had never seen anything so beautiful. Suddenly it buckled, and pain thrummed through her arms into her chest. She shut her eyes tight and let out a painful moan. *This has to work. Please let this work.* Panic began to overwhelm her. This was a mistake. She wasn't strong enough.

Adrastus' voice was soothing as he said, "Listen to the sound of my voice, little thief. You must welcome the sensation of your power. Don't fight it."

She hissed in pain. It was like a fever overtaking her. *Don't fight it. Accept it.* She needed this to work. Adrastus was offering her control over her magic. Control that would keep anyone from using her own power against her. And control that would keep her from hurting the people she loved.

She focused on the memory of her father standing tall and proud. Picturing him happy and safe, she took a deep breath and let the magic flow through her. The pain subsided as the magic began to weave and circle its way around their hands and around Adrastus' magic. When the last thread of it had been bound, magic rushed over their bodies. Adrastus held tight to her hands, keeping her from falling back due to the impact.

Lights of gold, silver, blue, and black encircled them, dancing around under the moonlight. Her sunlight and fire magic merged with his shadows and ice. Power rushed into her, aiming for her very soul. She felt it in every fiber of her being. She was hot and cold, day and night... it was everything she had expected and yet so much more.

Adrastus was looking at her with awestruck eyes. Somehow, she could sense that he was feeling it, too. The connection had been granted. Their magic had been shared. She was bound to the bastard prince of the Unseelie Court.

In the distance, Kelera heard hoofbeats. She scrambled in the sand, ready to meet whatever minions Samael had sent for them. Adrastus joined her, interlocking his fingers with hers. Horses cried out from above and she gasped as she looked up to see a horde of riders in the night sky. They left behind a trail of stardust as they galloped in the direction of the Unseelie Court.

Adrastus whispered in awe, "The Wild Hunt. A sign of what's to come."

Kelera's heart was racing as she glimpsed their faces. They rode with fierce determination, clothed in skeletal armor, not much different from the Night Riders. She leaned into Adrastus. "What are they doing?"

He shook his head in disbelief. "I think they're helping to give us a head start."

He tugged at her hand, pulling her away from the fearsome riders and whatever terror they were riding to meet. Kelera followed Adrastus. She had escaped a fate worse than death at the hands of Samael, but her journey wasn't over yet. No. It was only the beginning.

A cknowledgments
When I started this journey I was both terrified and exhilarated. I had no idea what would happen when I released that first series, and since then it has opened so many doors. Doors that led to new friends and adventures. I feel so incredibly blessed to be able to share these stories with you.

First I have to thank you, my readers, who have shown me so much love and support. I am honored to share these worlds and characters with you. The very idea of you coming along with me as we stare evil in the face, reclaim magic and discover beauty in new realms, is what drives me to be a better writer.

As always, I have to thank my family for their support. Without them, I would never have had the courage to take this leap. To my husband, Zach, who is my rock and always tries to bring a smile to my face (especially when the work becomes overwhelming). And to my babies... I can never express how much joy you bring me. You two are the greatest story of all.

Next, I would like to thank the brilliant writers in my writer's group: Danielle, Emily F., Emily H., Kate, Samantha, and Jess, who never hold back. You have shaped me into a better writer and have given me a thicker skin. You've taught me so much about my strengths and you have shown me how to build on my weaknesses. And through it all, you have given me encouragement, love, and support. I truly do not know what I would do without you all.

Lastly, to my beta team: Ardena, Catherine, Luna, and Christina. I am so grateful to have been able to entrust the roughest version of this book to each of you. Without your fresh eyes and guidance, this story wouldn't be what it is today.

One thing I have realized since starting on this journey is that it would be impossible without people around you who will love and support you. Through the ups and downs that have come with pouring my heart and soul into this story, every person mentioned here has kept me going.

My love to you all,
J.M. Wallace

A LSO BY J.M. WALLACE
  A Legacy of Darkness
A Legacy of Nightmares
A Legacy of Destruction
Heir of Embers and Ash (Claiming Elfhame Book Two)
Novellas and More
The Princess of Sagon: A Smuggler's Tale

About the Author

J.M. Wallace is a proud military wife. She has spent much of her adult life moving from place to place with her husband and their two children, making stories of their own. As a young girl, J.M. was fascinated with stories that she read and that she dreamed up on her own. Even when she was horseback riding, she was never in her own yard; instead, she was in an enchanted forest or riding into battle alongside brave knights. Today, she puts those stories to paper, to share with the world. She does this in the little pockets of her day between giving her kids snacks, naps, baths, and putting them to bed. *A Legacy of Darkness* was her debut novel.

www.jmwallaceauthor.com

CPSIA information can be obtained
at www.ICGtesting.com
Printed in the USA
BVHW080809290822
545757BV00006B/203